ONE NIGHT
IN MILAN

A Fairly Weird Tale

Eric A. Blair

Cover design by: Art Painter
Library of Congress Control Number: 2018675309
Printed in the United States of America

"The path to paradise begins in hell." — Dante Alighieri

TO LIVE OR DIE IN L.A.

Laszlo Nagy, the only child of Andras and Clara Nagy, passed underneath Santa Monica Boulevard speeding home on California Interstate 405 North. Next up was Sunset Boulevard and the Getty Museum. In moderate holiday traffic he was pushing hard. Weaving back and forth across multiple lanes at 100 MPH, he was unfazed in this moment by the possibility of a James Dean-esq crash ending to his story. Hip-hop artist Lupe Fiasco's *No Scratches* track continued to boom on repeat as it had the entirety of the three-hour drive from San Diego.

> *So before we hit a wall, heartbreak and it crashes*
> *Just walk away no scratches*
> *So before we hit a wall, heartbreak and it crashes*
> *Just walk away no scratches*

Suddenly and finally his phone rang. Immediately he shut off the stereo. It was Scarlet. The call he was waiting for. The most important call of his three plus decades on this planet.

"'L!" She always called him 'L' instead of Laszlo. Perhaps it was a term of endearment but more likely she wasn't confident in correctly pronouncing his full name. Either way he didn't mind. His feelings for her were singularly focused. Scarlet could call him whatever she wanted so long as she called. Seeing her name pop up as the incoming caller was better than any drug. The most exhilarating feeling he ever experienced. The most exhilarating feeling short of physically being in her presence. Presently this amounted to a total of five days: Two in New Orleans in September, two in Seattle a few days prior to Christmas, and the previous night in San Diego, New Year's Eve 2024.

"L!" She repeated.

"Yeah, Scarlet, what the hell?"

"What do you mean what the hell! Where are you?" she screamed.

"Me! Where are you?"

"You know where I am. I'm at the beach house in San Diego. Is it really you 'L. I mean—uh—I thought you were dead! Drowned!"

"I'm not sure" he retorted with sarcastic honesty. "I remember the party on the yacht. I remember hitting the water. Tasting salt in my mouth. I recall swimming toward the lights 'til I got to the beach. It all feels like a dream! I'm all fucked up! Scarlet... What the hell happened last night?"

"I don't know but everyone thinks you're dead. I heard them making jokes how they would attend your funeral and tell your parents how sorry they were!"

"Who? You must tell me who!" Laszlo swept across four lanes of traffic hitting the brakes to catch the exit for the 101 freeway toward Woodland Hills.

"I swear 'L, I didn't know a thing but the way they were acting I too assumed you were dead. I'm sorry. I'm so sorry!"

"Fuck that, Scarlet. I don't want to hear it," he punched the gas. "Tell me who! Who and why?"

"I don't know, honest. You must believe me! I would never! I'm like you. We are part of the group, but we aren't like them. We are good people. You're a good person. I love you 'L. You gotta believe me!"

"OK, OK... I'll believe you when you tell me who did it and why!" he pleaded again.

"Please believe me! You know I was fucked up too. The cheers after, after you went overboard, were led by Willow, Mike, and Abhi but everyone onboard partook. How could we not? I mean, we just saw Abhi push you overboard! I assumed the reason was history between you and Willow you never disclosed. My brother panicked and almost jumped in after you. I didn't know what to do. We were still on the yacht with them. How could we-"

Laszlo was in bad shape but miraculously almost home. He pulled in the far-right lane, slowed down, and in the calmest voice he could muster marveled: "Wait, wait, wait a god damn wait! Did you say Abhi pushed me overboard? As in, he pushed me into the bay on purpose?"

"Yes. I think so."

"The fuck you mean you *think* so?"

"Please don't be angry with me 'L. I don't have much time. When you went overboard, the boat sped away. Everyone else watching thought it was funny. 'Oh look, he went for a swim'. They howled with laughter. I rushed up to tell the captain to turn around. He shot me a weird smile and kept going. That's when I heard them making more explicit toasts to your demise. My brother Carlos also witnessed Abhi push you. 'L listen; you know Carlos has not been around this group before. He told me to call 911. He honestly believed they would be arrested when we got to port. You know calling the cops would've been suicide. I was so fucked up I couldn't believe it was real. I've been up all-night crying. I didn't think there was any... No way you made it to shore in your state."

"But why Scarlet? Why? These are my friends you're talking about. We go on trips all the time. I've known Willow nearly twenty years and you're telling me she toasted my death!" He took his hands off the steering wheel and raised them to the sky in disbelief.

"I don't know why 'L. They are crazy. Witches, I think. Masons or Rosicrucians, church of satan, scientology or illuminati. I don't fucking know. You must believe me. You know how much weird shit goes down at industry parties."

"No, Scarlet. I don't know. I don't participate. As soon as I see the costumes and candles and hear people getting excited for the ritual bullshit to come, I'm out."

"Yeah, well me too" she replied calmly. "I rarely even get invited to anything but the ski trips. Those bastards call me the communist black sheep of the group to my fucking face. Make jokes I'm only around to get sheared. But I know you've heard the rumors. I'm guessing you're talking or started asking questions. And probably you crossed one of them."

"Are you saying I deserved it?" he challenged her with a combination of hurt and anger in his voice.

"Fuck you for putting it like that. Of course not 'L! But what. You think you're invited 'cause of your looks. Nigga please!"

Taking the Topanga Canyon exit off the 101 Freeway toward his parents' home, a different question hit him. "What did they drug me with? Do you know anything at all?" He pleaded with Scarlet and the whole universe.

"I heard Willow and Mike talking on the balcony after we got back to house..."

"Tell me."

"Hold on, I hear someone. I think they're in the kitchen. I'm in the bathroom. I can't talk much longer."

"Fuck! Scarlet! You have to tell me."

"I'm telling you, listen! They gave you a witch's brew of shit. I don't know exactly. Don't know the quantities of each but I heard 'em on the balcony. And that shit was in addition to all the alcohol and drugs you did willingly! That's why I, why nobody thought you survived."

"I was an all-state swimmer. Of course I survived."

"You're not listening L'. The dude still talking about what a great swimmer he was in high school and college... Dying by drowning. That's part of the fucking ritual to these sick fucks!"

"Ritual! Like what? Witchcraft or voodoo or what?"

"Yes, probably. I don't know exactly, I'm not at their level and will never be allowed to reach it."

"Why not?"

"It doesn't matter. We don't have time for that now. You need to focus on getting away. You can look for answers to these questions when you are somewhere safe. Until then you need to be very careful. Even if you feel OK, you are under their necromancy."

"Necro—what? Sounds like you know more than you're letting on Scarlet! I know your voice well. We have spent countless hours on the phone but I'm doubting if it's really you. They've been able to fake voices for years."

"Stop with that! Trust me. Fear and paranoia will make it ten times worse. It's me and we don't have time for games."

"OK then if you're really Scarlet, tell me what they fucking drugged me with," Laszlo begged of her.

"I will tell you but then I must go. Necromancy, or brujería: ritualistic black magic. The drugs are only one part of the ritual. In your case the drugs were supposed to guarantee the spell works and you drown in the bay. The Latin term is maleficium. I would start researching there. Old books only. Whatever you find on Wikipedia or googling ignore... Better yet, do the opposite."

"What drugs did they give me," he begged for what felt like the thousandth time.

"'L, listen, you need to research the whole ritual not just the drugs. I don't know exactly what they gave you. Investigate Henbane, Belladonna, C2B, Ketamine, Datura Metel, Mandrake... And, uh... Ergot. Can you remember all that?"

"I think so. Yeah, I got it. I'm good. I mean, obviously I'm not fucking *good*. I got motherfuckers trying to assassinate me but talking to you is good. I fucking love you Scarlet."

"'L! Shut the fuck up with that. How are you gonna love me from six feet under. Breath and focus. Look this shit up. Come up with a plan to disappear for a while!" she implored in now whispered tones.

"I'll be good! You know how I do. Drink, smoke, shrooms on the regular. Fuck them! I made it out of god damned San Diego Bay! I ain't going out like this!"

"'L you don't understand. Please listen to me because I really do have to go. It's not going to be like the hallucinogenic trips you're used to. Will there be some hallucinations and synesthesia, yes. I know you can handle that. But whatever they gave you will above all cause disassociation and delirium. This is going to hit for weeks but the first week will be the hardest. Don't get weirded out. To get through this you will need to maintain a strong and clear sense of self. Use your brain and listen to your soul. Be courageous. Do you hear me 'L?"

"Yes" he replied after a hesitation revealing the lack of confidence in his assertion.

"Good. If you survived last night, I know you will make it. It's going to be rough. Remember to only trust old books on the subject. Pre-1913 is best if you can find one. Look for a triade on the inside of the cover."

"A triade?"

"Or triskele; same thing different term. Do you

remember the wine glasses you asked about at my apartment. The ones I got from Ireland with the three connected triple spirals."

"Yeah, sort of."

"Look for that symbol. It might be small but if it's there you can trust what it says and maybe mitigate the worst effects. Smoke cigarettes. Drink alcohol and try to pass out before midnight. Two-to-five in the morning will be the worst time to be awake. Make sure you are asleep. Do not—this is super important—do *not* dwell on any dreams you have. 'L you hear me?"

"I do. I swear. I got it."

"Good. Now tell me you didn't eat all those shrooms last night," she realized the ridiculousness of her question.

"Of course I ate them. But why should I smoke cigs? I quit years ago."

"Only if you feel like it. If things get bad or start to feel dark. I don't have time to explain. But no more shrooms and don't smoke weed or take any uppers. Drinking in moderation the whole time you're awake should help to numb the effects."

"That will not be a problem," he assured her.

"Drinking will help you sleep a little and hopefully you will pass for a drunk and not get detained. 'L listen, if you become delusional in a public place or disassociate, they can legally lock you up on a mental hold like Kanye. If you get confined in your current state of mind you will freak out proving the claim. Do you hear me?"

"I know."

"Now 'L, listen to me. I don't know definitively that they gave you all those drugs… But! It's a good bet you got most of 'em. You still with me?"

"Yeah Scarlet, I'm here."

"Good... I'm like you 'L, only in a different way. I get a small window into what is going on. They will never reveal the full picture. They will never reveal their true selves to us. Believe me. Willow told me one night when she was wasted —she couldn't tell me why—but she made it clear I would never be invited to join the coven. I swear 'L, I'm telling you everything I know. I'm so sorry she... They did this to you. I had no idea! I would've warned you if I did! You believe me, don't you? I would've warned you. I swear to everything that is good and holy! My God, 'L, you're alive! You're fucking alive! Focus on that. You must disappear ASAP. Always know, 'L listen, I had nothing to do with this. Do you believe me? Tell me you believe me. You must believe me!"

"I believe you Scarlet."

"OK" she breathed deep. "One more thing. You're going to hate me bringing this up now 'L but it's important so listen to me."

"I could never hate you, Scarlet. I love you with all my heart and soul and-"

"'L! Fuck! I gotta go so listen. For the next week you are going to be—despite your sorry state, outside appearance whatever—or perhaps because of it... You will be irresistible to witches. Not all witches. I don't know the details but be super careful not to indulge. I don't know the spell cast upon you. It could relate to me."

"Why would it relate to you? You said you aren't with them!"

"I'm not. But they know you visited me in Seattle. That was a week ago. We don't have time to get into our dating histories. The trip could've angered someone. You feel me?"

"I guess. Not enough for Willow to fucking try to have me killed."

"It's not important now... Under the spell you may feel

like you are being freed from your attraction to me."

"I could never feel that!"

"Shut up! I said that's not important... Witches, sorcerers, nercs and even some empaths will be irresistibly drawn to you. You must not act on it! I'm not saying this to be selfish or to deny you pleasure. You are a free man."

"Damn straight."

"But under the spell, if you act, one of two things will likely happen: the guilt you feel after orgasm will subsume your soul within this spell; or you will fall victim to an alternate, perhaps darker magic practiced by the one you have sex with. I must go. Don't call back. Don't text. Definitely don't come to my apartment. 'L do you understand?"

"Yeah of course. I'm drugged, not dumb. But you can't hang up on me with that shit. I have more questions. The portals, the post eclipse realignment you started telling me about last night, telling me to research. Does it have anything to do with this? The timing? I mean—why now?"

"I love you too 'L. Take care of yourself." Click and she was gone.

Fuck. Laszlo knew she wouldn't answer if he called back. Would only be putting her and himself in more danger. If Willow and Mike are awake it means they will soon find out he is alive. This realization both frightened and awakened him to the moment. While talking to Scarlet he stopped at the Arco gas station right before Ventura Boulevard. Not only stopped but went inside and as evidenced by the unopened pack of Marlboro Red '72s sitting on his lap, apparently purchased cigarettes. "Smoke if you got 'em," he lit one and made a right turn out of the parking lot. Moments later it was the familiar left onto Mulholland Drive. He finished the short cigarette before reaching his parents' home at the top of the hill, where Mulholland meets Canoga Avenue. As the clock on the console changed from 12:32 to 12:33 PM he pulled into the driveway. He was not ready to go inside.

Laszlo shut off the engine of his 2024 Genesis turbocharged G80. White on the outside with black leather interior it was the first car he ever purchased brand new. "Unbelievable," he said aloud. Like a poorly thought-out opening scene of a forgotten novel or shitty sitcom, his real-life story flipped upside down overnight. From New Year's Eve to New Year's Day. A mere sixteen hours. Stability in family and friends, an up-and-coming career in the entertainment industry, and his hope of a future and family with Scarlet all overturned. Worse, replaced by the need to leave it all behind and run for his life. He lit another cigarette.

His mind wandering all over the place on the drive up from San Diego, he now knew the truth. At least one version of it. He needed a story to tell his parents that was less than. Ha! Even if he knew the whole truth he couldn't give them all the details. He gathered himself to collect his thoughts best he could. You're coming down off the shrooms and the cocaine is long gone. Scarlet said the witches' brew would be hitting for days and in waves. Thank God for Scarlet. If not for her, he wouldn't even know what they gave him, and it would hit unexpectedly. It's one of the many weird things about psychedelic drugs: the unexpected can really make for a bad trip. His trip was only in its initial stage. Where he was going, he did not know.

Laszlo looked at the house from the car. It was a remodeled late-century four-bedroom four-bath in Woodland Hills with a view overlooking the San Fernando Valley. During his childhood and through high school they had lived down in the valley in a working-class neighborhood. His parents were immigrants from Hungary, a former communist satellite state of the Soviet Union. A few years after moving to California, his father took the US Postal Civil Service test. He was offered a mailman position which he continued in until his recent retirement. Laszlo's mother was a dental technician and worked full time until her even more recent retirement. Their big move up into the hills was afforded by a big bet on America. At the height of the Great Recession—the very bottom of the housing market in March of 2009—they put up their life savings to purchase the foreclosed home in a short sale from the bank.

Now is not the time for reminiscing, he told himself. It was time for action and the first step was to go inside. He went in through the front door and found his parents on the couch watching a recording of that morning's Rose Bowl Parade. Before he had the chance to greet them, his father started on him in the usual fashion— "Wow! You're back early and still look like dogshit."

"You really are back early" his mom continued. "We figured you'd go to your condo to sleep it off and maybe come by later. I haven't even *started* dinner but there are leftovers in the fridge if you're hungry."

"Thanks mom… I'll eat it later."

"How was the party last night? Did you remember to say hi to Willow for me?" she inquired after him as he made his way through the dining room toward the balcony.

"I'll be out here" was the only reply he could muster. Stepping outside he immediately lit another cigarette. It was a beautiful Southern California day. His phone told him it was sixty-five degrees, but it felt warmer with the sun reflecting off the… his mind wandered… off what? What was the balcony made of? It looked like cement. Does that make sense. Ugh. It didn't matter; focus: you need a plan, and you need one now.

He paced the balcony. At least it was sunny. How could one deal with a trip like this in a place like Seattle he questioned and refocused. Seattle. Scarlet lived in Seattle. What did he know? Only what Scarlet told him. He had been drugged and left for dead. Pushed to his demise. He hadn't slept but for a couple hours on the beach and was in bad shape. He had to presume that within hours if not already, the group—his former friends who for an unknown reason wanted him dead, would figure out he was not. His condo and his parents' house would be the first place they would look if they wanted to finish him off—and surely, they would —because having survived he was now a loose end. More dangerous than someone who went to the police; and they knew he knew he could not go to the police. Willow's family was far too connected. Recently he learned Mike was working for the government or military in a secret capacity. The only immediate option was to run.

Going into the kitchen he poured a whiskey over a single ice cube. The reality of his situation was bringing the darkness Scarlet warned about. Use your brain and drink only in moderation. He stepped back outside and instinctively lit another cigarette. He waived at a young woman who lived down street as she walked by with her two black labs. All around him it was quiet and peaceful. Inside his head it was the opposite. He imagined what the other neighbors might be up to. Out to brunch with family, sharing stories from their New Year's Eve festivities, or relaxing and recharging with a day in front of the television watching football.

That's it, football! Americans call it soccer. It didn't matter what he called it. His best immediate go away and figure things out plan was to go to Europe. Specifically, to Hungary. Any country outside the US would be significantly safer but Hungary made sense for three reasons. First, it will allow him to blend in because his name was common there. Second, he spoke the language. And third, a sudden move to Hungary would be less of a shock to his parents than an unfamiliar place. They could even visit without raising suspicion.

There was not a minute to waste. Less than an hour had passed since he pulled in the drive. He could still leave today. He knew most transatlantic flights left from the US in the evening and arrived the following morning local time. He pulled the slider door open. "Father please come out here as soon as possible."

"Smoking cigs again, son?" he questioned stepping outside.

"No. I mean, I am right now but it's complicated. I need your help."

"Of course, what is it? I knew the second you walked in the door something was amiss."

"I'll explain over dinner. The short version is that I'm in a perilous situation. I have a tremendously powerful group looking for me. I need to disappear tonight."

"Where are you going?"

"That's what I need your help with. I want to go to Hungary, to Budapest. Please find me a ticket leaving LAX tonight."

"Why tonight? You look like you need to sleep off whatever drugs you're on before going *anywhere*."

"I promise I will explain later. Please find me a ticket. I don't care what airline."

"Economy or does Mr. Big Shot fly to Europe on a whim need an upgrade?"

"It's not a joke father. This is an exceedingly grave scenario! And no upgrades. I may not be working for a while so the cheaper the better."

"You lost your job? Is that what this is about?"

"No! I said I will tell both you and mom over dinner. Please find me a ticket. I'll bring my credit card."

For a moment a slight sense of calm overcame him. He had a fairly decent escape plan that was in the initial stage of being executed. Now he needed to come up with a tale to tell his parents over dinner. It must explain the urgency without giving away all the details. Stick close to the truth because he hated lying to them. Laszlo lacked details and was sure to upset them terribly. Suddenly it him like the cold waters of the Pacific Ocean waking someone in an alcohol and drug coma: he didn't have his wallet. This was not itself the main issue he quickly realized. His passport, an emergency credit card and cash should all still be locked away in his safe. The missing wallet made sense as they may have taken it to delay the identification of his body. No, the missing wallet made him question something he failed to consider 'til now. It took him at least fifteen minutes but probably closer to thirty to swim to shore. This meant both his car fob and phone managed to stay in his pockets, and after all that time submerged in the salt water of the bay, both magically operated perfectly. Was he really the tragic figure running for his life. Or the luckiest son-of-a-bitch west of the Mississippi. Could be both or neither. Perhaps it was all the drugs talking to each other.

Despite finishing the whiskey, it was not an urge to urinate which sent him to the bathroom. He wanted to look himself in the eyes. The first thing he noticed is that he was still wearing the expensive new bright blue shirt he purchased for the occasion. It was lacking the fresh feeling it delivered the night before. His shoulder length blonde hair looked good for someone who woke up on a beach and had yet to look in a mirror. His arms were their normal tan color, but his pale face didn't match. Whose heavily dilated brown pupils buried in a sea of red veins was looking back at him. Am I a character in a Hunter S. Thompson novel? Or maybe this is all gibberish —a product of the demented imagination of a drunken sailor playing the role of Hollywood lawyer. Yesterday he believed he had it all figured out. Live life out where the real winds blow. Sleep late, have fun, get wild, drink whiskey, and drive fast on empty streets with nothing in mind except falling in love and not getting arrested. *Res Ipsa Loquitur.* Let the good times roll.

Looking down from the mirror Laszlo checked his phone: 2:22 PM January 1, 2024. Plenty of time to gather the essentials, have dinner and make a flight. But which flight? Better go see if his father has found one. He stopped in the kitchen for another whiskey before inquiring, "Any luck with the ticket?"

"Nothing. Every flight to Budapest tonight is sold out. I checked Vienna, Prague, Bratislava, and even Venice. Absolutely nothing leaving to Central Europe tonight under five thousand dollars."

"Please keep looking. I really need to preserve cash 'til I understand the situation."

"You know your mother and I will help, but we are retirees on a very fixed budget."

"Yes of course, father. I don't expect you and mother to sacrifice to pay for my sins."

"I don't ever want to hear you speak like that!" his mom scolded from the living room.

His father returned the conversation to the issue at hand. "I don't understand why it must be tonight. It's holiday pricing for a couple more days. If you leave the fourth there are tickets for under one thousand including taxes and a checked bag."

"Please! Please, listen to me... Why are you wasting time looking at other days? We will have the discussion we have time for, but I *must* leave for Europe tonight!"

He turned and quickly went back outside to the safety of the balcony. Refilled whiskey in hand Laszlo lit another Marlboro. The five senses are said to be the ministers of the soul and all of his were fighting each other for control. He needed to focus. Getting from here to his ass in a seat on a flight in the next four to six hours would under normal circumstances be an easy ask. Perhaps traffic would be more exasperating than usual or the rideshare driver annoying. But this was not a normal day or trip. If Scarlet was right, he might lose his sense of self at any moment. Use your brain while it still works. Five thousand for a ticket was costly but he could afford it. It was settled. He was leaving tonight whatever the cost.

What else needed doing? Go to the condo for his passport and cash. Pack a carry-on. The rest could be shipped later with his car... The book! Was there time to stop at a bookstore and look for the triskele as Scarlet suggested. It would have to be a specialty shop, and it was a holiday, not likely. Thinking of Scarlet forced him to again recall a dark depressed memory. This was the second time it popped in his head in one day. The first time was on the drive home right before she called. There was a folder. A police report in a manilla folder hiding in his parents' attic. He needed to find it and depending on time and his mental state look at it or bring it with him. It could hold the clue to figuring out why they tried to kill him.

OK, first thing first: smoke one last cigarette. Try to think of what else you may need he stressed, continuing the conversation with himself. Next step is going upstairs to find the folder. Then book the best ticket available and take a much-needed shower before dinner. The noise from a police siren rising from somewhere down in the valley concealed the sound of the slider door opening.

"I found some beautiful chicken livers at the farmers market last week. I'll make the mushroom soup you like and fry up the livers for dinner... Does that sound good? How do you want the potatoes?" she asked, her face a combination of motherly love and alarm.

Soup before lunch or dinner is nearly a must in Hungarian cuisine. "Let's fry the potatoes too. With the creamy garlic sauce so nobody on the plane will start up conversation." They shared a knowing smile.

"But this is no ordinary dinner mother. Should we call it the last supper?" He raised his glass knowing the comment would get a rise out of her.

"That's not funny. Your father already told me your mind is set on leaving for Europe tonight." He tried apologizing in their native Hungarian, but it did not accomplish his intent. She too switched languages and continued with the reprimand. They had not attended services since he was in high school, but his mother hated religious humor.

After a lengthy disapproving lecture of his last supper comment, she began to delve into her son's decision to leave immediately. "Your father tells me you have not explained who exactly is after you, or why?"

"I told him I would explain while we eat. I don't have much time."

"You have time to pace around out here drinking and chain smoking. No offense my son, but you're not exactly running world affairs or even a large corporation. Perhaps all the marijuana you smoke finally made you paranoid."

"Mom! I don't have time for this! We will talk during dinner. Right now, I need to focus. Purchase my ticket and with luck quickly find something in the mess of the attic."

"Oh, don't go up there. If you need an extra suitcase I have a couple in the guest bedroom closet you can take," she offered.

Laszlo lit another cigarette, took a drag, and blew the smoke up in the air. "I don't need a suitcase. I'm very sorry to have to leave you and father like this, but there is no other way. I will need your help. I don't need a suitcase because I'm not bringing one."

"What! You're not bringing even one?"

"No mom. I'll need you to go to my condo and pack some of my stuff into the car. After I get settled, I will send you money to have it shipped over. We will need to be discreet. Perhaps your dentist friend can take delivery for me."

"Oh my Lord! You're shipping your car. You're not planning to come back, are you?"

"I don't know that. Not any time soon. Not 'til I can figure out their motives... But you can come visit. You and father always claimed you would spend the summers in Hungary after you retire."

"That was our plan but with your father's condition now, he might not make it to this summer."

"I know ma. I'm truly so sorry I'm leaving like this."

"Oh, can't you stay a few days? Just until your birthday?" she pleaded with her only child. He apologized in Hungarian with a look signaling his departure which neither wanted was not up for debate.

With his mom heading inside to start prepping the chicken livers, Laszlo's father joined him outside. "Good news I think," he declared. "I found a cheap ticket. Only problem is it goes to Milan."

"OK, does it depart tonight?" he questioned the only relevant detail.

"Yes, 8:47 PM from LAX."

"Perfect. I can find a flight from Milan to Budapest or take the train. Doesn't matter."

"One slight issue," his father said worryingly.

"What is it?"

"Well, you know how superstitious your mother is and... So, the flight is only $605 but-"

Laszlo cut him off. "$605 is amazing! Thank you. Let's go

book it right now."

"Yes, so as I was saying its $605 but with taxes and fees the total comes out to $666 and change."

"Father, you know I don't care about that. We don't have to tell mom the price… I need to find something in the attic. Please book it now before it's gone. And thanks again for searching. This is great! I can spend one night in Milan and head to Budapest the following morning."

A WEIRD SCENE INSIDE THE CANYON

Riding a wave of emotion Laszlo furiously searched through boxes and two old filing cabinets. His flight was booked. The pressure to find the folder was mounting. Before beginning the search he was positive it was in this attic. With every passing minute the panic multiplied. It was stuffy and hard to catch your breath. Surprisingly a song he never liked, *Thru the Glass* by Stone Sour, was running on loop in his brain helping to calm him. He thought of Scarlet wondering whether she was completely truthful. Is it possible she told Willow and the gang he was alive. Did they find out through other means. And most importantly, would he ever find out the truth behind why they tried to kill him?

He wasted more than an hour in the attic before his mom called him and his father to the dining room. Having searched all the boxes without finding the report he was distraught. "I'll be right down," he shouted diving into the bottom drawer of the cabinet closest to the only little window. Yes! This is it. A weird rule of the universe had proven true again. The more desperate one is to find a lost item, the more likely it's hiding in the last place he or she looks. The elation at finding the report dispelled the frustrations of the search. Not having the nerve or the time to view it now, he decided to bring it with him. Safely in his seat on the plane would be the perfect time.

Despite the disastrous start to this new year, Laszlo attempted to convince his brain everything would be OK. Dinner was going to be tough. Saying goodbye after even worse. But they failed to kill him. Now he was taking the only step he could take: the next one. There was a plan, a ticket, and perhaps even the information to make sense of it all.

Dinner was set in the formal dining room with the fine china and silverware used only on holidays and special occasions. His parents looked a combination of curious, worried, and sad. Despite not having done it for years prior, his mom insisted Laszlo recite the Lord's Prayer before serving the meal.

Expecting to be immediately bombarded with questions about his sudden departure, he was surprised to be confronted with silence. The three of them slurped their soup without a word. He prepared the opening statements in his mind and was willing himself to begin when his mom asked, "Is that a bracelet on your left arm? It looks like one of those smart watches you didn't want for Christmas." Laszlo looked down at his wrist and there it was. But what? It looked like a smart watch but with a tiny face and no screen. He didn't know how to determine if it was on. It was too tight to pull off and it did not belong to him. When did it get there? How did he not notice? Had it been there the whole drive up from San Diego? The few minutes of relative calm he felt since finding the folder again turned to sheer panic. Could it be? It must be! They put a tracker on him.

"I have to go." He jumped from his chair.

"We just sat down to eat. You said your lift was scheduled for 6:00 PM?" His mother panicked for a different reason.

"It is. I'll be back. Ten minutes." Grabbing the scissors and duct tape from the kitchen junk drawer, he exited through the garage door in a near sprint. It was only a five-minute drive up to the Top of Topanga Lookout. Please let there be someone up here he kept repeating aloud as he accelerated first downhill and then up.

Reaching the left turn into the park he was relieved to see two parked cars. Their owners were occupied taking pictures near the edge. He threw the car into park and took a deep breath. Attempting to appear casual he got out and discreetly made his way toward the walkway. When an opportunity presented itself, he haphazardly duct taped the device into the passenger side back wheel well of a newer model Ford pickup before continuing to the edge. He pretended to be wowed by the view forever emblazoned in his soul. Gazing out across the valley an ocean of memories flooded his brain simultaneously. He recalled his childhood home in Granada Hills. Playing football in the street and skateboarding with friends whose names he could no longer recall. Swimming in neighborhood pools and at the Van Nuys Aquatic Center. Always begging parents, his own and those of his friends, for a ride to the beach.

Getting older he worked to save for an old Toyota he would drive up to this very lookout before and after his parents moved up to these hills. He recalled taking his girlfriend Heather on trips up and down the coast. Many of those trips started by taking a left out of this park. Doing so led one on a fun winding drive through Topanga State Park culminating at the Pacific. The ocean dead ahead at the intersection with Route 1. The Getty Villa on the left, Malibu to the right. He recalled stopping in secluded places on the way to smoke weed and make love.

More than a decade and many women passed through his life since those good 'ole days. Yet even now he considered Heather one of the great loves of his life. He also hated her. She cheated on him with an actor. Jeremy Piven at the back end of his HBO *Entourage* fame. She met him at a Playboy Mansion party he couldn't sniff back then. Heather was nineteen and

Piven was in his forties and already bald. It was hard to make sense of at the time. According to the government you can drive at sixteen, smoke cigarettes at eighteen and after turning twenty-one you're old enough to drink alcohol. The day he came of age and understood how nonsensical these timelines are is the day he found out she cheated. He understood now that subconsciously this was what led him to pursue his own career in the entertainment industry. "Fucking whore," he mumbled, still seething as the urgency of now returned. Quickly but remaining in stealth mode he made his way back to the car.

On the short drive home Laszlo realized the futility of his frantic effort to dispose of the bracelet. His ride to the airport was in one hour. Throwing the damn thing out on the way would have sufficed. Scarlet was right. He was not himself. This was more than merely being high on drugs. He was outside himself trying to remote control a confused barely playable character. How to focus on the present task at hand and do right by his parents. Having always sacrificed for him, they deserved it and much more.

Returning to the house Laszlo found them still seated at the table but not eating. "I'm sorry about that. I'm sorry about all of this. It's hard for me to explain what happened because I don't know the reasons. The only thing I know for sure is that I was drugged."

"I do believe you were drugged my son, that is obvious," his father lamented. "We remember you coming over on New Year's Day and after other celebrations hungover. Today is a different beast. Your eyes, especially your eyes, are completely different."

"Last week you told us Willow, Scarlet, Mike and more names I recognized will all be at this yacht party. What did they tell you about what happened last night?" his mom puzzled.

"I spoke with Scarlet briefly on the drive back. It's hard to know who I can trust because everyone aboard I considered a friend or an acquaintance thereof."

"Scarlet is the new one. The little Cuban hottie with the curly hair you went to visit in Seattle a couple weeks ago?"

"Yes dad, that's Scarlet."

"And you haven't talked with Willow?" his mom challenged. "You two have been friends and travel buddies since high school, or longer."

"Do I know Willow?" his father asked.

"Of course you do Andras. She has been here dozens of times over the years. The Jewish girl Laszlo traveled to Israel and Egypt with. Her father runs one of the big studios."

"She is not a girl anymore mother. She now controls the financing for her father's films and has her hand in a bunch of other pies. I can't even keep track of it all."

"So why haven't you talked to her?"

"Because Scarlet told me Willow, Mike and Abhi are the ones who drugged me. Their plan was to kill me."

"Oh my God!" his father quivered as he stood up from the table and headed for the liquor cabinet. "I need a whiskey."

"Andras! You are not supposed to be drinking with your condition," Clara scolded.

"Please make me one too father."

"Laszlo! Don't encourage his drinking." His mom was now visibly shaking. "I understand you *think* you're in love with this Scarlet woman, but you hardly know her. How can you trust her over old friends. You need to call Willow right now! You need to get this all straightened out before you leave."

"Mom, you need to perceive the situation unfolding from my perspective. Let's suppose I call Willow and she answers. What is she going to say. Will she admit to drugging me. Or the more likely scenario of coercing Abhi to drug me in exchange for God knows what. And when she denies it what do I do," he asked rhetorically. "I do what I'm about to do. I am taking a flight out tonight. Don't you see? If Scarlet is right and the goal was to kill me then right now it doesn't matter who the culprits are. Only that I get away before they have a chance to finish the job."

Laszlo's father rejoined them with a whiskey in each hand. "That's it… I'm calling the police!"

"Sit down!" Laszlo and his mother replied in unison.

"I don't understand," his mom continued. "You went to New Orleans with Willow in September and told me you had a great time. Then in October you guys went to Belize for her birthday. I don't know about the other two, but I refuse to believe Willow had anything to do with this."

"Mom, listen to me. Willow is not always the prim proper studio executive she presents herself as. I never told you because we squashed it, but she and I had a huge falling out like five years ago. She threatened to kill me back then! And beyond motive she has the means to dispose of a body. She always talks about studio business, but I know for a fact her family also owns hundreds of funeral homes all-across the country. Funeral homes cremate bodies. A murder case without a body is exponentially more difficult to prove beyond a reasonable doubt. Will a district attorney making low six figures bring murder charges without a deceased against a family worth, I don't know, five hundred million."

"This is all so unbelievable."

"I know mother. I'm so sorry I brought this upon us. Brought this madness into your home. It wasn't intentional but now that it's here I need to find a safe place where I can sober up. After that I will try to make sense of it all. Figure out the who, the why, and the weird."

"Don't be sorry. Tell me about the other two," she commanded.

"Mike Panelux is a weird dude. The more I learn the deeper the rabbit hole. No official title or position but he is a big shot with the fashion houses. You know the names: Gucci, Versace, Balenciaga depending on the week. Tall, dark and skinny with a beer gut. Supposedly Algerian born. Says he grew up in Paris. He claims to live in Dallas but is always somewhere else. I'm 99.9 percent sure he's a fed."

"Lots of people travel for business. Doesn't mean they're some sort of secret agent," his father quipped.

"Sure, some do. I know Mike travelled extensively— including internationally— during the height of COVID on a fake vaccine certificate... Not fake. It was real and recorded in the databases, but he didn't take it. He could do the same for others. It doesn't prove anything other than he is not who he portrays. He never reveals his inner monologue. Not even when drunk. The most superficial person I ever met, and I have lived my whole life in L.A."

"Why do you think Willow and Mike put Abhi up to it? I always found Abhi to be very polite when he came to pick you up. A bit chatty for my taste but he seemed harmless enough."

"Abhinov, if that is even his real name, hails from Hyderabad and is a complete phony. Convinced everyone he was an MBA student at Stanford. We investigated after some things didn't add up. Turns out he never attended any US institution. His existence is a monument to all the rancid genes and broken chromosomes that corrupt the possibilities of the American Dream; a foul caricature of himself, a man with no soul, no inner convictions, the integrity of a hyena and the style of a poison toad. He will shake your hand while using the other to stab you. A natural-born loser with a filthy-rich daddy who was forced to send his son away because no self-respecting family in the whole of southern India would allow their daughter to marry him. If you could find a modern doctor to perform a lobotomy on him it wouldn't drop his IQ a single point."

"Wow! You sound convinced he is the guilty party."

"Yes, I think he carried out the act but not of his own volition. He was offered something in return. He is so desperate to impress his father—to prove he made it in America—it made him an easy mark for Willow. For anyone in need of a sacrificial pawn."

"Fuck this Abhi guy!" his dad chuckled. "Does any of this have to do with Angie or Boston?"

"No, not at all."

"Your father hasn't had a single drink since coming home from the hospital... We love you and will try to help you in any way we can."

"I love you both."

"Let me finish, son. You need to, as you said, survive this and figure out who is behind it and why. That is only the start. You must learn and mature from this, or it will all be for naught. All these people you work with, your friends. The parties and this story from last night remind me of the characters in that movie with Leo and Tobey Maguire. You know the one. Your dad and I still put it on-"

"*The Great Gatsby*"

"Yeah. They smash up things and people, they're careless in their own affairs, and when things go awry, they hide behind their vast fortune and power and make other people clean up the mess."

Laszlo's phone vibrated. His ride to the airport was arriving in a matter of minutes. "You're right mother. I'm not without guilt. I allowed myself to be fooled by the industry and associated with trash people because of their wealth and fame.

I was happy to be along for the ride. I ignored their selfishness and watched them destroy people for nothing but spite or jealousy. And I excused it all because I thought I was protected. That I could straddle the fence, dip my toes so to speak without falling in. How wrong I was."

"Son, I'm going to keep this short. Take care of yourself and keep your mouth shut. You talk too damn much because you trust too much. It's not only Hollywood. Nobody in Budapest or anywhere else gives a rat's ass if you survive this ordeal except your mother and me... We love you."

"I love you both," he breathed, giving each a deep hug. He grabbed his backpack, double-checked the folder was where it was supposed to be at, and closed the front door behind him for perhaps the last time.

****

Laszlo opened the back door of his lift. He greeted the driver and put his backpack between his legs. "Says here I'm supposed to take you to LAX with a stop in Sherman Oaks?"

"That's right, sir... Hey, can I ask you for a favor?"

"Sure, you can ask."

"You mind taking Ventura Boulevard to my condo instead of the freeway. It's my last night in town. I'm feeling nostalgic or something weird like that. I'll tip extra. Cross my heart but hope to live."

"I suppose I could do that for ya," the driver responded with a hint of a southern drawl. "And where is it you're headed if you don't mind me asking."

"Italy. Milan to be specific."

"Never had the chance to go myself. Two years in Vietnam is all the international traveling this old dog was afforded."

Knowing he was headed to the airport raised Laszlo's spirit a bit despite the uncertainty. Surely Willow and company—though powerful in the industry—didn't have the means to take him out in the terminal at LAX. He had a few smokes remaining and was desperate for more alcohol. Overall, he didn't feel the terrible rumblings Scarlet warned about. "Amateur fucking witches," he cursed under his breath.

"What's that you say?" the driver turned.

"Oh nothing, all good back here thanks." He was inclined to reminisce quietly, but the driver seemed eager to chat.

"Are you excited to be leaving this god-forsaken town?"

"Yes and no. Jack Kerouac described L.A. as the loneliest and most brutal of all American cities. It's been home but I don't disagree. It's a jungle of confusion and anarchy surging with selfish and materialistic energy."

Catching a wave of green lights through moderate traffic they crossed Winnetka Avenue. "And what is it you do to make your living... If you don't mind me asking."

"Oh, well I *was* in the entertainment industry. Not in front of the camera. Contracts, legal stuff."

"No shit! Well then you *must* know my drinkin' buddy Peter Paul?"

"The name sounds familiar. I don't recall meeting him."

The driver looked in the rear-view mirror and made eye contact briefly before he continued, "Oh you're probably too young, an up-and-comer as they say. Peter has been around forever. Managed Fabio in the 90's and later worked on *Spiderman* and with the Clintons. He knows absolutely everyone."

"Sounds like an interesting character."

"Oh yeah! I missed him a lot when he was locked up."

"Did you say locked up. What for?"

"Conspiracy, fraud, drug dealing, but it went much deeper than that or him. He was forced into the role of scapegoat. Some Clinton appointed judge gave him ten years."

"Wow, that's wild, no I don't believe I've met him and now probably never will."

Only a few minutes from his condo Laszlo was desperate for a drink. Who the fuck was this guy. A Vietnam vet rideshare driver talking about a crooked lawyer with ties to the Clintons. His brain was racing again. Was this the set-up. Were they waiting for him at his condo. Could he cancel the stop and go straight to LAX. Or is that why they sent this guy, to guarantee he never makes it to the airport... No, fuck. His passport was in the safe. He had no choice but to go inside.

The veteran turned in the driveway and Laszlo directed him to the nearest entrance. "I'll be back in five minutes." He checked for the folder and headed upstairs with his backpack. His place was on the second floor. He took the stairs instead of the elevator. The hallway was empty. There were no signs of forced entry on his door. Turning the key, he opened the door slowly, reaching in before entering to turn on the lights. The condo was a one-bed one-bath without much furniture or places to hide. Soon he gave himself the all clear.

The passport and less cash than he remembered were quickly gathered from the safe. He threw a few days of clothing into his backpack. After filling an empty water bottle with vodka for the ride to the airport he remembered to grab a jacket that was too warm for Los Angeles. It would serve him well in through the Hungarian winter. He pulled the door shut behind him but didn't bother to lock it.

Minutes later he was back in the car proceeding toward the Interstate 405 South entrance ramp headed for Los Angeles International Airport. Laszlo marveled at the idea of time itself. Past new year days were always spent wasting away on the couch or in bed. Six hours passing by quickly and virtually uneventfully save for the need to pass the blunt or pay off a bet on the big game of the day. And yet today, only six hours prior, he was driving in the other direction waiting for the call from Scarlet. Fucked up and clueless to the witches' brew. No recollection of the intentional push from Abhi. All before there was a plan, a ticket, or the search for the file. Before the painful conversation with his parents interrupted by the unnecessary trip to tape a likely tracking device to a stranger's car. Taking a big swig of straight vodka, he leaned back in his seat. Outside the traffic slowed due to light rain. He would've been content without a word for the rest of the ride. It was not to be.

"As I was tellin' ya before I'm just a nobody rideshare driver. But I pick up a lot of drunk celebrity types and—I guess —I must have that I'm safe to confide in face because most are like an open book back there where you're sitting now."

"Oh yeah," he replied not even feigning interest.

"And I too have my stories of the good 'ole days coming home from war to the sexual revolution. But these popstars of today," he continued without the slightest reciprocation from the back as drunken celebrity antics was the last thing Laszlo wished to discuss. "It's weird... All the travel and fun and blah blah blah they yappity-yap, the one thing all of them seem to revere is this museum here. The Getty. And you wouldn't believe it, well you're in the industry so perhaps you would. People say it's the most important occult site on the West Coast. Can it possibly be true. A purported art museum. Some go so far as to claim the Book of the Illuminated is hidden in tunnels carved into the bedrock. Others swear it houses the original Rothschild Bible. I've heard stories claiming it's the depository for the real birth certificates of the sacred bloodlines who control the entire entertainment industry. Oh... And I almost forgot the secret basement chambers filled with stolen occult art going back to Babylon. The grated black cube visible to the street, on the right of the curve as you go up, is the ventilation chimney for the underground facilities. Supposedly the tunnels leading to it originate at the Houdini estate in Laurel Canyon." Taking both hands off the steering wheel for a second, he made the air quotes gesture, "Or so they say."

Traffic suddenly halted approaching Santa Monica Boulevard. The rideshare app continued to show him reaching LAX with time to spare. "You know about Laurel Canyon's history?"

"Not really. It's a popular spot to take pictures of the Hollywood sign," Laszlo replied without increased enthusiasm for this new topic.

"Sure, but anything more interesting?"

"No, not really."

"I figured, most don't. Well, everyone knows if you take this exit west, you're going to hit the Pacific Ocean in Santa Monica. And if you go east its Beverly Hills and then Hollywood."

"Correct."

"Ok, so going east you first hit West Hollywood. Then, two blocks after the Chateau Marmont, there is a restaurant called Laurel Hardware. This is where you make the left on Laurel Lane to go up. Normally I recommend folks stop there and try a Gangster cocktail, but I surmise you're not interested now seeing as you're leaving us."

"Oh, I'm always interested in a good cocktail. What's in it?"

"Cucumber vodka and fresh watermelon juice. The perfect way to start the day if one is to go explore the Canyon. The restaurant is in a building with a long history of its own, but we don't have time to get into that now. Anyway, as I was saying... If you make a left there on to Laurel Lane and keep straight, it will turn into Laurel Canyon Boulevard."

"Ok, yeah, I've been up that way before," he replied hesitantly, again unsure if this was leading somewhere other than his safe arrival at airport departures.

"When I was younger most everybody went up there to hike and for the views and whatnot. Now it's a goddamn tourist trap. Netflix premiered a series during COVID about Laurel Canyon being the place where the 1960's peace movement and hippie counterculture started."

"Haven't seen it," Laszlo replied honestly, now curious as this was a show about L.A. history he was surprisingly not familiar with. "I thought the movement started in San Francisco?"

"Oh sure, after the festival in Monterrey and 1967's Summer of Love, San Francisco, and Haight-Ashbury specifically became the phenomenon. But it all started right here in this canyon on our left. The Doors, The Byrds, The Mamas and the Papas, Zappa, Alice Cooper, David Crosby, Neil Young and Buffalo Springfield all lived in that there canyon. And, for a time, so too did Charlie Manson—he was a houseguest of one of the Mamas, I'm blanking on her name," he admitted apologetically. "But that's not the weird part, man. The weird part is all their fathers were high level military conducting the god damn war in Vietnam at the same god damn time!"

"No way!" Laszlo snorted, again wondering who this driver was and what kind of trip he was embarking on.

"Yep, it's true, I swear by it. Late in '63 when Kennedy was assassinated, we had no front-line troops in Vietnam. Then, in '64 we got the Gulf of Tonkin incident—a false flag —and boom! Newspaper headlines and political outrage on television sending a generation of our boys off to Southeast Asia to die for nothin'"

"Indeed sir; I do know about the Gulf of Tonkin."

The thought made him feel terrible, but Laszlo asked himself the question anyway. Who was the more capable driver at this moment. Not free of alcohol sober driver but real world capable. If one is prohibited from driving at fifteen and not sixteen, why are people suffering after fifty years of PTSD allowed to drive. Better question: what kind of evil is willing to spend unimaginable fortunes to send young men to war and not take care of those lucky enough to survive and return home. Vietnam being the only foreign country this veteran visited was the first thing he shared. Now, post-retirement, he is forced to drive Hollywood actors to the airport for a few bucks to make ends meet. Bloody hell.

"You know about Tonkin... As I was sayin', guess who was the goddamn commander in charge of the naval fleet at Tonkin. Admiral George Morrison, father of Jim! Jim fucking Morrison. Can you believe *that*. The father fabricates an attack on a US Naval vessel which is then used by the press to drum up support for an illegal war. At the same moment in history the son is thrust into the narrative as an icon for the anti-war hippies!"

"I'm sure the press was blind to the connection."

"Fucking blinded by the light! But listen my friend, the saying goes: once is happenstance, twice is coincidence, and three times is *fucking* enemy action. The happenings here in Laurel Canyon during this time were not happenstance. You ever hear of MK-Ultra?"

"Sure, the CIA program run by Allen Dulles where they gave people LSD to alter their brain. The first known attempts of wayward empire attempting to mold citizens into assassins. It was released publicly during the Church Congressional hearings in the mid-70's."

"Exactly. And it was Francis Zappa, father of Frank, who ran the West Coast chapter of the operation. I call it experimentation, from Edwards Air Force Base in Lancaster,

California. Twice is coincidence." Before Laszlo verbalized a response, he continued, "But I promised you three.

"David Crosby was much more than the son of Major General Crosby. David Crosby, the anti-war activist member of supergroup Crosby, Stills, Nash & Young is the spawn of a nearly endless list of war mongers. US Senators and congressmen, governors, Supreme Court justices, Revolutionary and Civil War generals, signers of the Declaration of Independence, and a whole hive of thirty-third degree masons. But if you aren't yet impressed with Mr. Crosby's lineage, according to the New England Genealogical Society, David Van Cortlandt Crosby is a direct descendant of Founding Fathers and Federalist Papers' authors Alexander Hamilton and John Jay.

"I say all that to say this: If there is a network of elite families shaping major events across a long, perhaps ancient timeline, well, it's probably safe to say Crosby is a bloodline member of such a clan. This would explain why his semen was in such demand in certain circles, because I can't believe it was due to his looks or talent. But otherwise, a normal, run-of-the-mill kind of dude who happenstance shined upon as one of Laurel Canyon's brightest counter-culture stars."

"Captivating history is all around us. I do recall reading Jim Morrison was Scotts Irish and claimed his lineage back to Robert the Bruce, King of Scotland." Laszlo offered his contribution to the topic. The traffic was moving again. His vodka in a water bottle nearly empty. Refocusing on making the flight he couldn't wait to finish this ride and enjoy his last two cigarettes.

The veteran too refocused on the road ahead. Laszlo wondered what he was thinking for a second before being thrust into viewing all that had transpired over the last day from a third-party perspective. The weird scene playing on loop with *Thru the Glass* as the only song on the soundtrack—

How much is real? So much to question
 An epidemic of the mannequins contaminating everything
 We thought came from the heart
 But never did right from the start
 Just listen to the noises
 Null and void instead of voices
 Before you tell yourself, it's just a different scene
 Remember, it's just different from what you've seen

 I'm looking at you through the glass
 Don't know how much time has passed
 All I know is that it feels like forever
 But no one ever tells you that forever feels like home
 Sitting all alone inside your head

He remained in this trance state until the right turn into the airport and the brights lights of the monstrous LAX sign woke him up. "International I gather?"

"Yes, sir."

"Don't forget to add the tip for taking Ventura," he was reminded.

"No, sir, I won't. Appreciate the ride and have a great night."

Laszlo checked to make sure the folder hadn't miraculously jumped out of his backpack. It was there safe. He thanked the driver again, slammed the door and immediately lit a cigarette. The busy holiday crowd was not conducive to his mental state, but reaching the terminal gave him a sense of calm. "Almost there." he mumbled. Make it through check in and security and a whiskey at the bar nearest the gate is your reward. In a little over an hour, he would be off to Budapest via a short layover at London Heathrow followed by a night in Milan.

A few minutes later he exhaled the last puff of his second smoke and headed for the Virgin Atlantic counter. At check-in the nancyfied Dylan Mulvaney character looking at his passport asked if he was OK. "Just a mean New Year's Eve hangover."

"It's alright, you don't need to tell me, but don't *lie*. I've been there. You on some kind of ride right now." Dylan proclaimed with both arms flailing. As he did, Laszlo saw the logo for the airline behind the counter turn bright and float up and away. Making a quick turn to his left and looking up in an effort to track it he nearly fell. It soon merged with the lights and disappeared through the ceiling of the terminal.

"Peoples is going viral for the crazy shit they be sayin' and doin' up in the air. Behave yourself Mr. Nagy or they's gonna duct tape you to a seat. If you know what I'm sayin' blink thrice," he smirked with a little high-pitched laugh. Laszlo stared at him but said nothing. "*Anyway...* Here is your boarding pass. It's a packed flight. Your seat will be assigned at the gate. Thanks for flying Virgin Atlantic."

"Thanks," Laszlo muttered as he walked away. Even in this state of mind he knew better than to upset an employee at a US airport. They have all been programed with some weird god complex and must not be offended or you will find yourself talking to federal agents instead of flying. One wrong pronoun thrown at this clown who—somewhat ironically—has misgendered himself, and he'd be off to some hole in the depths of LAX.

Laszlo's hatred for the song, *Thru the Glass*, was longstanding. At least since his colleague in New York City, the only real friend he made during his short time living there, would play it on repeat as loud as the stereo could blast. Now, here he was walking the terminal attempting to traverse the hell that is the LAX TSA checkpoint on a holiday, running for his life and drugged out of his mind, and the song was his security blanket, his proverbial teddy bear.

I'm looking at you through the glass

Don't know how much time has passed
All I know is that it feels like forever
But no one ever tells you that forever feels like home
Sitting all alone inside your head

How do you feel? That is the question
But I forget, you don't expect an easy answer
When something like a soul becomes initialized
And folded up like paper dolls and little notes
You can't expect a bit of hope

So while you're outside looking in, describing what you see
Remember, what you're staring at is me

Passing through security without issue, thirty-six minutes remained before they would close the gate. He stopped at the first bar he came across. All the airlines post-COVID seemed to be dealing with the issue of unruly passengers by cutting people off after only a few drinks. Not in business class, but in this moment, he was fortunate to have a cheap seat. Telling the flight attended he was poisoned with a witches' brew of drugs would not make him a sympathetic character. He needed drinks down the hatch so he could pass out for the long flight. Scarlet warned nighttime would be more difficult. A dark episode during the flight would fulfill Dylan's prophecy of getting taped to his seat.

"Hi... Can I have three shots of tequila and your strongest IPA please."

"Would you like the sixteen ounce or twenty-two, sir?"

"I'll have the tall one and bring the check as well." He had two shots down and half the beer was gone when he regained appreciation for his surroundings to notice a couple of weird looking guys at the corner of the bar eyeing him. Jesus! I hope they don't try to talk to me was his first thought. Oh God! Is the song merely stuck in my head or have I started singing aloud was his next concern. Doesn't matter. He grabbed his bag with the folder and looked at his phone: 8:11 PM. Twenty-two minutes to make the flight. Raising his glass in a toast "To the gate!" he downed the last shot of tequila before finishing the beer.

Laszlo arrived at the gate for the flight to London to find a long line of passengers waiting to board. Fortunately, he also spotted another bar only yards beyond it. "Shot of Jameson, sixteen-ounce Guiness, and the check please." The barkeep delivered the drinks and asked if he was heading to Ireland. "No, Milan... But I try to live by the old Celtic axiom: Good people drink good booze."

"When I was growing up in Ireland," the keep replied, "I learned when you raise a glass of Irish whiskey the classic toast is 'Slàinte,' it's a Celtic word that translates as 'good health.'"

"Interesting." Laszlo slammed back the Jameson, "In Hungarian our word for cheers similarly translates as 'to your health.'"

After quickly finishing the Guiness he was the last to board. Walking down the jet bridge he found a short line of passengers slowly entering the aircraft. Inspecting the boarding pass he did not see a seat assignment. Stepping aboard, he showed it to the flight attendant assuming he was too drunk to spot it himself.

"This is super weird. I have never seen this before. You do not have a seat assigned. Wait here," she instructed. He waited in the galley as she spoke to a colleague before disappearing back up the bridge.

Laszlo watched as the passengers who boarded before him stowed their bags and took their seats. It wasn't long before the flight attendant returned, "Follow me." He proceeded behind her to row eleven on the left-hand side of the aircraft. Both seats were occupied. The flight attendant spoke to the stunningly beautiful young brunette sitting on the aisle and she stood up. He was notified this was now his seat and the attendant and woman headed for the rear. The middle-aged man sitting in the window seat couldn't have been happy about the switch of seatmates. Laszlo pulled the folder out and stuffed his backpack in the overhead bin. Tossing the folder on the seat and sitting down on top of it he fastened his seatbelt for departure.

AA MEETING

"Excuse me... Excuse me, mate." The man sitting in the window seat reiterated with a hand on his shoulder. "I'm terribly sorry but I need to use the restroom."

Laszlo attempted to jump out of his seat but was restrained by the belt. "Ah... Yeah, no problem... Give me a second." Standing caused him to remember where he was and why. The surrounding passengers were all eyeing him a bit more than would be normal. He must have done something weird in his sleep to draw their attention away from the entertainment screens. No matter. He had made the flight without a major issue. Continuing to stand he surveyed the cabin. They were at cruising altitude but almost everyone was awake. He surmised he hadn't been asleep for long and didn't recall any weird dreams.

With his seatmate returning it was his turn. He grabbed the folder and took it with him to the restroom. There wasn't any turbulence, yet his balance was off. He was nauseous but in command of his faculties. He took note of how little he urinated considering the two airport beers and wondered if that had anything to do with anything. Washing his hands after he looked in the mirror and decided he looked no worse than earlier at his parents' house. Surely that was a win he theorized before asking the only important question: are you ready for what the contents of the report in this folder may reveal?

Making his way back toward seat 11B he was excited to

see the dinner service cart nearing him. Again, he sat down on top of the folder. He had not looked at it. Decided he would not look at it on the plane. Too dangerous with his mind altered. Not thinking about it again before landing in Milan felt appropriate. "Good evening, gentlemen. I can offer the beef or vegetarian?"

"Beef" they replied in unison. It was the same flight attendant who seated him. "And to drink?" He requested the red wine and window seat quickly followed with "I will have the same."

As the flight attendant set his wine on the tray table Laszlo asked for a second. "I promise I'll behave. I'm a very easy-going person but my clavicle is broken, shattered to be precise.

"Clavicle?"

"Yes, it's this bone here," he pretended to wince from the pain of moving his left arm up near his right shoulder. "Obviously it's not possible to put a cast on so they gave me very strong painkillers. I forgot to bring the prescription and airport security confiscated my pills... Even the slightest turbulence feels like torture."

"I can't right now." She sounded sincerely concerned. "I'll come back through after we finish dinner service."

"Is that true mate? You've got a shattered clavicle? I'm James," he offered his hand.

Laszlo shook it introducing himself with a wink. "Sure, shattered it in college."

"Nice try, anyway. Are you afraid to fly mate or merely a drunk?"

"A drunk having an awful day," he immediately regretted revealing how he felt.

"Fuck. Sounds bad mate," James opened his little bottle.

"I like to drink before I attempt to eat this shit anyway." He raised his plastic cup. Laszlo raised his as well and seconded him with a "Fuck it!"

"Put your butter on top of the beef container," James instructed after downing half his cup.

"Excuse me?"

"If you place the cold butter packet on top of the hot beef now, by the time we finish our drinks it'll be soft and spread easily on the roll that otherwise has zero flavor."

"Oh, ha! That's smart. Are you an Australian *mate*, or you just play one on long haul flights?"

"Irish. Born in Dublin." James remained stoic for a moment before smiling. "I moved to New Zealand more than two decades ago," he clarified as the flight attendant walked by and inconspicuously dropped two more little bottles in Laszlo's lap. He offered one to James who readily accepted. "No way she bought the clavicle story. I think she *likes you* Laszlo."

"Maybe but I'm going to slip her a tip to be safe. We still have over eight hours remaining."

"Plenty of time for you tell me about your god-awful day," James slammed the remnants of the first bottle.

"One would think but it's exceedingly complicated." Focusing on his meal, Laszlo promised himself he would not reveal the danger he was in to this stranger.

Eating in silence his thoughts grew far darker than at any point since finding out Abhi pushed him intentionally. Scarlet, his love for her and the warning she gave him was saving him. Would it last? Why was he on this flight running away? What was there to save? His whole life was back in LA. Family, friends, home, and career all washed away in a single day. The assured uncertainty of everything all at once left him utterly without will. He was a corpse. A head on a body of flesh and bone travelling through time and space. His spirit, his soul missed the flight.

Talking positively about starting over worked back on the ground but in the air he was lost. He understood the spell was hitting fiercely now. It will wear off. You will feel better. Don't do anything stupid. Do not get arrested was the new refrain taking hold in his brain. Despite this he couldn't stop the escalating anger. Willow, Mike, and Abhi were the most likely culprits but there was another level to this hell he couldn't help but contemplate. His mother put forth the question during dinner: Are you sure Scarlet can be trusted?

An internal debate was unfolding. Would it be safe to call Scarlet from another phone. Perhaps he could use Jame's phone upon landing.

"Hey mate, are you OK?"

"Umm, yeah. Long day as I said."

"Well here comes your lady friend," James nodded toward the front where the flight attendants were preparing for their trip back through the cabin to collect the trash.

"Thanks for the reminder," he reached into his pocket and pulled a hundred dollar note from his wallet. James watched as he folded the bill into a little square.

"Damn mate, a hundred. I thought you just wanted wine. For that I'd expect a hand job after they dim the lights." They laughed loud enough to turn a few heads.

As she approached, he noticed her name tag for the first time. "Thank you, Amy." He slowly handed the tray to her with a little corner of the bill showing between his index and middle fingers. She took it and moved on without saying a word.

Without booze at least for the time being, he decided talking to James would be preferable to talking to himself. "So let me guess. You're taking the long way to New Zeeland from Los Angeles to stop home in Dublin?"

"Nope, not going to Ireland. I wouldn't spend a night in London if you paid me mate." James acted as if the question posed was absurd. "Stopping in Florence for a few days is the only reason why I'm heading east. My kids live in Los Angeles. I have no one in Ireland. It's not my country any longer. And Dublin is only a few steps behind London in turning into a complete shithole."

"I've been through Heathrow a bunch of times but haven't left the airport since before COVID. Is London truly as bad as some are reporting?" Laszlo inquired.

"It's god-awful. A suicidal culture symbolic of a disconnected mass of humanity. England as a whole is like some stricken beast too stupid to know it is dying. Perhaps it's the backlash and bad karma of empire. The natives are good at turning food into shit and beer into piss and not much else but watching football; but the asylum seeker is where the danger lies. Not because of their migrant status, but the disproportionate number of military aged males is destined to lead to strife. A couple decades ago London had a particular idea of itself: post-Thatcherite property owners reconciling modernity and tradition, globalization, and national self-determination and where, finally, racism was mostly a thing of the past. It was a socially mobile, law-abiding land of high trust, low corruption, the rule of law and religious toleration. A model for the world of an open society with a cultural and historical belief in individual freedom and unassailable rights going back to the Magna Carta."

Laszlo pondered James' passionate position for some time before following up. "And there is no righting the proverbial ship?"

"Never say never but in my opinion the time is exceedingly short. Modern British people are tolerant to a fault. Is that tolerance finite? There will come a point where the breakdown of relations between the British public, the state, and British Muslims is simply irrecoverable, after which there is no telling how it plays out. Without a drastic course correction, my belief is England will be fully under Sharia Law in one generation."

The cabin lights dimmed and many of the passengers were now sleeping or attempting to. This made him uneasy. If James fell asleep, he would be utterly alone in this aluminum tube now approaching the east coast of Canada. His aerospace engineering cousin had—while flying together to Heathrow many years ago—explained that ninety-nine percent of all commercial airline accidents happen either in the first sixty seconds after take-off, or, the last five minutes before touchdown. He did not recall the reason, but the idea of falling from the sky at this moment was weirdly comforting.

The darkness of the cabin and the growing darkness in his heart was lifted by Amy. She came unnoticed from the back of the cabin, stopped briefly to lean down, and whispered in his right ear. "Wait a couple of minutes and then come up to the galley between economy and business class."

Until now Amy had merely been a means to an end: alcohol; but as she strutted toward the front, Laszlo took note of her shapely figure and long black hair. Had James been right. Was she flirting with him. Was she mile-high clubbing with passengers on a regular basis? Wait... No, it couldn't be. She was a witch! He was irresistible to her exactly as Scarlet warned. His mind, running to this point on alcohol and a drug cocktail, received a mass injection of testosterone.

"What did she offer mate?"

"Ah... Nothing; only that I should go up to the business galley in a few minutes."

"I knew it! She loves you mate."

"Oh stop," Laszlo deflected to disguise his inner dialogue. "She is being discreet about giving me more wine is all. Are you still thirsty?" He released the seatbelt and stood up in the aisle.

"Yeah, clean her out mate."

Remembering to grab the folder he couldn't bring himself to look at, Laszlo cautiously made his way forward. He heard giggling as he approached. Slowly pulling aside the curtain he found Amy sharing pictures on her phone with two other members of the flight crew. "Thanks for the tip." She didn't look up, continuing to scroll left. "All the wine we have is down there in the bottom right. You can stay up here for a little while if you want to stretch your legs."

"You're a lifesaver. Thanks!"

"Sure, whatever. Only rule is to be quiet and don't make a scene."

"I won't. I'm chill, promise," he leaned down to grab a couple bottles. "Hey, would it be OK if my friend comes to stretch his legs too?" he coaxed.

"Whatever. Like I said, don't be loud. Everyone in business is asleep." She joined one colleague heading toward the back as the third disappeared through the curtain forward.

He was now alone in the galley with a nearly limitless supply of little bottles of wine and beer. He did not locate any liquor. The set up was not going to solve his life's problems, but it would absolutely numb them for the remainder of this flight. The plan was simple. Go hard and fast. Pass out and catch a little shut eye before arrival.

He pulled the curtain slightly astray and soon caught James' attention. Waiving at him to come forward he placed his right index finger over his mouth to signify obedience to the silence Amy requested. There was only one possible hiccup. The folder was still in his hand. He was not in his seat. The amount of alcohol at his disposal was significant. He needed a plan. There was no good place to hide it. No way to guarantee he would remember its location or find a clue he left himself before being forced to disembark. The best immediate option was to stick it down the front of his pants. He did exactly that and pulled his shirt down over top just as James pulled the curtain aside. Not exactly a *James Bond* move, but he was a drunk entertainment lawyer not a highly trained secret agent.

"What happened?" James questioned entering the galley.

"Nothing weird. Amy said we can hang here and drink so long as we're quiet," he handed James two bottles of red at once.

"Fuck yeah mate!" James quiet screamed as he clicked his two little bottles against each other. "Slàinte!"

"To our health!"

Old souls and new best mates, James & Laszlo; Laszlo & James—soon found themselves in a heated discussion regarding the inner workings of a yet to be named winery. The only major sticking point being the name. Specifically, whose name would come first. It was hotly debated for some time before James tabled the issue for the time being by changing the topic.

"What's your business in London, Laszlo?"

"Same as you, a layover to Italy. I'm going to Milan for a night and then Budapest."

"Laszlo, Budapest, Hungary... Yes, it makes sense now."

"Yeah, a very Hungarian name" he confirmed. "My parents escaped in the last days of the communist regime. They were political refugees in an Austrian camp for a year before getting the green light for a green card to move to the US."

"No shit. A son of refugees. You probably hate me for my

comments regarding asylum seekers earlier, huh?"

"No way, buddy... Most legal immigrants in the US like my folks share the same security concerns. All the military age males coming across the southern border is a disaster for social cohesion for a multitude of reasons."

"Yeah, its fucked," James concurred as Laszlo grabbed two more little bottles.

"There's been a meme going around on US social media about the topic. If the migrants were mostly young single Latina or Asian women with cooking skills and a desire to settle down, instead of military age males, all the liberal white 'Karens' would form brown-boot deportation units overnight," Laszlo recalled laughing at this funny because it contains a deep truth meme yet again.

James chuckled before inquiring further about Laszlo's history. The wine now flowing in his veins, he again forgot his dad's admonishment about not being an open book with everyone. "We are Hungarian, but the borders changed with the world wars. My grandfather's property spanned across what is modern day Romania, Ukraine as well as Hungary —right where the three countries modern borders meet. The Romanian region is a place English speakers know as Transylvania."

"Dracula!" James snarled, lifting his top lip to expose his red wine stained teeth.

"Yes, Dracula...Loosely based on Vlad the Impaler who is a national hero in Romanian folklore" Laszlo continued, "but Vlad was imprisoned by the most revered king in Hungarian history: Mátyás."

"Dracula imprisoned. I never heard *that* part of the story."

"Yes, and King Mátyás also founded the first professional standing army of medieval Europe, the Black Army of

Hungary. He reformed the justice system reducing the power of the barons. Promoted the careers of talented individuals chosen for their abilities rather than their social status. His royal library, the Bibliotheca Corviniana, was one of the largest collections of books in Europe. Hungary became the first country to embrace the Italian Renaissance during his time as king."

"Interesting. Be right back."

While James used the bathroom Laszlo observed the first light of the new day peeking in the emergency exit door window. In the local time zone, it was now the morning of January 2nd. Flying east overnight—in addition to putting distance between him and his pursuers—had shortened what would be a long winter night of darkness from over thirteen hours to nine. Four hours remained before they would arrive at Heathrow. It was a destination he again wanted to reach safely.

Upon his return Laszlo noticed the front of James' pants, "You wipe your hands on your pants buddy?"

"Fucking turbulence."

"Funny that, I didn't feel any turbulence out here, mate."

"Oh shut up and get me another one!" he demanded. Laszlo obliged and they each opened another little bottle of red.

"So, you grew up in Los Angeles?" James returned the conversation to its earlier vein.

"North of in the San Fernando Valley. Pretty standard working-class upbringing until high school."

"What changed?"

"Two unrelated things both opened my eyes in a similar way. I became a prolific swimmer. In addition to attracting women, swimming afforded me opportunities to travel all over California and later the country."

"Travel does change one's perspective on life. And the second?"

"The other was a so-called conspiracy theorist teacher who mentored me. He grew up ostracized speaking out regarding his beliefs that Oswald did not act alone in committing the assassination of President Kennedy. He spent half a semester each year attempting to convince his students it was the CIA and Israeli intelligence working together for various reasons. For most of his students JFK was ancient history. I gave him a fair hearing and ended up agreeing with many of his views—not merely on the assassination but corrupt government ties connecting to big government lies."

"Indeed," James finished his cup of wine. "But government lies are as old as government itself. If JFK was already ancient history when you were in high school, what possible relevance remains in 2024?"

"In my more optimistic moments," he spoke slowly contemplating the obvious pessimistic view of his future currently, "I continue to find it relevant for two reasons. The first is the current presidential candidacy of RFK Jr. The Kennedy's are, to the large and wealthy boomer generation, still American royalty."

"That's true mate, that's true" James interrupted him suddenly excited about ancient history. "It was a couple weeks before I left New Zealand. There was RFK Jr. on Alex Jones' show declaring he can prove the CIA was responsible for the assassinations of his father and uncle in a court of law."

"Right," Laszlo finished his cup. "But not only on Alex Jones. He is making the same claim on the campaign trail and to mainstream media."

"Ok mate, pass me one final-final little bottle and finish your thought. I need to go back to my seat and pass the fuck out."

"It's complicated. It comes down to the battle for a free internet and free speech in the information war. In the wake of JFK there was no internet for the likeminded to connect. No social media, only their daily physical circles. And so, if you questioned the official story, you were branded the 'conspiracy theorist'. It caused a tremendous amount of cognitive dissonance for many people to accept the big lie, to live the big lie. For the feds, it served as a poison pill in the body politic which continues to generate a political and social cancer. The assassinations of the 1960's set up the public by confirming to the intel agencies—and their masters—that a majority of the populace would accept everything fed to them by mass media and not believe their lying eyes. And this is why today we live in the matrix of lies."

"Exactly! The control matrix is being implemented globally *right now*." James declared with the conviction of someone actively working on it. "Their tools of control are legion and growing more sophisticated. The banking and financial system is to keep us in debt and locked into a constant cycle of work and consumption. Social engineering and divide and conquer strategies are to keep us distracted and at each other's throats. Technology keeps us plugged into a simulated reality, oblivious to the higher realms. They pervert religion to keep us trapped in fear and shame, disconnected from our true selves because without discernment there can never be a united opposition to their power. *1984* wasn't meant to be an instructional manual. But we live in a world of doublethink by Orwellian definition."

"You're right of course. The time to stop it is very short. Orwell wrote the year into the story, but it was not his original title for the novel. His editor or publisher, I'm blanking, but one of them changed it from *The Last Man in Europe* to *1984*. Modern citizens—like the proles of *1984*—are largely focused on football weekends and Disney vacations as the highest attainable goals in life. The proles never wake up.

Not only is there no revolution to end the tyranny and provide a happy ending, but there is also no hope of one, ever. That's why so many found it terribly frightening. The party's power is both absolute and permanent. Achieving a permanent entrenchment of the power structure eventually becomes the goal of every empire."

"The printing press helped for a bit though. It's a historical rhyme to the present war for a free internet. To wage an information war against the system before the planet is locked down through surveillance mechanisms. As we've already seen in Canada, mate, they will shut off access to your bank account for peacefully protesting. Implementing central bank digital currencies and eliminating cash is every totalitarian's wet dream. For our own safety naturally. Removing our rights is always done in the name of protecting us."

"Sure, there is hope in the first amendment... The Catholic Church waged a massive campaign to ban books across Europe after the invention of the printing press. Alternatively, Protestantism imposed universal literacy on the populations it controlled because it mandated the faithful have direct access to the Holy Scriptures. As literacy boomed so did economic and technological development much like modern tech has vastly improved productivity and communication. The Protestant sects modeled, by accident, a superior, efficient workforce. It was the reason Germany and Austria-Hungary were for nearly two centuries at the heart of Western development, even if England was the eventually winner of the Industrial Revolution."

"C'mon mate, let's go get a little shut eye. Before you know it, they'll be coming around with bloody muffins and telling us to prepare for arrival."

"I'm right behind you. Need to take a leak first." Alone in the bathroom, Laszlo couldn't help but look at himself in the mirror again. What would Scarlet think of this person, he wondered. Would he ever have the chance to get lost in her eyes again. Unlikely, how would she even recognize him. He didn't recognize himself. Just who *was* this character staring back at him. And why was he waving a razor-sharp hunting knife around. It may or may not be risky to turn your back to a person, but never ever turn your back on a witches' spell fueled by a drug cocktail.

****

James was putting his tray table down when Laszlo woke up. Amy asked if he'd like coffee with his muffin. He hadn't slept long and did not dream or, as the first nap of this flight, did not remember it. No recall meant nothing for him to dwell on as Scarlet warned.

"Coffee?" Amy inquired for the second or third time.

"Umm, ugh, yeah, yes, coffee... Please!" he eventually muttered rubbing his forehead.

"Don't worry mate. I grabbed a couple more little bottles to help us recover but eat the muffin first. You were in the bathroom for a long time. I was getting worried about you. I almost went to check if you were OK but then saw Amy knocking. You appeared on your own accord shortly after."

"I was merely having a little chat with the man in the mirror." He flashed James a half-hearted smile while pulling out the folder still safe in the front of his pants and putting it back underneath him.

"You sure are protective of whatever is in that folder, mate. I don't suppose you're inclined to share?"

"Can't even bring myself to look at it so I don't know what to share. But I can't imagine it would be interesting to someone not privy to the details of the situation I've got myself in."

"Understood mate." James sipped his coffee silently for a few minutes. "So, what do you do in L.A.?"

"I work in the entertainment industry. Mainly contracts and discovery. In common law jurisdictions like the US and England, discovery is an important part of the legal process before going to trial. It's when each side is compelled to show the other the evidence they plan to admit to the court."

"A lawyer! You're a goddamn conspiracy lawyer are ya! Ha!"

"Well, yeah, I was until a couple days ago."

"Ah I understand. You were fired or laid off and this is the cause for your bad day."

"No, not fired. It's more complicated. I can never go back to that life. Not that I want to. Fuck Hollywood. It looks glamorous. Everyone looking in from the outside is ready to sell their soul to get a piece of it, but I haven't seen anyone left unscathed. The song *Hotel California* summed up the whole industry decades ago: *You can check in any time you like, but you can never leave.*"

"Don't take this the wrong way, but did you not, mere moments ago, tell me you are leaving the industry?"

"Have you seen my face in the media or movies?"

"No, mate."

"Exactly... I drove to the fucking hotel with bags packed, went inside, and waited in line at the desk. Right before checking in-"

The ding of the Boeing's P.A. system sounded. The pilot instructed the flight attendants to prepare the cabin for landing and the passengers to fasten their seatbelts and put their chairs in the upright position. It was a perfectly timed interruption for Laszlo, stopping him from giving James the 'cliff notes' version of an industry wide tell-all book.

After the announcement, he decided to steer the conversation in another direction. "We will be landing shortly. You haven't told me a single thing about New Zealand?"

"What do you wanna know mate?"

"Hmm... Well, I read that COVID NAZI Prime Minister finally stepped down or was replaced recently. Any thoughts on the new guy... What's his name?"

"Luxon, Christopher Luxon; one World Economic Forum puppet took the reins from another. He is already selling out to BlackRock—I'm sure you've heard of them—the New York based investment firm. The world's largest asset manager... Luxon is your typical socialist. A prim little wanker. Publicly he is married to a woman but probably likes little boys if you get my drift. A vegetarian and a secret teetotaler."

"Teetotaler! Holy hell! I haven't heard that word in *forever*."

"Listen," James used a more serious tone than at any time up to this point. "Kiwis, New Zealanders, made a tremendous contribution to the Allied effort in WWII. First against Rommel in the Africa campaign and later in Italy. Point of fact: New Zealand's 2nd infantry division were the first troops to reach Florence, liberating the city and forcing the Nazis to blow up the bridges over the Arno River and retreat north. Today, like much of the rest of the former empire, we are a shell of what we were even one generation ago. The submission to the COVID despotism you brought up is not a mere symptom of a dying breed, but a cancer metastasizing through the whole of the body politic."

The Virgin Atlantic Boeing 777 popped out under the clouds into light rain. Laszlo and James stared silently through the window as the giant airliner banked hard to the left and aligned with its assigned runway. They heard the grind of the landing gear and minutes later felt the slight bump of touchdown. "We made it, mate," James announced seconds before Amy went on the P.A. to welcome them to Heathrow. James didn't know his story. Nobody on the flight did. From San Diego Bay to London in the UK.

"We made it. What a fucking trip."

Sitting on the wing of the massive plane and feeling the rain and wind hit his face was enthralling. Outside the glass, staring into the cabin through the window, Laszlo watched as he and James continued to chit-chat. The passengers around them were becoming increasingly restless as the aircraft taxied slowly toward its gate. Continuing to stare inside watching himself, he couldn't help asking: How does it feel? I am more at peace than what feels like *forever* came the refrain. He had passed a test of sorts. Was transported to another place not merely physically, but spiritually. No, he wasn't in Hungary yet; but Willow, Mike and Abhi were far away. Powerful as they were in California, it had been mere hours since they could have discovered he survived. Assuming they knew his location, it would still take them time to formulate a plan. His plan was set. In a couple hours he would be on the next flight to Milan. And tomorrow around this time—if nothing went awry —he would be taxiing to the gate at Liszt Ferenc International Airport in Budapest.

The aircraft came to a stop. The seatbelt signs were turned off. Laszlo rejoined the other passengers inside the fuselage. He quickly stood and opened the overhead bin. Stuffing the folder in his backpack he looked down at James waiting patiently. "Do you have enough time to grab Bloody Marys before your flight to Florence?"

"Was about to ask you the same."

"Cool. I'll wait for you at the top of the jet bridge," Laszlo turned and began to inch his way forward.

He thanked Amy for her "hospitality" as he exited and

still feeling at ease glided to the top of bridge. He stopped to wait for James as promised. A few minutes went by and soon a few more. Most of the passengers he recognized from sitting near him all passed. There was plenty of time before his flight to Milan, but he desperately needed to use the restroom.

The flood of people hurrying off turned into a trickle when he finally spotted James. And not only James, but the beautiful young woman who was his initial seatmate at departure. Each pulled a carry-on bag with their outside arm while their inner arms interlocked, looking very much like a couple. All the peace he felt since touchdown was sucked from his soul and instantly replaced by an ominous dread.

One of the only advantages of being in the entertainment industry he still valued was the constant of new beautiful young women on the scene. He was not one to be easily impressed. She was olive skinned with dark hair. Exactly his type. A black jacket covered her top and was seasonally appropriate, but she matched it with a black mini-skirt and thin black mostly see-through leggings. And the outfit was a mere side-show to six-inch-high silver pumps. Is this what she was wearing back at LAX or did she change on the flight. He wasn't sure of anything except in Kansas he was not. She pulled her arm from James' and extended her hand forward. "This is my wife Ava," James announced.

LOVE AT FIRST SIGHT

After the introduction in the jetway, James, Ava and Laszlo entered Heathrow Terminal 3 with the goal of finding a bar for a quick Bloody Mary brunch before departing for their respective destinations in Italy. James was excitedly telling Ava how quick the flight passed thanks to Laszlo. He recounted how he slyly tipped Amy at the beginning and how this led to them getting drunk on wine in the galley. He even brought up the winery partnership which garnered a nod of thoughtful approval and a "Sounds like an interesting idea," from Ava.

Marching with them to the right of James, he was not in lockstep. He didn't say anything and wasn't actively listening. The last three months had been the most tortuous of his life and it all started in New Orleans. The bad vibes or juju, voodoo, the occult associations and weirdness—looking back now—it all stemmed from that one weekend. But it took time to manifest. New Orleans as it unfolded was exciting and full of possibilities. It's where he met Scarlet. So how did everything go so astray he nearly ended up dead at the bottom of the bay.

His mind was racing hard and fast like the phone call with Scarlet. Why was he allowed through the gate at LAX with no seat assignment. Once through, if there was a single empty seat farther back why would the flight crew not seat him there instead breaking up an already seated couple. And when Amy did break them up, why did James allow his beautiful young bride to be moved without a word of protest.

Nothing about this trip was adding up except Ava's

outfit. Judging by the number of males, and females, who couldn't help risking a neck strain to get a doubletake, he was not hallucinating as to *that*. She really did walk off a ten-hour-redeye in an outfit that screamed: Take me clubbing right now!

"Are you heading to Florence as well, Laszlo?" Ava walked like she was on the runway but acted like there was no one staring at her.

"No, Milan for one night and then Budapest tomorrow."

"You absolutely must come to Florence if you haven't been."

"I wish but the timing doesn't work for me now," he remembered to be vague.

"Oh Laszlo, you simply must meet the holy trinity," she persisted. "Michelangelo, Leonardo, and Raphael. The three giants of the Florentine High Renaissance all live there! We could live there too but this guy is wedded to New Zealand." She gave James a playful elbow to his lower ribs.

"There it is." James first pointed and then put his right arm around Laszlo. "The Curator Bar. I knew it was in terminal three." They sauntered in with all eyes on them. Or, more accurately, on Ava. Not bothering to wait for the occupied hostess the unholy trio sat themselves at the last open high-top table near the bar. The walls were a weirdly shaped wooden paneling. The large counter housed pastries, sandwiches and coffee. A full bar followed with track lighting making it much brighter than a non-airport pub. Everything including the tables and chairs were sitting atop a black and white checkerboard floor.

The waiter appeared quickly. All three ordered the same 'Classic Big English' brunch. Fried eggs, Cumberland sausages, back bacon rashers, baked beans, oven roasted mushrooms, and skin-on fries; and of course, three Bloody Marys. Ava announced she did not drink on the flight but slept nearly the whole time. She then convinced them to also order a round of tequila shots to 'open their palates' for the big meal. Turning, the waiter headed back to the kitchen.

Ava moved to face Laszlo, "Have you been to Milan before?" she made intense eye contact and held it.

"Only for a single day many years ago. My friend Willow-" He caught himself opening a story he told many times that would never be the same. "A few old college friends and I spent a day there as a planned long layover. It was on our way to Israel and Egypt for a summer study abroad."

"Sounds *amazing*," she twisted her left wrist to point her thumb at James. "Milan is where I met this guy!"

"That's great!" he responded before asking the most obvious question in the long history of obviousness. "Are you in the modeling-fashion world, Ava?"

"Yes. I mean I was, "Until he rescued me." She now placed her hand on top of James' and gave it a squeeze.

"Awesome. Did you ever work with Mike Panelux by chance?"

"Panelux... You meet so many people. I don't think so. Doesn't sound familiar."

There must be several dark stories behind Ava's casual 'rescued me' comment Laszlo noted as the waiter arrived with the tequila shots. They thanked him and quickly slammed them back after toasting Italy. He wished to dig deeper into Ava's career in fashion, but James broke in to reveal, "Our new mate here is a big shot Hollywood attorney hiding a dark secret. He wouldn't divulge specifics even at his most drunken state. Have you noticed he guards that backpack like he's got the goddamn Shroud of Turin in it?"

Before she could say anything, Laszlo did, "Shroud of Turin? James, you saw the folder. It's merely a report about an incident a few years back. Nothing to do with the church. I swear to God."

"Oh, don't mind him Laszlo. James has secrets too. Did *he,* divulge to *you,* the fortune he spent building a doomsday bunker four-freaking hours south of Auckland in the middle of nowhere."

"Not the cost and not even its existence." The waiter appeared and set their meals and drinks in front of them.

Ava grabbed her Bloody Mary first, "Let's toast these to the apocalypse." James and Laszlo joined without protest, clicking their glasses and again drawing the attention of the bar with an enthusiastic: "To the Apocalypse!"

James and Laszlo grabbed their silverware. Ava admonished them to wait. "Gotta capture it for the 'gram," she pulled out her phone to take a picture of their meal.

"Ava has millions of Instagram followers," James boasted, giving his own homage to the obvious.

All three dug ferociously into the first bites of real food since Los Angeles. Seeing Ava's phone forced an internal debate in Laszlo's mind. To call Scarlet or not was the question. Obvious arguments for and against were holding a heated debate deep in his subconscious. Unable to resolve the conflict with reason, he resorted to emotion: I want to hear the sound of her voice.

"Hey buddy, my battery is dead. Could I use your cell to make a quick call?"

"Mine too, mate. I'm sure Ava won't mind," she grabbed it and reaching across handed it to him.

Laszlo excused himself from the table and made his way toward the terminal hallway. Dialing the numbers he realized there were only three phone numbers he knew from memory. His parents and Scarlet. It would be prudent to jot a few others down just in case. He listened to it ring as his brain pleaded with the universe. Please pick up, please! It went to voicemail.

He made two more attempts with the same result. "Fuck!" he barked loud enough to garner a couple of looks.

Turning to walk back to the bar he realized Scarlet may return the call. But when. In a few minutes he would be parting ways with James and Ava. What if Scarlet called later. Would Ava answer. There was no reason for them to talk if she did, but he didn't know Ava and Ava was—had been—rescued from the industry. Crap. He should not have called. Fuck. He could tell Ava not to answer if the number calls back, but that's an invitation to do the opposite. Fuck. Fuck. Triple… Fuck!

Having nearly convinced himself there was no way Scarlet would return an international call from an unknown number considering the circumstances, an idea hit him. Email her but not from his account. He used Ava's phone to create an email address Scarlet would recognize as him, but Willow, Mike and the rest of the world would be oblivious to: triskele.glass.sale@gmail.com. Easy enough. Now for the message:

> *Hello Valued Triskele Customer,*
>
> *We appreciate you signing up for Triskele updates and are happy to announce the grand opening of our new physical location in London.*
>
> *We are relocating our call center. If you need to speak with us regarding your purchase, please contact us via this email address.*
>
> *Thank you,*
>
> *Triskele Inc.*

He erased the outgoing calls off Ava's phone and before returning to the Curator Bar remembered to check the departures board. James and Ava had finished with their meals and a second round of Bloody Marys was being delivered. "Thanks," he set the phone on the table in front of Ava.

"We're both delayed. Only twenty minutes for me. Your

flight to Florence is now showing a 3:22 PM departure."

"Of course, Heathrow strikes again" James sighed.

"He supposedly hates it but continues to book us through here" noted Ava.

"What are your most hated airports, mate?"

Laszlo thought for a second, "Atlanta makes the list... and O'Hare definitely does. Denver creeps me out-"

"What's wrong with Denver?"

"Nothing with the city and I love to go skiing in Colorado, but I fly direct to Aspen now. Denver airport is weird and super creepy. Look into it. There is a masonic inscription on a time capsule, gargoyles with flashing red eyes, and the murals are satanic. One of the murals, painted years before 2020, has a huge group of mostly young people, male and female. They are masked like we were for COVID. And the various masks are flags from countries around the world. Like some shrine to the global mask cult. It's not conspiracy theory. I had a long layover and went to see them for myself because I couldn't believe the pictures on the internet. Recently public pressure forced them to take the most egregious of the murals down. I refer to it as: The New World Order of the America's Hunger Games Capital Denver International Airport."

"That's a mouthful mate," James smiled as they raised their glasses again. "To the New World Order of the America's Hunger Games Capital Denver International Airport" they chanted in perfect unison.

"Ava loves the *Hunger Games* movies, don't you sweetie?"

"I do."

"Ok, then check this out." He turned to Ava to confirm she was listening and then immediately back to James. Tempting as it was looking Ava in her eyes, doing so for long could lead to trouble. Any more than a few seconds was like staring at the midday sun. With the latter you could lose your sight but with the former it may be your soul.

"My ex," he paused and thought about it, "my ex, ex, ex-girlfriend," he smiled. "It's been a few years, but I digress. Anyway, she graduated from a school in Boston called Phillips Academy Andover. Have you heard of it?"

"No, mate."

"Ok so it's one of two rival high schools. Phillips Academy Exeter is the other. Boarding schools like in the UK where you live there full time. Anyway, they are Skull & Bones schools. Both Presidents named George Bush, and a host of other top scumbags are confirmed members of the gang. It's crazy hard to get in. The running joke on campus is: 'My father was a happy congressman. He had to become a Senator to get me into Andover'. But seriously, it's eighty thousand dollars a year for high school. Orders of magnitude more difficult to be accepted than an Ivy League college."

"*Seriously*? I never even heard of it," Ava looked at him over the brim of her glass and he looked down at the table.

Laszlo took a big gulp of his Bloody Mary. "Seriously… But I'm getting distracted from the point. All that background is because I want you to understand the level of institution we are talking about. So, returning to *The Hunger Games*. I'm dating this woman who is a graduate of Andover, and the first movie is coming out. I did not read the book. She is adamant we must see this movie. OK, are you following?"

"I'm tracking mate." James looked eager for him to complete the thought.

"OK, we go see it. The next day, perhaps days whatever I don't remember, she casually reveals it was well understood among her peers, again we are talking the children of the .0001 percent, *The Hunger Games* is the blueprint for the future of society. I pushed her to explain. She tells me we are not talking about the game itself which takes up much of the plot, but the way society is structured post WWIII. This means the war was already being planned back then. It is to be followed by a *Hunger Games*-esq brave new world with large open-air prisons, no calories above subsistence level, and no travel outside your assigned zone for the 99.9%!"

"No way mate. I'm all for an elaborate fantastical theory of the future but there is too much coordination required. Any random bloke with a conscience playing a minor role could reveal their machinations."

"Way... The projects are compartmentalized. Need to know. And what media company is touching the whistleblower in the unlikely event one dares to run afoul of such a group. But this was all years before I learned about the World Economic Forum and fifteen-minute cities, and all that. I was quite shocked."

"What was your ex's reaction to seeing the movie?" Ava wondered.

"Hammer meet nail. That right *there* is why it's still so unnerving. She was interested only in how the visuals, plot, and entertainment value came across on the big screen. How would a middle-class father of two taking his daughters to the Saturday matinee in Tulsa interpret it. The plan she shared with me; the ideas embedded in the story being a model for the future was an inevitability she did not question. She did not know or give a specific date. Her assumption was in the medium term. Before we reached middle age. And this was more than ten years ago now. She was only twenty-one at the time."

Ava, James, and Laszlo sipped their drinks in silence for a few moments before James asked, "So, Laszlo, based on these conversations with your ex and members of these secret societies—whatever, however—we define them. How do they see the information war playing out in the lead up. The ideas we discussed on the flight. Censorship and suppression of speech by the giant internet oligopolies. How would your ex describe the present. One of Orwellian doublethink. Or is it more Huxleyan? Because from my perspective sports, movies, entertainment generally, though produced to be 'predictive programming' are mainly a huge distraction. Most cannot— like you coming from within the industry or your ex—see through to its true purpose. Any given show on a given night of Netflix and chill will not resonate at a higher level than an escape from a shitty day, shitty boss, the rent due or some combination thereof. Huxley believed 'People will come to love their oppression, to adore the technologies that undo their capacities to think.'"

"I hear you, James. Most of my life Huxley was closer to the target in the West and Orwell in the communist regimes. The COVID operation proved the desire for totalitarian control Orwell warned against was dormant and waiting right below the artificial surface; and not only the desire of the controllers, but a weird and desperate need by the unthinking masses to submit to arbitrary and absurd rules without questioning." This distinction started not an argument but a back-and-forth in jest between two likeminded men.

"The victim of mind-manipulation does not know that he is a victim. To him, the walls of his prison are invisible, and he believes himself to be free."

"A generation of the unteachable is hanging upon us like a necklace of corpses."

"Subliminal projection is intimately associated with mass entertainment, and in the life of modern human beings massed entertainment plays a part comparable to that played by religion in the Middle Ages."

"We are at the mercy of a vast mass communications industry, concerned in the main neither with the true nor the false, but with the unreal, the more or less totally irrelevant."

"The very concept of objective truth is fading out of the world. Lies will become history by way of algorithmically controlled deep-fakes created in silicon valleys."

"War, debt, and the planned obsolescence of humans replaced by AI robots: These are the three pillars on which the destruction of Western Civilization is founded."

"If you know the truth it will drive you stark raving mad."

"Guys... Guys...Please!" Ava interjected. "You're both right. We are living in some weird dystopian timeline where Orwell and Huxley have morphed and were given steroids. Laszlo, you told us about the fancy pants boarding school in Boston, yes? England is the same. Do you know that Huxley was Orwell's teacher at boarding school. Eton to be specific, in Berkshire. It's similarly known for its wealth and connections. It has produced like twenty British Prime Ministers, Ian Flemming of Bond fame and the most well-known parasitic economist of the 20th century: John Maynard Keynes. But we must not lose hope. These old institutions will soon be overturned like a powerful but inbred and retarded royal who flips the chess board while winning because he spies himself too smart to need an unfair advantage."

At this the three new friends broke out in uncontrolled laughter before raising their nearly empty glasses for one last toast: "To the Royals!"

****

The Airbus A320 was taxiing for take-off. It was scheduled as a nearly two-hour flight from Heathrow to Milan Malpensa International Airport. Laszlo was in seat 26A. The folder was in his backpack between his legs. Before bidding farewell to James and Ava they exchanged contact information and made promises to get together soon. There were no issues with his boarding pass or seat assignment. The single-aisle plane built to carry more than one-hundred passengers had approximately forty souls on board.

He plugged his phone in to charge from the USB slot in the armrest and checked his messages. Laszlo replied to his mother but there was nothing from Scarlet, Willow or anyone from the San Diego trip. Wishes of Happy New Year from work colleagues and others he would likely never see again were ignored and deleted without emotion.

As the plane reached cruising altitude the seat belt signs were turned off. He was already searching for tickets from Milan to Budapest for the following day. There were two options on Lufthansa with whom he could use his points from a partner airline. He booked the first one leaving the following morning, January 3rd, 2024, at 10:25 AM. Outside the sun was shining brightly above heavy cloud cover below. Laszlo felt quite relieved at this moment. By deciding to spend a night in Milan after his father found him this flight, he was going to save more than $4,000. That money will help extend his runway to figure out his new life outside the entertainment industry, outside the US.

Next up on the to do list was transportation to central Milan and a place to spend the night. A male flight attendant asked if he wanted something to drink. He requested "Whatever pilsner you have, thanks" without looking up from his phone. He soon found the best option for transportation was an express train direct from the airport to Stazione Centrale di Milano in under sixty minutes. The cost was twelve euros. His beer arrived and he raised it slightly. Silently he toasted Scarlet, Budapest, Milan, and a new beginning!

Sipping his beer, Laszlo attempted to catch a glimpse of the English Channel now below through the heavy cloud cover without success. His mind wandered to what this night and his new life might look like. The words of the philosopher

Dante Alighieri soon helped focus his thoughts. Dante's *Divine Comedy* was the most important poem of the Middle Ages and the greatest literary work in the Italian language. And though not mentioned by Ava as being one of the greats still alive in Florence, it was Dante's use of the Florentine dialect which is largely responsible for establishing a standardized Italian language. By writing in Italian vernacular rather than in Latin, accessible only to highly educated readers, Dante influenced the course of literary development. He was responsible for making Italian the literary language of Western Europe for several centuries. Who better to gain inspiration from in this moment.

> *In that book which is my memory,*
> *On the first page of the chapter that is the day when I first met you,*
> *Appear the words: 'Incipit vita nova'*
> *Here begins my new life.*

He repeated the lines dozens of times and was eventually transported to the place his new life began three months and eleven days prior: New Orleans, Louisiana. There, on the afternoon of Friday September 22, 2023, he met Scarlet.

Willow, Abhi and other friends all had rooms at the Four Seasons NOLA for the weekend. Laszlo had a work commitment he couldn't now recall. He flew in only for one night. Mike owned a condo close to the hotel and suggested Laszlo stay with him. "It's the fall equinox, you know this crew ain't gonna be doing no sleeping." True as that statement sounded at the time of the offer, when he arrived, Mike was not answering the buzzer for the condo or his phone. He tried Willow who answered but was quite annoyed to be bothered at the early hour of 2:00 PM. She promised to dispatch her friend Scarlet with a spare set of keys to let him in.

Laszlo waited and waited as the sky turned more and more ominous. It was now 3:11 PM, ninety-five degrees with one hundred percent humidity, and he couldn't even get into the lobby. The air was sweet as a sugar cane plantation; and you could smell the river and really smell the people, and mud, and molasses, and every kind of tropical exhalation. A few cars went by, none stopped. He tried Mike's phone and the buzzer again but still no luck. He was about to head to the gas station at the next block when—from the same direction— he saw a woman that could be Scarlet jogging toward him. As she got closer his hopes rose to a feverish pitch. The woman approaching him was gorgeous and his type to boot. Sweat beaded her olive skin and wet curly hair. She was wearing a colorful bikini top, skimpy black shorts, and flip-flops. She must've been at the pool when Willow asked her to come, he determined.

"Are you Lezollol?" she butchered his name as she slowed to a walk. "Sorry I took so long. I had to stop at three shops to find rollies."

"It's cool." How could he possibly be mad at her timing when she shows up looking so damn edible. "Yeah, it's Laszlo. I'm sure Mike has papers, a bowl or something we could smoke out of upstairs."

She went inside and he followed her into the lobby. "I smoke blunts and always roll 'em with real tobacco leaves." She made her way toward the elevator. Turning back over her left shoulder she caught him checking out her legs and ass, "You like?" Scarlet hit the button for the eighth floor.

"Love. Fine as hell *and* you roll blunts with real leaves... Wanna make a baby?" The elevator doors opened.

"I got a man." She punched him playfully in the stomach as they stepped in, "And I'm a good girl so don't be getting no ideas."

Inside the condo they found Mike passed out on the couch. An empty bottle of rum, a few lines of coke, and a half-eaten bowl of pasta adorned the coffee table. Laszlo snuck up and smacked his bare stomach where his tank-top had folded up over his beer gut. "I've been outside for over an hour motherfucker!" Mike opened his eyes for a second, turned inward toward the back of the couch, and muttered something awful that he could only assume was Creole for 'Let me die here.'

Scarlet took a seat at the dining table opposite the couch with her back to a slightly cracked window. He didn't see the lightning but heard the thunder boom as the sky opened and let loose.

Completely unfazed, she pulled a large bag of weed from a small pocket and threw it on the table. "Come sit down and break that shit up. You break; I'll roll" she declared with sass and a fire that made him desire her more than any woman he ever met.

Sitting in silence across from each other, Scarlet was deeply focused on the task of rolling the blunt. Laszlo was deeply focused on Scarlet. Her fine high forehead sloped gently up to where her hair, bordering it like an armorial shield, burst into curls of shimmering black. Her golden green eyes were bright, big, clear, wet, and shining. Her cheeks were filled with life, pores breathing close to the surface from the strong still youthful pump of her heart. Her body hovered delicately on the edges of perfection, slowly gathering speed down the runway of female fertility. She was undoubtable enjoying the freedom of flight that comes after teenage angst and before the pre-menopausal instinct to settle down. Something he never considered now washed over his thoughts like a tsunami: Modern women get too much of the blame for putting off motherhood.

A quarter of an hour after meeting downstairs he watched Scarlet light the blunt. He knew his life would never be the same. This day would either become the story he shares with their future children as to how he met their mother, or it would metastasize into the missed opportunity which would be his life's great regret when he closed his eyes for the last time. Like attempting to drive a piece of papyrus between two stone blocks, there could be no middle ground.

You haven't even smoked yet. Don't start talking crazy he lectured himself. Your worst enemy, he reflected, is your nervous system. At any moment the tension inside is liable to translate into visible symptoms.

"Willow says you two have known each other for years?" Laszlo attempted to appear casual to mask his internal passion.

"Yeah, since before COVID. But I hear you two go even further back, have been besties since college."

Scarlet passed him the blunt and followed up without giving him the chance to breathe. "Have you and Willow ever dated?"

Laszlo took a big hit and contemplated her question as he held it in. "We haven't." He blew the smoke in Mike's direction. "In the beginning I don't know. It's a good question. Now... Now it couldn't work. We have been riding the friendship train for far too long. We know each other too well to put up with each other's bullshit; if that makes sense."

His reply—sensible or not—caused Scarlet to pause and allowed him to counterpunch. "So, who is this man of yours you mentioned. Is he a big star or the big money behind the scenes?"

"Oh no. He is none of that, he's a nobody."

"A nobody? Then why is someone like you with him?"

"I mean he is not in the industry. You haven't worked with him. A regular nice guy from a good home. He'll be taking over the family business, smart and caring."

"Smart? I doubt it. He let you come to New Orleans for the weekend with *these* animals unescorted." In disbelief he nodded at Mike, still dead on the couch.

"My freedom is a must. It's part of the deal if you want to be my man. I take care of myself Mr. Laszololo," she proclaimed, again butchering his name.

"That's Mr. Nagy to you, my dear. And I don't care what kind of superpowers you possess. If you were my woman, I would not be comfortable with you travelling with this group alone."

He puffed the blunt a second time. Passing it back he changed the subject. "Have you been to NOLA before? Are you interested in its history? Or the voodoo black magic whatever the proper term is for that weirdness?"

"What! Do I look like a *witch* to you, my nigga?" she exhaled right in his face. This caused them to both burst out laughing until he commented awkwardly, "Well, I think you're fire. If you do turn out to be a witch, I'll happily take a non-speaking role as the stake."

"'L... Imma call you 'L if that's OK. You don't know me so let me just tell you. I'm Cuban and Dominican. I know about this Candoblé, this Yorbuba, the Santeria; OK, you feel me... I know about it; but I don't play. I'm a good girl. I came to party, dance, have fun and that's it." Laszlo held in the smoke from the blunt he was again holding in his right hand, and gestured understanding circles with his left index finger before exhaling in agreement, "Yeah for sure. I feel you. You don't play. I'm only making small talk."

"I ain't got no time for small talk" she winked, leaning forward and stealing the blunt back.

Sitting in silence as Scarlet checked her phone, Laszlo peered over her shoulder through the window overlooking the famous French Quarter. A light rain lingered but the storm had passed. The sun was trying hard to break through the clouds and cast shadows of the old buildings. Presently it was illuminating only the tiny corner of the room where Scarlet was seated, as if heaven was shining down on her, and her alone.

"'L, play some music," she demanded.

"What are you in the mood for?" He turned it around hoping to learn about her tastes.

"I told *you* to play something."

"OK, alright... Beyonce it is."

"Nigga! I told you I don't play," she scowled at him facetiously before an exchange of smiles signifying an understanding without the need to elaborate. Laszlo put on a jazz mix which eventually garnered a positive review, "This is dope! When in Rome..."

"I can do any genre depending on my mood," he offered her a way out if she wanted an alternative.

"Same. Except sad love songs. Ugh. The worst. And Michael Jackson knew, he told us. You know about that 'L?"

"I do. I think it's one of the reasons they did him so dirty before killing him."

"Yo! You're right, it was one of the reasons. The first huge star to disclose music frequencies were weaponized even before the lyrics. It has an extremely powerful effect. If you pay attention to modern mainstream music, you'll notice a pattern. It's almost always about love, sad love, lost love, past relationships."

Laszlo lifted his right hand and placed it over his heart. "I have never been dumped by Taylor Swift. I swear."

"'L stop it. You're too much. Funny dumb, but listen... They want us hung up on the past. To be sad and love drunk. It's very artificial and done on purpose because when you're doubtful and in a low space, you become easier to control and manipulate. This is why it's equally vital to tune out of mainstream music as mainstream news or movies."

"Don't allow yourself to be chained to their rhythm,"

Laszlo concurred.

"Exactly," Scarlet extinguished the last bit of life from the blunt in a square shaped green-resin ashtray with four small silver elephant heads for its base, one in each corner. "So many people live without questioning. Like my man's parents. We try to tell 'em and they're polite people so they listen but their routine never changes... And that's the large majority. Can you imagine living like a so-called normal person?"

"You're chillin' listening to a few P. Diddy and Lady Gaga tunes prepping dinner. Later you turn off the music to put on CNN or the BBC to catch the news. Another clone starts the main headline featuring some bought and paid for political hack talking about 'defending democracy'. This is followed by a glowing report about Bill Gates philanthropic efforts in helping to bring new vaccines to market. Another distinguished minister on the take pops in to promote a digital ID to keep us all safe. The Secretary of War makes a heartfelt plea for more money to fund the killing fields in Ukraine. The grand finale is John Kerry, who has again flown half-way across the world in a private jet to give the same speech about the climate crisis to the same people, who also flew there private." He showed Scarlet a wry smile and she playfully continued the bit.

"Initially you're grateful we have such altruistic politicians and billionaires who truly care about the downtrodden, the well-being of people and our planet. But then the back end of the news hits and it's filled with a racist Donald Trump being indicted again followed by an update on the Andrew Tate sex trafficking case. This section of the 'news' makes you very angry. You curse at the TV and decide you will NOT become a victim. You will fight back against such fascism. You angrily open social media to signal your virtue by writing an Orwellian-esq two-minutes hate post... Finally feeling better you're ready to call it a night. You switch to the Disney channel or perhaps relax with a Harvey Weinstein movie starring Tom Hanks and a load of supporting actors who attended parties on Epstein's Island of sex-trafficking and blackmail." Scarlet tilted her head to the left and let the sarcasm on her face show she understood the game well.

"What the fuck y'all yapping about?" Mike groaned without showing any further signs of life.

"We were wondering if there was any booze in this place you didn't drink?" Scarlet fired the opening shot.

"Or drugs!" Laszlo mocked, simultaneously realizing he and Scarlet should've done the remaining cocaine before Mike woke up. "Is there more coke or is that all of it? I could go for a bump before I shower."

Hearing the word coke caused Mike to immediately sit up and snort one of the remaining lines on the table in front of him. "Aghh!! There it is. NOLA day two let's go!" He was still seated but now turned to face the table. "There's beer in the fridge and booze in the freezer. All the drugs are in Dean's suite at the Four Seasons." He was referring to Jonathan Dean; the great-nephew of actor and singer James Dean of Rat-Pack fame, who—as far as Laszlo had witnessed—was interested in nothing other than blowing through his trust fund as quickly as possible. "Don't worry about it being with Dean," Mike attempted to assure a distrustful audience. There's is plenty to go around. And, in celebration of the equinox... I was going to keep this as a surprise, but I can't help myself. We have a bunch of mescaline should you care to partake." Mike boasted joining them at the dining table.

"That's dope. For sure we want some" Scarlet spoke for them both.

"Mike, I was about to call you out for making me wait outside but it seems you redeemed yourself without trying. I read Aldous Huxley mentioned the discovery of adrenochrome in *The Doors of Perception* and likened it to mescaline."

"Comparing chrome to mescaline. Sounds like he never tried it," Mike spoke with a confidence that only comes from experience.

"Bro is that an eye of providence tattoo on your left shoulder?"

"Damn! Good *eyeing* it, 'L. I've known him for years and never recognized it." Scarlet noted.

"It is. I was dumb when I was young. Most people don't notice it because of the other tats. Hell, most people don't notice it's on their god damn currency," Mike chuckled.

Laszlo decided this was an opportunity to use the 'Overton Window' opened by Mike to probe Scarlet's worldview. "Speaking of the dollar... Among the odder theories I've seen is that Adam Weishaupt, founder of the Bavarian Illuminati, killed George Washington after the American Revolution and took on his identity as President of the United States. It's wild, but there were no photographs back then and everyone wore wigs. Travel between D.C and the states took weeks or longer. If two people looked similar, how could anyone but his wife know for certain. Proponents of the theory point out Washington's portrait on the one-dollar bill closely resembles that of Weishaupt."

"Oh, hell no Laszlo, don't go there. Do *not* get Scarlet started or we gonna be up here all night talking about secret societies" Mike warned, his voice pitching higher. "I need to hit these streets. Down shots and meet me some sexy men!" Everyone agreed to table the topic for another time.

Showering and sipping a beer Laszlo was engulfed in nervous excitement for what the night may bring. For him, and for Scarlet: the good girl with the angelic face, perfect body, open mind, timeless old soul, and—most importantly in the present—an absent boyfriend.

Ding, ding, ding... The PA system of the Airbus returned

him from the stifling heat and humidity of New Orleans to the nearly empty, cold, and dry cabin of the plane beginning its descent into Milan. He again took notice of the happenings outside his window. England's thick cloud cover now a memory replaced by the snow-capped peaks of the Ligurian Alps. Its majesty surely persisting even as his view below was replaced with the Piedmont, the drainage basin for Italy's longest river, the Po. Finally, and most spectacularly, the last section right before landing in Milan took them over the edge of the Apennine Mountains. Twenty minutes of grandeur surely worth more than all the mined gold from every epoch before the invention of the airplane. Landing in Aspen Colorado was no less spectacular. It was merely familiar. The adage familiarity breeds contempt wasn't accurate in this context. It merely allows one to suspend their awe in order to breathe.

The imminent touchdown in Milan was an exciting relief for several reasons. The most pressing being a desperate need to urinate. The only thing remaining on his to do list was booking a room for the night. Without much consideration he decided it was smart and to his advantage to wait. The closer to check-in he booked the room, the less time those bastards back in L.A. could have knowledge of his precise location. He was happy with how the trip progressed so far. He managed to avoid the worst-case scenarios Scarlet warned against. All through the remaining descent, touchdown, and exiting the airliner with his folder safe in his backpack, his brain whistled the old tune:

Jimmy crack corn and I don't care
Jimmy crack corn and I don't care
Jimmy crack corn and I don't care
Jimmy crack corn and I don't care...

Big old owl, with eyes so bright
And many a dark and starry night
I often heard my true love say
Sing all night and sleep all day

Jimmy crack corn and I don't care
Jimmy crack corn and I don't care
Jimmy crack corn and I don't care
My master's gone away

Plodding through the terminal Laszlo continued to whistle his way toward passport control. He entered the first restroom to finally release the pilsners from his liver. "Oh dear God!" he begged for mercy, nearly throwing up. He turned immediately without relieving himself and quickened his pace. He spotted another restroom about a hundred yards straight ahead.

Entering the second bathroom he was met with the same repugnant smell. This time, with the line for passport control approaching, he had no choice but to suck it up. Whilst doing the deed his upbeat mood was similarly replaced with something foul. He washed his hands and eyed himself in the mirror. The desire to run from the wicked stench was overrun by visual disturbances. At ordinary times the eye concerns itself with such problems as where?— How far?— And situated in relation to what? Here, questions of place and distance ceased to exist. He could perceive life only in terms of intensity of existence, profundity of significance, and the spatial pattern of relationships. He spent some time in contemplation of these profound questions before a man entering the space polluted his mind's eye. He turned to leave and promptly vomited in the trash bin.

SOUL BURN

After the unceremonious arrival in Milan, Laszlo was pleased to skate by passport control without garnering special attention. Making the long trek through the lower arrivals level of terminal one to the train station, he made one quick stop for a shot of tequila to cleanse the taste of puke from his palate and grabbed a beer for the ride. The train platform was sparsely populated. He easily found a window seat when it arrived. Barring a delay, he would reach central Milan before sunset.

In an abundance of caution, he deemed it wise to further delay getting a room for the night. Staring out the window the outskirts of the city were the antithesis of the historic center toward which he was traveling. No fancy cathedrals, world-renowned shopping plazas or beautiful women heading to five-star restaurants in exotic sports cars. Instead, Laszlo witnessed a bleak scene reminiscent of the outskirts of Bucharest or Kiev. Farmland gave way to endless rows of run-down four to ten story block brick apartments with laundry pinned to balcony clotheslines. Old billboards long made unreadable by weather corrosion fluttered fitfully like pennants. A menacing wind howled as the train picked up speed. Shuttered storefronts were covered in graffiti like the apartments surrounding them. The streets were massed with garbage and old vehicles of all shapes and sizes parked with no discernible system of getting out should one desire to do so. He noticed a group of women dressed in full burqa talking, and many groups of young North African men in western clothing riding bicycles or playing soccer. Laszlo's thoughts drifted first to his previous trip to Milan with Willow so many years ago, and then to their most recent trip: Belize, the weekend of October 20, 2023, exactly four weeks after New Orleans.

He and Willow were on the same flight out of LAX arriving in Belize City hours before anyone else. They shared a ride from Philip S. W. Goldson International Airport to Ambergris Caye on a Tropic Air Cessna. Upon arrival on the Caye, they were met by the welcome team from Victoria House and transported by golf cart to the spa resort on the southern tip of the island. After a quick dip in the Caribbean and refreshing showers they headed to The Hidden Treasure Restaurant and Lounge. Arriving a few minutes before it opened for dinner at 5:00 PM local time.

Seated promptly they ordered Don Julio margaritas to start. Willow was the planner of the group. As they perused their menus she went through the itinerary again, a topic already covered on the flight and again while swimming. "Today is a beach and drinks day. As you know, I don't like to plan any major activities for the first day in case anyone gets delayed."

"Of course I know. We've been to like thirty or forty countries together. And how many times to Vegas, gotta be pushing a hundred now," he smirked. Annoyed as one can be considering his presently pleasant circumstances.

"Shut up because tomorrow is the big day. I will need your help to corral the unruly herd."

"I got you," he assured her taking a big sip and focusing in on the menu.

"What time is the van coming in the morning?" Willow quizzed him.

"7:00 AM... And no one is less enthused by the early start time than me."

"I know but morning is the best time to snorkel. The Belize Barrier Reef is the second largest reef in the world after Australia's. We cannot *not* do that shit... After, there is a van to take us to the helipad. If someone does miss the van from the villa they can meet us there for the helicopter ride over the Great Blue Hole. What time does the helicopter leave?"

"It leaves at 10:45 AM sharp."

"You da man! We don't have time to stop for lunch because this crew will order a million drinks, and we'll never make it to Rio Frio Cave. *So,* the driver will be picking up our lunch and drinks for us to consume on the boat ride to the mainland. The cave is known for its massive cathedral-like chambers and the pics I saw were awe-inspiring. We will be there during the hottest part of the day which is perfect timing if I do say so myself."

"Sounds like the perfect day" he cheered because the waiter finally returned to take their order.

Willow went first requesting the Seafood Treasure. A whole lobster tail with fresh snapper fillet & shrimps, grilled and served with a garlic lemon butter sauce, coconut white rice and seasonal char-grilled veggies.

"I'll have the same. Thanks... Speaking of Vegas," He looked at Willow, "Have we come up with a better plan for New Years Eve?"

"But you love Vegas Laszlo!"

"I do love it, and I *love* winning money... But we've done it so many times. And I like to play poker which can be such a rush but takes a long time to play out. It's not like playing a few hands of blackjack against the casino. You have to bide your time, let the cards play out. Wait for some sucker from Kalamazoo, Michigan to turn out. Be dramatic while drinking six or seven light beers in four hours 'til he assumes I'm drunk. Play the part. Start talking loudly. Ask the table if we should do a round of shots. Then, when he thinks he has it all figured out thirty-six hours into his first journey to the desert: Bam! I flip the fucking nuts. That means winning hand in poker lingo… Dogs get buried with their favorite chew toy, and suckers must apologize to their wives because there is no money left for dinner and a show."

"You're a fucking savage Laszlo."

"A savage living a heartbeat from the edge of the American Dream… But there is a good reason for not doing Vegas again."

"What!"

"I know you know. C'mon, that's the only place you and I fight. It's always someone else in the group bringing the drama except in Vegas."

"Don't even fucking go there" she warned.

"I ain't trying to relive details here but we had some dark times stemming from that shit."

"That shit was all your fault Laszlo!"

"I admitted as much but it was not intentional. I didn't mean to harm anyone. I got drugged and fucking robbed."

"We all got *fucking robbed* because of you" Willow countered.

"Still, that shit should've stayed in Vegas. You brought it back to Hollywood and made a big damn production out of it. I'm not the first drunk dude to get taken advantage of by a hooker in Vegas."

"No, but she got you how you get people at poker. Face it, that night you were the out-of-water fish getting hustled. It resulted in everyone staying in our suite having their cash, jewelry, designer handbags, and fucking work laptops stolen."

"You're right," he was forced to concede. "That bitch got me fuckin' good. Got us good because of me." Luckily the waiter came with the food and interrupted before this escalated. He changed the topic by bringing up better times. Their first big trip together.

"Now that I have again admitted I was in the wrong, will you please finally reveal what happened when you 'lost' us on the Milan layover to Israel."

"We've *been* through this. I lost the group. Instead of wasting time looking for you guys I did all the things by myself."

Laszlo wasn't buying it, never would, "You did all the things and showed up to the airport on time with no pics, no souvenirs, and not mad at us for leaving you. Color me suspect."

Digging into the food in front of them it was now Willow looking to change the topic. "Cairo was the illest part of that trip. Remember the pyramid race?"

"Of course I remember The Pyramids."

"No, not the day-time trip with the big group. I'm talking about late night. We went to a hotel rooftop bar out past El Nour Mosque. It was the only place still open and serving booze in the whole city according to our concierge. There was a rickety old elevator we could only ride two at time to go up to the roof."

"Oh yeah, its fuzzy but you're ringing a bell." He tried to recall the details as the waiter delivered another round of margaritas.

"We cleaned them out of beers quick" Willow recounted after a toast to Belize. "Then they brought us the house vodka which we worried was going to make us blind but drank it all anyway."

"Oh yeah… How could I forget. It was like ether, the shit that makes your soul burn slow."

"And for a small tip the dude added hashish to the tobacco in the hookahs."

"Agreed, dope night."

"Tom—I think it was Tommy—came up with the idea for the pyramid race. It was stupid late, or early, approaching sunrise. And the terms were that when the morning call to prayer started each group: Tom's group, your group and my group, would race to the Great Pyramid. We could use any means of transportation, which added an interesting twist. Tommy was a sick fuck, but in a good way. Nearly all the cabbies are Muslim and would therefore have to pull over for morning prayer."

"I remember everything now. My team lost. The bet was the last group to have a member touch the Great Pyramid loses. He or she would pay for everyone's dinner and drinks the following night."

"That's right! You lost and that's why you always pretend to not remember," Willow teased.

"Don't sleep on the snapper," he pointed his fork at her untouched fillet. "It's the best thing on my plate... Tom's group found a Christian taxi driver first and were way out in front. Our two taxis were neck-and-neck from the bridge over the Nile and across Giza all the way down Al Haram."

"Neck-and-neck 'til we jumped out of the taxis. You took off thinking I had no chance to beat you in a footrace," she grinned.

"I know how it ends. A cold hollow sound. A furious clatter of hooves approaching from behind," he recalled utterly dejected as if experiencing the loss for the first time. "You paid some guy to borrow his horse. Caught up and passed me with only a few yards to go. It was sunrise over the Great Pyramid of Giza—the oldest and only intact member of the Seven Wonders of the Ancient World—and my role was the tired, sweaty, drunk, pissed off loser... Thanks for the memories."

Finishing the last remaining bites on his plate, Laszlo forgot about the past and looked to the future. Declaring, not to Willow, but broadly to the universe: "I really wish Scarlet could've come."

"I bet you do. I've never seen you lovesick like this in twenty years."

"She's fucking perfect. I'm going to marry her," he announced.

"Shut up. Nobody is perfect. You hardly even know her."

"We've been talking every day since New Orleans, talking for hours."

"And that is why she is not here now," Willow fired back.

"What! Why?"

"Don't buy her bullshit excuse. There was a fight with her man about how much time you two spend talking on the phone."

"Really? Scarlet told me he was super chill. She was free to do whatever she wanted."

"She *was*, until Mike posted the video of you two dancing at The Jazz Playhouse on Bourbon Street."

"That was nothing. I wasn't all up on her or anything like that."

"No, but you two couldn't take your eyes off each other. It even came through in the video. You were in perfect harmony like your eyes were tethered or some weird shit. If it was flipped and you were my man dancing like that with another female, it would be a huge problem."

"But Willow," he protested, "Everyone knows nothing happened."

"Not everyone. Her man don't know."

"That's fucked... Scarlet told me her brother was taken to the hospital after getting in a car accident."

"See, she isn't perfect. She lied to you about her man not letting her come."

"I need another drink." He looked for the waiter.

"Don't get fucked up too early. Everyone else should be here by the time we get back to the villa."

"You know I drink when I'm upset. Or when sad and feeling lonely. When I have company, I consider it obligatory. If I can't eat, I may have a few but only until I feel hungry again. Otherwise, I never touch the stuff, unless I'm thirsty." He eked out a smile to hide how upset he was.

"How do you know Scarlet anyway? In New Orleans she told me you two go way back so it's kind of weird I never met her before," Laszlo observed.

"Scarlet was besties with my little sister for a year, perhaps longer. She did a couple things for Disney at the time. She was always over at the house. Her and my sis were all excited about working together on a project dad was involved with."

"What project, a feature?"

"I don't remember. This was like freshman-sophomore year-ish. Anyway, one day she came over and told us she was moving back home to Seattle to help her mom. My sister tried calling for months. We didn't hear from her again for years."

"Don't fucking leave me hanging. How did we get from there to her joining us in NOLA?"

"She called me out of the blue one day in the fall of '21. Gives me a sob story about how her Disney money is gone and she lost her job teaching school because she refused to get vaccinated for COVID."

"Why didn't she get a fake certificate from Mike?"

"She wasn't in contact with him either at this time. When I say she left L.A. without a trace, that's *exactly* what I mean. Poof! Here one day and gone the next until the phone call."

"Ok, so what happened? You got her work?"

"I offered, was honest with her. Told her she would need to pay her dues again. Do a couple commercials and bit roles. You know how it is. My sis was in London working on her master's degree. I put Scarlet up at my condo while she was in town for a month." Willow finished her margarita.

"So, what happened?" He was desperately curious now. "What was she in?"

"Nothing. I reconnected her with Mike and we sent her to auditions. She showed zero enthusiasm or drive. She's so damn cute she should've got some kind of work. When I followed up with casting, they always said the same thing; she had the deer-in-the-headlights look of someone who ran away from home and popped up in Hollywood three days prior. It didn't track with her work history, her Disney experience... Long story short, Mike gave her the fake vaccine certificate for the auditions. As soon as she figured out it would work outside the studios, well, that was it. Next day she went home to Seattle and got back into teaching. This time she kept in touch and knowing she is an avid skier, I invited her to Steamboat Springs. For some reason you didn't come with us on that trip."

"I was in Hungary with my parents."

"Yeah... Anyway, she's friendly with the group now and when I invited her to NOLA she said yes straight away."

"I get it now" Laszlo said confidently. "She left initially because Disney tried to flip the script on her. Take her from after-school special to sex symbol. She's smart, witnessed the pre-thirty meltdowns ala Brittney, Miley, the whole damn club. She came back because she needed the money, but her head wasn't in it."

"Oh shut up!" Willow became visibly upset. "The only one fucked in the head is you. People don't make it in the industry because they don't have what it takes to be a star. Full fucking stop. Trust me, Scarlet ain't perfect. She isn't Snow White, and you are *nobody's* Prince Charming."

"I'm a buffoon who for better or worse has met all the stars. Scarlet shines brighter than them all. She has every-fucking-thing to make it and you fucking know it."

They sat in silence for some time while Willow played on her phone. Laszlo ordered another round without asking if she wanted one too. He went to the bathroom without excusing himself. After the drinks came, they moved on as old friends do by toasting to the future.

"Thankfully it appears we will be able to travel freely going forward without the vaccine certificates." He wanted to probe Willow about Mike's connections.

"Cheers to the end of that bullshit," she raised her glass again.

"I'm curious. It didn't occur to me during the trip to Switzerland. I mean, Mike is in fashion, not medicine. I didn't expect him to be so anti-vaccine and certainly not the person to be supplying countless people with counterfeit cards?" he asked hesitantly.

"All he told me at first was they weren't gonna Tuskegee *his* people. But later when I questioned him, he elaborated and told me not to worry. Said they were not fakes. Meaning they were processed and in the database globally."

"Globally?"

"That's term he used. Fashion or not he is a fed, remember that."

"Seriously? A fed like he works for the government and

the rest is a cover story?"

"Yeah, he has never been forthcoming with me as to what he does exactly but it's for the government, sanctioned by some government. That's pretty much all I know. I met him right after he started at NIH, the National Institute of Health. This was years before COVID, so I didn't think much of it. But I found out he was granted security clearances back then. He never mentions his time at NIH anymore... Randomly he invited me to Ukraine a few months before the war broke out."

"Holy Shit. This is too much. Algerian immigrant works his way up from fucking intern in Paris to a major player in the industry by thirty-five, but wait, also a sidetrack mission working at NIH before the largest pandemic psychological operation in a century. Make it make sense. Is he a warlock? Bastard child of some European royal who won't claim him as an heir publicly, but set up him for success... You never questioned any of this?"

"Questions don't necessarily bring answers. You know that. And occasionally they lead to big trouble."

"I'm going to confront him."

"Shut up! You're drunk. What's that going to accomplish? You think he is going admit to anything? No! It's only going to cause drama and ruin everyone's good time."

"I don't give a damn. It's almost 2024. Time for these motherfuckers to be exposed and held to account. We've been lied to on a scale most people's brains cannot comprehend. If you ever wondered how people would act during tyranny and fascism just look how they acted during COVID.

"How many of us in the industry are Jewish? Your family attends synagogue. You know half-of-mine was murdered at Auschwitz. We both have forebears who did or did not escape. But almost universally people in our industry were compliant dupes of authority or worse. They strapped on their jackboots and started goosestepping. Viciously attacking decent people for standing by their principles of freedom, bodily autonomy, skepticism of government and big pharma. The questioning of authority, free speech, and resisting totalitarianism was met with ridicule... Many were worse. People were shut out of deals for not conforming to the narrative. They scream 'never forget' but virtually all who did so forgot why consent to medical procedure became a part of the Geneva Conventions. People across our industry—in front of and behind the camera—many who I respected and admired, who's entire brand is being rebellious truth tellers, revealed their inner coward and willingness to repeat propaganda while simultaneously smearing those who were speaking truth to power and trying to dismantle the false establishment narratives.

"Fucking Rage! Rage Against the Machine required vaccine passes for their shows last year. Fuck Rage! And now," Laszlo cursed after taking a deep breath, "Now these same people—the same motherfuckers--are putting their COVID behavior in a memory hole because they lack the character needed to admit they were wrong and change. I didn't want to know this about them. But now I do know it and I can't un-know it. I'm mad as hell."

"Jesus, Laszlo, you're talking about *fucking* Hollywood. There's a better chance of a politician owning up to some shit. We're not in a college classroom making arguments for universal rights and justice. Yap, yap, yap. You think you're so clever, but most people find it annoying. Who the fuck are you? You're not going to change this world. It's time to get yours before you're old and dead. The bigger the business and cash money involved the more who are willing to conspire to get it! That's fucking Life 101, and you didn't have to pay for it or sit in a damn classroom for a semester to learn that lesson. I just gave it to you, yet again, for free! I suggest you start using that oversized noggin' before someone uses it like a watermelon for target practice."

"Thanks, again, for the life lesson. I want to have fun tomorrow and you're right, Mike won't disclose shit to me. I won't even ask. But! Before we head back to the villa let me ask you something about Hollywood."

"Fine, hurry up."

"You watched "*The Hunger Games*."

"That's not a question... What the fuck!"

"Relax..." Laszlo advised enunciating both syllables as slowly as possible. "Chill for a second. Breathe; not only you but all of us. We watched or read *The Hunger Games*, *The Matrix*, *Star Wars*, *V for Vendetta*, *Brave New World*, *1984* and on and on and we instinctively know who to root for. The Resistance! And yet, in so-called real life, we continue to tell each other, as you just now told me, to submit. Submit because you cannot win. Do you know why the above and so many more dystopian stories are popular but utopian ones are not?"

"I don't and unfortunately I don't think I can stop you from telling me so hurry up because I don't give a shit."

"The only well-known utopian tale—if we want to call it a tale—is Adam and Eve in the Garden pre-sin and ultimately not a happy ending there either. Virtually all other attempted works about utopian society are science fiction set in a time and place so far away as to be unbelievable. Inconceivable and unbelievable to most. Dystopia, alternatively, is almost universally understood across all cultures. Most societies have examples of specific periods in their history that were literal hell on earth scenarios where the living wondered why the dead should be so lucky."

"Ladies and Gentlemen, the next and final stop is Milan Central Station. All passengers must exit the train." The announcement was replaying alternatively in Italian and English as Laszlo felt and then heard the brakes doing their best to bring the train to a stop. His backpack was safely between his legs and being in no rush, he waited for the other passengers to disembark before doing so himself. Feeling pleased at his arrival despite the unnerving Belize memories his brain served up on the ride, the plan was obvious: walk around the station and find a spot that served beer. Drink beers and book a room for the night.

Exiting the train, he followed the crowd toward the lights of the main hall. There were more than twenty platforms and it being early evening people were scurrying in all directions. Walking from the covered outdoor portion into the station's vast main lobby he was immediately struck by its grandeur and elegance. Imposing arches, marble pillars, high ceilings and large windows merged with bronze sculptures and lamps to form a nearly flawless example of neoclassical architecture.

Fine decorative details of lions, eagles, flowers and vines played backdrop to statutes of allegorical figures in classical dress and busts of Michelangelo, Leonardo da Vinci and Dante. The ceilings depicted significant events in the city's history including the construction of Milan Cathedral and the triumphant 1796 arrival of Napolean Bonaparte after his victory at the Battle of Lodi. This ancient beauty and grandeur intertwined with fancy shops, cafes, fast food, and massive posters of provocatively posed men and women showing off the latest line of undergarments from the cities famed fashion houses.

Laszlo sat down at a small circular table with two slices of pizza and a Drago Verde—an American style lager brewed locally. The time had come to book a room, but his mind instead wandered back to Belize.

Contentious as dinner with Willow was that night, they'd had worse. What did he miss that rose to the level of her wanting him dead. The remainder of that evening passed pleasantly. The following morning only Kim, a mutual

Japanese friend who worked at one of the big Wall Street firms, joined Willow for the 7:00 AM pick-up to the reef. Mike, Abhi, and Dean had not returned to the villa after going to San Pedro for an after-party with some guys they met at the beach bar on the Caye. Laszlo was awake and alone waiting for his ride to the airport. Overnight he had received a frantic call from his mother. His father was rushed to the hospital. The outcome appeared dire.

DINNER AND A SHOW

It was after eight in the evening. On his fourth beer in a now mostly empty station, Laszlo booked a room. Under normal circumstances he would rent a private apartment, but this was a not a normal night. A hotel with cameras and security was the smart play. The B&B Hotel Milano Aosta is a three-star hotel across the plaza from the station. He secured a single room for under one-hundred fifty euros.

Leaving did not start off with good vibes. The initial majesty of the station had seemingly left with the passengers. All that remained were the asylum seekers peddling umbrellas and groups of homeless drunks arguing loudly in Italian. The giant posters of nearly naked models were still around watching over him, but they had turned ugly. Advertising is such a racket. Misleading and false solutions to deceptively created problems that do not exist, or the product cannot solve. The soul feeds on truth and beauty like the body feeds on nutritious food. To eat right and exercise is hard work. Instead, advertising sells the quick fix to lose weight forgetting to tell you the little pill will destroy your endocrine system. Get plastic surgery to deal with the excess skin caused by the rapid weight loss and you too can buy these $165 undergarments.

Advertising is the anti-thesis of beauty. A building, sculpture, painting, story, or music; art is fundamentally the act of creating something beautiful. A mother, a teacher, anyone with love and good intentions bestowing knowledge upon another is art. But this! It demeans! A net negative for the soul and wallet. The same way eating junk food sold at the station McDonalds is destructive to the body. Vulgar indignation weaponized within his soul. Sorrow filled his heart for all the people who unknowingly walked into this station with this madness scientifically developed to induce them and their children into poor decisions.

The east side exit of the station was filled with more homeless drunks. A few had already passed out. Feeling the light rain upon his face, Laszlo looked down on them without any of the disdain he held for advertising executives. He was in solidarity and had a quiet understanding—if not appreciation —for their lifestyle. However acquired, their poverty had freed them from accepted standards of behavior. In different, previous times, he would've looked upon them with pity or worse, but they were not unlike his old gang; his former friends whose wealth and power freed them from common decency, responsibility, and accountability. Why is the heavy lifting always done by the middle-class, he wondered. Like the English during the inter-war years, it was only the innate need of the majority to keep up appearances which kept the wheels of civilized society churning in former empires with long expired use by dates.

There was no line at check-in nor issues with his booking. Going up to the fifth floor he used the keycard to enter room 515. The red digits on the alarm clock showed 8:34 PM. He locked and bolted the door before emptying his clothes onto the bed and securing the folder in the safe. Diving straight into the report was something he considered in the elevator, but again decided it was better to postpone. He was in desperate need of a shower and would feel better after raiding the mini bar. Then he would look at it and with the information safely tucked away in his brain he could leave the backpack in the room and enjoy a carefree dinner.

Entering the tiny but modern and clean restroom he turned to the mirror to look himself in the eye once more. He looked exhausted; moth eaten. Very pale, with bitter, new but likely ineradicable lines. The good news was he felt in control of his faculties. Forty hours had passed since his final ready-to-rock New Years Eve mirror check back in San Diego. In those forty hours, accounting for the time saved by flying east, he had traveled more than six thousand miles by plane, train and automobile. There were meals, countless drinks, a pack of cigarettes and he vomited in a public bathroom. He had not washed his face, brushed his teeth, showered, or changed clothes. The urgency was justified. Now safe and sane for the moment he felt disgusting. He immediately stripped naked and tossed everything he had been wearing including the boat shoes purchased specially for the occasion in the trash. Good riddance.

Brushing his teeth felt great. Scrubbing from head to toe was equally satisfying. Next, he turned the water as hot as it would go and sat down, transforming the small room into a makeshift sauna. A jumble of memories raced through his mind in no particular order of time or importance. At one point he dropped to his knees and said the Lord's Prayer. He added verses of his own at the end thanking God for saving him, begging for the safety of his parents and a chance to see Scarlet again. He even swore off alcohol and drugs before asking for forgiveness in advance because he was going break that promise in mere minutes.

Drying off and putting on clean clothes he noticed it was now 9:33 PM. He grabbed a couple little bottles of whiskey from the tiny fridge and reconsidered his situation. Promises to heaven or not, he needed a drink. First, it was only day two. Scarlet warned the worst of the spell would last a week. Second, she warned nighttime would be worse than daytime. It was eleven hours to sunrise. Third, arriving in Budapest tomorrow he would want to celebrate his escape. Three days later, on the sixth of January, it would be his birthday and surely another night out. It was settled. Enjoy tonight and starting January 7th he would stop all the nonsense that led him here. Move forward free of Hollywood and the bad habits it fostered.

Having packed only a backpack in a panic his outfit was a random assortment of bright colors he would normally never wear together. It was loud, especially the bright yellow brand-new high tops he was gifted more than a year ago but never previously wore. With the bathroom steamed out he sized himself up in the mirror on the back of the hallway door. His uncombed wet hair was ready to go. Despite his face looking ghostly compared to his tanned arms, the steam opened his pores. He was pale but not lifeless. No razor meant shaving would have to wait, but he felt confident he could pass for a character able to afford the tab in a high-end Milanese restaurant.

The only remaining to do before leaving was to look at the report. The whiskey gone, he opened a little shooter of tequila and put the folder in the safe without opening it. It was not the time. In the exceedingly unlikely chance the report showed what he feared, it would destroy all he accomplished in the last forty-one hours. His very survival would be in doubt not because of Willow but by his own doing. Making the flight to Budapest in the morning would become a fifty-fifty proposition at best. He briefly left his body with that thought and hovered outside the window of the hotel. First looking in the room, before glancing down at the drunken homeless passed out on the steps of the station. There but for the grace of God go I.

Presently reunited with his bodily flesh still safe inside room 515 of the hotel, Laszlo grabbed his phone, room key, and wallet. The glass used for the mirror in the elevator was different, perhaps less polished or more concave than the one in his room. He did not like what he saw. It made for a long, lonely ride down. In the lobby he noticed something he missed while floating outside his window looking in: the rain had picked up considerably. He sprinted back across the street to the station where a dozen or more asylum seekers were selling umbrellas. A handful spoke English and he began to haggle over the price. The initial opening offer was thirty euro. Having no reservations, no fixed timetable for the night, and previous experience haggling at the famous Khan el-Khalili bazaar in Cairo, Laszlo was up for this game. He shook hands with Muhammed and introduced himself before continuing to walk toward the west end of the station. Muhammed followed and incrementally dropped the price by a couple euros until they reached the gate and fifteen euro. At this point he exaggerated his time spent in Cairo, "C'mon bro, I know how this goes. I lived in Zamalek for a year. I'll give you five." They exchanged stories and pleasantries for a few minutes before Muhammed agreed to five. Laszlo then gave him a twenty and motioned for him to keep the change. "In sha Allah, I hope you find a more suitable hustle."

The plan for the night was devastatingly obvious. Find a nearby restaurant for a nice meal and drinks. Follow dinner with many more drinks at a nearby bar. Go back to the hotel and pass out before 2:00 AM. Walking south past hotels fancier than his own, he noticed a little place called Barzac Tradizione. Peering in through the all glass front it looked the part. Red and white checkered tablecloths covered round tables sitting below hanging copper lamps. Each gave off a warm low light in front of a brighter exposed brick open kitchen in the back. A large wine selection covered the side walls. A cold gust of wind and the flimsiness of his cheap new umbrella reassured him this was the perfect place.

He was escorted to a table in the back left corner. Knowing the service in Europe can be painstakingly slow from the US perspective, he asked the hostess for a Negroni to start. Laszlo sat down with his back to the wall. His waiter quickly delivered the menu, and the Negroni—a gin apéritif made with vermouth and Campari. Gazing around the dining room he found roughly half of the two dozen tables occupied by a diverse crowd. Tasting the aperitif, his mind wandered farther afield.

Back outside, he was peering in to see himself sitting alone sipping the drink. A celebratory dinner this was not. It did not look the part. He looked defeated. A hunched over old beast staring back. Not even realizing the person outside the glass was him. Only half his iris was showing with blood shot white below. This was not an individual to have a staring contest with. He floated up and over the street for a second. The magnificent external finishes of the train station from above took his breath away. Moments later he was transported back to Seattle-Tacoma International Airport, only two weeks prior, December 21st, 2023.

His standard routine on all trips was to welcome himself with a local drink at the first bar in the airport terminal. This was different. It made sense; his whole life was different after meeting Scarlet. Why risk ruining the big weekend with her by getting too drunk. They spent a lot of time talking on the phone since New Orleans but much of it had been fluff. Other times they didn't talk at all. Laszlo at his condo in Sherman Oaks and Scarlet in Seattle, each with the phone on speaker. Cooking dinner or doing other chores. One of them would play music. It was the most amazing feeling to want to be with someone so much talking was optional. And to know she wasn't with her man or someone else. He always wondered where he was and received the same story each time. He lives on the other side of town near the family business. He works late.

Then one magical mid-December afternoon she called at the usual time and gave the usual rundown of the day at school before casually telling him they broke up. She played it with a poker face he would've been proud of. Gave away zero information. It was mutual was all she divulged. They had grown apart so why go through the holidays faking it. Laszlo pushed for more. She never relented. Nothing until one night she lamented being alone for her birthday on December 22nd. Shyly she asked if he would come celebrate with her. He did his best to play it cool. She sweetened the offer by telling him the plan was for them to see comedian Katt Williams. She next disclosed going to the show was originally a surprise Christmas gift meant for her man. Now she was begging him to come instead. The eight days between the invitation and the trip was the least productive of Laszlo's adult life. Virtually every second awake well spent daydreaming about the memories to be made.

Pacing past the bars of concourse A, his phone buzzed with Scarlet's response to his "I'm here" text.

"5 mins which terminal?"

"1/A."

"cool 3 mins away"

"What u drive?"

"911" was the reply. He exited into a surprisingly warm and clear late December Seattle afternoon. Seconds later he spotted her. Laszlo jumped in and they attempted a quick hug. Scarlet sped away with his still ajar door slamming shut from the acceleration.

"Black on black Porsche 911, nice. I love cars so it's pretty weird I never once wondered what you drive. Or whether you even owned a car."

"Got it when I turned twenty-three and the second half of my Disney earnings were released by the trustee. I considered selling it when I was fired during COVID, but I just couldn't part with my baby... Anyway, how are you? How was the flight? Thanks for coming 'L,'" she smiled, turning briefly to make eye contact.

"Thanks for inviting me. You look great; beautiful... You said we wouldn't have time to go to your place before dinner, so I tried to come ready."

"You're good, chill. It's only twenty minutes from here but who knows at this time of day." She accelerated onto interstate 5 North showing him her lead foot despite the high heels being temporarily off.

"What's the fastest you've taken her?"

"A little over two hundred."

"Kilometers?"

Scarlet hit the brakes as the traffic ahead all did the same. "No silly... Miles. Not in the city but Eastern Washington is rural as fuck. You can get away with anything out there. What cars have you taken over two hundred?" Laszlo never drove or rode that fast in his life. Luckily it didn't take him long to realize that if there was ever an occasion to tell a white lie, this was it.

"Same... A little over two but on the autobahn in Germany between Munich and Nuremberg. My buddy from Bayern has an AMG Benz that's a station wagon. Can you believe that shit. They still drive station wagons over there and they're dope. BMW too. You can get 5-series Beemer wagon with M specs. But you know how L.A. is... Thirty is cruising speed. The first state to legalize weed because it was the only way to slow the road rage epidemic." They exchanged knowing smiles. "I can show up late to my own funeral in L.A. and blame the traffic. Nobody will bat an eye," he reckoned.

"Did you tell Willow, Mike or any of our mutual friends you are coming to see me?"

"Hell no! I'm keeping you a secret forever. I've never told a single soul you exist because I don't want people to know how wonderful you are."

"Oh shut it!" She gave him a flirty backhand to the gut.

"I'm serious. When I'm around you I don't even breathe right. It's no longer instinctual. I'm conscious of each breath and every heartbeat." She giggled but he could tell he was overdoing it. Making her uncomfortable. Scarlet pulled a blunt from the console.

"Light this shit," she implored with a look confirming he needed to slow down with the heavy-handed come-ons.

He hit the blunt hard. Tilting his head back he slowly released all the smoke through his mouth only to draw it back in for round two through the nostrils. He told himself to relax. Turning to his left he blew it all into Scarlet's face. This drew a playful smack to his left thigh as intended. In Hollywood the saying goes: 'all press is good press'. When a man falls hard for a woman the way Laszlo had fallen for Scarlet, every touch is a good touch.

"I've been so stressed lately but now it's all lifting. I'm so happy you are here. 'L, we gonna get fucked up tonight! You ready?"

"Fuck yeah let's go!"

"Self-restraint was the original sin. Let us lose ours if only for a few hours." She returned the blunt and raised the volume on the stereo. He stared at her thighs while puffing it as she concentrated on fighting the traffic.

"Of all the records in the world you're bumpin' this when you come pick me up. Now I know for sure you're *the one*." He did his best to rhyme along with Lupe Fiasco:

> If you love her, don't ever send her to Mally Mall's
> Homie if she lonely she might end up in Macauly's claws
> Coming out the closet over goblets down at Mardi Gras
> The fame, champagne, walk of shame lobby call
> My re-position was a bad condition of activism
> I'm ammunition for abolition, missions attacking systems
> But they not after listens, unless it's dropping on Activision

Are we apps or are we bodies filled with apparitions
Operating applications, stuck inside an Apple prison
Chicken hackin' downloads and updates that lack religion
Or... Are we more?"

Laszlo didn't know the rest of the lyrics. He turned hard toward Scarlet during the last line as if to ask whether the question: *Are we more*, pertained to them personally.

She dodged his punch and deflected instead of countering. "Are you excited for the show tonight, 'L?"

"Fuck yes!"

"First, you're taking me to a place I've never been. It's the best Italian restaurant in Seattle. It's going to be expensive 'L. I hope you didn't forget your wallet and our deal. I get us into the show. You pay for the fancy pants dinner and drinks!"

"Pay? I must've been high for this conversation. I swear you told me the plan was to dine and dash," he earned another playful slap to his thigh.

"The restaurant, Spinasse, is in South Capitol Hill close to the club hosting the show. They're known for their incredible handmade pasta and traditional cuisine from the Piedmont region of Northern Italy. The whole menu sounds amazing. I think we should do Meno Degustazione."

"Sure, whatever you want. What is it?"

"It's everything! Family style. A few bites of every antipasto, main course, sides and dessert."

"Great idea. With the food order settled we can focus on the drinks menu," he grinned as she took the East Madison Street exit.

"Damn!" Laszlo cooed as Scarlet stepped out of the Porshe. He noticed the snug fit of her short green dress while driving, but now the front and back were both on full display. He twisted her around with his right arm and then raised his left pretending to wipe the sweat from his forehead. "I wasn't expecting Seattle to be hotter than New Orleans!" She attempted to smack him again, but this time failed. With a single move he grabbed her around the bicep before slowly but aggressively moving his hand down her arm. Not to defend himself but to clutch her by the hand. It was a short walk to the restaurant, yet it seemed a long time their hands were clasped together. Long enough for him to discover every magnificent detail of it.

Her cheeks were flushed. She met his tight grip and held it close to her side. He looked down upon her for a moment. She was glorious like the morning sun but somehow pained, desiring, or worse; made ashamed by his desire. Their eyes for a moment met. What treasure she promised! A queen's ransom of temperament. Hastily he looked away, disengaged his imprisoned arm. He was weirdly terrified. She was so much more than he could ever be worthy of.

Laszlo opened the door for her and gently put his other hand on her lower back as she stepped inside. They were led through a dining room adorned with lace curtains, fine art replicas of the masters of the Italian Renaissance, and noodle sheets draped over the open kitchen. He pulled the chair out for Scarlet and the hostess lit a candle. A more perfect setting for a late December sunset dinner he could not imagine.

As agreed, Scarlet ordered the Meno Degustazione to share. "Can you recommend a drink to start us out?" he questioned the waiter.

"We make an excellent Negroni. It's a traditional Italian aperitif served before a meal to open your palate and stimulate appetite."

"Great, one for each of us please."

"'L, you didn't ask what's in it or if I even wanted one silly."

"It's cool, if you don't like it order something else... What's your biggest pet-peeve? Outside of the classroom I mean. Not the kiddie stuff."

"People who are afraid of silence but have nothing to say so they constantly run their vapid and meaningless tongues for no god damn reason. Not dead but also not alive, soulless clones in human form."

"Wow... That certainly gets to the point as to how you really feel about me," he smiled.

"'L! Shut it! Your soul is the part I'm falling for. It's the exterior that's getting rusty. Begging to be traded in for a newer model."

"I deserved that. Well played."

"What's yours?"

"Um... Fake people. I realize everyone says that about California by default but its more, it's the manipulators. Every interaction is transactional but everyone pretends it's not. You can't trust anyone unless you've known them *forever.*"

"I feel you 'L, but I must also warn you. Watch out. I like manipulating people and I'm good at it!"

"What, are you for real?"

"Yeah, I'm an empath."

"A What?"

"I have like super-empathy. I can perceive people's feelings even if they don't intend to communicate them to me."

"Whoa, weird... OK so would you describe yourself as a psychic... Or a witch, or what?"

"No! What did I say 'L? Empath! I told you in New Orleans I'm a good girl. I want to help people. When you say witch it has a negative connotation. Like the Kardashian Coven where they chew through the men. Use 'em up and spit 'em out. I'm not like that."

"You say empath, but I will call you an enchantress." He teased and was thrilled to see her blush. "OK, so Miss Scarlet my enchantress, what am I thinking right now?"

"You are starving and severely parched," she purred as the waiter set the Negronis and appetizers on the table.

Raising their glasses Laszlo made a toast: "To a wonderful weekend and a cherished birthday for my enchantress!"

"Don't play 'L... But seriously, thank you for coming it means a lot," she put her drink down. "Everything looks so delicious."

"I am absolutely loving this one, try it." He put a bite on his fork and fed it to her.

"Oh my god, love," she agreed before swallowing. "Is that the cavolo?"

Laszlo looking down at the menu still open next to him affirmed it was, "Yeah, the kohlrabi and radish salad with anchovy vinaigrette and parmigiano. Hungarians love kohlrabi too. There is quite a bit of overlap between Northern Italian and Hungarian cuisine." He attempted to sound informed on a subject he knew nothing about.

"Where's the sexy dress from?" he was hoping to learn about her tastes in the few days remaining before Christmas.

"Oh, it's off the rack, nothing special."

"Off the rack or not you make it rock!" he smiled.

"Here," she pushed the burrata balls in his direction. "Try a piece of cheese to match that cheesy ass attempt at game."

"Well, rack or not I think it looks great. I don't think the high-end stuff is worth the price."

"Agreed, but I definitely take the samples Mike gives me for free."

"As would I... Which reminds me. We are in this Northern Italian restaurant. Milan is Northern Italy. Everyone knows it as one of the fashion capitals of the world."

"For sure."

"And they need to label their products as made in Italy, but we know most textiles get made in China. So what they've done instead to keep costs down is bring in workers. Not directly to Milan, but they set up manufacturing facilities in cheaper areas nearby. Despite the outrageous sticker prices and 'Made in Italy' labels they are produced by Chinese workers."

"I didn't know that, but it makes sense. Not that it's good for the locals but makes sense from a business perspective."

"Anyway, I don't care about the workers," he grinned. "Not that I don't not care, but not where I was going with this. So, the workers come from China and only go home once a year for two weeks when the factories in Italy shut down for Chinese New Year. The Chinese calendar is lunisolar, so the new moon determines the dates of the festival. Well, in 2020 Chinese New Year started on January 25th and went until February 11th. OK. You follow?"

"I think so."

"Think it through. We are talking about a *metric* fuck ton of Chinese workers," he smiled and took another bite. "It's many tens of thousands of workers that all go home at the exact same time. What was already spreading there?"

"Oh shit. COVID."

"Exactly, COVID started in Wuhan in late 2019. By early February the outbreak is nationwide."

"But weren't flights shut down?"

"Not international ones. The Chinese shut roads, trains and flights internally. But all the factory workers were allowed to go back to Italy."

"Holy fuck 'L, I remember."

"Two weeks later Northern Italy becomes the first European hotspot."

The waiter appeared with the pasta course and the bottle of sauvignon blanc Scarlet picked out. Laszlo was delighted to see Scarlet taste and compliment the braised rabbit filled agnolotti. Ordering rabbit at a restaurant in Boston many years prior led to huge a fight with his ex-girlfriend. In hindsight it had more to do with their eventual break-up than it should have, considering their mutual attraction mental and physical. His continued jabbing on the topic after the dinner itself—asking if she would eat rabbit in a *Hunger Games* scenario—no doubt annoyed her more than a male could ever grasp.

"This is going to sound crazy Scarlet, but to this point I gave you only the intro and rising action portion of this China to Italy COVID tale. Are you ready for the climax?"

"I'm dripping with anticipation," she vowed.

He smiled, "So my friend from Michigan and I are texting at this time trying to figure it out, you remember the early days before the lockdowns. It was all day news hype, but we didn't know anything... One day he sends me an article from the Catholic Diocese in his town, Lansing, Michigan. It's like the first week of March and the TV is showing overwhelmed hospitals in Northern Italy. Now listen to this. The article states there is a Saint Corona," he paused for effect, "And! This Saint Corona is one of the Catholic Patron Saints of... Wait for it, pandemics!"

"C'mon 'L, I haven't had *that* much to drink. You're

making this up. Is this a gullibility test?"

"It's not. I swear it. I will send you the link," he insisted. "Now take another drink because it gets even weirder. The remains of Saint Corona are memorialized in Anzu, a town in, you already know what I'm going to say: Northern Italy near the factories at the epicenter of the corona virus outbreak."

The waiter presented the bottle of Sangiovese Laszlo selected and the main secondi course was delivered. There was beef caramelized in an onion and honey sauce stuffed inside a savoy cabbage, milk-braised pork and pan-roasted gnocchi, and a butter poached halibut with pickled turnips and herbed potatoes.

"Damn 'L everything looks so yummy!"

"Amazing. Thanks for bringing me here."

"I drove but don't forget who's paying the tab," she sassed him once more.

"I got you. And I know you're enjoying it 'cause you didn't ask if I we should go smoke a blunt between courses."

"Hell no! I'm not getting up now, but I do have more rollies in the car. We can blaze before the show. It's not far." They sampled each dish and sipped the wine. Catching a buzz for the first time, Laszlo assumed Scarlet must be there as well.

"Do you like your job 'L?"

"It pays the bills," he paused, pondering if she was asking to see how deep he was tied to the industry. He recalled Willow's account of Scarlet's time at Disney and leaving abruptly. "I'd like to save up and open a restaurant... I once had an idea for a novel, but who has time to read anymore. Hell, I keep scrolling if I see a video's runtime is more than sixty seconds."

"What's your novel idea?"

"The protagonist gets into a big pickle. Some major

trouble where a powerful antagonist wants him dead; but at the last moment through luck and sheer will he gets out of it just in time to slay the proverbial dragon. People love that story. They never tire of it."

"I understand your sarcasm regarding the novel. It's like saying you as a Hungarian American are going to move to Mexico to open a low-priced, high-volume taco stand. Yet a book can also become influential not through converting tens of millions of casual readers, but rather gaining the attention of the very few, *who*, at the given moment, have or seize power. Karl Marx and Sorel were not great marketers of their ideas. But their readership included two, Lenin and Mussolini, who had the power to remake Europe... What I'm trying to get at 'L, is you should write your story without thinking of a target audience... Do you know who Miyazaki is?"

"The Japanese author and filmmaker. Yeah, for sure. He got some Oscar nominations. I think he won at least one."

"Ok, 'L listen. A major reason why Miyazaki still hits is because it's fairy tale and not power fantasy, which makes it ring truer. The audience can identify with the protagonist because they represent the best in us but are still relatively minor to the greater mysteries going on."

"Interesting take; perhaps you were meant to be a critic and not on-air talent."

Scarlet took a big gulp of wine and glared at him. "I hate you... Listen, 'L, think how the hero myth rituals are conceptualized. The sacrificial victim or hero, usually young, may be a central figure in the ceremony. Perhaps they are crowned or even hailed a living god, but even then, they play but a small part in the vast cosmology the proceedings are attempting to affect. There is no certainty the ritual, performed perfectly, will fix the cosmic wrongs. Attempting to satiate the entity they're trying to please can lead to making the world worse off. The hero's actions and avoidance of death are merely their best shot.

"Contrast this with today's superheroes who are repeatedly portrayed as saving the world. All our fates constantly hinged on their actions. Whereas, in Miyazaki's films, the world traces its own ancient and inscrutable path, pulling people into its processes when necessary. The best those engulfed by such machinations can do is protect their loved ones and not hurt the innocent."

"Interesting. The individual characters in Camus' stories are often powerless to affect their own destinies, especially in *The Plague*. I think it's the goal of all globalist totalitarians, but as Elon Musk argues it's a dangerous game. Human progress is not linear. Societies succeed and then forget and devolve. Knowledge survives only to the extent it is traded and translated to other groups. The likely outcome of a one world system is stagnation followed by devolution without the possibility of revival because critical knowledge will be either forgotten or forbidden and then lost."

"Listen 'L, all I'm hearing is excuses. I know what's stopping you, fear of failure. You were a successful student and athlete. You are successful in your career. You think yourself capable of success outside of L.A., but it requires taking a big risk."

"I hear what you're saying, Scarlet. I hate to say it but you're right. I have a story I want to tell. I hope you will play a role. I have strong feelings for you. Not exactly a shocker. You don't need to be an empath or psychic to feel what I feel. I know how to *game* a woman in a Hollywood club. My desire is to win your heart the old-fashioned way: chivalrous dedication and-"

"'L! Stop. Chill. I invited you because I like you. But you're too much with all this right now. I ended a years long relationship only two weeks ago."

The waiter's return was perfectly timed to help Laszlo re-engineer where this was going. "Did you two save room for dessert?" he inquired.

"Do we have time for dessert? Or does that course not come until we get home?" Laszlo deadpanned before wincing in reaction to receiving a stiff kick to the shin under the table.

"We do but I couldn't possibly eat any more. How about we get one last round and the check. We can go blaze before the show," she suggested.

Scarlet lit the blunt and they sat in silence in her car. Laszlo had a million thoughts running through his head and every single one related to the angel sitting to his left. She said she liked him. That was great. She was still silent about why her last relationship ended. He had hoped it was because she liked him more but her comments about its recency indicated that was unlikely. The breakup was clearly still bothering her. He couldn't imagine anyone cheating on her and was therefore uncertain how to proceed.

"'L," she exhaled. "You haven't even smoked yet and you're zoned out. Get excited! We are about to see Katt! He dumps on everyone and everything!"

"I'm excited," he imitated but internally he was a mess. He didn't know how to behave around her now. It was easy to play it cool on the phone when she was far away and had a boyfriend. But now she was right here and single and telling him to chill. They smoked and exchanged stories of other comedians they had seen or met. He faked interest but was desperate to get out of the car and to the show. Hopefully it, and a few more drinks, could change the energy between them.

They began the short walk to the venue with the wind picking up and the temperature having dropped significantly since arriving at the restaurant. Laszlo walked alongside her with his hands in his pockets. He could've used the cool down in temperature as an excuse to put his arm around her. He was sure she wouldn't reject his hand if he grabbed hers. He was physically capable of performing such actions but mentally he was not. They continued in silence for what felt like forever but was not more than five minutes before he saw *it*. He had seen it a few times in Hollywood, but not often. *It* was subtle and immediate. Like she pushed a button and turned herself on for a show in front of a live audience. Marylin Monroe singing happy birthday to President Kennedy did not glow brighter than Scarlet in this moment. It was magic.

He experienced it in New Orleans briefly, but this was another level. Scarlet had drawn attention at the restaurant as beautiful people do. Now they could not look away. Cars were slowing and rolling down the windows to get a glimpse of her. Men didn't care if their girl caught them staring. The women didn't catch the men staring because they were equally enthralled. Laszlo and Scarlet strolled past the line and the bouncer opened the ropes before they reached him. She didn't acknowledge or address him other than a "Thanks." He too stared unabashedly. They entered without showing an invitation or identification.

The place was like any small comedy club in a major US city but there had been no signage outside. It was modern but not fancy. The usher took them to an empty table in front, to the right of the stage. They ordered double tequila shots to start. The opening act started his routine. They moved their chairs closer together so they were centered and right next to each other. Scarlet seemed to be enjoying herself immensely. Hitting his thigh or playfully slapping his chest with the back of her hand when the punchlines were delivered and the club erupted in laughter. Sitting to her right and thus slightly behind her line of sight, he gazed upon her more intently than all the rays of the sun magnified through a single focal point.

Time, drinks, and laughter combined to restore the magic of the evening. Exiting the club into heavy rain, Laszlo instinctively grabbed Scarlet's hand. "Let's go back this way through the park" she implored. "Cover me," Scarlet pulled his arm and ducking down against a building pulled a rolled blunt from her purse. She lit it and hit it before standing and eventually exhaling. "We are in the northwest corner. If we cut that way" she pointed, "The car will be right there."

The universe was again in harmony. His fortune changing hands faster than chips in a Vegas casino. "Do you believe we have souls, Scarlet? Souls of different ages perhaps but something universal?"

"I don't think we have a soul," she countered. "The soul has us. Our ever-evolving selves inhabit these bodies of ours for a short time. My body is not the master of my fate. I can collaborate with it and to a large extent direct it, but my soul is merely a noisy passenger. The captain resides elsewhere," she leaned back releasing a large puff of smoke into the dark, wet, night sky.

They maintained their trajectory toward Scarlet's vehicle. She passed the blunt back. "'L, listen, even the ancient Egyptians divided the soul from the body. Today we call it conscious and unconscious but not understanding how the unconscious part functions we ignore it. Now you don't really know me yet so I want you to know these are thoughts I'm having now. A conversation we are having. I don't fully know what to believe, you feel me?"

"I feel you. I'm here for it. Keep going."

"The entire purpose of the mysteries or so-called ancient pre-Abrahamic religions was to achieve immortality by reconnecting the soul or unconscious with God and the cosmic. Modern science speculates we don't have free will and everything is unconsciously decided before we even make the decision. That's because we are spiritually blind and not aware of the other parts of the soul."

"I've read some of this 'science' as well," he recalled. "Ancient Eastern, Celtic, Greek, Christian, Muslim, and Mesoamerican religious practices—hidden in plain sight—but found in every part of the world, believed so for millennia.

Today it's challenging to even find a record of them because they go against everything we are taught to cherish in this materialistic illusion."

The late-night December sky opened up and the heavy rain was ceremoniously joined by the gods of lightning and thunder. "Is this normal?" he questioned.

"Its energy. It's the spirit breathing. Imagine if the body were a computer and the spirit was the software. The soul is like a cache in the form of electromagnetic energy. It is not of the body, nor the spirit."

"Analogies are fantastic teaching tools but I'm fucking serious Scarlet! That's an electronic Palmerian gate we are headed toward!" he surmised as they approached arm-in-arm... His whole world changed in an instant. Only the rain remained.

She spun him around like an unsure Celtic Dancer, "There is nowhere to go because we are already here. Embrace the flashes 'L! They either have our number—or if we are not yet so lucky—will get us soon enough. Feel the fourth dimensional plane 'L, here change occurs at a slower pace, these are different times. We must state our intentions clearly as we walk together to empower our hearts with the light of the realms we wish to occupy, and the realities to which we shall ascend. Let go of the external. Observe without attachment. Feel the light as it integrates our souls, forever aligned."

Reaching the car, Scarlet walked him to the passenger side. "You have to drive," she kissed him on the cheek and fell inside. "I'm too exhausted." Laszlo closed her door and walked around the back. He adjusted the seat and mirrors and set the navigation for home. The rain continued. Pulling onto the highway ramp there was another flurry of lightning over the park through which they trekked minutes earlier. "Pure essence, and pure matter, the two have joined into one and are shot forth without flaw, like bright arrows from a cosmic three-string bow," Scarlet yawned, and seconds later fell into a deep slumber.

BEAUTY AND
THE BEAST

"Sir, good Sir," the waiter woke him. "I can see you are overly tired, but we are closing. You can't stay here." Laszlo reoriented himself and, grabbing his umbrella, walked out into a clear Milanese night sky. His first thought was Scarlet. Soon followed by the folder he foolishly left in the hotel safe. What if somebody got in his room. Calling himself a moron, he quickened his pace and within minutes re-entered room 515 at 11:21 PM. The room appeared untouched and the folder as he left it. Recounting the first day in Seattle he understood now was not the time to look at it. It was early in the night. He was disassociating almost as much as being present. He threw it back in his backpack. The rain had passed. The room felt small. Knowing many hours have passed since he used the credit card to book it made him uneasy. A decade after spending one day in Milan, it was time to see what the city offered on this January night.

Laszlo stepped through the glass doors of the hotel lobby and made a left. He stopped in a little shop to purchase two shot sized bottles of whiskey to keep him warm on the way to Via Dante: the famous walking street known for its high-end boutiques, restaurants, cafés, and bars. The street is flanked by elegant multistory palaces running from Sforza Castle to Duomo Square, the heart of Milan.

Nothing behind you. He urged his brain to focus on the

future as he wandered down an empty side street. It was now past midnight meaning the calendar had flipped to January 3, 2024. Today would be the day he flies to Budapest. New beginnings would be his theme for the night. That and getting shitty drunk so he could pass out for a few hours before heading to the airport.

On that note he drank the second whiskey. He could now see Sforza Castle about a half mile away. The streets were unusually quiet. Few shops remained open. He passed only a handful of people, none of whom struck him in a particular way. Car traffic was similarly sparse. He eventually came upon a street vendor asleep in a chair next to his stand. Laszlo woke him and asked for a Peroni Crystall, a light lager. It cost three euros. He tossed him two two-euro coins which in Italian circulation have Dante's portrait on the obverse side. "Grazie. Keep the change." Turning, he cracked the beer and heard a harsh craw. Looking up to his left he spotted a crow perched on a black poplar tree.

Reaching Sforza Castle and making a left onto Via Dante, Milan was transformed. The long wide avenue alight and alive was buzzing with energy. Couples walking slowly and talking intimately. Groups of local teenagers doing weird teenage things. Tourists taking selfies. Glamorous people sipping drinks while sitting outside in the cold because they wanted to see and be seen. He stopped dead in his tracks to gulp his beer and appreciate the scene. Before long he noticed how different it was here from the train station. There was a large police presence and no homeless or asylum seekers.

The expensive glitzy storefronts and posters of nearly naked models were again juxtaposed against the beauty of the architecture in a weird duality. The bustle interspersed with loud wails of drunken fury and lamentations resounding through the starless air. He couldn't understand them but what his eyes saw, and ears heard, did not align. Beautiful people dressed smartly and smiling. Outwardly a scene taken from a picture in a tourist guidebook but with voices loud and hoarse. Strange tongues and horrible language sounding angry and pained, a tumult whirling in the dark night. A turbulent and restless vortex of bad vibes stretching from the castle to the cathedral in the center square.

Frozen and unable to fight or fly, he stood still in the street as the crowds parted around him. Was he dreaming or was it the drugs? Was it the spell? Perhaps the drinks and lack of sleep? He contemplated sitting down where he was when he spotted the entrance for the Palazzo Cordusio Gran Meliá. It was a five-star hotel he dismissed as too expensive to book a room for the night. He recalled it advertised a cozy interior garden bar. He willed himself to put one foot in front of the other with the promise of drinks and safety from the madness of the hordes presently swarming him.

Slouching slowly across the red brick circle drive he stepped into the marbled lobby and was met with greenery accented with hints of bright yellow, red, and purple flowers. The pictures of the bar area online failed to capture its magnificence. The ceilings were high—at least thirty feet—and the lighting was low and warm as it emanated from behind the bar mirror which reached nearly to the ceiling. The furniture was modern. The chandeliers were old world. The only thing that looked out of place was he.

Surprised to see the place completely devoid of patrons, Laszlo plopped himself in the middle of the bar. A middle-aged extremely tall dark brunette paused her task of re-turning glasses to their proper place and greeted him, "Buongiorno."

"Buongiorno, may I please have a shot of tequila and your cocktail menu," he assumed correctly she spoke English to be working at such a place. "On second thought, never mind the menu. Make the tequila a double and a Peroni as well please."

"Where are you from?" she inquired setting the shot and

beer in front of him.

"Hungary."

"Really? I would've guessed the states."

"You're right, Hungarian from Los Angeles here for the night before going to Budapest. It's a long story," he admitted and smashed the tequila. "I will have another when you get a moment."

"Look around. Nobody here; without you I spend all the moments making the glasses sparkle."

She delivered another double tequila and introduced herself, "My name is Bella."

"That's beautiful, great meeting you. I'm Laszlo."

"You know Laszlo I like Hungary immensely. I dated a Hungarian man many years ago. And what he tells me is this: Leonardo Da Vinci—I'm sure you know—he lived in Milan for a time and designed and painted and made many other works."

"Yeah, sure."

"Leonardo went to Hungary at the behest of Sforza, the Duke of Milan, and was commissioned by the Hungarian King Matthias Corvinus to paint a Madonna."

"That's cool... I thought I knew that history, but every day is an opportunity to learn something new," he quipped as she leaned back against the bar pulling out her phone.

"Did you go to Sforza castle Mister Laszlo?"

"Walked by it minutes ago. I have not been inside."

"You must go if you are here. Leonardo did the Sala delle Asse."

"What? I don't have time-"

"It's a trompe-l'œil. It makes the great hall appear to be a pergola created by the interwoven limbs of sixteen mulberry trees whose canopy is an intricate labyrinth of leaves and knots on the ceiling… Do you want more shots?"

"Not yet, I'm feeling dizzy. I can't miss my flight in the morning. Weirdly I feel like smoking cigarettes, but it will have to wait… What happened to your Hungarian boyfriend?"

"Oh, so many things. We were very immature. Working and traveling all the time. But I learned a lot of history from him."

"Like what?"

"Well like another one of the greats, Michelangelo, was sentenced to death by a Médici, Pope Clement. Michelangelo hid for two months in a small chamber under the chapel in the Basilica of San Lorenzo. With light from only a single tiny window, he made charcoal and chalk drawings which remained hidden until the room was rediscovered in 1975."

"I believe you about the death sentence, but Michelangelo painted the Sistine Chapel at the Vatican. Was he pardoned?"

"Yes, he was eventually pardoned by the Médicis, and the sentence was lifted so he could complete work on the Sistine Chapel. And believe this, he also did the Médici family tomb in Florence."

"Sounds unusually incestuous. Kinda like modern day Hollywood. I'll take another tequila now. I must be going soon."

Bella wasted no time serving him another. "You got a mob package between your legs?"

"Excuse me?"

"Oh, I'm just teasing Mister Laszlo. But you are looking down so often. It must surely contain something of great value."

"Nah," he feigned laughter. "I'm the only person in the world interested in the contents of this here bag. It's nothing but an old police report," he divulged unnecessarily.

"An old police report which you're guarding like it's the holy grail. If its value is not materialistic, is it spiritual?"

"Stop it Bella, it really is nothing, personal shit. It's different in the US. Everything is recorded."

"Sure sweetie, I wouldn't know. It's only a weird recurring dream I have where I travelled the US and the whole world as a top model starting at fifteen years old. Before washing back up here at one of the most exclusive hotels in Milan listening to drunk *gentlemen* such as yourself. Surely I know nothing about secret police reports. But let me ask you this: Do you even understand the significance of its contents? I don't think you do. You look fearful and desperate Mister Laszlo."

"Damn," is all he could muster.

"Did I hit a nerve?" she sneered before disappearing to the back. He grabbed his bag and went to the restroom. It was the anti-thesis of the airport. It was filled with lush greenery and inconceivably smelled better than the grand lobby. Looking at the man in the mirror he advised the person staring back: do not reveal anything further to this woman. Have another drink and pay your tab. Avoid Via Dante and take the side streets back to the hotel.

Returning to the same seat at the bar there was no sign of Bella. A female customer was now sitting two stools away. At first glance she appeared to be about the same age as Bella but lacking the genes of a former model. Taking a swig of beer and a closer look changed his mind. She had the appearance of an old hooker who had finally found her place in life. Women practicing the profession were found at hotel bars all over the globe. Plying their craft alone or in pairs tempting drunk business travelers with the promise of a good time. Her presence forced him to recall Scarlet's warning about witches being drawn to him. She looked fit to play the part. Not a hot modern 'good' witch but an ugly Middle Ages caricature.

Bella returned and the two women hugged across the bar and began talking furiously in Italian. After a few minutes Bella poured three tequila shots. "This is my friend from the old days. Her name is Emilia. This shot is on the house!"

"Great. Cheers! Nice to meet you, Emilia." He assumed she must have been a designer or agent but not wanting to be rude asked, "So by the old days Bella, you must mean you two worked together, modeled?"

"We did, yes. I didn't last as long in the industry as Bella," Emilia answered for her friend. "All the travel and long days wore me out. It's toxic to your health. From what I hear around town not much has changed."

"I would venture Mister Laszlo knows about our industry. He is from Los Angeles," Bella revealed.

"Is that true. You are in the industry?"

"No, not fashion. My friend- Or more accurately somebody I used to know very well, is."

"What do you do in Los Angeles?" Emilia probed.

"I've never been in front of the cameras. Contracts, but that's the past... The last few days I have been living in some weird movie about my own life. An unwillingly bystander thrust into playing a role he never signed up for."

"How so?" Bella urged him to continue.

Laszlo sighed, "I shouldn't tell you this, but you probably won't believe me anyway. On New Years Eve, only three nights ago, an old friend tried to have me killed in some sordid occult ritual I don't yet fully understand. I was able to escape but I'm basically on the run. I will never work in Hollywood again and worse: I may never again see the one I love."

"That's terrible to hear. We certainly know how it is. You will get past it and be better for it." Emilia encouraged.

"I hope so. With the exposures of the last few years at Nickelodeon and a certain powerful producer going to jail, I was hopeful the violent casting couch gangsterism was finally coming to an end."

"Not a chance." Bella knowingly set three more shots on the bar. "These are on your tab, Mister Laszlo... A producer or photographer may get in trouble or retire but there are always hundreds more looking to take their place. The old guard industry magicians behind the curtain, the ones bankrolling the whole edifice will never be revealed to the public or go to jail."

They downed the shots and Bella persisted, "It's weird and more horrific than the public can imagine. And we've been out for years." He was now curious how many years exactly. "You wouldn't believe what is expected of the talent."

"Try me, I dare you!" He smiled and immediately realized the flirtation was inappropriate.

"OK. You've seen the reports on TV. Us models are made to not eat and—at least in our time—would smoke cigs and do cocaine to stay skinny," she asked rhetorically. "Well, what do you think that kind of, um, shall we call it a diet, does to your skin?"

"Nothing good..." he trailed off.

"Exactly, so then we are sent for skin treatments. Do you know what that consists of?"

He knew it wasn't rosy like the advertising of vitamin E lotions. "I'd guess there are some bad chemicals in those products but no. I must admit I have no idea."

"They put hundreds of little pricks in your face and inject you."

"Oh yeah, Botox..." He hesitated, realizing it couldn't be that. Botox was for middle age wrinkles, not young models.

His admonishment was immediate in the form of a decidedly sarcastic reply of, "No," followed by silence.

"Ok I realize that was dumb. What do they inject you with?" he pleaded.

"Stem cells taken from the placenta of a mother with skin tone and DNA precisely selected to match your own," Bella explained without batting an eye.

Emilia shook her head knowingly but moved the discussion to a different vein. "They've been publishing weird science like this for a hundred years but have known and used the techniques for far longer. The human mind, for example, creates reality based on what it believes to be true. And the more the process is amplified and installed in the conscience of the collective masses, the more effective it is. They project what they want your mind to see and the more people who see it, the less someone not taken in by the deception themselves will have the courage to call out obvious falsehoods. This applies not only to a brand, film, or musician, but the whole picture of society in the mind's eye."

"For a couple of drunk former models, you two have some interesting insights. Are you both from Milan originally?"

"No, Bella is Florentine. I was born in Verona. It's east of here, northwest of Venice."

"Verona, interesting... Are you a Capulet or Montague?" He jokingly referenced the two families from *Romeo and Juliet*.

"That is not the only Shakespearean play set in Verona, Laszlo."

"Indeed, we can debate the conflict between friendship and love in the context of *The Two Gentleman of Verona* if you prefer?" he smirked.

"Even most locals don't know the plot of *Two Gentleman*. You must be a big fan of Shakespeare or especially well read."

"Remember I worked in Hollywood so it's something I must know. The studios have made virtually all of Shakespeare's plays into movies starting back in the silent era. Then they remake them with modern plots and stars. Even science fiction like Star Trek copies Shakespearean storylines."

"I have noticed and wondered why there are so many remakes and sequels."

"Because Satan might rule the earth, but he doesn't have to ability to create. Same with his followers. They take the creation of another, destroy its beauty, add their symbolism, and then market it to an unsuspecting public while patting each other on the back in a huge circle jerk of depravity," Laszlo roared with anger directed at his former friends and colleagues. "Please get my tab, Bella. I need to go."

With Bella turned facing the back bar, Emilia put her left hand on his right thigh. "Would you like to be our friend? Our lover for the night Mister Laszlo? Not romance, but a friend who gives a benefit. We will give you all the benefits you desire in return."

"My apartment is only a few blocks away," Bella confirmed her willingness to participate with a sultry look. She handed him a pen to sign and momentarily held his hand. It was tempting. Though older than him, Bella was still a proverbial ten by locker room standards. Laszlo had partaken in a handful of threesomes when he was single. But Emilia—smart and pleasant—was too ugly to tempt him. Too weird of a creature for him to view sexually.

"Um… Thank you. I'm flattered," he caught his breath while sharing a quick, deep glance with Bella before reaching down to get his backpack. "I must go."

Exiting the hotel and turning right toward a side street, Laszlo was overtaken by his love for Scarlet. She warned him. She helped him when all the others were out to get him. They had crossed through the portal in Seattle and their souls were now forever joined as one. In the morning he would go to Budapest. Soon after, the nightmare of the present would reach its climax. Not long after she will join him in a reunion of epic proportions. Surely as the sun rose that fateful morning in San Diego, the final scene of his story will end with he and Scarlet riding off into forever. Holding hands while the credits roll.

THE APPROACHING STORM

Returning to the street vendor a half mile from Via Dante, Laszlo again woke him. It was now 2:03 AM. He purchased another Peroni and headed in the general direction of his hotel. He spotted a small park and figured it a good place to relieve himself. While doing so, and simultaneously able to watch himself do it, like a bird perched above, he was able to grasp two things at once. First, he needed to fully understand the second day in Seattle with Scarlet before reading the report. And two, the weird part, he now felt an ability to disassociate at will. From Milan. From anywhere to any other place. The vivid recalls of New Orleans and the first day in Seattle he felt powerless. It was the influence of the spell and the drugs which swept him away. Now he knew where he wanted to go so he did. He placed the nearly empty backpack on a bench. Sitting down on it he took a sip of beer and looked up. Moments later he was transported through the low, fast-moving clouds.

It was a little after nine in the morning Seattle time: Friday, December 22nd, 2023. Laszlo opened his eyes to find himself alone amongst the black satin pillows and sheets of Scarlet's bed. He looked around the room recognizing each familiar detail. She passed out on the drive and again immediately after coming upstairs. He fell asleep only recently after spending most of the night in a weird dream like state re-living the previous night from his arrival to the storm in the park. He held Scarlet as she slept while simultaneously scrutinizing the room. Her bedroom was the polar opposite of his. A king-size bed in a small room with furniture which you could not see. Not because it was invisible, but because every inch was covered with various personal items: jewelry, clothes, books, candles, electronics, and trinkets large and small. The walls were similarly an organized mess of posters and pictures from around the world. He knew her to be well traveled but not to this extent.

Being mindful of not overdoing the drinking the preceding day, he felt strong. The smell of fresh brewed coffee emanating from the hallway was but a bonus to jump out of bed and give Scarlet a big happy birthday hug. He relieved himself and brushed his teeth before announcing he was awake, "Good morning beautiful, the coffee smells amazing," to no reply. He checked the kitchen and dining area, the living room, even the second bedroom set-up as an office and clothes storage. He looked everywhere including out through the sliding doors to the balcony but Scarlet was not to be found. A raven, not a crow, he was certain because it was wedge tailed and croaking deeply, was perched on the black iron banister.

He assumed Scarlet stepped out to grab breakfast items. Perhaps she was going to make a sensual breakfast in bed for them to share. Adding sugar to his coffee after locating the cream in the fridge he made his way back toward the bedroom. To his surprise, Scarlet now occupied the balcony. Her back facing him holding a coffee mug looking out over the Seattle cityscape. He watched her for a while, but she wasn't doing anything. Not a singular thing. Merely sipping coffee with one hand on the balcony railing holding his whole universe together.

"Good morning," he stepped barefoot onto the cold balcony floor.

"Morning, 'L... I'm sorry about this weather. Another

cloudy day in Seattle. I hate that it's like this while you are visiting."

"Oh, c'mon don't take it so personal Scarlet. It's the weather. Only a poet would take the weather so personally. You're not a poet, are you?"

"No, silly. I'm a teacher who had a great time last night. Thank you for taking me out."

"My pleasure."

"I wish you could've come for longer, stayed for Christmas."

"Me too. I want to stay but my father is ill. I must be there for my mom. It's probably the last Christmas we will spend together."

"I know 'L, I like that you prioritize family."

"And we'll get to be together for New Years."

"Yes! I'm so excited!" she squeezed his hand briefly. "The pics of the yacht are *crazy*. It's massive."

"And the pics of the rental Mike secured are dope too. We are right on the beach and there is an infinity pool and hot tub... You have a nice view from up here. My condo in Sherman Oaks is OK. I look up at Stone Canyon Park."

"It's nice from up here 'L but it's crazy down on them streets," she smiled. "I love it, it's home but the people are wild. Everyone's has six gigs. They DJ or paint and are learning to code, while starting a company that's going to be disrupter, except they're not sure which industry it will disrupt. Some teach yoga but that's not enough to pay the bills, so they have side hustles as a bartender or barista and drive ride-share... You see the empty store front on the corner there?" she pointed.

"I can see a few empty ones. The one across from Whole Foods?"

"Yeah, that used to be a burrito joint. Bomb burritos! Homemade tortillas, line out the door at lunchtime. I would stop after school to get my fix. Anyway, people found out it was owned by a Filipino couple who hired some Mexican ladies to run it, and they started protesting, ranting it was cultural appropriation."

"Damn, I believe it but like I don't want to."

"Believe it. They got death threats and moved out to the burbs somewhere. This was more than a year ago. So now we have another empty space and no burritos."

"Not even breakfast burritos, I'm hungry," he chuckled, receiving a pinch to his left nipple.

"I have everything here to make us brunch. I went shopping a few days ago in anticipation of your visit. Two bottles of champagne and fresh oranges for mimosas too. We can eat, drink and be merry. My little brother Carlos said he will stop by later. I am really excited for you to meet him. He is coming to San Diego for New Years!"

While Laszlo squeezed the oranges, Scarlet made breakfast: fried egg, bacon, tomato, and gruyere cheese in an English muffin with rosemary potato wedges on the side. They decided to eat on the balcony at the little round table for two.

"Thanks for driving home and taking care of me last night 'L. I was *on* one."

"Anytime, thanks for taking me to the show."

"I told you Katt would be fire."

"Show was fire and then we caught that lightning storm in the park. What a night," he inhaled a bite.

"I don't recall a thing after the show," she declared.

Why would she say that. Did she truly not remember or was this her way of telling him she got too drunk. That she didn't mean or regretted all the soulmates talk. His heart sank into his stomach. The food stuck in his throat as he attempted to speak, "The eye sees more clearly in dreams than does the imagination awake."

"Oh 'L, listen, I had some *crazy* dreams last night. I can't remember now but I woke up feeling I had travelled somewhere—we travelled—yeah you were with me."

Laszlo felt better and interrupted, "That wasn't merely a dream Scarlet. It was raining and lightning and we danced in the park. You exalted the heavens. Described how we were floating because we crossed into another dimension. I was fucked up too, but it was real."

"We danced? In the park with no music? What!"

"Yeah, you spun me around and then I picked you up and we were spinning together," he laughed. "Then I tripped. We fell but you were fine and jumped right back up."

He received a kick to the shin. Scarlet turned her leg to expose a bruise on her left outer thigh. "I guess that's what *this* is from."

They finished eating outside and went inside for a round of mimosas and to roll the first blunt of the day. She plunked herself at an angle to him on the brown leather L-shaped sectional and put her feet up on his lap. "I hurt my calves too. You owe me a foot massage clumsy."

Outwardly he feigned protest, "Call me names if you wish but we both know the five-inch heels are responsible here," he pinched her right calf.

"I'll roll and you massage, deal?"

"Deal," he agreed, pinching himself to confirm he wasn't dreaming.

Enjoying the perfect start to the day Laszlo massaged her legs. Smoking the blunt in silence he was more at ease than in many years. Previously only the ocean could deliver such peace of mind but being with Scarlet surpassed even the Pacific. He tickled her perfect feet with the bright green nails matching the color of her dress from the previous night. Smoking and drinking had him somewhere between wanting to suck her toes and attempting to probe deeper. Best to go the latter route first, he decided. "Do you really believe in portals, Scarlet?"

"Sure."

"Truly... Like you and I went through one together last night?"

She hit the blunt hard and held it in. "'L, listen, I consider myself open minded. I think quick and talk fast and —as you know—smoke a *lot*," she exhaled. "I also change my mind. Often. But to answer your question, yes. I believe in the possibility of portals. If I said it last night, I definitely meant it at the time... Are you familiar with Project Looking Glass?"

"I think so. Are you talking about the research being conducted in particle physics, like the hadron collider at CERN where they supposedly found the 'god' particle?"

"Yeah, I think Looking Glass is something bigger, but you nailed story being fed to the public."

"Do you think something more nefarious is happening there?"

"Good question. Physics, science in general, is like a weapon in that it can be used for good or evil depending on who is wielding it."

"Yikes that's bad news. CERN being government funded has me leaning evil."

"It could be, sure. So, listen, qubits exist in a state of superposition."

"Q-what?"

"Qubits is a concept in Quantum Mechanics where

objects can exist in two or more realities simultaneously through a phenomenon known as Quantum Entanglement."

"Holy shit Scarlet! I read an article about a physicist on my flight here who created a theory like this. I may be wrong. It was a fluff piece, biography not science. Sorry to interrupt, keep going."

"OK so with this phenomenon, qubits can be made to communicate with one another instantly, regardless of distance in time and space. This is where the whole Project Looking Glass part becomes supposition. One idea is nefarious actors are using it to predict the future. Not like a science fiction movie plot gone wrong but imagine using non-public advanced AI to feed it data collected in real time globally. Giving them the ability to predict the very near future, perhaps only seconds, with near flawless accuracy. The most obvious use case would be to predict and front-run global financial markets."

"Weird, reading the article that was my first thought, predicting financial markets. The motivation to do so is obvious, the ability to win the lottery over and over. I had no explanation for the how."

"Cash rules everything around me," Scarlet sang the hook from the early 1990's Wu-Tang classic.

"You know about quantum mechanics and real rap from before you were born. Have I told you yet—*in this dimension*—how much I love you."

He received a stiff heel to the groin. "I told you at dinner to stop with all the love bullshit. We're chilling and talking here... Listen because the second theory of how the portal is used is significantly more dangerous in the wrong hands. The location of CERN must be public because of its size. It's more than fifteen miles in circumference and like five-hundred feet deep. And, perhaps not coincidentally, its built on the site of a Roman Temple to Apollo that was known as The Gateway to the Abyss."

"Of course, they enjoy throwing it in the public's face. Deception in plain sight is some kind of weird fetish these fuckers have."

"Exactly 'L; and check this out: CERN's former Director for Research & Scientific Computation, Sergio Bertolucci, is on the record admitting the Large Hadron Collider could open otherworldly doors to another dimension, possibly allowing something to emerge from it."

"OK, I'll assume he really said that. My question is: If there is no clear cash money benefit but there is the potential for an apocalyptic hell being unleashed, why? For what purpose?"

"One theory is our dimension, the playground of duality, is the highest dimension the dark forces can reach and is their most abundant source of energy. They cannot ascend higher, and the lower dimensions do not have enough energy to sustain them. Destructive by nature, they are unleashing their minions, the so-called scientists at CERN. The plan is to mislead these lost souls into opening the portal and allowing an army of dark spirits to enter the third dimensional plane of Earth."

"Insane."

"It is... But they know the awakening presently transpiring will bring an end to all their systems keeping humanity enslaved. Without our energy they will be forever relegated to the lower realms."

"So, not to get too dark here Scarlet, but you're saying the goal of these entities is to open a portal to a dimension bursting with malevolent apparitions whose power will be summoned by, through—whatever—the portal, in order to stop the awakening by means of a mass human sacrifice."

"Yes."

They sat together in quiet contemplation for some time before Laszlo broke the silence, "Do the portals or the theories thereof relate in any way to-"

"Hold that thought 'L," she jumped to her feet. "I need to pee. I will refill our glasses before we go down another rabbit hole."

Alone for a moment, Laszlo contemplated everything. Scarlet wasn't merely beautiful, she was beauty. The Goddess of Beauty animated. Lively sparkling eyes growing ever brighter when she talked about something she was passionate about. It wasn't temporary and it wasn't magic, it simply was. The fantasy of New Orleans was becoming reality. She had invited him into her temple. Was feeding and nourishing his body and soul. The duality of the present presented itself with uncertain terms. Being with Scarlet was the only place he wanted to be. But to be with her was to leave his dying father and mother at home. Being home for Christmas meant leaving Scarlet alone, with her ex-boyfriend near in time and space. If only there was some way he could occupy both dimensions at once.

Scarlet returned handing him one of the champagne glasses and plopping on the couch exactly as before, placing her lower legs across his eager lap. "I was going to ask when you poured the last round. These glasses, they're amazing. They sing when we clink a toast. What is the engraving? Do the triple spirals have significance for you?"

"Oh yeah, I've had these for years now. Got 'em on my trip to Scotland and Ireland for the Beltane Fire Festival. I had no idea it meant anything at the time. I thought they looked cool so I purchased them as a fun souvenir. What's weird is no one has ever asked me about it. Not my little brother, who is late and hasn't texted. Not my mom or friends or anyone. Nobody before you ever asked if the symbol has meaning. I know now it has to do with fertility: life, death, and rebirth...

And since you asked, I also have a candle with the same symbol. Want me to light it?" she stood up.

"Sure," he blurted attempting to be casual. Scarlet offering to light a fertility candle with him was another sign from the Heavens. Not that he needed any more convincing.

With the candle burning and his liquid courage growing he started to massage her again, now mid-thigh. She slapped his hand and discarded it in one motion, "Behave! My brother could be here any minute."

He moved back to her calves and the conversation returned to physics. "I started telling you about the article I read on the flight. It was about a Princeton University physicist. I'm blanking on his name but it's not important. He is credited with discovering M-theory. Have you heard of it?"

"Maybe," she hesitated, pondering and taking a drink, "I'm blanking too but I think it has to do with string theory."

"Damn you're smart. Yes... It attempts to unify string theory according to a set of symmetries called string duality. Now maybe you understand what that means, but I sure don't. The point is, the interesting part to me is the connection to CERN and the portals we are talking about. M-theory speculates there are eleven dimensions."

"What does the M stand for?"

"That's the most fantastical part. According to the Princeton physicist who came up with the theory it stands for mystery magic membrane."

"You're fucking with me 'L... Mystery magic physics?"

"I'm not. Everyone believes they possess at least one of the cardinal virtues, and this is mine: I am honest to a fault... Seriously, look it up. Mystery dude has won the Fields Medal which is the Nobel Prize of Mathematics, the Issac Newton Medal, and the Albert Einstein Award. All for this eleven-dimensional magic theory."

Scarlet did look it up and found the professor on Wikipedia. "Holy fuck, 'L, you're right. His name is Edward Witten."

"Told 'ya," he crowed.

"OK... I'll have to believe your silly ass next time."

"Every time."

"Yeah whatever, 'L listen... I find it interesting that his theory has eleven dimensions. I think he may be one off and there are really twelve."

"I'll listen to your theory on twelve but must first note the Italian philosopher Umberto Eco conceived of ten realms in his work of speculative history set in Milan: *Il Pendolo di Foucault.*"

"Noted... You're Jewish but not practicing or not orthodox like Willow, is that right?"

"Half-right, non-practicing Jew from a Christian family. My Grandfather was a Christian minister who married my Jewish grandmother during WWII as the Nazis were closing in. Everyone else was put on a train to Auschwitz but they never suspected she, the wife of a minister, could be a Jew. Her whole family, my family, more than thirty in all were murdered at Auschwitz," he recalled with tears in his eyes.

"Damn 'L, I'm so sorry for bringing it up. I had no idea."

"I know. It's OK... Everyone from that part of the world has similar stories. The eastern front was a bloodbath that wiped out millions of all faiths and ethnicities. On the Christian side my teenage grandmother hid deep in the well for forty-eight hours while the Soviets came through. Her father went down first and built a shelf for her to sit on because rape and pillaging was so widespread. He was an unarmed non-soldier in civilian clothing shot dead in front of his church because at sixty years old he was still capable of picking up a rifle and becoming a future combatant. Then after the war the communists took power and took everyone's farms. Being Cuban I'm sure you know about *that*...

"Of course, taking the land didn't release you from having to work it, only you now had to give away the fruit of your labor for free. Anyway, it's complicated... I don't attend any services, but I try to keep faith and hope alive. A spiritual belief that ultimately evil will be defeated or transcended. I guess you could call me gnostic, but only if I get to define what gnostic means," he cautioned. "Anyway, tell me about the twelfth dimension."

"That's so crazy but yeah, I'm gnostic too... I asked because I'm wondering if you know about the Book of Enoch that was found among the Dead Sea Scrolls. It was left out of both the Torah and the Bible."

"I haven't read it but it's one of the reasons I don't subscribe to any orthodoxy. The whole what's in, what's out, and who makes those decisions. It reminds me of the Edict of Milan, or Mediolanum, the Celtic name for Milan before Roman times... For centuries a Christian could be killed or tortured merely for their faith. One day in Milan the Emperor declares Christians are good and are now protected under the law. If you killed a Christian the day before, you—the killer—was protected by the authorities. Do it one day later and now the killer would be executed under the authority of the same Emperor."

"Absurd. That reminds *me* of the Vulgate, Saint Jerome's Latin translation of the Bible. Jerome wrote it in the late 4th century and then a measly 1100 years passes before it becomes the Church's official version at the Council of Trent."

"Right, the council also known as the Catholic Church's Counter-Reformation. Totally a nothingburger, unrelated to the creation of the Jesuit Order."

"Or the Gregorian calendar replacing the Julian." she added as they shared a knowing smile confirming their understanding not of Church Canon, but each other.

Scarlet lit another blunt and after exhaling returned to, "The book of Enoch talks about twelve portals. Though if they all lead to a dimension different from our own the total would be thirteen dimensions. At any rate, close to the eleven number the professor theorizes."

"Thirteen lines up interestingly with Aztec and other pre-Columbian Mesoamerican belief in thirteen levels of creation. The highest level was called the 'place of duality' and occupied by the god and goddess of fertility," he interjected.

"Whoa, that does align... Is the number two-hundred significant in Aztec mythology?"

"No... Not recalling anything."

"Because the other story I find interesting in Enoch is the two-hundred fallen angels. Now it's not that I necessarily believe in these old texts. I find them compelling because the very powerful people who run our world believe. Regardless of literal historical truth, that makes it super interesting. Don't you think?"

"Yeah, I feel the same. I like to know what the enemy is thinking," he winked. "So, what does it say about the angels?"

"The first book, The Book of the Watchers, is the story of the fallen angels and it says these angels had sex with human women."

"No wonder Jews and Christians both hate it. That's like the serpent seed theory where Eve was impregnated once by Adam and once by the serpent. Thus, everyone is either of the good or the evil bloodline all the way down to modernity."

"Makes sense they hate it but that's not where I was going 'L. It's more practical to what is playing out in the world today. The ultra-wealthy sitting atop our human pyramidical power structure believe in and adhere to the rules laid out by these ancient often secret belief systems. According to the story in Enoch, the fallen angels not only have sex with human women but share secret knowledge about magic and seduction, ultimately leading to the angels being expelled from heaven. Now, keep that number two hundred in mind. it's not approximation. It's the exact number given," she divulged... "OK... Now what do you about Kazakhstan?"

"*Borat!*" he smirked. "Seriously not a lot. I do know it's a huge country and landlocked. It was part of the Soviet Union. I know the Kazakhs were pissed about how the movie portrayed their country. And I also know the opening scene of *Borat* where he leaves his Kazakh village was filmed in modern day Transylvania, Romania," he claimed, taking the blunt from Scarlet. "Not far from where my grandparents were born."

"I did not know about the film but also not where I was going... But you're right, Kazakhstan is the ninth largest country in the world by land area. It stretches from Eastern Europe to Western China. The southern part near its largest city and historical capital was first settled more than three thousand years ago. But check this out: they recently built a brand-spanking new capital in the north called Astana. Throughout all this history there was virtually nothing for hundreds of miles in this location near modern day Astana but a small outpost on the Great Silk Road. The ancient Turkic word for the region translates as virgin soil. During the Soviet period in the last century its Russian name was City of Virgin Lands and still its inhabitants numbered only in the tens of thousands," Scarlet explained before pausing to hit the blunt.

"This is interesting, keep going," he urged.

"Yeah... So, in the middle of nowhere Eurasia over the last twenty years they built this brand-new city, Astana. UNESCO, the United Nations Agency, immediately gave it the title: City of Peace. Massive palaces and government buildings, skyscrapers housing financial institutions, multiple colleges founded in partnership with many of the world's leading universities, and giant sports complexes were all erected in record time. Additionally, there is a neo-futurist entertainment complex larger than ten football stadiums that is the highest tensile structure in the world. It houses shopping, golf, canals, and cobblestone streets, even an indoor beach resort. All for a population barely over one million even today."

"I have heard a little something about this," he exhaled.

"Cool, so 'L, listen. I told you to keep in mind the two-hundred fallen angels, remember?"

"Yeah."

"OK... Have you heard about The Palace of Peace and Reconciliation?"

"No."

"In the middle of Astana, a London based architectural firm built this palace. It's probably the most important firm in modern architecture. They designed Apple's campus in Cupertino, Beijing International Airport, the new World Trade Center, and a bunch of other projects you would recognize. The firm is run by a private equity company called," she paused, "'L guess!"

"I have no idea."

"Third Eye!" She waited for his reaction.

"Now it's my turn to claim you're fucking with me, Scarlet."

"I'm not, trust. This palace..." she remarked making air quotes before taking the blunt, "Is a pyramid. It serves as the permanent venue for the Congress of Leaders of World and Traditional Religions which is made up of two hundred members. The apex of the pyramid is based on the United Nations Security Council meeting room. It has exactly two hundred seats and meets there once every three years. The pyramid itself is two hundred and three feet at its base and two hundred and three feet tall."

"I get it. It's like you said, it's not about what you and I believe but what the freaks in control do. And the shit they keep hidden and worship in secret. They clearly have massive plans for this place, Astana. And we know the plan goes way back. Hell, the first President Bush gave his 'New World Order' speech to Congress on September 11, 1991."

"Exactly, 'L, Astana was nothing back then."

"They have been planning for a long time. Based on what you told me about it, I think this mostly unpopulated so-called virgin soil will be spared in WWIII. It will likely host the negotiations for a peace treaty post-war before serving as one of *The Hunger Games* envisaged capitals of the new world order. Headquarters of the fallen angel bloodlines post-apocalyptic one world religion and government. The apex of evil's final attempt to eradicate the righteous."

"That's so fucking dark but I love it and agree with you 'L. My ex said I smoke too much and chastised me for making everything into a conspiracy. But we are the same. We can go down super deep rabbit holes without internalizing it as definitive truth. We can talk openly knowing a misunderstanding will not lead to mistrust."

"No mistrust here save for the raven I saw on your balcony this morning."

"Huh?"

"I couldn't find you but there was a raven on the balcony. And you're teaching me so much about this Book of Enoch… The only aspect of his story I know is that Enoch was the son of Cain. And according to all three of the Abrahamic faiths, when Cain kills his brother Abel, he doesn't know how to dispose of the body until he sees a raven kicking up dirt," he snorted.

"Shush it," she mouthed and kicked him playfully.

"Listen, that reminds me I forgot something. In Astana there is also a massive tower meant to embody the Tree of Life."

"Of course there is. And let me guess: the new city will be smart and is scheduled to be completed by 2030."

"Yup, they have us focusing on everything unimportant, lie about everything of note, and mask their plans for a totalitarian future in symbols."

"Yes, but the hope is people are seeing, or should I say, 'eyeing' this stuff."

"I used to feel hopeless with how few could see obvious lies, conspiracies, whatever you call it. But they fucked up with COVID. I don't know if it was hubris or relying too much on an AI model created by their own programmers."

"Or they couldn't postpone any longer because Project Looking Glass showed the timeline needed to be altered."

"Oh! Interesting take—I don't know—but that shit failed. It was diabolical and many are suffering but it unleashed forces of societal transformation that are impossible to control. Yes, they've been planning and preparing for this for a very long time. But they have fundamentally underestimated the human spirit. They've underestimated the power of human agency and misunderstood the unstoppable force of the truth vibrations activating humanity.

"...When we talked on the phone a couple weeks back you mentioned wanting to have kids-"

"My little brother texted. He can't come 'til tonight. I guess it's the two of us. What do you want to do today? Is there anything you want to see in Seattle?"

"I'm looking at it right now."

"C'mon 'L, tell me, there must be something."

"I'd like to cook for you tonight. We can go out if you

prefer."

"No, I want you to cook for me. What's on the menu?"

"Do you have any allergies or preferences?"

"No allergies. I love seafood, steak, pasta... I love to eat and drink as you've witnessed."

"Hmm... How about seared scallops in a garlic basil butter sauce over angel hair to start, and a bone-in ribeye with mashed potatoes and sautéed veggies for the main?"

"'L that sounds amazing. I'm so excited now!"

"Only thing is I don't bake, so dessert is all you," he couldn't help hinting his desire.

"You're a dork. Attractive enough and smart but a huge dork... I'm going to pop the other bottle of champagne. Later we will need to go down to the grocery."

She shimmied back in and leaned from the waist to seductively refill each glass with her cleavage mere inches from his face. He stared. She caught him. They both laughed and this time she sat down right next to him with her feet firmly on the floor. They toasted and kept eye contact for a moment. He hesitated but she did not and pecked him on the lips. "I really like you 'L but I'm not ready yet. Please don't be mad."

"What's there to be mad about. I'm eating and drinking with my favorite person in this whole dimension. All the damn dimensions."

After a few moments he remembered his question. Not the best timing but timing was never his strong suit. "On the phone you mentioned wanting to have kids was the reason you didn't get the COVID jab. How did you know back then it could cause fertility issues?"

"I didn't. I had no idea but a hunch something was amiss. Then my brother convinced me to investigate. All the pressure and coercion by governments and media only confirmed my decision. Not questioning science became this weird political mantra. I didn't even consider fertility until Mike warned me against it in L.A."

"Makes sense. Willow told me in Belize that Mike worked for NIH years ago and has security clearances. Did he tell you that?"

"No but he always knows things before they happen. He said he didn't know if this was the big one but to resist any mandate. The harder the push, the coercion, incentives for taking it or punishment for not will be the clue to avoid it. It cost me everything. Almost everything; I had a career I loved teaching geometry to eager students at an expensive prep school. It paid well with amazing benefits. After being let go I couldn't find anything. I thought I was going to end up teaching yoga to hipsters on a brewery rooftop," she laughed, but Laszlo was not amused to learn these details. "I was broke and breaking down. I started losing my hair. I went back to L.A. and stayed with Willow because I didn't know what else to do. That's when Mike got me the fake vaccine certificate. Having burned all my bridges at the prep school I honestly felt fortunate to get the babysitter position I have now."

"I'm so sorry you had to go through that ordeal. You made the right decision. Held your ground against the largest and most sophisticated psychological operation in history and came out stronger."

"I know that now."

"It's weird. I read an article last week by a Japanese doctor from the Institute of Molecular Oncology in Milan..."

"Milan again. Did you live there or something?" she interrupted.

"No, I've only ever spent one day in Milan. Long story, Willow-related but unrelated to where I was going with this.

But I have been experiencing a weird delta with COVID and Northern Italy. Like last night, I let you pick the restaurant. I didn't suggest Italian cuisine. You picked it and it reminded me of the Lansing Diocese Saint Corona connection."

"That is weird. Tell me about the Japanese doctor."

"I can't remember his name, Hiroshi perhaps."

"For someone in the industry you are really bad with names 'L."

"I know. Nobody could ever pronounce mine right as a child, so I told myself names aren't important. Decided in like third grade I would judge people on character as evidenced by their actions. But I digress…

"The good doctor is in agreement with colleagues who have been censored like crazy for proving miscarriages and still births are exploding in highly vaccinated cohorts. But he goes further. He is claiming the protein in the jab can go from the placenta to the fetus. Even if the child is never vaccinated for COVID their body will produce the spike protein."

"Yet another theory turns to conspiracy fact. Mike is an asshole, but he saved me."

"Producing the spike means the child has the potential for all the side effects like myocarditis, cancer and a generally weakened immune response requiring a lifetime of pharmaceuticals supplied by the same companies who made billions off the poison shots."

"It's going to leave a Nile long trail of tears in its wake."

"Who would deny the three letter government acronyms never stopped the MK-Ultra research they were caught doing in the 1970's. Imagine how much they have learned since and pat yourself on the back. You did not submit to the largest mass formation version of a fear-based trauma inducing dissociative mind control weapon to ever be released on an innocent and unsuspecting public."

"Damn 'L, you got a fucking dark heart, but I love how you explain this shit without the bull." Scarlet refilled their glasses and lit another blunt.

"Damn, where did that come from?"

"I pre-rolled a few in anticipation of you coming," she admitted.

"Oh-cool, I was worried it was a magic mystery blunt you summoned from a dark realm," he teased.

"I'm saving the dark magic for after you make me dinner," she retaliated without missing a beat.

"Good one Scarlet. You're witty without a trace of dork. If only I found you physically attractive, we could be a thing."

Scarlet looked at her phone and sighed. "Carlos isn't coming at all. I swear I'm the black sheep of the family. Nobody ever comes to visit me. I always end up having to go to their place."

"Don't make a big deal out of it. I'll get to meet him in San Diego."

"You're right. Finish that drink so we can go to the grocery. There is going to be a storm later."

Throwing on sweatshirts and shoes it was only a split second before they exited her building into the street. A strong wind was made sharper cutting between the tall buildings, but the sun remained in control breaking through the high cloud cover. "This way," she took his hand and led them in a northerly direction. "Now I'm sure you know a lot of this but follow me for a minute. I want to take you back in time for effect."

"Take me *Back to the Future*," he attempted his best Doc Brown impression.

"You're too much. Listen, Ivermectin was vilified as 'horse paste' despite its inventors winning the Nobel Prize in

Medicine. And we've discussed countless absurdities on the phone. Shutting down parks, beaches, gyms, and churches but keeping fast food joints and liquor stores open."

"Open? They were deemed essential!"

"Exactly, then they told everyone to inhibit their breathing with masks even when not confined in close quarters with the sick. Douse themselves in carcinogenic chemicals for protection. Fucking follow floor arrows around the grocery store for their safety!"

"Motherfuckers paved a road to hell with blind obedience masquerading as good intentions."

"They did but stick with me, 'L.'"

"I'm here."

"As late as March of 2023, the federal government did not allow the unvaccinated number one ranked tennis player in the whole world to fly into the country on a private jet to play a sport which by its rulebook is socially distanced. And the tournament they prevented him from participating in—The Miami Open—was in *fucking* Florida where they did away with the COVID nonsense two years prior. The clubs were hosting parties for thousands of people nightly."

"I know. I was practically living in Miami at the time."

"I know you know but I feel it's necessary to highlight the absurdity for your mind's eye before you hear the point I want to emphasize."

"Which is?"

"To use that dark heart of yours and imagine this dystopia: Years before we ever heard of COVID, the Chair of Harvard University's Chemistry & Chemical Biology Department was working for the U.S. Department of Defense *and* secretly working with the Chinese Communist government at the Wuhan University of Technology."

"What was he doing at Wuhan?"

"His expertise is in injectable self-assembling nanocircuits... Now imagine that a pandemic breaks out providing the cover and impetus to inject self-assembling nanocircuits into billions of people and none of the three-letter acronym public health authorities even bother to check what's in the vials because they are all captured. Bought off or brainwashed into believing that vaccines are god. That would be weird, wouldn't it 'L?"

"What is his name?"

"Dr. Lieber. He was arrested in Boston a few weeks before the rest of us were locked down. Now, if that's not weird enough for you, here's a fun fact: Professor Lieber holds the record for the largest pumpkin ever grown in Massachusetts. More than two-thousand pounds!"

"No way. I believe the nanotech part. But I've never heard of a pumpkin so huge!" he smiled. "Have you met Kim from New York. She went to law school with me and Willow?"

"Yeah, I like her. She came on one of the ski trips."

"The first time I learned about nanotech was from Kim the weekend of Obama's Inauguration in January 2009. Kim worked on the campaign. She was invited to the Staff Ball at the armory in D.C. and brought me as her guest. The Obamas' are there and the usual suspects along with the campaign staff. Jay-Z did a set which back then I thought was really cool. He performed *99 Problems* but replaced bitch with Bush. Crowd pleaser to say the least... Long story short, Kim tells me she is being offered a job in the National Nanotechnology Coordination Office. And I'm like *wow*, Obama is creating an office for nanotech, that's cool. She reveals he isn't creating it; it's been around for a decade already."

"Holy Shit."

"Right? On that timeline, assuming government never

makes tech with a military application public without at least a five-year runway, we are now thirty plus years deep into the era of nanotechnology."

At the store the vibe between them was completely synced. Neither wanted to waste time. Both enjoyed the back and forth over selecting the perfect cut of meat and picking a complimentary wine. Laszlo selected an oaky chardonnay for the scallops and Scarlet chose the full-bodied Barolo to highlight the main course. Being out in public with Scarlet was almost as much fun as having her all to himself at home. She wasn't wearing a fancy dress and high heels as the night before but there was still something magical people couldn't help but be attracted to. He knew the real magic was her choosing to spend time with him over anyone else.

Returning to the condo they unloaded their haul onto the counter. Scarlet grabbed the corkscrew from a drawer, "It's early but I'll put the water for the pasta in a pot so we have an excuse to open the chardonnay."

"Great idea. There is wisdom in wine and freedom in beer, but be careful, tap water is laced with fluoride… I can open it," he offered. "Why did you get filo-dough?"

"So I can teach you an easy dessert. That way, *in the future*, you can make your date a proper three-course meal," she teased.

"I'm listening. What's your recipe?"

"Mold the dough into little cups and coat each one with butter before baking. While that's in the oven, mix enough mascarpone with honey, vanilla, and cinnamon to fill all the cups. The exact ratio doesn't matter so it's super easy. Next, cut up a variety of fruit. I have raspberries, blueberries, and kiwi so I'm going to use those. A couple minutes before the dough is ready, pull it out. Fill each cup with the mascarpone mix and top it with the fruit. Toss it back in the oven for a couple minutes and voila! Dessert is served!"

"Now I'm excited," he mirrored her earlier comment. "I guess this is a good time to tell you I brought a surprise. Not a birthday gift per se… Something I want to share with you."

"I love surprises!"

"It's not a big deal but I have a bottle of Hungarian dessert wine. My dad gave it me many years ago and I never found a fitting occasion to open it."

"Aww, that's so cute. Hopefully I will get to meet him."

"I hope so too… It's a rare bottle of Tokaji wine he brought back from Hungary years ago. Tokaji is the most renowned dessert wine in the world."

"I've never heard about of it, but I believe you."

"You probably have heard about it without a reason to note it. It gets regular mentions in pop culture, from Bram Stroker's *Dracula* to an episode of *Mad Men*.

They sipped the chardonnay and began dinner prep as Scarlet lit another magic blunt. He cut veggies and she cut fruit. "Are you happy in Hollywood? I mean, you seem to be doing well from what Willow told me."

"What did she tell you?"

"Only that people like working with you even though you aren't the typical type. You don't go to premiers of projects you're involved with. Forget or ignore people who are the power players in town."

"I can't argue with that take. The business is uglier than most. On the surface is the cruel and shallow perceived rightly as superficial by outsiders. Deeper through the heart of the industry there is a trench filled with the promise of riches and fame where thieves and pimps run free and good people are used up and thrown away like trash… But you were in long enough to know this. I looked at your IMDb. Why did you suddenly quit?"

"It's a long story. I don't want to talk about that now," her eyes glazed over. She looked away. Her right hand grasping the edge of the table as if to anchor herself. The oxygen was sucked from the room. It felt like all of Seattle went silent and the vibe turned somber for a moment.

"OK… We don't have to talk about it. Let's change the topic by staying on topic."

"Huh? 'L? You hear yourself… You high as fuck my nigga."

"Fuck yeah I'm high. Your Cuban ass be rollin' these blunts fat like a cigar," they laughed until he forgot what he was going to say and continued with dinner preparations.

"Oh yeah… Same topic but the music side of the industry…" He couldn't even get the words out before she cut him off.

"It's worse. Absolutely everyone is a degenerate, trust."

At this they were laughing again only not the with same nonchalant attitude of moments earlier. They both understood the evil. Their laughter a respite against horrible truths. "Seriously," she continued, "like Katt joked last night. I believe they're taking everyone out next year, cleaning house."

"I hope so but who is they? Are there any good guys?"

"I believe there are. I need to believe the good guys are coming," she whispered. He reached across and set his hand on top of hers. He understood this was no fairy tale monster. She had come across a real malevolent force that breathed in this world.

Scarlet pulled her hand away and poured them each another glass of chardonnay. "I'm telling you 'L, Drake and Diddy are going to have a terrible 2024."

"You think Drake had XXXTencation murdered?"

"I didn't say that."

"But you heard about the pic he posted of Drake?"

"Pics... Shit, 'L, I saw the video."

"Damn. And Diddy too?"

"Yup."

"Really? Do tell because I assumed he was a fed for years," he wondered how she could possibly know all this.

"The gun rap with J-Lo he beat back in the day is nothing compared to what's going to come out."

"And what is that?"

"I don't know the specifics. I see bribery, extortion, sex trafficking and murder in his astrological house of troubles." They exchanged wry smiles.

"Wow. Video evidence of such charges usually leads to people talking and making deals, but what do I know. I took the one mandatory semester of criminal law a decade ago. My only experience beyond that is working with a cast member of *Law & Order SVU*," he admitted. "I do recall a lawsuit filed by Beyonce's employee. I didn't know about this stuff back then. I chalked it up to a disgruntled employee who got fired trying to milk their wealthy former employer."

"Not merely an employee. That is how they deflect and lessen the allegations. Her name is Kimberly Thompson. A drummer who played in Beyoncé's band for seven years. She filed a lawsuit and requested a restraining order. She accused her of extreme witchcraft including the murder of a pet kitten, magic spells on her lovers and gang stalking. Do you know what the fuck gang stalking is?" Scarlet raged such that he couldn't help but wonder if it was something she had been subjected to.

"Umm... Under the law I think its characterized as 'Organized Stalking', extended harassment by multiple actors working in concert against the victim."

"Sure, that's the legalese definition. A victim would say it's being under surveillance 24/7, home break-ins, personal property and automobile vandalism, theft, pet torture, electronic harassment, slander campaigns on social media, chemical assaults, and income sabotage persisting for many years and intended to produce isolation, psychological and physical illness, destitution, homelessness and even incarceration."

"That's so fucked. I can't imagine being subjected to all that. At the level you're talking about it must be very well funded. Likely linked to Cointelpro and MK Ultra. Former government trained bad actors now working in a private capacity."

Scarlet excused herself to the restroom and he stepped out onto the balcony. To the northwest he caught the last moments of the winter solstice sun peering through the clouds before saying goodnight. The thick, dark, and more ominous clouds emerging from a south westerly direction appeared poised to take their place. Scarlet's prediction of an impending storm was about to be fulfilled.

EVE OF THE DRAGON

His spirit reconnected to his body still sitting on his backpack in a park in Milan, Laszlo checked his phone. It was 3:33 AM and he needed to be at the airport by nine. There was a message from his mom reminding him to call when he landed in Budapest. There was no reply to the email he sent Scarlet from Ava's phone in the Heathrow restroom. He did not learn anything about his own fate from the days in Seattle, but he did gain an understanding of Scarlet, a depth of character underneath the public persona. He realized she regretted not the past but a lost future. Not what had been but what could never be. The dreams of her youth would never be fulfilled. Not because she lacked the talent, but because her soul shined too bright to succumb to the darkness required to make it in the industry. That is why she walked away at the exact moment she was given her opportunity to become a household name. A Hollywood starlet.

Back at the street vendor, Laszlo was surprised to find him awake. He too was surprised, "My friend you are back. I did not expect you to come again. It is so late. My name is Luca," he extended his arm. One of Laszlo's pet peeves was a clammy limp handshake. Luca, however, shook his hand so hard and for so long he didn't know how to get it loose. Eventually extricated, he was handed a Peroni without having to ask.

"Before I assumed you didn't speak English, Luca."

"I was exhausted but now I'm awake. I studied in Boston for two years. Where are you from?"

"California, but my ex-girlfriend graduated from Andover in Boston. Did you hear of it? It's a prep school attended by America's ruling elite, like the Bush dynasty."

"I have not… I do know the Bush clan is related to the most powerful Italian family through Catherine de Médici, who was also Queen of France."

"Interesting, I didn't know that. Wish I could stay and chat more Luca, but I have an early plane to catch. Grazie."

"Bonjourno."

Catching his flight was merely an excuse. He had plenty of time to return to the hotel but did not wish to do so. He needed to revisit what he feared almost as much as the contents of the report in his backpack: New Years Eve. Laszlo took a deep swig of his cold Peroni. Zipping his jacket, he set off across dreary late-night Milan on a course heading away from Sforza castle in a northwesterly direction.

He looked up into the sky to find it bereft of clouds. A warm San Diego sun was shining on his face, and he could feel the hot sand between his toes. It was 4:23 PM local time, December 31st, 2023. Scarlet had sparked the blunt exactly at 4:20 PM. It passed first to her little brother Carlos on her right and soon made its way around the circle from Carlos to Mike, Willow, Kim, Abhi, Dean and his new friend, before finally reaching him standing to Scarlet's left. Laszlo was the last of the group within a group, those staying here at the beach house Mike secured for them, to reach San Diego after getting stuck in traffic leaving L.A. He joined the larger group of everyone scheduled for the yacht party in the middle of a late lunch a half mile up the beach. Scarlet was friendly with him, but he didn't feel a deep connection like Seattle. She mostly focused on introducing her brother to everyone and the associated small talk. No matter the night would surely work its magic.

The women didn't hang on the beach for long, opting for last minute shopping and to prep for the night's festivities. Laszlo hung with the boys until dark throwing the football back and forth without much purpose and engaging in light banter completely devoid thereof. Nothing out of the ordinary before heading in for pre-shower shots of tequila. He had purchased a whole new outfit for the night. White pants—which Mike approved of despite it being well past Labor Day—he paired with a blue dress shirt that was the most expensive he ever purchased and a brown belt. Always brown and not a black belt with a blue outfit was a mantra Mike had coded deep into his brain. He even ordered a pair of new but faded looking blueish grey boat shoes and wore them without socks. He found this gross as his feet were always sweaty, but for a night like this First World sacrifices had to be made. Caring about his appearance to such an extent was exceedingly out of character, but tonight was different. Tonight, he was to spend the most magical night of the year for new relationships with the woman he had fallen in love with over the last three months.

Embarking started at 8:40 PM for the six-hour cruise scheduled to leave the harbor at nine sharp. Immediately high-end bottles of tequila and vodka were brought forth to cheers of "Happy 2024" and a chorus of "Shots! Shots! Shots!". Moments later someone dumped a *Scarface* sized pile of cocaine out on a tray and Laszlo and Scarlet joined the line to get the night started. Dean arrived with his new boy toy and littered the ship's kitchen counter with baggies of weed and plates of edibles, mushrooms, little pellets of mescaline, untold sheets of high-powered blotter acid, more cocaine, and a whole galaxy of multi-colored uppers, downers, screamers, and laughers.

It was not ten minutes after they set sail before one adventurous couple from the outgroup grabbed Willow by the hand and the three of them went off to 'break in' one of the bedrooms. Laszlo asked the bartender for a round of shots and beers to be brought upstairs. He grabbed Scarlet's hand. They made their way up to the deck as the light illuminating from the city merged with a waning gibbous moon in the clear star-laden early night sky. Beautiful as it was, he wasn't interested in the view. Laszlo had Scarlet in his sights. She was wearing a shoulder-less white dress that fit tight as can be. Her lovely olive skin sparkled as if it was responsible for the stars shining in the sky and not the other way around. All beneath the perfect canopy of her long, dark, curly hair which had been slowly driving him mad since the fortuitous first sighting in New Orleans.

Over the next couple of hours nothing noteworthy happened. More shots and trips below deck for bumps of cocaine or other drugs. The conversation was initially superficial. How lucky they were to get such good weather. The amazing dinner spread. Where in the world everyone was planning to travel in the new year. Everything was going perfectly as he had envisioned. She was mirroring him and keeping eye contact with those gorgeous green eyes. Carlos was mingling on his own. Scarlet engaged him as though no one else mattered. "I want to tell you about something 'L. Remember the discussion we had about dimensions and calendar shifts last week?"

"Of course."

"Well, I started researching the switch from the Julian Calendar and that led me down a big rabbit hole related to the upcoming eclipse this year."

Willow re-emerged from downstairs with Mike and Abhi carrying bottles of champagne. They were in a celebratory mood. Laszlo wished he could be alone with Scarlet. As the new year's toasts began anew, he couldn't help himself. "Tonight is nothing more than an excuse for us to get fucked up. According to the Julian and many other calendars," he shared a quick knowing look with Scarlet, "there are numerous different new year's celebrations globally. Most of these calendars have been in use much longer than our current one."

"That was like thousands of years ago. Even India celebrates new year's today," Abhi declared. "And we have not only Hindu but regional calendars like the Tamil and Malayalam."

"It's a global world now. How could we travel and trade without agreement on something as basic as date and time." Mike challenged.

"I don't think you two understand L's point," Scarlet came to his defense. "He is questioning why the current calendar—the one where we celebrate the new year tonight—won out over all the others."

"It won because over time it was shown as the most accurate," Willow professed.

"That's not true," Laszlo countered. "Most calendars are lunisolar, meaning they incorporate both the sun and the moon and are thus conceptually designed like the Babylonian calendar. This is significant because the Julian, the old Roman solar calendar which became the Gregorian Calendar, is what we use today."

"The Catholic Church adopted it by decree only in the 16th century. England and its dominions, including in the America's, continued to use the Julian until 1752," Scarlet explained. "For the sake of argument let's concede its accuracy post the change. Is the global adoption of something so fundamental as the calendar—how we keep and record time —not evidence the Roman Empire never fell but instead morphed to become the Catholic Church."

"I love a good conspiracy theory, but I don't believe in the bible." Mike testified.

"It's not about what you or I believe Mike. The question is: have powerful people like emperors and popes been motivated to deceive. To manipulate something as fundamental as what year it is to solidify or gain more power in their time, thus affecting all future time," Scarlet challenged.

"This is too stupid to be true," Abhi droned his usual refrain when a viewpoint challenging his hardened worldview was presented. He disappeared below deck.

"I propose we start the new year on April 1st," Laszlo grinned.

"Everyone can be in on the joke," Scarlet continued the troll.

"You two are crazier than I thought. Or do you have better drugs you're not sharing?" Mike questioned.

"I'm sober." Willow, Scarlet, and Laszlo all declared in a universal admission of the opposite.

"Listen guys, the various histories and timelines of the calendar are super interesting. The French revolutionaries adopted a metric calendar from 1793 to 1805. One week was ten days, one hour a hundred minutes, and one minute consisted of one hundred seconds. New year shifted from the 1st of January to the 22nd of September."

"The fall equinox!" Willow and Mike exclaimed.

"No," Scarlet continued, "It's the anniversary of the founding of the French Republic. The ten-day week was meant to disrupt the traditional, sacred seven-day cycle. To birth a more egalitarian era. Napoleon finally restored sanity after twelve years."

"Sounds like pre-Marx communism to me. Stalin tried to impose a new calendar as well. He cut the week to five days. Days were assigned colors and workers assigned colors 'equally', except if your spouse or family had different colors you would have different days off. Essentially an attempt to destroy the traditional family."

"Laszlo and Scarlet cannot stop fighting against communism. We won. Let's all enjoy the new year!" Willow raised her glass for another group toast.

"No, seriously," Laszlo began to a chorus of low laughter.

"Every time you say 'No, seriously' it's like your signal," Willow snickered.

"It's Laszlo's equivalent of the bat signal. It lets us know he is about to spew some wacky theory," Mike followed on.

"Seriously, mockery won't shut me up. It's possible to hear evidence of a novel theory without accepting it. You can make up your own mind. Alternatively, you can run away like Abhi."

"Let's hear him out," Scarlet urged.

"I can cut the sexual tension between these two with a butter knife," Willow asserted. Mike shook his head in affirmation.

"The Chinese New Year doesn't start until February 2024 on our calendar. It's going to be the year of the dragon. Chinese as in China: the second largest economy in the world run by a totalitarian *communist* dictatorship the West has not defeated." Willow gave him a dirty look, but Laszlo pressed on. "Anyway, the Chinese calendar is thousands of years old and has eleven real animals that still exist and one mythical one, the dragon. Why would the Chinese calendar have eleven real animals and one mythical one?"

"This sounds like some religious voodoo to explain away dinosaurs and science in order to claim the earth isn't billions of years old," Mike protested.

"I didn't say that. I'm merely pointing out that Chinese

and every other ancient culture describes dragons. In Europe there are many surviving texts, instructions if you will, for wizards and witches to craft brews with many different ingredients that all exist in the natural world *and* dragon's blood.

Carlos joined them bringing reinforcements of champagne, cocaine, and a fat blunt. "That looks like a Scarlet rollie," Laszlo observed.

"You learned a lot in Seattle," Carlos noted.

This led Willow to comment, "You went to visit Scarlet in Seattle... Wow, that explains this."

"Explains what exactly?" Scarlet queried.

"Why you dumped your man right before the holidays, Scarlet."

"It's not like that... 'L and I are good friends. We have a lot in common." Nobody believed her but only he was annoyed. Why would she use *that* word: Friends. She could've deflected in another manner.

Laszlo desperately wanted to talk to Scarlet alone, but she moved next to her brother. "Carlos told me about a theory I found captivating, however improbable, on our flight here. Tell them, Carlos."

"Uh, it's wild but a Bavarian historian of the Middle Ages proposed that the Holy Roman Emperor Otto III and Constantine VII fabricated hundreds of years of the then in use Julian Calendar. Among other evidence, he notes that if the Gregorian calendar was really introduced in AD 1582, there would have been a discrepancy of thirteen days between it and the Julian calendar it was replacing. True solar time was used as justification for its introduction. However, the astronomers and mathematicians working for Pope Gregory found the adjustment needed to be only ten days. It's complex math but if you do the computation relative to solar time this leaves roughly three centuries over counted."

"You are definitely Scarlet's biological bro." Willow quipped. "Much of European history from the time is also recorded by other civilizations, is it not?"

"Sure, its recorded but the timelines don't have to equate because the other civilizations you cite were using their own lunisolar calendars during the possibly fraudulent period in question."

"I see your point regarding the lunar calendars, but modern science has radiometry that would unequivocally show a gap of hundreds of years." Mike asserted.

"I said the same, but Carlos had a clever response. Tell 'em," Scarlet urged.

"My sis gives me too much credit, I didn't come up with it. There does not need to be and cannot be a break in physical chronological time as dated by modern science. The question is simple. Why was there so little progress for centuries and was the history of the period altered in some way."

"Wouldn't the Black Death explain it?"

"It could and it certainly existed but what if it was overhyped like COVID. What if all those people were burned to death not because they were contagious carriers of disease but because they refused to go along with the narrative. The church has a long history of killing heretics."

Laszlo would normally be uncommonly interested talking about such theories but at this moment in history all he wanted was to speak to Scarlet alone. Unfortunately, time was not going to cooperate. It was nearing midnight in the Pacific Time Zone and everyone gathered on deck for the big toast. When the clock struck twelve he kissed Scarlet on the lips and met a closed mouth. She gave him a big hug, placing her head on his chest in a manner that let him know there would not be another. He stood perplexed and alone while she proceeded to hug her brother, Willow, Mike, and the others.

He too ended up embracing a few people who came to him but was again standing alone and looking out into the darkness of the Pacific Ocean to the west when Scarlet grabbed him by the hand. "'L come with me." She pulled him toward the back deck where they were finally alone. Assuming she didn't want the others to see them before, he again kissed her on the lips. She pulled away.

"'L, stop! I told you in Seattle and a billion times on the phone. I'm not ready for a serious relationship," she grasped his left hand with both of hers and looked him in the eyes. "Please, 'L, I know it's New Year's, but we are on our own timeline. Don't be mad at me."

"I'm not mad about waiting but why did you call us friends?"

"Who cares what they think. You want Willow and Mike gossiping about us. You know how they are. It's still our night."

"If you say so. Are you going to sleep with me—sleep in my bed with me—tonight?"

She pulled his hand up around her shoulder while moving close and grabbing him around the waist in a long embrace. "Of course, silly... Did you eat a lot of shrooms?"

"The usual. I don't want to get fucked up too early. We should go down and take some mescaline and dance the night away."

"That's a great idea but listen... I want to tell you about the eclipses, remember?"

"We didn't really get into it, no."

"I want you to research it 'L, don't trust me. I mean, trust me, but don't trust me blindly, do your own research. I'm giving you a synopsis before everyone else comes back because you know if they hear us, they'll accuse of us boring their night with more theories… 'L this is the weirdest shit ever."

"Tell me."

"I researched it, but you look it up yourself cause its crazy!"

"You know I always do the research unless it comes from you. I believe anything coming from you wholeheartedly, even it requires doublethink" he smiled thinking she would understand the reference. She did understand and hit him playfully on the arm.

"I know you remember the total solar eclipse we had across the US in 2017. You told me about going camping near the line of totality with friends."

"Yeah."

"OK, well there is going to be another total eclipse this year in April."

"Cool, you want to come camping with me?"

"No, maybe, but listen. In between the date of the one in 2017 and the upcoming 2024 eclipse there was another total solar eclipse over South America."

"OK, I don't recall that one. Did you go to South America?"

"No. No, I don't remember it either. I only started researching this last week after you left Seattle. So, if you remember we talked about different dimensions, ripples in time, and portals."

"Of course, how could I forget."

"OK so when I throw this glass overboard," she threw her champaign glass into the bay to prove a point he could've understood without such a display. "See the ripples from where it hits the water spread out evenly in all directions."

"Yeah, and I see the shrooms you took are kicking in" he

shot back facetiously.

"I'm serious, look this shit up. I want your honest opinion before we leave San Diego… OK, so as I was saying, ripples in time. The date of the South American eclipse was in the middle of the two in the US. *Exactly* in the middle. From the 2017 eclipse to the 2020 it was 1211 days. From the 2020 eclipse to this upcoming April 8th, it's again 1211 days. Look it up."

"I will, but my understanding is eclipses aren't rare."

"They aren't but what they don't tell us is some are more important. I don't know why yet but remember how adamant Willow and Mike were that we go to New Orleans not over Labor Day but for the equinox. It's because they have some beliefs they don't speak about. She is Jewish and Mike atheist, but I know that's just the public face they present."

"I don't think they're scientology."

"I don't know. They never fully explain things to me," she trailed off and took a bump of cocaine. He handed her the remainder of his champaign and did the same.

"OK, so 'L, imagine the 2020 eclipse is my champagne glass hitting the water and the ones before and after are the ripples in time, past and future. Do you understand?"

"Ah I guess, I'll look up the dates for sure. That's funky."

"Cool, but listen, you'll have to look up more than that. The path of totality of the two US eclipses, 2017 and 2024, form an X over Chesterfield, Missouri. And do you what's in Chesterfield," she asked rhetorically and continued: "The Pfizer facility where they developed the COVID shot!"

"Really, that's quite the coincidence."

"Coincidence my ass! What day did they start administering the jabs?"

"I don't know, a few days after the 2020 election."

"On December 14! The date of the eclipse in South America exactly 1211 days before and after the totalities in Chesterfield!"

"Whoa. OK if that's for real, and I'm not doubting you, that's weird. But as for tonight, let's go eat some mescaline and dance in the moonlight."

Going below deck they found the expected: old pop music turned up and the lights mostly off. Scarlet elbowed him in the stomach and motioned toward Carlos dancing with Willow's little sister. They found Kim, Mike and Dean devouring the coke. The bartender poured another round of tequila shots.

"You two are fucking sober as fuck," Dean yelled cutting out two massive lines. Scarlet went first and he was right behind. "WowWee! I'm good for now," Laszlo breathed in. "As you all know, I live by the old maxim everything in moderation," to a few chuckles and a sarcastic 'Yeah right, buddy," from Kim. The sarcasm from Kim wasn't surprising but what Scarlet did next was.

"Too much of *almost* anything is bad—except sex and champaign—Oooh that I can *never* get enough!" she screamed and began twerking against Mike singing along with the hook from Brittney Spears *Gimme Gimme More*. Mike took Scarlet by the waist and was grinding behind her doggy style. Before Laszlo could react, Dean walked up to Scarlet from the front thrusting his pelvis in her face while placing one hand on top of her head and pointing mockingly in his direction with the other.

He turned without reacting and went back to the top deck where Scarlet had embraced and reassured him only minutes earlier. He looked down at the water cold and choppy. He knew attempting to swim ashore from here was suicide, but how could he stay? The mockery made him feel an outsider; and feeling an outsider increased and intensified his contempt. It was nineteen minutes past midnight. His whole life passed overhead. Caricatured in the clouds now slowly descending over the bay. Scarlet came upstairs after some time. She must've noticed the three whites of his eyes for she stopped her approach short, made no mention of his soul, the first witness to his blood running cold.

"What are you doing up here all alone?" she asked while keeping her distance some six feet away.

"Keep away from me you fucking whore. Twerking on Mike like some glorified pole. Singing about you can never get enough sex; but giving me pecks reveals a lack of respect. Fuck you! Fuck your brother and your whole family too! I'll say it again bitch, 'cause I no longer care about you!"

She approached him cautiously, "I know you're upset, but you must listen. I feel safe with Mike and Dean. You know they're gay. It's only dancing and having fun. It's not real. It's acting, playing a scene. With you it's different. You care about me and that's amazing, but it makes it real and real is hard."

"You feel safe with them but not with me!" He spiked the shot glass into the ocean. "Let this ripple your brain. We're not friends Scarlet. I want you to be my girl. We are not friends! We can *never* be friends."

SCOPATA DI MAGIA NERA

Feeling the splash of water hit his body made him cold and angry. An expensive looking black sedan with tinted windows sped away into the darkness of the cloudy Milanese night. "Motherfucker!" he screamed, throwing up double middle fingers. Laszlo wasn't positive but it felt intentional. The vehicle either swerved into a puddle to dirty a stranger without cause, or it was on purpose, a warning meant for him. Could it be. It was 4:14 AM on the morning of January 3rd in Italy. This meant it was the evening of the 2nd back in California. Enough time had now passed for Willow and company to recover, figure out he was still alive, track his location, and plan something nefarious. I'm not going back to that hotel was his first thought. He looked at his phone. He was a ninety-minute walk from the train station, just east of the Ippodromo Snai San Siro: A huge complex housing a stadium, racetrack, and amusement park. Keep it moving. Be observant of your surroundings and head in the general direction of the station. Around 6:00 AM it will start to crowd with morning commuters. Taking the first train to the airport seemed prudent.

The Santana song *Black Magic Woman* was the tune currently in his head. At first it made him uncomfortable. It brought the question of Scarlet's true nature to the forefront of his mind. He did his best to again wipe the twerking scene from his memory. That could be explained away. Ignoring the fact she watched him get thrown overboard and later returned to the beach house with the culprits now made her highly suspect. Not calling the cops was the right move, but she didn't even offer an excuse. Whatever, excuses are like assholes, even the devil has one.

The band continued to play his favorite adaptation of the song. The critical difference being this version of the song combined the original Peter Green version with Gypsy Queen, by Gabor Szabo. Gabor was an innovative guitarist who combined elements of jazz, pop-rock, and his native Hungarian folk music. And anything to do with Hungary and everything to do with leaving this night in Milan behind was comforting.

Yes, I got a black magic woman
She's got me so blind I can't see
That she's a black magic woman and
she's trying to make a devil out of me

Don't turn your back on me, baby
Yes, don't turn your back on me, baby
Don't mess around with your tricks
Don't turn your back on me, baby
'cause you might just wake up my magic sticks

You got your spell on me, baby
Yes, you got your spell on me, baby
Turnin' my heart into stone
I need you so bad
Magic woman I can't leave you alone

Scarlet's betrayal was replaying deep in his thoughts when he was awoken to danger. Looking ahead at the gasoline puddle rainbows reflecting in the streetlight his vision and focus aligned to find a gang of asylum seekers dead in his sights. From afar they looked menacing and rough. He had no band, was marching alone. A *West Side Story* remake would not here be born. Perhaps another time he would've run from this

place, but with all he had gone through he was not afraid. He looked each one squarely in the eye, daring them to find out why. Laszlo saved their leader for last, but he too stepped aside. That's when he knew that for at least this one night, there was not a soul alive who possessed the power to make him abide.

Cutting through a park he was still angry and looking for a fight, when he passed an old man sitting on a bench holding a sign: Efesini 6:12. He knew it was a reference to the New Testament book Ephesians, purportedly written by the Apostle Paul while imprisoned in Rome. The exact verse meant nothing to him. Getting closer the man made non-confrontational eye contact while repeating in Italian, "il Vaticano è la testa e Firenze è la sua coda." A verbal biblical argument with an old Italian man was not the action he was seeking.

Attempting to recall the verse with his head still turned, he ran into a woman. She looked how he imagined Bella must have looked at the prime of her modeling career. Tall, dark, and beautiful; she was dressed in all black and had to be freezing without a coat. "Scusa," he managed to utter while gawking her up and down.

"Buongiorno," she handed him her phone. "Look." There was a translation app open. In English it read: My name is Giulia; do you like me? He looked her up and down again shaking his head in the affirmative. She grabbed the phone back. Typing furiously before showing him the offer: penis suck here 150 euro, fuck here 300, full service my apartment 600.

"Here?" he questioned aloud.

She took the phone again and showed him the translation: police do not care. She pointed behind the old man to a playground not illuminated by the lights along the walking path. He hesitated for a moment before agreeing to go to her apartment. She grabbed his hand and off they went back in the direction from where he had come.

Walking in silence his mind raced. This had to be what Scarlet warned about. No way this woman was a streetwalking whore. Who was she and where did she appear from. He was equally drunk and not interested when Bella offered the same. He looked at her and kept eye contact briefly. That settled it. Fuck Scarlet. She had left him for dead and continued the cruise. Probably grinding on everybody like the whore she was. All modern Western women had been turned into whores. It wasn't their fault. The culture celebrated it. Hollowood promoted it and social media fueled its fire. What a fool he made of himself falling for Scarlet. Everything she ever said was probably a lie. She was the key to the whole spell, he now realized. It wasn't the drugs making him crazy. It was her. Now it would soon be over. He would again do as he pleased. A weird ritualistic cleansing this would be. Scarlet's soulmates and timelines bullshit would be extinguished in an orgy of pleasure celebrating this moment right here, right now. Gratifying this urge was exactly what he needed to break free of Scarlet's spell before starting a new life in Budapest.

Making a left out of the park, Laszlo was surprised to see a whole street of women on offer. They were standing or strolling, alone and in pairs. Giulia ignored them but a few made a pass at him anyway. Tempted he was not, for these women looked like Emilia, used up and spit out by the game of life. Guilia soon pulled him to the left again into a small corridor with three doors, one in front and one on each side. She let go of his hand, pulling keys from her purse and leading him in through the door on the right. She flicked the lights to reveal a clean modern lobby and hit the button for the 3rd floor.

"Welcome to my home," she announced upon their arrival.

"Thanks, it's nice," he looked around.

"It's small but it has everything I need." The apartment

was indeed small with an open floor plan. To his right was a tiny kitchen with modern cabinets and appliances. In the living area to his left the furnishings were from a bygone era. "Make yourself comfortable. Mister I didn't get your name?"

Suddenly recalling the app he was surprised. "Holy shit! You speak English?"

"I speak. Please put the donation on the table. I'm going to freshen up. Be right back."

"Wait a minute. You approached me with translations. Didn't say a word on the walk and now you are speaking fluently?"

"It's not you... Mister?"

"Laszlo."

"It's me. I must protect myself out there with the men in the streets. Many have not even fifty euro."

"You started me at one hundred and fifty."

"Some people negotiate, others fall in love. You know how it is."

"No, I don't. I didn't show you any cash. I told you I have six hundred. You trusted me and brought me back to your place?"

"I trust. You're an old soul. I think we were friends in a past life or something," she giggled and disappeared into the bathroom.

Pulling the cash from his backpack without the slightest urge to look at the report therein, he tossed it aside. Laszlo spread out the currency to show each of the six one-hundred-dollar bills. Oh shit. "Hey! I have dollars not euros. Is that OK?" he shouted at her through the door.

"Yes, relax... Make yourself at home."

Before sitting, he took a short stroll around the room.

This wasn't an apartment shared by multiple women working the street below. Guilia lived here full-time. There were pictures of friends and family, mementos, and a collection of books. The furniture was old but not worn, classy; with a multitude of pillows and throws of various colors inviting you to get comfortable. The walls were covered with reprints of the old Italian masters, mostly Raphael. Prostitution is said to be the world's oldest profession, but certainly not the most indecent. He wondered if art had always been used for nefarious purposes. Theft of course, forgeries and money laundering from mobsters to politicians and vice versa. The modern art world was no doubt an elaborate payment scheme to work around money laundering laws. Trust fund babies calling themselves artists and selling ridiculous pieces of trash for millions of dollars was the plumbing for ugly businesses like child trafficking and murder for hire.

Guilia reappeared. His mind and body were lifted from the depths of repulsive darkness to a new world filled exclusively by an alluring light. She was wearing only a red crotchless jeweled g-string. Her eyes proclaimed: I'm ready now. "Want a bump of cocaine? It's clean."

He took the bump. She collected the money before leading him into a dimly lit bedroom. Laszlo knew there was no need to compliment her; she got what she wanted but he couldn't help himself. He told her she looked beautiful before beginning to kiss her neck. After a few minutes allowing him to explore her body, she pulled him onto the bed. Their eyes met for the first time since the walk. To his surprise, she kissed him deeply on the mouth while sticking her tongue down his throat. Their legs intertwined at the foot of the mattress. With his little head draining the blood from his brain, the insanity of the last few days was spirited away. Laszlo felt like himself again for the first time in months. He pushed her down and climbed on top, continuing to kiss her on the lips before moving down. He teased one breast with his fingers while sucking on the other, switching back and forth, taking his sweet time as there existed no other. Soon he was fully erect and grinding her hard. She let him do as he pleased, which only encouraged him more. She was surely enjoying this play for no actress could fake it better, an amazing performance he would retell and make lore.

Now prone, with his head between her legs, his hands extended to massage her perfect breasts. He bit the inside of her upper right thigh and glimpsing up, watched as she licked her lips. Taking control, Giulia pushed his face to the left. Raising her pelvis slightly she jammed her wet pussy into his mouth. He kissed it gently for a while before turning her lower body around. Slowly removing the G-string and then smacking her ass. "Again!" she breathed. He spanked her once more before jumping back in between her legs. He delighted in giving her cunnilingus, there was no need for her to beg. Soon his tongue found her anus to be equally divine. He rimmed it slowly at first and soon went deep inside. He was careful and gentle in the back, but with his fingers he rammed her fast and hard in the front. She thrust her hips in rhythm with his lips as an orchestra of pleasure cried out from within.

Left with no doubt Giulia was enjoying herself, it was he who was finally free. Like a piece of cake so delicious you never want to swallow, he chewed slowly. He was content to continue but she pulled him up by his hair. Kissing him again before they switched positions. She teased his cock for a moment then swallowed it whole.

He took her by the hair thrusting hard until she could take it no more. Starting to gag she lifted her head, "Enough Mister Laszlo, please fuck me instead." He shook his head yes and mouthed the word "doggy," getting behind her his mind was focused and naughty. Laszlo ran his hands down her back, gently at first before slapping her ass. He teased her cunt with his cock for as long as he could avoid temptation, finally sliding it in, feeling elation.

"Hard and fast!" she commanded him as if there was any other option. He held her first at the hip, followed by the shoulders. Her pussy vibrating in conjunction with his heartbeat. Her skin was so smooth it revealed her age. She was at least a decade younger than he. Her long brunette hair smelled like a woman's hair should.

Continuing to thrust as fast as he could, the urge to cum never came. Eventually slowing, and taking notice of her curves, he gently ran his hand down her spine. At this she pulled away and turned over. "Look me in the eyes when you cum inside me." He got on top of her in missionary with his legs outside hers. Grabbing Giulia's hands from her side he lifted them over the shoulders. With eyes locked he inserted himself deep inside and was again thrusting with all his might. He knew this couldn't be real, he knew it wasn't really her, but for a moment he imagined Guilia was Scarlet and immediately released his seed into her.

He collapsed onto the bed. The blood returned to his brain. The reality of what he did hit him. The warning from Scarlet made him cringe. He closed his eyes and attempted to ignore the pain.

"Hey! hey, mister don't fall asleep."

"I won't." Be nice, he told himself. Giulia is a lovely woman. You are wholly responsible for what transpired.

"Sit up, take another bump."

"Thanks... Can I have some water? And a whiskey or any hard liquor?"

She returned still naked with water in one hand and whiskey in the other. Setting the water on the nightstand, she handed him the whiskey and slid under the covers.

"I noticed you are a fan of Raphael. Are you from Florence?"

"No, but I love the Palazzo Pitti. A vast, old palace in

Florence on the River Arno. It's my favorite place in the whole world. It has many works by Raphael. The inside is beautiful, but the courtyard is more amazing: a short passage leads you to a small second chamber and then to a third with a fountain of Giambologna's Venus in the center of the basin, peering fearfully over her shoulder at four satyrs spitting jets of water at her from the edge… And yes, as you noticed, my favorite of our so-called holy trinity of Italian masters is Raphael. He is from the town where I was born, Urbino. Do you know where that is?"

"I don't, but I recall reading Raphael was close with the Médici Pope Leo the 10th. Leo was the pope at the beginning of the Reformation who excommunicated Martin Luther, and… I'm blanking on his name but a fellow at Cambridge University published a well-researched claim that Martin Luther believed the pope to be the Anti-Christ, and by extension the Catholic Church the synagogue of satan."

"I don't know about *that.*"

"I'm not sure it's true. Merely something I read… Can I have another bump while you tell me about Urbino."

"It's about a three-hour drive east from Florence, close to the Adriatic coast at the foothills of the Northern Apennines. The Apennines run almost the length of Italy starting here in the north near the Gulf of Genoa all the way south to Sicily. The highest peaks are in the central range at Gran Sasso National Park near Lazio. There are hundreds of kilometers of trails to go horseback riding and mountain biking in the summer. And of course, in the winter we ski."

"I love to ski!" he interjected but stopped himself from what he would normally do and rattle of all the places in the world he traveled to ski, "We will have to save skiing for another day."

"In Urbino we have the Palazzo Ducale. It's a UNESCO

world heritage site. There are many works by Raphael, my favorite being La Muta. And one of the earliest depictions of the saints Faith, Hope, and Charity, along with their mother Sophia: The Widow of Milan. It is also the birthplace of a pope, Clement but I don't remember which one. I don't care for that pope stuff though they did commission these great artists. And why have so many called themselves Pope Innocent? I think those innocent popes were probably the worst."

"I think you're on to something Guilia. I will have to research these so-called innocent popes. It's a tell as we say in poker."

"Exactly Mister Laszlo. Like when someone prefaces a story with: you won't believe this, but I swear it's true. You know they are about to tell a falsehood. An exaggeration at a minimum." Laszlo shook his head up and down in agreement and wondered if he was hallucinating or dreaming. Yes, he was in Italy. Nevertheless, he was getting schooled in history, art, psychology, and geography by a street walking whore he paid six-hundred dollars to fuck.

I'm going to roll a joint for us. Then—if you don't have another donation for me—it will be time to leave."

"A joint will be amazing. I would like to stay but I have a flight to catch. I can't risk cutting it close because I have a witches brew of drugs in my system," he declared.

"What did you take?"

"I don't know. I was poisoned on New Year's Eve and thrown off a boat. I'm running for my life... I really shouldn't be telling you this."

"You should have told me before. No more cocaine for you. And no weed either."

"That's what Scarlet warned too."

"Scarlet? Is she the good witch in all this. The one helping you?"

"I don't know, but she told me to not smoke or do any coke."

"Did she tell you not to fuck me?"

"What?"

"Did you think about her when you came inside me?"

"How do you know... I mean, why would you think I?"

"I've been down this path, the path in the park where you met me many hundreds of times... You are different. You will get through this, but you need to go now."

"OK, but can I get a hit of the weed first? It always calms me down coming off the cocaine."

"Always? Is this always right now? Your average weekend? Or are you in Milan running from real witches or weird apparitions? Having spent the last hour with you, I do not know. But you need to know yourself. Knowing yourself is how you will get to wherever it is you need to be. Weed will not help you. You say they are after you and trying to murder, to assassinate you. Do you know where that word originates?"

"No"

"In the West we call it weed or ganja, marijuana, cannabis, a hundred different fucking names. What do they call it in the Islamic world?"

"Hashish?"

"Exactly; don't question yourself. You need to be very sure of yourself as I have already told you. Muslims who were to be martyred in carrying out suicide missions for Allah were drugged by their handlers with hashish, earning the nickname hashishins. This is the basis for our word meaning trained killers: assassins."

"But you're going to smoke it," he protested.

"My life is not in mortal danger at this moment in time."

He put his clothes on and grabbed his backpack. Giulia gave him a hug and a dusty grey hardcover book of considerable width.

"Take it. It's the only English language book I have on the subject. It's a reasonably good translation of ancient texts. I hope it can help you counter their spell. Remember, casual curses operate most effectively in the preconscious, marginal areas. This is why you should not smoke weed. Black magic is most effective against an erratic hyperconscious state, so no more coke or any uppers."

"Where did you get this book?"

"New Orleans."

He opened it to look at the inside cover and there it was, the triple spirals. "What does this mean?"

"It's a triskele. The idea that everything important in life comes in threes. A very important concept in Celtic tradition. Life-death-rebirth, spirit-soul-body, mother-father-child, past-present-future, power-intellect-love. Also the orbits of the sun, moon, and earth… Rituals are performed every December 21st or 22nd at specific sites according to ley lines and the sun beam."

"The winter solstice?"

"Yes; do you know about Newgrange?"

"Tell me."

"It's a prehistoric monument in County Meath, Ireland, located on a rise overlooking the River Boyne, west of the town of Drogheda. It is an exceptional grand passage tomb built during the Neolithic Period, around 3200 BC, making it older than Stonehenge and the Egyptian Pyramids at Giza. Newgrange is the main monument in the Brú na Bóinne complex. It consists of a large circular mound with an inner stone passageway and cruciform chamber. It has a striking façade made mostly of white quartz cobblestones and is ringed by engraved kerbstones. The triskele features on the entrance stone. It's ten feet long and four feet high. It weighs five tons and is widely considered the most famous stone in the entire repertory of megalithic art.

"Give the old priest some change," she insisted, closing the door behind him. Laszlo went downstairs and stepped outside into an approaching dawn, the street a dark grey. The shadow of a tree fell abruptly across the sidewalk and ghostly birds began to squawk anew. There was unease in the cool and windless air. He zipped up his jacket and hastened his pace. He had an hour to make the first train.

TERMINAL REGRET

Thirteen hours after arriving, Laszlo was scanning the large electronic timetable in a crowded Milan Central Station. He took a deep breath to calm himself. It was 7:03 AM the morning of January 3rd, 2024. The next express train to the airport was scheduled to leave at 7:11 AM. He knew the trip was less than an hour and his flight was scheduled to depart for Budapest at 10:25 AM; perfect. He used his credit card to purchase a ticket and found an open seat in the second to last car.

The train pulled away from the station and a few raindrops began sliding down the window. Still dark outside, all he could see was his reflection. The crazed anger in his eyes before now replaced with sorrow and regret. He didn't listen to Scarlet. Fell for the temptations of a witch. Fucked her without a condom no less, proverbially face-planting in a ditch. The cocaine was still in his brain and without any booze to tame the madness this was going to be a long trip to the terminal. And not the normal bad trip he might attest to after a night of too many shrooms. No, having his old second grade teacher pee on his leg like a dog he could've dealt with. This was a darkness he would not easily banish from his mind.

The first stop was Porta Garibaldi and most of the remaining empty seats were taken by travelers carrying bags large and small. Though he could not understand them, he heard the excitement in their voices. Heading off on a new adventure or happy to be returning home from one in Milan. Was there another like him, also on the run. The odds seemed unlikely, not something he would bet on.

'Every one of my regrets has produced a song I'm proud of.' The quote attributed to Taylor Swift had wormed itself into his subconscious. For him, fucking Gulia on this night in Milan was not apt to lead to similar artistic accomplishment. How different it turned out from what he planned. A New Year's Eve cruise that was going to fan the flames of his new romance. The next episode of his how I met your mother story that began in New Orleans. Instead, a walk of shame and ride of shame would soon beget a flight of shame. All leading to the last stop: A lonely deathbed of regret. He had fancied himself worthy of Scarlet. Of being her soulmate. Of kissing her on New Year's Eve and living happily ever after. Yet without even having the guts to see what the police report may reveal, forty-eight hours later he fucked a street whore. Sex without love is as hollow and ridiculous as love without sex. Willow and crew might not have killed him physically as intended but this was worse. The train slowed and he wished it would crash. He wished he was dead. This better be rock bottom he said aloud, wishing for the sun to come out.

The train stopped to add a few additional souls at Saronno and continued. Moments later the brakes squealed again. They came to a stop. Looking out the window he could see a hotel, some retail shops and what appeared to be a school or library. He was getting hungry and really needed a drink. Shots before going through security and then finding a spot near his gate to eat and drink wine sounded like a fine plan. He decided to kill the remainder of his time on the train by attempting to look up the witches brew Scarlet described. He opened the book from Giulia. The irony did not escape him.

He peeked inside the front cover again to make sure the triskele had not magically vanished before looking in the back. He was pleased to find another larger triple spiral engraved inside the back cover and surprised to see the book had an index. He flipped to the first drug Scarlet mentioned,

Henbane. He learned its use went back to ancient Rome where the priestesses of Apollo used it to yield oracles. In the Middle Ages it was used in Goetiatic sorcery to conjure spirits and lightning storms. Ingestion causes delirium, disassociation, and hallucinations. The effects last three days or longer depending on the power of the witch casting the spell and the mental determination of the spellbound.

Flipping to the next one, Belladonna, he already knew it meant beautiful woman in Italian. He learned this was so because it was used by women as far back as Cleopatra to make the eyes more seductive by diluting the pupils. In larger quantities it can kill and was used to by the wife of Emperor Augustus to poison him. Witches use it in flying ointment and call it the devil's cherry because of its cherry-esq sweetness and black color. The entry concluded with stressing the unpredictability of its effects because it is a tranquilizer of inhibition.

With the train squealing to a crawl once more, he began to flip through the large volume at random. The section on Celtic Goddesses caught his attention when he came across Morrigan. Her name means 'phantom queen' and she is a shapeshifter associated with bodies of water and the foretelling of doom. She is also described as being the patroness of revenge, magic, prophecy, witches, and the night. At times, Morrigan is featured as one of three sisters while other times she is a singular figure. In artistic representations Goddess Morrigan is young, with long flowing dark hair; strikingly beautiful yet intimidating. Her clothing is black and very revealing. As a shapeshifter, she is known to take the form of a crow or raven.

He looked to find it was 8:18 AM and with the train having restarted there was plenty of time to make his flight. He would soon be going through security, drinking, and getting on the plane to Budapest. The book largely confirmed what Scarlet and Giulia advised. The effects would last for days before wearing off gradually.Taking other drugs was a bad idea because he needed to stay true to his nature. Scarlet had been honest after all. It made him feel even more terrible for a moment before relaxing. She told him to look for the triskele and he had found it. She told him the contents of the brew. Looking them up confirmed the disassociation she warned him about and he experienced. She also warned about other witches being attracted to him and the book confirmed the devil's cherry was powerful in dulling inhibitions. He still regretted fucking Giulia but felt better knowing she was a Morrigan. Not a witch but a goddess. She helped him when he was spellbound and unable to help himself. He needed to remain vigilant a few more days and the madness would end.

Passengers were now standing nervously and forming a line at the doors. Laszlo looked outside to find the morning sun peeping through clouds and fog. The scenery was now rural. They were getting close. He dove back into the index to see if there was anything else to uncover and soon discovered the Kelpie. An aquatic spirit in Celtic lore often depicted as a powerful and beautiful black horse inhabiting the waters of Scotland. It too was a shapeshifter taking a male human form. Kelpies are malevolent beings, delighting in drowning their victims. "Holy fuck," he said aloud. The yacht Mike chartered for New Year's Eve was named 'Sea Horse'.

The train pulled into its stop at Malpensa International Terminal One. Everyone was in a hurry to disembark but Laszlo sat in his seat shaking. This train ride had revealed all. Willow and Mike were without doubt behind his attempted drowning and Scarlet did what she could to help. How could he have doubted or blamed her. She was in no position to know. When she found out she did what had to be done to keep herself and Carlos safe. As soon as he made it to Budapest, he would write her a long email explaining everything. It would include an invite to join him in Hungary. He felt confident she would accept.

Entering the lower arrivals level Laszlo unzipped his jacket and made himself at home by stopping at the first bar and ordering a triple Jameson with a single ice cube. He enjoyed sipping it for a few minutes before paying. He soon reached the elevator to go up to the departures level and found a long line of several hundred. Must be all the people from the train he surmised and continued walking. He passed an escalator that was out of service and then a second one. He tried to reason with the men working, "It's OK, I'll walk up the stairs, no problema." They were not amused and pointed back in the direction he came. He did as instructed and the same scene was replayed at the first set of escalators. He went back to the bar for a to-go beer before taking his place at the back of the line. It was 8:44 AM. His breakfast would be cut short but with everything he learned on the train, his impending flight, and a stomach happy on whiskey, this was the best he felt in what seemed like forever.

Continuing to hold the book carefully like a long-lost treasure, he chuckled before placing it in his backpack. What would customs and security agents in Budapest think when he arrives on a one-way ticket with nothing. No clothes or personal items. A toothbrush and toothpaste in a nearly empty backpack with an old book on the occult and a Las Vegas police report. If only his name didn't give away his ethnicity. He could really fuck with them before revealing he speaks the language fluently. He imagined a warm handshake welcoming him home. Going outside and having the taxi take him directly to his favorite spot for a quick bite: A butcher shop also selling ready to eat meals like sausages aptly named Porkthroat.

The elevator was large. From his viewpoint it appeared to be taking more than twenty people at a time. He needed to pee and recalled the horror he felt in the bathroom here the previous day. His one night in Milan had its surprises, positive and negative. He did a rough calculation: $5,000 (direct to Budapest ticket), minus $666 (Milan ticket), minus $600

(Giulia ticket) minus $200 (drinks with Bella and Emilia ticket) minus $150 (hotel shower ticket) equaled roughly $3300 saved.

He tossed the empty beer into a nearby recycling bin and peeked over the long line ahead. It was now 8:50 AM. The large elevator was slow because the crowd was anxious. He watched the doors open. Instead of twenty people going up, thirty attempted to squeeze in. The doors could not close. There was quarreling in loud voices and precious time passed as the sixty second one floor roundtrip and return of the machine was slowed by human selfishness to the detriment of all. The scene played out more dramatically each time. Frustration building as wasted seconds turned to minutes. Was there another elevator? Could he give the escalator workers twenty dollars to let him pass? All other options required getting out this line, so he did. He grabbed another beer from the bar. Turning back to the elevator he casually made his way toward the front. The big glass doors opened and he charged. With a thumb in his beer bottle to preserve his score, he battled the hoard for a place aboard.

Unsuccessful at this first attempt he found himself at the front of the line. Upon the lift's return, the crowd behind thrust him into the glass on the back side. Mission accomplished. The doors soon parted and human sardines were loosed upon the departure terminal. It was nine on the dot and all was calm. He finished his beer and relieved himself in a properly maintained bathroom without issue.

Exiting, he noticed empty stairs leading to a food court on the third floor. Tempted, he instead searched for the Lufthansa desk to check in for his flight. The Malpensa departures area is not laid out like most large airports he had traversed. Instead of a single long row of airline after airline, there are twenty ovular desks with a couple airlines on each side. He circled back and forth until he became dizzy and realized it was now 9:29 AM. He immediately asked the first person in a uniform. They sent him back in the direction of the elevator. He picked up his pace. When he noticed the desk for Air Canada he jumped the line to the front.

"Please help me I'm going to miss my flight. Please point me in the direction of the Lufthansa desk."

"Lufthansa..." the young man continued to type away without looking up from his screen. "Lufthansa is Terminal Two. You are in Terminal One."

"No way I double-checked."

"Terminal Two. There is a bus at the end of the drop-off area leaving every fifteen minutes. Next," he waived his hand at a couple in line.

Panic hit him immediately. Sprinting outside through giant glass doors he was met with a flurry of activity and a light drizzle. Looking in both directions he saw neither a bus nor taxi stand. He pulled a hundred-dollar bill and some smaller denomination euros he had remaining and began to wave it at cars. "English! Anyone! Terminal Two! Please help me! I must make this flight! Terminal Two! English! Please!" The frantic scene played out and when his desperation reached its climax an angel appeared in the form of a young, very obese Tony Soprano character.

"Come, come," he said signaling him towards a three series BMW. Tony bear-hugged another man and they exchanged a few words in Italian before the man disappeared inside. "Terminal Two?"

"Yes, quickly; please!"

Tony opened the passenger door with his right hand while simultaneously grabbing the cash from Laszlo with his left. He was hot and sweaty with distress. He pulled off his jacket and threw it and his backpack on the floor. Tony jumped into the driver seat and sped away. "It is ten minutes to the other terminal. We will be there in five." Weaving through traffic and accelerating through a curve Laszlo believed him. He watched the time tick away: 9:38... 9:39... 9:40... 9:41... 9:42. As promised Tony pulled into the drop-off area as the clock changed to 9:43 AM.

"Thanks," he grabbed his backpack and headed for the entrance in a full sprint.

"You forgot your jacket!" A bombastic voice boomed from behind. He turned to see Tony standing next to the driver's door holding his jacket high in the air.

"Keep it!"

Inside he found a long line of people circling the ropes toward a giant desk for Easy Jet. He asked the first uniformed person where the Lufthansa desk was. The man shrugged and extended his index finger on his right hand toward a large 'Information' sign about fifty yards away. He hurried toward the sign only to find there was nobody manning it. That was OK but he suddenly recalled his jacket. More excruciatingly, his passport was in the front inside breast pocket. Running back outside Tony was gone. He haphazardly searched his backpack without success. He backed up slowly toward a bench still scanning for Tony's BMW. There would be no flight today without a passport. Lowering himself slowly onto the bench with a sick feeling in his stomach, he felt the passport in his front-left pant pocket.

Again in full sprint he soon reached the information desk where there was another passenger being helped. He didn't hesitate to interrupt. "Lufthansa! Please! Where is Lufthansa, I'm going to miss my flight!"

"Lufthansa is Terminal One," came the reply. "No! No! No! That can't be! I was there! They told me Lufthansa is two!"

"This terminal is Easy Jet only. All other carriers operate from Terminal One. There is a bus leaving every fifteen minutes."

Laszlo turned and without further protest limped toward the exit. He stopped at the large electronic screen. There it was: Flight 223 Milan to Budapest, Gate C17, Terminal One, On-Time. It was 10:08 AM when he placed his backpack on the bench in front of Terminal Two. Using it for a pillow he curled up in fetal position and fell asleep.

****

Discombobulated and delirious, Laszlo awoke on the bench outside Terminal Two. His phone showed it was 10:42 AM the morning of January 3rd. How was this possible? He dreamed, the word wasn't accurate, had re-lived the night in Vegas with Willow and Mike when he was drugged. The prostitute drugged him and robbed the room. How can a dream lasting thirty minutes replay every minute detail of that which took eight hours awake. Was it all a dream? The drugs? He intentionally left his body to float above and check out the scene: there he was sitting hunched over on the bench. Every plane at this terminal was Easy Jet. He could see another terminal a few miles away. Everything seemingly checked out. He re-entered his body, got up from the bench and went inside.

Checking the big board inside confirmed the date and time showing on his phone. He spotted another flight to Budapest at 3:15 PM. There were so many questions about his missed flight and the Vegas dream. It could wait. He went looking for breakfast and said a quiet little prayer to no God in particular begging for the mercy of an available seat. At Briciole Bar he ordered a prosciutto and pesto panini with extra mozzarella and two Peroni lagers.

The first order of business was to book the flight. There were multiple seats available and without much consideration he picked one and entered his information. It did not go through. A long error message appeared. He entered his personal, passport and credit card information again. Another error. The drinks came and he slammed the first Peroni without breathing. Instead of trying the third-party site again he went directly to Lufthansa's website and entered his information. Yet another error message. It was not insufficient funds but rather a vague violation of European Regulations. The specifics were left a mystery but there was a link to a giant online depository of regulations relating to the purchase and sale of tickets by non-EU citizens and permanent residents. Whatever. It was only 11:05 AM and his sandwich arrived on schedule. He cut it in half, something the kitchen should've done before plating, and dove in.

Smashing the panini helped him feel better physically. Additionally, it focused his brain so when he received the same EU regulatory error attempting to purchase a ticket from a different third party, he became deeply concerned. He immediately called his credit card company. First the automated message and later a live person confirmed the card was active with no limitations in the EU and enough available credit. He next called United Airlines—a Lufthansa partner— with whom both he and his parents booked most trips. The gentleman took his information and confirmed his frequent flyer membership. He seemed eager to help but apologized for putting him on a brief hold. After a few minutes it was explained that accumulated miles couldn't be used to book this flight. Laszlo supplied his credit card and other information verbally. After the "Thank you sir, please hold while I get your confirmation," he was met with a verbal denial. No explanation was given other than, "You must contact your credit card issuer."

"I just did that!"

"I'm sorry sir, you must contact your credit card issuer."

He slammed the beer bottle in disgust drawing the attention of patrons and staff. What the hell is happening he wondered. Willow and Mike would not have known he was taking the train as opposed to a taxi to the airport until minutes before when he purchased the ticket. And he did not want to believe they wielded such power, either real or occult, as to slow it down. Fucking with a genuine American passport also remained exceedingly hard. The Supreme Court has so far protected the freedom of movement as a fundamental right. A limited hold on his credit card was their attempt to trap him. By now they certainly realized he was alive. All they had to do was call in a favor from a banker working in risk management or a similar role at a government agency. A temporary hold on certain transactions would come into force while an 'investigation' of allegations was conducted as standard procedure.

Knowing it was nighttime in California he hesitated before relenting. His simplest and surest course of action was to wake his father. He called both phones until his mother answered. "A text saying you made it would've sufficed."

He caught the sarcasm but there were pressing matters to discuss. "I'm OK. Don't panic but I didn't make it. I missed the flight. I'm still at the airport in Milan."

"I was worried that would happen. You were not well when you left here Laszlo."

"Mom! Stop! Did you forget why I left. I know for sure Willow and Mike are the ones trying to kill me."

"How?"

"It's a long story. No time now. Please wake father. I need his help."

"Oh my God!"

It was a quarter to twelve Milan time when he got on the phone with his dad who understood the situation. "I'm going to fix myself a cup of 'joe' and book the ticket. I will call you after I forward the confirmation to verify you received it."

"Thank you, father; I'm really sorry I woke you." Closing his tab after getting a to-go beer, Laszlo headed for the bus to bring him back to Terminal One.

With the immediate firestorm handled, his mind returned to the one that unfolded six years earlier at the Palazzo Hotel in Las Vegas. After his breakup with his only adult love from Andover whose name he could never bear to mention, it was Willow and her new friend Mike who planned a 'get over her by getting with someone new' weekend in Vegas. It was the first time he splurged on himself so egregiously. Spending—wasting—tens of thousands of dollars in a single weekend not in search of a good time but to forget past ones.

Exiting the elevator on the 51st floor, the suite at the Palazzo fit its billing as a palace. Thick oak double doors led into a marble foyer decorated with Italian art before opening to a large living space with a fireplace and grand piano. There was a full kitchen, bar, and a large dining area with a table for ten. Outside a wraparound balcony with strip views housed a private pool and sauna immersed in a garden. Four immaculate bedrooms and six baths filled the remainder of the nearly 8,000 square foot suite.

The night planned down to the finest details as insisted upon by Willow started off as expected. He couldn't see it at the time, but it was all antithetical to what he should've done to get over an ex. Don't waste money. Save it for a better future. Don't look for a one-night stand. Hang with his boys and conjure a better plan. But he succumbed to the lure of the lifestyle, and later to the cult of the in-group fancying itself as the gravitational center of all Las Vegas, if only for this singular night. Finally, and most destructively, he submitted to the woman at the club.

The facts of what happened after dinner he could recall only from what he was told and the police report. He didn't remember the ride to the Wynn or going inside. Not one single memory of their group table, the waitress or what he ordered. He didn't even have a clear image of the woman who seduced and drugged him. Only a vague feeling deep in his gut that she was the most alluring woman in the whole world. He would've given her all his money if she only asked; was dying for a moment of her affection. She had other plans. Spiked his drink with Propofol is what the report showed. Stole his wallet and the belongings of everyone in the room. She disappeared into forever save for a single clue. The hotel security photo of the two of them in the elevator. Laszlo stumbling as she pushed him in. Riding up to the suite and going in. She robbed everyone, not only him. It was a set-up, standard procedure. He didn't need to look at the report to know how it happened. There are two ways to be fooled. One is to believe what isn't true; the other is to refuse to believe what is true: the harlot that Vegas night was non-other than Scarlet.

Waking in the Palazzo suite the next morning he did not understand what had unfolded. Everyone was chill except for Willow who unloaded. She barged into his bathroom while he was going number two. Slapping him across the face she started screaming. There was nothing he could do. He didn't remember a thing. He apologized to everyone and reimbursed all their losses.

The bus was approaching Terminal One. No longer clueless he now understood he was deceived by Willow and Mike. They used Scarlet to do it. Knowing he didn't remember her they did it again. The final 'fuck you' was using her to lure him onto the yacht where Abhvi was ordered to deliver the shove meant to finish him.

"Fucking assholes," he said aloud as he rose from his seat. Wandering around the terminal after grabbing a Peroni he came across the desk for Lufthansa. It was directly behind the Air Canada desk. That prick sent him to Terminal Two on purpose. Surely all employees at the airport knew the much smaller Terminal Two was Easy Jet only. But why? Did he hate his life? Or rude Americans? Not saying 'Bonjourno' or waiting in line? No explanation could suffice. Only a truly horrible person would intentionally cause a stranger to miss a flight. No more interested in seeing the basement of this airport than LAX, he decided to avoid the Air Canada desk.

Laszlo remembered his father hadn't called yet when his phone pinged. Momentarily he was distracted by hearing a couple speaking Hungarian. It was a quarter after twelve and the email was his confirmation for the flight to Budapest in three hours. Perfect. He purchased a pack of Marlboro Reds and spent the next hour alternating between smoking outside and coming inside to purchase another Peroni. Nothing out of the ordinary happened save for one gentleman he witnessed urinating in a corner inside the terminal. He was hidden from the crowds, but it caused him to wonder anew about the foulness of the bathrooms in this place.

Exchanging "Bonjourno's," the smiling young woman at the Lufthansa counter took his passport, swiped it, and began typing into the machine in front of her. After a few moments and without an explanation she picked up her phone and dialed. Speaking in Italian he could not understand the conversation. Pausing, she explained they had her on hold. She asked if his ticket was recently purchased.

"Yes, only an hour ago."

"No problema. You are confirmed. This happens sometimes when the booking is at the last minute and not directly with Lufthansa." With each second that passed he became more agitated. "They want to speak with you," she handed him the phone.

"This is Laszlo."

"Good day, sir. Kindly verify some information for me."

"Sure... Can you explain what the problem is. I've never

been asked to speak with someone on the phone when checking in for a flight."

"No problem, sir. I can see your flight confirmation here. I must verify I'm speaking with Laszlo Nagy before we can resolve the issue."

"You just said there is no problem so what issue is there to resolve."

"Kindly, sir, I need to verify your identity before I can continue."

Fully verified, it was explained there was a small issue because his ticket was recently purchased with United Airlines rewards points and a known accounting error between the two airlines' systems had not been fixed. Every last-minute cross carrier ticket purchased with points thus had to be input manually. It was routine. All he needed to do was 'kindly' hold for five minutes while the appropriate department was contacted.

Waiting he attempted to listen in on the conversation of a Hungarian couple standing to his left waiting to check in. With the noise of the airport and the hold music playing in his other ear he couldn't understand the apparently heated discussion. They moved through and so did three more groups before he asked the woman behind the counter if this was normal.

"What did he say?"

"He said it was a known issue. I've been on hold for almost fifteen minutes. Has your computer updated?"

"No, I cannot do anything here. You must wait."

"Thanks."

A few more minutes later the music stopped. "I apologize for the wait, sir."

"Am I all set?"

"Unfortunately, the appropriate department is not replying to my messages. Please continue to hold."

"Wait! You said five minutes!"

"Kindly, sir, I have raised your issue with my manager. It will be resolved shortly. Please continue to hold."

"No! This is ridiculous. I have a confirmation number!"

"I know sir but there is nothing I can do about this issue."

"Ok, then book me another ticket. I will pay for it with my credit card. You can refund the points or not. I don't care. I must be on this flight."

"I'm sorry sir, I am not authorized to do that. To book another ticket you must call directly or go to our website, www.lufthansa.com."

"I know the fucking web address you dipshit!"

"Kindly, sir, please hold."

"No! I need to use the restroom. Fix it and I'll be back in fifteen minutes. My flight is in an hour. Don't fuck this up. I have to be on this flight!"

He handed the phone back to the agent, "He put me back on hold. I need to use the restroom. Kindly keep this line open for me." Confronted again with an overdue trip to release the beers, he found the nearest bathroom to be the most acceptable yet. Looking in the mirror he looked calm. Too calm considering what was taking place. There were no more flights to Budapest until the next morning. He was not going back to Milan for another night. He attempted to reason with himself. Willow and the gang did not have the power to do all these things. His credit card, yes. But they could not stop him from boarding an international flight that was already paid for and confirmed.

In line to grab another Peroni, Laszlo was sure the two

women in front of him were speaking Hungarian. It had been years since he had seen them in person but from the back and side view, they were dead ringers for his mom's friend and her daughter. Without acknowledging he recognized them, he said "Good day" in Hungarian. Both turned, neither said a thing but each gave him a dirty look. They about faced so quickly he couldn't even be sure it wasn't his mom's friend. "Weird" he said aloud.

Back at the Lufthansa desk the hold music was still playing. It was now 2:18 PM. Under one hour until the flight was scheduled to depart. He still needed to get through security and to the gate. Even cutting the line that would take at least ten minutes. At 2:22 PM he got good news. "Sir, I have escalated the issue to my manager who was able to contact the appropriate department. It should be only five more minutes."

"You said five minutes at the start of this. What are the chances I'm flying to Budapest today?"

"One hundred percent. Sir, kindly hold five minutes."

After ten minutes with his frustration filling the whole of the terminal, the hold music stopped. A woman introduced herself as a manager.

"Mr. Nagy, my colleague has been keeping me up to date on your situation. I have escalated your issue from my end. We should hear back from the appropriate department shortly."

"Shortly! Your colleague said five minutes more than an hour ago!"

"I understand your frustration but there is nothing we can do on our side."

"I have a confirmation number!"

"I understand, sir, but you are showing as having flown with us this morning on the same route and now you have purchased a ticket with points."

"I missed that flight because some asshole at Air Canada... Never mind, it doesn't matter. I missed that flight."

"I understand that sir, but it has caused a flag within the computer system coordinating between the two carriers that I do not have permission to resolve. I have escalated the issue with the appropriate department."

"Be honest. I'm not flying today."

"Your gate will close in about twenty minutes. I would say it's fifty-fifty to be, as you say, honest. Please hold."

He slammed the phone handle on the counter and screamed loud enough to momentarily freeze nearly every person in the large, loud terminal.

As the minutes continued to tik-tok away he was convinced there was no hope. He didn't know who to blame and didn't care. He was tired and defeated. He should've landed in Budapest hours ago. He should've paid the five grand and never came to Milan. He should've never trusted Willow. He should've moved to the Midwest and become an engineer instead.

"Sir, good news! The issue has been resolved. Please pass the phone to the agent so she can print your boarding pass." He did as instructed without so much as a thanks. It was 2:55 PM.

A minute later he was again running through Terminal One with boarding pass in hand. Winded, going up to security, he managed to exhale, "Bonjourno." He pointed to his departure time and was granted permission to cut the line and caught his breath as they scanned his nearly empty backpack. He glanced at the sign for directions to his gate and made his way post haste. Passing C15 he saw the sign for C17 to Budapest and slowed to a walk. He knew it was all for naught. He watched the gate agent shut the door to the jetway. Only an onboard emergency could be deemed sufficient cause to re-open it. Having missed a second flight his reaction was the same as the first. He found the nearest bench. Used his backpack as a pillow and prayed for someone to cover him in six feet of dirt.

SABALI

Waking on the bench opposite Gate C17, Laszlo immediately checked the time: 4:20 PM, January 3rd. I could really use a joint right now was his first thought before recalling a weird surreal dream. Again it seemed to last far longer than the one hour he was asleep. The short sequence played on repeat hundreds of times. The first night in Seattle. Specifically dancing in the storm and going through the portal except it wasn't Scarlet he danced with. It was Giulia. And it had always been Giulia. It was Giulia he met in New Orleans. It was Giulia at dinner, and it was Giulia who would be coming to New Year's Eve. It was like Scarlet never existed. There was and had only ever been Giulia.

Shaken, he stood and headed for the exits contemplating how much time had passed. How much of this was real? The only immediate move was to leave this god-forsaken airport where he had spent eight of the last twenty-four hours. The past, like a dream, is a curious thing. It's with you all the time. A single hour never passes without your subconscious thinking of that which had been. Yet what's it got to do with the present, he wondered passing a bathroom. The sight of the bathroom brought back the smell and it's the smell that really gets one going. The past was no longer a memory, he was living it. All that transpired made him desperate to leave the airport immediately. He made his way to the nearest trash can and vomited.

Once again on the Malpensa Express Train headed to Milan, the carriage is filled with chatter. The conversing voices combined with the wind and noise from the tracks to nothing but a distant shallow hum. Putting the dream down yet another memory hole, his brain spun with a singular thought: Will I ever see Scarlet again? Is it possible she is the woman who robbed me in Vegas? Aware of what was happening, he couldn't help but indulge himself for a brief moment in New Orleans when he saw her for the first time.

The wild promise of mystery and beauty lighting his world on fire. A rare creature, one of a kind, a unicorn who treated people as carefully as if she was a plain Jane. What's the point of a successful escape alone? He recalled meeting her and his heart sank down to his stomach as he realized how much his soul loved hers. No matter what her past was. No matter what she had done to him. Would he ever have a chance to tell her how she moved him? All other women did not exist in the same universe as she, her soul and spirit were one, imbuing the beauty of her body with the essence of life itself. She is the physical manifestation of the unity sought for by the great philosophers throughout the ages.

Nothing to do but sit alone inside his head, Laszlo knew he needed a plan. He looked at trains to Budapest. The next one didn't leave until the morning. He ran a search for rental cars and pulled out his earbuds to put Damien Marley's *Patience* on replay:

This is how the media pillages
On the TV the picture is savages in villages
And the scientist still can't explain the pyramids, huh
Evangelists making a living on the videos of ribs of the little kids
Stereotyping the image of the images
And this is what the image is

You buy a khaki pants
And all of a sudden you say you a Indiana Jones
An' a thief of the gold and thief of the scrolls
And even the buried bones
Some of the worst paparazzi I've ever seen and I ever known
Put the worst on display so the world can see

And that's all they will ever show

So the ones in the West will never move East
And feel like they could be at home
Get tricked by the beast
But a where dem go flee when the monster is fully grown?
Solomonic lineage we dem still can't defeat
And them could a never clone
My spiritual DNA that print in my soul
And I will forever own, Lord

Sabali, sabali, sabali, yonkontê
Yeah, sabali, that's patience
That's what the old folks told me
Sabali, sabali, sabali, kiye

At the Castellanza station, a tall dark-haired beauty, perhaps Goddess Morrigan in a different human form or a clone, boarded the train. Despite ample open seating she plopped down directly next to him. He felt and showed zero interest in her and went back to the task at hand. He knew one-way rentals were more expensive and yet still couldn't believe the offers. A mid-size car was in the $150 a day range plus a 'one-way fee' of $4000 which was taxed at eighteen percent. He had made his bed. The only option was to spend another night in Milan. He couldn't bear to face what the police report might show. He decided right there that no matter what was to come, he would not look at it until he made it to Budapest. He stared aimlessly out the window at the setting winter sun across the piedmont, praying for patience.

Discovering the world before this world
A world buried in time
Sabali, sabali, sabali, kiye
Uncover with rhymes, it gets no realer
Ni kêra môgô

Are we born not knowing, are we born knowing all?
We growing wiser, are we just growing tall?
Can you read thoughts, can you read palms?

Huh, can you predict the future, can you see storms coming?

The earth was flat if you went too far you would fall off
No, the earth is round if the shape change again
Everybody woulda start laugh
The average man can't prove of most of the things
That he chooses to speak of
And still won't research
And find out the root of the truth that you speak of

Scholars teach in Universities
And claim that they're smart and cunning
Tell them find a cure when we sneeze
And that's when their nose start running
And the rich get stitched up, when we get cut
Man a heal dem broken bones in the bush with the wet mud

Can you read signs, can you read stars?
Can you make peace, can you fight war?
Can you milk cows, even though you drive cars
Huh, can you survive, against all odds, now?

The train, his personal train, was off the rails. Nearing the midpoint on the journey of life, his clear path was lost. Yet it could not be solved tonight. Sabali. Patience. One step, one night, one day at a time is how he would reach Budapest.

Arriving at Milan Central Station did not sprout the excitement of the previous day. He headed first for the ATM to ensure he would have enough cash. He was not surprised to be denied. He called the bank again who verified the funds were there and available. They could not account for the error but apologized profusely. He told himself to be patient. Screaming on the phone was not going to fix his situation. He thought it best to relax with a beer and slice of pizza. Heading in the direction of the same little pizzeria as the day before he took notice of an inscription on the wall of the station: *Nessun maggior dolore Che ricordarsi del tempo felice Nella miseria.* The English translation underneath read: There is no greater pain than to remember a happy time when one is in misery. This was a line of Dante's poetry with which he was not familiar, but it fit his situation perfectly.

Eating at the same table as the previous night he could not believe his eyes when James and Ava strolled in and got in the line.

"Mate!" Laszlo shouted, stood and gawked. He had to be dreaming. Why would they be here.

"Laszlo! Holy shit! You are still here!" James exclaimed as he made his way over and bear hugged him. Ava followed but the hug from her did not cause him to leave his feet.

"James, I told you to message him in case he was still here."

"How was I supposed to know he missed his flight."

"How do you know I missed it?"

"You said one night in Milan. Logic will surmise you got too drunk and missed it, mate."

"I'm not going to tell you what happened at the airport because it will only upset me. You wouldn't believe me anyway. What are you two doing here?"

"Ava will tell you." He pulled out a chair for her, "I'm going to grab us a couple slices and beers."

"I can't believe we ran into you Laszlo, how fortuitous. Hearing you were coming here I got nostalgic and called a few friends I know who live in Milan. Long story short, they are having a celebration tonight and insisted we come. You're invited too! We will need to go to our hotel first to freshen up. Then we will have a proper dinner and drinks before we go... Sound good?"

"It really is amazing we ran into each other. I don't have anything planned so yes; I will join you."

"Great. Our hotel is the Portrait Milano. It's a converted old seminary in the largest public square in the fashion district, the Piazza del Quadrilatero."

James returned with two ginormous slices of pizza and six beers. "Ava, did you tell him where we are going tonight?"

"No, let it be a surprise... Remember to meet us at the hotel by nine."

"OK, I like surprises. Is there a dress code?"

"Milanese dress is the same as L.A. Wear whatever you like with confidence."

"How was last night mate?"

"Mostly uneventful," he lied. "It was raining so I grabbed dinner at a little spot not far from here and went to sleep it off."

"That was smart. I see you are still protecting whatever you're hiding in that backpack. Have you got any news from back home?"

"No. Nothing."

"Speaking of Hollywood, mate, do you know why it's *called* Hollywood?"

"The preponderance of Holly Trees?"

"Don't start," Ava warned.

"I have to... Everything they teach in school is garbage."

"It's cool," Laszlo reassured him. "I'm interested."

"Matthew Guirke was an Irish blacksmith who moved to South Carolina in the early 19th century. A skilled craftsman, his various occupations are recorded as horse-breeder, dentist, and real estate agent. He traveled west from Charleston eventually establishing himself in an area near Los Angeles where he built a cabin. He purchased a racetrack and started a small community. Matthew named his homestead after the village where he was born: Hollywood, County Wicklow, Ireland. He died in 1901 and is buried off Venice Boulevard in Rosedale Cemetery near the daughter of Rasputin."

"*The* Rasputin? The Siberian peasant turned Christian mystic who befriended and influenced the last Tsar of Russia?"

"Why would I make that up?"

Passing a group of asylum seekers as they went outside, James took notice. "Parasitized Western leaders planned and unleashed an immigration policy that has altered the fabric of our societies. I can feel the resentment of the Milanese. It's how I felt the last time I went home to Dublin. Imagine if you walked into your house and the furniture had been changed. The personal photos on the walls are not of people you recognize. The family dog was given away or worse by Islamists who are forbidden by their god to keep dogs as pets. Your children are not safe to walk to school. If they make it there without incident the teacher may be grooming them to be trans... This is Western Europe now. What existed for centuries, if not millennia, is being extinguished in an orgiastic suicidal empathy."

Laszlo didn't disagree. "We can credit our parasitic leaders with a bevy of bad policies. History demonstrates the need for a faith in a system, usually based upon a belief in a god or gods. The Soviet Union and its satellite states lacked this cohesion and lost the ideological war, then the cold war, before pulling down the statues of their former leaders. The West hasn't fallen yet, but a large segment of the population resents its own history and heroes. Combined with very low birth rates and the asylum-seeking population having the demographics and a strong desire to establish Sharia Law, it follows they will seize power within two generations at most... Then your daughter won't be *allowed* to go outside to be assaulted unless she is accompanied by a male family member.

"It's not all doom and gloom, guys. We will be old or dead in two generations anyway. Let's go get ready so we can have a great meal and celebrate. A fabulous Milanese night awaits... Laszlo, where is your hotel?"

"A block over this way," he pointed east.

"Cool, go freshen up and meet us at nine. Do you remember the name of the hotel?"

"Portrait Milano in the fashion district."

He lied about his hotel. He didn't have one. Didn't want to spend the money. Didn't want to give away his location and wouldn't be able to sleep if he did. Perhaps he would hook up with Ava's friend at the party and go back to her place. The thought made him think of Scarlet but when he checked his email there was no message. Probably for the best, for now.

This part of the city appealed to him. A bohemian atmosphere with art galleries, period apparel retailers, music shops, and vintage bookstores. A city like Milan always houses plenty of not quite certifiable lunatics walking the streets, and they tend to gravitate in these places because you can hang about and conversate with like-minded people for a long time without spending much money. Inside a men's store he found a red polo shirt he liked and purchased fresh socks and underwear. He used their restroom to clean up and change, throwing his old clothes away in the trash for the second time in twenty-four hours. Checking himself out in the mirror he felt refreshed.

Out on the street he attempted another ATM withdrawal and was denied. His card worked to book a room the night before. It worked at the retailer moments ago. It worked at restaurants and bars in the city and at the airport, but he couldn't take out cash. Cash afforded anonymity. If Willow and her gang were freaking out about him surviving, and tracking him via his credit card transactions, cutting his access to cash would be a priority. An idea manifested. They didn't know he had made friends here. What a lifesaver it was to run into James and Ava. He will insist on paying for the meal tonight without disclosing why. In the morning he would meet them at the train station and ask James to purchase his ticket to Budapest. When the ticket was secured, he would call his parents and Scarlet before dumping his phone in the trash. Brilliant. He gave himself a proverbial pat on the back. He now felt lucky to have missed his flights. Disappearing in a large city like Budapest with tens of thousands of other males with the same name was a good idea. Doing so without his pursuers being able to track him there was fucking genius. Accidental genius but next level nonetheless.

Feeling smart and fresh with time to kill he decided to check if Luca was manning his stand. He could hang out until dinner without spending much money or going out of his way. Passing by the little bench from whence he was transported back to Seattle made him think of Giulia. More accurately his second dream at the airport where Giulia replaced Scarlet in the thunderous portal scene. How could it be. A person could spend a fortune on psychotherapy exploring a topic like that. He believed psycho-the-rapist of your mind was a more apt title for these witch doctors. He could never be taken in by such a grift.

Presently approaching the stand, he found Luca to be in deep discussion with another middle-aged man. "Hey! Mr. Peroni. I apologize I forgot your name. I thought you had a flight this morning. Did you miss it?"

"It's Laszlo and yes I missed it," he grabbed a beer. "Do you take cards? I'm out of euros."

"Of course. Meet my amico from Paris, John." The friend extended his hand and Laszlo shook it.

"Milton, John Milton."

"Nice to meet you, John. Did Luca say you were from Paris?"

"Not originally of course. Having the namesake of one the greatest English language poets in history I get asked the question often. My parents were in the fashion industry. We moved to Paris when I was a child."

"Ah OK, that makes sense. Are you in fashion as well?"

"Yes, I'm on the buy side and spend a fair amount of time here in Milan."

"Ever come across a guy named Mike Panelux in Paris?"

"No, but I don't socialize inside the industry. Even here in Milan I spend most of my free time hanging out here drinking with my amico Luca."

"Milton—of *Paradise Lost* fame not my Parisian amico here—was born and buried in London but his favorite city was Florence," Luca avowed.

"Seriously?" John and Laszlo both wondered aloud.

"Oh yes. He traveled all over Italy and was granted two months in the Vatican Library with the privilege of the librarian personally guiding him through the collection. In Florence he was known to visit Galileo who was under house arrest for going afoul the of the Council of Trent and the Jesuits but allowed an extensive collection of books. In his *Defensio Secunda*, Milton proclaimed his admiration for Florence above all, because of the extensive private academies there, most famously the Médicis."

"This is why I love this guy. He knows everything about Italy. He knows more about Milton than I do, and my god damn name is John Milton."

It was 8:40 PM. "I gotta run gentlemen. Appreciate the conversation and the beer, Luca. In case I don't see you: good night, good morning, and good luck!" They bid him adieu and he avoided Via Dante and all heavily populated streets on his trek to the hotel. The darkness of the previous night had not set in but there was no reason to tempt fate. He assumed dinner was going to be pricey but worth it and wondered what the surprise celebration would bring. His phone showed it was nine on the dot as he passed through a massive seventeenth century gate with two imposing columns adorning its sides. On the inside he found a majestic baroque central court with restaurants, boutiques and Ava standing in front of the entrance to the hotel.

"Yay! You found it," she hugged him.

"It's beautiful. I love it... Where's James and more importantly where are we going to eat? I'm starving."

"He needed to take—in his words—a huge dump. He went back up to the room. It might be a few minutes. He is blaming the massive quantities of the shitty red wine you two consumed on the flight to Heathrow for his lack of intestinal fortitude."

"I'll be sure to let him know I feel wonderful myself. I hope the restaurant is close by because I'm *simply ravenous*."

"Relax. We are going to eat here at Beefbar," she pointed to his right.

"I have not heard of it but based on the name alone I approve."

"It should be fantastic. Started by a Michelin-starred chef the first location was in Monaco. They have since expanded to the usual suspect locales: Saint-Tropez, Santorini, Saint-Barth and now here. Our experience has previously exceeded expectations... What do you think of the square, Laszlo?"

"I love it. I feel like I've been transported back in time to another world."

"Funny you should say that. The hotel website calls the gate you entered through a 'sumptuous portal' and explains the wrought-iron decoration above the columns symbolizes the merging of divinity and philosophy. It was built in 1564 at the height of the Counter-Reformation. The Council of Trent introduced the innovation of seminaries to educate priests. The Archbishop of Milan–the future Saint Charles—

was among the first to implement it, making this seminary the second oldest in the world."

"Of course he was among the first. Charles *organized* The Council of Trent along with his buddy Loyola who founded the Jesuits. His uncle was a Médici and pope during this period. Milan was the largest diocese with three thousand clergy before the Great Plague of Milan decimated the city... Sorry to interrupt, Ava."

"No, it's interesting. Are you a church historian or something?"

"No, definitely not. It's weird. The last three years I keep coming across various pieces or having articles forwarded to me by friends. It's like a big rabbit hole. The more I learn the more interesting the larger picture becomes... Shall we go inside and grab a drink while we wait?"

She reached into her purse and pulled out what at first glance appeared to be an ultra-short barrel silver Beretta pistol. "Jameson whiskey aged 18 years. I'm married to James. I always come locked and loaded," she smiled handing him the flask. He took a deep pull, paused, and then another before reluctantly giving it back.

"OK, Laszlo, listen to this. After your buddy Saint Charles, this place has remained at the heart of Milan through its ups and downs. The Austrian Empress Maria Theresa used it as well as the Hapsburg General Radetzky, for whom the classic Johann Strauss piece is named. After Napolean took the city, the Cisalpine Republic housed its Ministry of War here. At the sunset of the last century two floors hosted the atelier of Mario Bellini."

"What's an atelier and who is this Mario character?"

"An atelier is the workshop of an architect. Mario Bellini is the greatest modern Italian architect. People hear the word architecture and they think old buildings like the ones surrounding us. But Mario was exceptional at designing modern products like calculators, cameras, and televisions. And before you say those are no longer modern products because they have all been replaced by the smartphone, know that Steve Jobs was so fascinated by Bellini he came here. Right here, perhaps to the very floor we are staying on, to propose a partnership for Bellini to design Apple products."

"You know an awful lot about this hotel."

"I looked it up before we left Florence in order to convince James to splurge on the room here. He's a total cheapskate now that we're married."

"If you don't mind me asking, how much was the room?"

"1,700 euro."

"For one night?"

"Yes."

"Jesus" he said aloud. Dinner was going to be expensive. "Can I have another shot while you tell me about the surprise?"

Ava handed the whiskey pistol back and unloaded: "The party is at Santa Maria delle Grazie."

"No way! That's where The Last Supper by Leonardo da Vinci is. I looked it up. You have to reserve a ticket months in advance to get in there even during daytime."

"It's not light out and we are not tourists, Laszlo. My friend's birthday is tonight. He is a Sforza... Like the castle. Like the former Duke of Milan who was Leonardo's patron. The remains of his ancestors are buried beneath the building."

THE LAST SUPPER

Following the host to their table, Beefbar felt like a classic steakhouse should. Elegant but not flashy. The walls and tables were rich chocolate rosewood, and the chandeliers emanated a soft warm glow like a fireplace. There was classical music playing so quietly you had to concentrate to hear it. Laszlo was still coming to terms with who and where they were going after dinner. If he was going to be living in Europe how fortuitous it was to make such well-connected friends.

When the waiter arrived, Ava asked which cocktail on the menu was the most exotic. "Ah yes, that will be the Giostra D'Alcol. This means it is a carousel of alcohol. It is a tradition called polibibite and its defining characteristic is surprise."

"Laszlo here likes surprises. I would like to know what's in it?"

"Yes, of course miss. It has Fusetti—what the English call bitters: an aperitif with a base of rhubarb, orange, and herbs; Tuscan red vermouth; Cedrata, it's a soda made from a fruit like a lemon, but bigger and not so sour. The rim of the glass will come garnished with chocolate and cheese."

"Cheese?" They all questioned in unison.

"Yes miss. Padano is a local favorite similar to Parmigiano Reggiano but aged longer to bring out a nutty flavor that pairs wonderfully with the chocolate."

"I'm in."

"Me too."

"Let's all ride the carousel together."

Waiting for the drinks, there were two topics he was curious about. The first was what Ava meant when she said James saved her from the industry. The second was aimed in the other direction. "James, I've been wondering about the bunker you built in the boonies. Was there a specific event, either past or future potential thereof that focused your attention. Or did you simply get to the point where you had the resources and therefore it made sense to do it?"

"Both. The question—my question driving my whole worldview is—are the minds that make up our civilization awakening to the new realities of their society, or are they simply degenerating further into frivolity. And this corresponds to the internet freedom issue we discussed but it's bigger. We are entering The Fifth Industrial Revolution. A new phase combining big data, artificial intelligence, robotics, nano and biotechnology. I'm sure you know this."

"And a cold Third World War using fifth generation warfare is simultaneously being fought," Ava added.

"My wife is a wise woman. Globally it began with 9/11. Now here this first week of 2024 we live in a world splintered by a multitude of fault lines."

The carousel was delivered. Laszlo goaded them, "Yesterday we toasted the apocalypse. Order Out of Chaos seems appropriate for this conversation."

"It is but let's toast a fun night in Milan instead," Ava suggested. "And let's order everything now and we can share as it's brought out."

"Perfect... I must try the veal meatballs for starters and the Kobe carbonara. And a Peroni please," he ordered and immediately regretted not waiting for Ava to go first. She selected a wagyu fillet in bearnaise sauce, miso spinach, truffle fries, and seasonal veggies.

James took hold of the flask and took a shot in front of the waiter. Daring him to say something he passed it to Laszlo, "We'll also have two tomahawk ribeye's, the tuna sashimi and two bottles of your cheapest merlot."

Ava grimaced at hearing the word cheapest, but James was oddly pleased. Dinner was going to cost Laszlo more than the train ticket but with many bottles on the list over a thousand euro, the two cheap merlots meant his plan remained intact.

Would James catch on, he wondered. Should he tell them the whole story. The meeting at the train station was a wild coincidence. But so was sitting next to James on the flight while Ava was moved. No, he needed to be friendly but keep his situation a secret.

"I apologize. I finished the whiskey. I'll pick up the check in exchange for the kind invite to the party... Let's return to the fault lines you mentioned. I find it interesting because it defines my own thoughts more succinctly. Wherever one stood regarding COVID in 2020 or even late 2021, if they remain asleep to the realities of the COVID tyranny now, what are the odds for the future?"

"It's easier to fool people than to convince them they have been fooled," Ava lamented with a quote attributed to Mark Twain.

"Exactly. Attempting to convince true believers the lockdowns and vaccine were a mistake is impossible. Instead, the rest of us need to internalize their truth."

"What truth is that mate?"

"The psyop, the psychological operation intended to induce fear. The mass formation psychosis perpetrated on us all, for many, made fear into a virtue. Many of those afflicted will justify that virtue for the rest of their lives. They will subconsciously and in dangerous cases consciously attempt to multiply fear to again feel the moral superiority bestowed upon them by the media during COVID. A generation of the unreasonably fearful is hanging upon us like a necklace of corpses."

"I agree Laszlo. A large swath of the COVID fascists will never admit they were wrong. If the perpetrators are held to account or at a minimum removed from power, we can move on. The same cannot be said for 9/11. This is why I argue it's the beginning of the consolidation of global power. Now you can go back much farther in time and show wrongdoing within the agencies. Yet even in the 1970's there was still the threat of public exposure and Congressional oversight. Post 9/11 that element is completely gone. Now the Congress critters and media in the US and across NATO are all run by counterintelligence. My opinion is 9/11 exposed the intel agencies internally. Meaning the good guys—and many did exist—realized the agencies they worked for were completely compromised and working for globalists. The real patriots who had fought against communism in Southeast Asia weren't innocent, they weren't evil, they were people. Some would go on to become economic hit men overthrowing tin-pot dictators for American corporate profits. Life isn't black and white. But with 9/11 the good guys, the patriots that remained who understood what happened the day it happened. The guys-"

"And women," Ava implored.

"Yes, those agents who knew aluminum planes can't bring down steel framed buildings, no plane hit building seven, all the rest... They quit the agencies en masse."

The first couple appetizers hit the table. "I see your point, James. If it was a huge intelligence failure the people responsible should've been the ones to lose their jobs but they did not. It was the lower ranking good guys who quit in disgust and the bad actors responsible remained in place and were given significantly larger budgets to hire new recruits lacking the institutional knowledge of the old guard."

"Good call ordering the veal meatballs, Laszlo, they're delicious," Ava raved licking her fingers. "Try 'em while I give you my take: The common theory of 9/11 is that it was a pretext for invading the Middle East for oil. But we know oil is not as scarce as the media portrays and the mob figured out a long time ago that everyone makes more money if you split the business instead of playing war games. My contention is we—the West, NATO—went into Iraq not as revenge for 9/11, not for oil, not for WMD, and not even to secure Israel. We were on a *real* treasure hunt. Mesopotamia as you guys know is located in the Tigris-Euphrates River basin and home to the oldest city states in what is now modern Iraq. Cuneiform, the earliest known logo-syllabic writing system older than even Egyptian hieroglyphs, was originally developed to write the Sumerian language of Southern Mesopotamia. Their greatest king is the subject of the oldest book in the world, The Epic of Gilgamesh. In the late 1990's the first lines were discovered on clay tablets and by 2003, mere weeks before the invasion of Iraq, the BBC wrote a piece detailing the finding of his tomb and a system of canals they likened to 'Venice in the desert'. Then it disappeared from the news permanently."

"I told you she was a wise woman," James gloated as the remainder of their meal was brought out.

Eating, drinking, and raving about how amazing the food is, the conversation slowed but did not cease.

"I never bought the oil story," Laszlo agreed. "Oil is fungible. Iraqi, Saudi or West Texas crude can all be refined into fuel or plastics. Comparatively, a thousand-year-old undiscovered manuscript of such significance is more valuable and worth fighting over; especially to the members of an occult secret society that worships the ancient deities memorialized in such a text. But going on Fox News and declaring we are going to invade Iraq to free the Epic of Gilgamesh from public discernment and hide what it may reveal to only those with access to the basement of the Skull and Bones frat house at Yale University is not a *casus belli* for war. If we acknowledge how much of what we are fed daily, what we can see with our own eyes is a lie, we must assume history as taught to the masses in public schools is significantly more corrupted because more people have had an interest to corrupt it; and because it was infinitely easier before the internet, cameras, the printing press, ad infinitum. If the past is a fabrication, then our present is an illusion and the future a machination."

"I agree with your premise about historical lies Laszlo, but we must fight the present battle," James advised and raised his glass to a toast of "Fight!" by all three. "As you know Laszlo, even the term 'conspiracy theory' was introduced into public consciousness by the CIA after the assassinations of the 1960's to discredit people who did not believe the official narratives. Post 9/11 the need to hold together the official account reached new lows. David Ray Griffin's *Cognitive Infiltration* describes how rogue elements in government intended to disrupt the 9/11 truth movement. Movement meaning the organized study of the evidence by independent investigators whose findings profoundly contradict the official version proffered by government and mainstream media. Griffin cites the writing of Cass Sunstein who headed the White House Office of Information and Regulatory Affairs to support his assertion that a flat earth conspiracy theory was launched behind closed doors for just such a nefarious purpose."

James sipped his wine and Ava continued. "Griffin argues, I read it as well... That the promulgation of flat earth theory created several beneficial distractions for the 9/11 conspirators. The first was associating the 9/11 truth movement with flat earthers seriously discredited the former in the eyes of any rational person who might stumble onto either theory. Additionally, over time, its scope and directive evolved such that those still talking about both conspiracies with anything approximating equal attention became near zero. It's all flat earth now. This is easily discernible by doing an analysis using Twitter—I mean X's—advanced search function. The perpetrators wrested tremendous utility toward themselves by framing flat earth as the grandest conspiracy of all. The big one. The only one that truly matters, thus making all other conspiracies relatively trivial. This results in millions of otherwise decent people focusing on a flat red herring instead of all the real conspiracies we know need to be exposed so the guilty can be brought to justice."

After a toast to 'Justice', James assured him: "I'm technically very savvy and have a foundation in physics to intuit how much someone else might know about the same by their use of terminology and how they couch their arguments. My purview is broad enough that I've had some wonderful discussions with friends who are esteemed mathematicians. One was a Dean with a PhD from Oxford. Another specialized in Differential Equations and Chaos Theory. In any event, some of the flat earth technical arguments are quite cunning. In fact, too cunning to have been formulated by a scientifically illiterate flat earther. Some number of so-called flat earth proofs could only have been constructed by someone who has a foundation in physics and is clever enough to couch them such that they're not easy to refute. These particular demonstrations were crafted with extreme malice of forethought by men who understand precisely how the world works.

"Consider this, Laszlo. What other conspiracy theory directly and only benefits those who might have created it? The answer is there is none. Flat earth is the only conspiracy where the tight knit conspirators are supposed to be every single physicist, mathematician, astronomer, cosmologist, geologist, chemist, cartographer, and engineer; be they

Christian, Jew, Muslim, Hindu, Buddhist, agnostic, American, Russian, Chinese, and on and on instead of the deep state, alphabet agencies, satanic child sex trafficking rings beholden to interwoven secret societies. This is the only point that needs to be drilled into those who don't know what to believe."

"James, do you know-"

One second Ava, I want to finish my point... These front accounts arguing flat earth are an abomination. They're obliquely shaping the worldviews of many well-intentioned but naive and vulnerable people. It's not hyperbole to call it mind control. Deceit designed to drive them to engaging in behaviors the deceiver knows can only harm. This is not a trivial problem. Ruining the discernment of millions of otherwise well-intentioned people by stealth is on-its-face immoral. It's a violation of the unspoken rules of engagement and it infuriates me."

James picked up his glass and waited for Laszlo to comment. He looked at Ava.

"Not to change the subject gentleman... But I found it interesting when I met you outside Laszlo, after passing through the gate, you made the same comment James did."

"That I had gone back in time?"

"Yes... But instead of going back, I would say you two were transported to or experiencing a different timeline altogether. Are you familiar with Project Looking Glass?"

"Yes."

"OK, so these events we are discussing are massive timeline altering ones whether they be active or reactive. My perspective is COVID had much in common with flat earth and two big differences... Scientists from around the globe, from the World Health Organization to national health bureaucracies, prestigious universities and hospitals, professors, doctors, nurses, and administrators all went along with it. But unlike flat earth, they were financially incentivized to do so. This is the first difference."

"That's a big difference," Laszlo agreed "Now it's admitted and documented that US funded gain of function research in Wuhan, China was in involved in creating it. They also lied about very safe and cheap treatment options like Ivermectin. The reason as we now know was the need for emergency authorization of vaccines. So, they closed beaches where people could get vitamin D to boost their natural immune systems. They prescribed Remdesivir to kill the sick and used the PCR test in the exact way its Noble Prize-winning inventor said it should not be used. It wasn't scientific. It was to drive up case numbers in order to convince billions to inject themselves with an experimental treatment. Taken together, the mitigation measures and jabs prescribed by the authorities caused infinitely more harm than the virus. And the whole lot of 'em went along: officials, reporters, big-tech executives and the whole medical establishment. And not just went along, they censored and shamed those who were brave enough to question the narrative. Took away their medical licenses and canceled them on social media… But I digress, what is the second huge difference?"

"Harm and retribution," Ava offered.

"Wow! I was thinking of something else but you're right. Please elaborate."

"Well, historically there have been societies who believe in flat earth and perhaps society—entire civilizations even— were set back. But, no individuals death could be attributed as the direct cause thereof. You could believe the earth was flat and still run a business or bring the kids to visit with grandma in her final moments. Additionally, once you learned otherwise how could the deceived prove an evil intention and seek retribution. With COVID, the evidence is quite substantial and the harm, comparatively, immediate and attributable. I don't wish to see individuals take retribution because the sheer scope would cause massive societal upheaval and a failure of much of the infrastructure of modern life we take for granted. However, I believe it would be wholly justified."

"You're right Ava. The harm caused is mindboggling. Mate, what was your line of thinking?"

"Well, hearing her out, I think its related to Ava's argument as well as your use of the word splintered earlier. Conceptually I was thinking about timelines. There is much we don't know yet but many of the experts who were censored claimed various versions of what to me is a similar tale. Basically, the shots alter DNA permanently. Not necessarily in everyone who received one because it's also come out that various batches were quite dissimilar. From placebo, to effective, ineffective, to more experimental and even containing nanotech that can assimilate within the body. Considering who was in charge and the billions of people injected it makes sense that the experiment was significantly more complex than a simple binary comparison of a placebo group to an active mRNA COVID variant. Now, the evidence of all this will come out over time. The great question is whether some combination of evil, hubris, and being for sale, led them to inject large numbers of people with a substance that alters the DNA of not only the recipient but in utero or semen, such that it is passed down to the next generation. For if that's what was done, then we have the most timeline altering event I can think of: the literal splintering of humanity. What those sick fucks might call a transformed or transhumanist future."

"Apologize for the interruption. Would anyone care for dessert, coffee, drinks?"

"We have time," Ava announced.

James took the initiative, "Three espressos, three shots of Jameson, and three spoons for one triple chocolate mousse brownie cake with caramel gelato to split."

"We have an hour, but I will need to go freshen up before the party. Laszlo, be warned," Ava smiled, and he felt his face flush for seemingly no reason but her charms, "My friend will introduce himself to you as Dr. Lecter."

"Umm, Ok. I swear you said he was a Sforza?"

"He is, but officially they died off centuries ago. Most of the royal bloodlines intermarried post-Reformation and became less public. The French Revolution was the final warning to go incognito. Rule from the shadows as the saying goes."

"So, I shouldn't tell him about the book I'm writing?"

Ava froze briefly but James understood the joke and they laughed it off.

"He is a genuine, good person. The only reason he uses Dr. Lecter as an alias is because Thomas Harris—the novelist who created the character famously portrayed by Anthony Hopkins in the *Silence of the Lambs*—was inspired by the 20th century serial killer known as the Monster of Florence. The character is highly intelligent and cultured. A descendent of nobility tracing his roots to the Milanese families Sforza and Visconti."

The drinks hit the table and Ava continued without noticing. "Laszlo, returning to Project Looking Glass. James is very knowledgeable about CERN, the large hadron collider on the Swiss-French border. Are you saying Project Looking Glass is tied to, or uses the collider, of which there are many smaller ones around the globe. Or do you believe CERN is only a front to hide the true nature of the activity being conducted there?"

"I'm not sure. My friend Sca- my friend from Seattle believes it's been a portal since Roman times. She ties it to Project Looking Glass because of a whistleblower who claims CERN is an attempt to build a portal because at a certain point in the future humanity wakes up to their deceptions and the demons stealing the energy from our dimension are defeated. So, if I understood her correctly, these demons are desperately unleashing more and more chaos to change the timeline such that humanity never awakens."

"But unleashing more chaos only leads to moving the timeline closer to the present and humanity waking up sooner," James surmised.

"Exactly."

"The way James first described it to me was that it's like playing the Mega Millions lotto. Winning the jackpot will change the course of your own timeline. You can move from struggling to abundance without the learning and working for many years it normally takes to build wealth. However, if you don't win and continue to throw more and more money at the lotto, you remain poor, and the end of the game comes ever closer as you grow more desperate."

"The idea of the timeline shifting makes sense to me but not the who, where, and why as it relates to CERN? Was there truly a portal there in Roman times or is this only possible with modern technology. Is the location merely symbolic?"

"Mate, think of this way. A ley line is a straight fault line in the earth's tectonic plates. Through these cracks in the plates there are very powerful magnetic energies released. It is documented that Alexander the Great was instructed by Aristotle to take control of the major centers located at intersecting ley lines. This is why he appointed his top general, Ptolemy, to rule over Egypt. The Great Library at Alexandria was commissioned by Ptolemy and famously later burned down leading many to question how many of those manuscripts ended up in Rome; but now I'm digressing...

"Throughout history megalithic structures have been strategically built on top of these ley lines: Stonehenge, Ziggurat, The Pyramids of Giza, and The Temple of Apollo at Delphi being the most famous examples. Many ancient philosophical and spiritual figures knew this now hidden knowledge and meditated or prayed on these lines and at megalithic centers, elevating their electrical auras and intellect, connecting them to a higher spiritual self. This belief system was an amalgamation of the Egyptian god Toth, and Hermes—the Greek god—not the French fashion house," he smiled at Ava. "During medieval times anyone with knowledge of Hermetics was designated a heretic and sentenced to a horrible death. Even knowing how to read and write if one was not a royal or clergy could lead to charges of heresy. Then in the 15th century the Corpus Hermeticum was brought to Florence by an agent of Cosimi de' Médici. Subsequently Médici sent a whole platoon of agents to scour European monasteries for other lost ancient writings."

Swallowing a bite of mousse and gelato Laszlo puzzled, "Mate, this is all very interesting but bottom line: Is it a good thing or evil?"

"Ah, good versus evil. Freedom fighter or terrorist. These are the most existential of questions. In 2022, Elon Musk posted about CERN on his twitter account. 'Please let me use CERN large hadron collider: I am normal and can be trusted with a demonic technology unlike anything the world has ever seen'."

"That's a real tweet?"

"Yes, but what does it mean? He can be controversial. Some will take the message at face value without knowing any history. Others will dismiss it as mocking conspiracy theorists though they themselves lack knowledge of basic physics. Most people react to the world and make it fit their own perspective. Anything that causes cognitive dissonance is dismissed or explained away. Great inconsistencies in their lives cause no greater disturbance in the force than an incoherent storyline in a scary movie being watched by a young couple making out."

"We need to leave soon and I must run upstairs first," Ava reminded the guys.

"Of course, sweetie, hold on for one minute. This is all I can tell you Laszlo, I'm sharing everything I told my wife, everything I know to be real. Imagine from birth you were raised believing you belong to a bloodline separate from our divine creator. That you are in service to masters who believe *they* are the light of this world irrespective of whether society at large would judge their actions as good or evil. As you grow older, you are taught the more chaos and fear you can generate in the outgroup, the more pleased your masters are with your work; and you receive an abundance of earthly blessings which most can only dream of."

"Damn."

"Now imagine you feel in your soul something is not right. What do you do? Stroll down to the library of Alexandria and check out a book? You learn and it causes positive changes in you. Oh! You've reincarnated to the next timeline. Congratulations. Books are now electronically altered, and your master possess the technology to find and kill you for the thoughts you hold in your mind. You must understand there is a very old and evil faction of entities behind Project Looking Glass. It all connects back to the ley lines because the rediscovery of ley lines in the 21st century is revealing the secrets of our shared past. Apocalypse is the Greek word for unveiling."

At this—without a word—all three raised their glasses for the second time in thirty-six hours and toasted, "To the Apocalypse!"

THE DARKENING

The future is a place in time everyone reaches at the same rate of sixty minutes an hour, wherever she is, whoever he be. Presently, it was 12:12 AM on the 4th of January 2024. Laszlo had removed the brass-colored mask of a generic male figure that, save for its color, was identical to all the other male masks given out at Dr. Lecter's birthday celebration. He came upon a dumpster and looked around. Seeing no one, he took off the velvet green robe with three gold stripes running from each shoulder to the wrist and tossed both items away. The mere happenstance of running into James and Ava was surprising. James calling the apocalypse an unveiling gave him illuminati vibes the whole ride to the party. Those items he was willing to chalk up as coincidence. Being asked to don a mask and robe by a man using the alias Dr. Lecter to hide the fact his royal ancestors are buried underneath the five-hundred-year-old convent named for the Virgin Mary where DaVinci painted The Last Supper was too much to inhale. He immediately excused himself to use the restroom and made a run for it.

Keeping a brisk pace heading east on Corso Magenta, he couldn't help wondering how it all tied together. The odds of him getting invited to a party like this in the midst of being on the run from Willow and Mike were infinitesimally small; like winning the lottery two weeks in a row small. Enough time had now passed that Willow and Mike could in theory be in Milan. They could've been at the party wearing masks. He couldn't help recalling how Willow had disappeared without explanation that day in Milan so many years ago.

Was she acquainted with Dr. Lecter? Nothing made sense but the inconsistencies of it all could not be explained away. He purchased a pack of Marlboro Reds and a Peroni from an old lady with a stand similar to Luca's.

Taking a drag and blowing the smoke high into the night sky he felt hauntingly alone in the middle of an enchanting metropolitan night. Young bar staff and the like loitered about talking loudly. Wasting the moist poignant moments of this night and life, watching the clock, waiting for closing time. He felt as if he was the only person awake in a city of sleepwalking clones. That was an illusion, but when one walks through a crowd of strangers it's next to impossible to see them as more than waxworks. He began to ponder James' comments regarding not only CERN but physics more broadly, AI, nanotechnology, and the predictions of an advancing singularity. The promises of great benefits to society and the ominous warnings.

"Mister Laszlo! Mister Laszlo of Los Angeles!" came the call from a familiar sounding voice he did not recognize.

Looking to his left he immediately identified Bella before noticing Emilia. Crossing traffic they met on the southeast corner. Laszlo opened with a veiled version of the question punching him in the gut, "Where am I, the smallest big city in the world?"

"Do you remember us? I am Bella and this is my friend Emilia."

"Of course I remember. It's just weird cause I don't know anyone here and I keep running into people."

"I'm surprised you remember us. You were very drunk last night. Come we are going to Bar Magenta," she pointed to her left at an old five story residential building with a big Heineken sign at ground level.

"Ah, OK, I'm going to smoke a cigarette on the way."

"Nice to see you again. We can sit outside so you can smoke as much as you like," Emilia explained while nudging him toward the bar with a gentle hand on his lower back.

He sat down at a black plastic round table with a black plastic ashtray surrounded by four wrought iron black chairs. Bella and Emilia went inside with the promise of bringing him a shot of whatever they were having and a Peroni. True to their word they returned minutes later with shots of tequila, red wine for themselves, and his beer.

"The tab here will be cheap. My friend is bartending tonight," Bella announced implying he would be paying.

"You two aren't working tonight?" he casually questioned indicating he knew they were, but not at serving drinks.

"No tonight we are free… What about you Mister Laszlo? Did you miss your flight to Budapest?"

"How do you know I missed it?" he responded suspiciously.

"Relax, I'm sorry. I don't know. We had many drinks last night and you told us your flight was in the morning. Are you still stressed because of the report you don't care to speak of in your backpack?"

"I apologize. It's been a weird day. And no, it has nothing to do with the backpack." He lit another cigarette… "We are but a day in this world, and in that day the fashion is changed a thousand times."

"Mister Laszlo what do you mean?"

"He is quoting Dante," Emilia noted, "But I don't understand why."

"You two are both models," he turned first to Bella. "*Were* both models," he faced Emilia. She returned a less than friendly grin as he again pondered the randomness of running into them and the impossibility of anyone, ever, on any timeline seeing Emilia as a model, wanting her image to represent their brand.

"No offense," he took a sip of beer pondering why he should not leave immediately. "But neither of you stayed in the business after you were no longer in front of the camera. Surely there were opportunities... What I'm getting at is fashion takes up so much space and time in people's heads but is it not trivial? You mentioned some negatives last night. Is there anything positive. Is there any more to it than a distraction tax collected by a few big fashion houses?"

"A distraction tax! I love it. Let's toast to that," Bella suggested, and they did, slamming the tequila shots. "It wasn't glamorous in front of the camera. It gets exponentially worse behind the scenes."

"How so?"

"You are still not in control. Every minutia is scripted by the machine. Lacking a sensible story and not knowing who the author is, you must simply do as you're told... One of our favorite jokes—how we would cope with an absurd request or day—was to clip our heels or declare 'There's no place like home'. Today they would call it a safe word to alert the other models there was something wicked behind the curtain."

Emilia didn't hold back. "Living through it yourself, you would have to be evil to continue. To play that role and become a destructive force in the life of an innocent soul whose life will mirror your own after being discovered."

"Wow... Sounds more depraved than Hollywood. In your day, who would you say were the best and worst houses to work for?"

"All of 'em exist on some level of *Dante's Inferno*," they both laughed.

"In the US Balenciaga has been receiving some awful

accusations lately," Laszlo extinguished his cigarette.

"Oh, I agree," Bella said without hesitation before Emilia went into details.

"Disgusting from its origin to the present. Balenciaga is the epitome of a luxury house. It was founded more than a century ago with close ties to the political elite from its origin. During the 1960's, the brand's most enthusiastic clients were socialites such as Mona von Bismarck and Pauline de Rothschild. In the first years of this century when we got our start, Balenciaga became a *must* in celebrity circles. Yet it was a weird fandom. The likes of Madonna, Nicole Kidman, Jennifer Garner, Justin Bieber, and Kim Kardashian never appeared truly excited about the pieces, the collections as we call it. It was fake. There was no organic appreciation. It was all driven from above through agents. An informal wink and nod that if you are Balenciaga talent you will find success across the entertainment landscape."   .

"They appear to be obsessed with the sexualization of children. Not only Balenciaga but the fashion world and much of Hollywood. The backlash in the US really gained steam last year as they tried to normalize their sickness and push the boundaries of what is socially acceptable. Has the industry always been like this and why?"

"Yes... Balenciaga has been a part of this mess for many years. Short answer: A whole lot of them are pedophiles. Even worse, the occult elite behind the pedophiles running the industry engage in the systematic abuse of children for aims so evil I hate to even contemplate. We—the models and celebs—are presumably used to normalize the gruesome imagery with the broader public," Emilia took a deep breath as she tossed back the remainder of her wine.

"Have you heard of Kim Noble?" Bella inquired.

"No."

"She is a survivor of trauma-based mind control who paints symbolic images. Uses the imagery to depict the abuse she was subjected to as form of art therapy. It's hard to understand her story because she claims to be thirteen different personalities who all have their own artistic style. She has been featured by the usual suspects: Oprah, Anderson Cooper, and the BBC. In one series of paintings, *Fire From The Sun*, she portrays children aged two or three in various stages of play with fire and human limbs. The children are all light-skinned Sistine-style cherubs, some covered in blood. The children do not appear to be distressed. Each scene is composed against a similar beige stage, otherwise devoid of context, but suggestive of a director or audience watching."

"That is so dark for so many reasons. Tell me something you saw personally. Was there something another model was doing that you just couldn't bring yourself to do?"

Bella stood up. "I'm .going to use the ladies' room and grab us another round. Tell him about penis cream."

"Oh God! Yeah, so everything is taken to an extreme, probably the same in Hollywood. I took a lot of dick in the industry. It is what it was, but somehow this shit was still weird, ritualistic."

"Penis cream? What the actual hell?"

"Ok, so you've heard of stem cell therapies, I'm sure... When we first got our start all the rage was these stem cell creams. They were quite expensive but we would receive them free in gift bags. Now the stem cells supposedly come from either the placenta or the foreskin of circumcised little boys."

"That is weird. You rubbed this on your face?"

"Yeah, but that's not the part which grossed us out. It gets worse. After a while some of the models concluded the creams worked even better if they emptied their partners semen from used condoms in with the cream and mixed it all up."

"Gross!"

"Yeah, so then maybe another year later the new fad became applying fresh semen directly like a facemask. But not only in private. Because everything is taken to the extreme, at some shows, people literally had partners and photographers, gay male makeup artists—whoever was around—jerking off and rubbing it on the models faces while their hair was getting done."

"No way, what, why?"

"Because still warm semen right before show time is most effective became the mantra."

"That is too stupid to be true," he borrowed Abhi's line for the first time and lit another cigarette."

Bella rejoined them with the reinforcements.

"Thanks for asking Emilia to share the penis cream story. I'm sure it will leave its mark." He recalled the experience at the convent earlier and wondered aloud. "Is all this sex, dark magic, satan worshipping—and I saw glimpses in Hollywood too—is it all wrapped together? Meaning, is it a bunch of true believers or merely desperate people doing anything for fame? The all publicity is good publicity mindset?"

"At the lower rungs it's the later. Goes back to the old saying the greatest trick the devil ever pulled is convincing people the devil doesn't exist. It's a competitive game. Every year tens of thousands of the most beautiful people in the world move to Milan, Paris, New York, and L.A., determined to become famous. Very few ever make it. It's not a meritocracy. The ones who end up on top are the ones willing to do anything to get there. Most newcomers in the industry are atheists. Anything seen as capable of furthering their career from secret societies to satanism, sex magic, witchcraft, it doesn't matter. Whatever fad or deal books the next project is viewed as a potential steppingstone infinitely better than a side hustle. The people running the show have more defined beliefs, often hardened ones. But the models do as they're told."

"Interesting, it seems to be the same in Hollywood. I've been wondering if the all publicity is good publicity mantra was intentionally created by the industry to maintain a semblance of control over the image of celebs. Understanding periodic disclosure of unsavory info would inevitably come to light."

"Of course, Mister Laszlo. This unsavory underbelly is the fuel that keeps the entertainment industry running. If you are a public figure and attempt to expose another public figure these transgressions can and will be used to shut you down. We are dealing with people that are—believe themselves to be —witches and warlocks beholden to no one. And they have a myriad of ways to deal with enemies who are exposing info on the person behind the persona. It might start with lawsuits and bribery, but if that doesn't work it expands to gang stalking and hitmen. The money at stake is too great for it to be any other way."

"Do you two remember the Tom Cruise and Nicole Kidman film *Eyes Wide Shut*?"

"Yes, it was super hyped pre-release and then all the critics hated it."

"Yes, I always wondered why... The film depicts a black magic scene where robed women circle a leader, then drop their clothes to become naked. Later there is a massive orgy where all the participants wear masks to hide their true identities. It hints that this satanic-sexual black magic ritual also involves sacrifice and murder by implying that one of the women is killed at the end. But we will never know the director's true vision because he was found dead a few days after turning in his final cut. With Kubrick gone all we have is the version approved for release by the editors and studio bosses. Did he cut a deal with the devil? It sounds silly but many people in the US suspect the late great filmmaker directed the US government's Apollo moon landings of 1969 to 1972. Do people in Italy believe humans walked on the moon back then and never again?"

"As kids we did, sure. It was taught in school and to believe otherwise was crazy. But then you grow taller and find out Santa Claus and the Easter Bunny aren't real, and adults lie all the time. Now more than fifty years have passed and the farthest up we can send a human is 700 kilometers. The moon is 385,000 km away."

"Wait how high is the space station?"

"It orbits the earth about 420 km up."

"And NASA's space shuttle program?"

"It maxed out around 620 km altitude... You see the problem with continuing to believe?"

"Yeah; but I questioned it for two different reasons. The first being the government killings or coverups of JFK, RFK, MLK and Malcom X, not to mention Vietnam, meant the US government in the late '60's was a huge fraud. Secondarily, the film and pictures don't look right. Now, I'm not a math person and arithmetic education in the US is lacking at best, but if your numbers are right the Apollo program took men to the moon for the last time in 1972 to a distance of 385,000 kilometers away; and did so with less computing power than is in my pocket. Since then, no man or woman has gone higher than 700 kilometers?"

"Correct."

"Wow that's weird. I was taught it was too expensive to go back to the moon and they found nothing interesting there. This is a plausible explanation but for manned flight to go no higher in any direction than 700 km in altitude since- I- I can't believe it. At best, it means NASA has been a huge grift siphoning billions per year which could've been better spent or saved... Future civilizations will look at television as akin to lead in the drinking water driving the Romans mad slowly over time."

Bella stood again but this time grabbed him under his left bicep. "Come. Let's go inside and get another round of shots." They did as she requested. Inside, the women left him alone to use the ladies' room together. Laszlo attempted to look at the street outside but could see only his reflection. *Hotel California* came on the jukebox. He sensed this a sign from the cosmos to leave and did so without paying the tab or saying goodbye.

Alone again heading east on Magenta Corso he was desperate to get out of Milan and fast. He could go see Guilia or even disassociate to some faraway fairyland with Scarlet, but those options were not solutions. There was one place he could rely on for cheap beer and a friendly face to kill the hours before the morning train: his amico Luca's stand.

Contemplating his situation brought forth harsh realities. The money spent picking up the group tab at Beefbar went down the drain. James would not be buying his train ticket in the morning. It was unlikely his card would work. Willow and company were probably not physically in town, but they had certainly re-grouped and deployed assets against him. Scarlet had not emailed. He looked at his phone with derision. He needed to dump it and soon.

What was the plan. He tried to book the train ticket online and was again met with an error. He checked his balance. There was more than enough for the expensive car rental. Throwing caution to the wind to see if his instincts were right, he attempted to book a midsize sedan at full price. Just to make sure he tried it twice. Then, doubting the bank's application, he booked a room for the night. This time the charge went through. If he wanted, he would have a room at the same hotel. There was no other explanation than he was being fucked with. He could spend all his money in Milan but leaving was not an option. If he could go back to his car when Scarlet first called, crashing on purpose might be the right call. He hated playing the victim but what could he do, he was stuck in Milan without a clue. Two flights were unsuccessful and now the train too. He couldn't rent a car, what the fuck was he to do?

Think, Laszlo, think! He was fit but walking across the Alps in January was a crazy option. Stealing a car would be momentarily easy but it couldn't succeed; he would need to pass hundreds of cameras to leave. Approaching Luca's he decided on a second attempt at his last plan. Overpay for the beer on his card and have Luca pay for his train ticket. This was now plan A and he really hoped it would work; plan B might as well be named Z, for there was no other option he could foresee.

Wondering whether he would find Luca awake was answered before he arrived by the friendly booming voices of both he and John Milton.

"Amico, look… Laszlo is back for another Peroni."

"Laszlo!"

He was pleased they each greeted him with hugs as he did not wish to shake hands with Luca. He accepted a Peroni and lit a cigarette.

"Listen, Luca, I'm having an issue purchasing a train ticket. Can you charge my card and buy it for me or give me cash? One-way to Budapest. Leaving first thing in the morning."

"Of course he will," John assured. "But we are in the middle of a heated conversation here… Tell us how you see this war in the Ukraine progressing?"

Metaphorically joking Laszlo physically ducked for cover. "Talk about a loaded question... Umm... My family is from that part of the world. Hungarian but spanning the modern border. I hate fascists and communists with equal vigor and believe most wars are like chess between well matched opponents: fought by pawns and rooks until a stalemate is reached and the board is reset preserving both royal families."

"I love this guy! See Luca, he gets it."

"No, he doesn't know how far down the rabbit hole we have progressed. That's his canned line for when the war comes up in Hollywood dinner party conversation. Nobody can disagree with such a statement without outing himself as an authoritarian."

"OK then catch him up and we can see how he really feels." John nodded toward Laszlo's pack of cigarettes indicating he wanted one.

"OK, amico, we are discussing the war in a much larger historical context. We know the governments of Italy, France, the US, and most of NATO are captured and beholden. We can name the usual suspects: The World Economic Forum, The Bank for International Settlements, The Council on Foreign Relations, Bilderbergers, or The Club of Rome it doesn't matter we have gone deeper. Behind these organizations we know there are secret societies which we can delve into but don't need to because the secret of the Freemason and the Rosicrucian is the same as the secret of the Jesuit. There are different actors at the bottom of their pyramidal structures but at the top these powerful armies serve the same demons."

"Laszlo, you must know Thomas Paine?" John tested.

"Of course, English-born American Founding Father, French Revolutionary, philosopher, and political theorist. He authored Common Sense: the most influential pamphlet of the American Revolution inspiring the Patriots in 1776 to declare independence from Great Britain. He personified the Enlightenment-era ideals of free speech and human rights. One of the few Founding Fathers who was staunchly anti-slavery."

"Sure, that's the US textbook version. It's hardly his whole story, for if it was, he would be celebrated along with the other famous fathers of The Republic. Paine became notorious for his attacks on his former allies, who he felt betrayed the revolution. He promoted reason and freethought, and denounced Freemason George Washington as incompetent and a hypocrite. After returning to the U.S. from Paris, he died in 1809. Only six people attended his funeral as he had been ostracized for his ridicule of Christianity and his attacks on the nation's leaders, the majority of whom were also Masons... Luca, get us another round. Grazie amico.

"Freemasonry is an occult order which has its roots in the ancient Mystery Schools. It is astro-theological in nature, which is the worship of the heavens. In his book *The Origin of Freemasonry*, Thomas Paine asserted their history can be traced back to Celtic Druids, who can be traced to Egypt and ultimately the Babylonian Mystery Religion. But the Celtic and Germanic Middle East migrants to Europe after the fall of Babylon were not able to control the people using this hidden knowledge. It was lost for much of the dark ages until the Knights Templar reignited the Mystery Religion of Babylon in Europe. Ultimately branching off into many organizations, including the Masons. They claim to be direct descendents of The Knights Templar through their fourteenth-century members who took refuge in Scotland and aided Robert the Bruce in his victory for independence from the British Crown. Ultimately, Paine concluded all religious institutions, whether Jewish, Christian, or Muslim, appear to be human inventions. Set up to terrify and enslave mankind and monopolize power and profit."

"I'm not sure whether it's you or Paine I should toast,

John; but this damn well explains why Paine is not celebrated in US textbooks. Now please tell me how the hell all this relates to your disagreement over the war in Ukraine."

"Yes, of course. Luca and I have been at this for some time now. Basically, we agree the war in Ukraine is a precursor to a hot Third World War. A historical rhyme of the Spanish Civil War of 1936 to 1939 where the combatants first engaged before the start of the second global conflagration."

"Where we disagree," Luca paused to take the deepest hardest drag off a cigarette Laszlo had ever seen, "Is whether it's all fake like a game of chess where the royal court— the opposing black and white royal courts are in cahoots— determined to end the game not with victory for their side over the other, but merely with the killing of the pawns before they think to unite against monarchic rule."

"We agree that is the game but there is no opposing royalty," John implored. "All European royal bloodlines are Khazarian. The Khaganate controlled the Silk Road from Ukraine, across Kazakhstan, to Western China for centuries. Mostly they survived as slave traders and bandits, stealing and kidnapping along the route when opportunity presented. The Khazar King and his inner circle of oligarchs were all practicing ancient Babylonian black magic, including occult ceremonies featuring child sacrifice and drinking human blood. But there is no real secret behind these ancient occult ceremonies. It is all Baal Worship. The worship of the Owl.

"Eventually fed up with the theft, kidnapping and other crimes against their people, Russia formed a coalition to surround and destroy the Khazars. But the Khazar King had a well-developed spy network through which he obtained prior warning and escaped to Europe with their vast fortune of stolen gold. Initially they laid low and regrouped, while assuming new identities. In secret, they plotted revenge against Russia and continued their Babylonian child and blood sacrifice rituals, believing Baal would eventually give them the whole world and all its riches. In reaching the British Isles, they enlisted Oliver Cromwell to help accomplish their invasion. Murdering King Charles I and establishing England as a safe haven."

Luca brought them another round of beers, "My amico here is not without knowledge but still he lacks the foundation. Your namesake John Milton described Cromwell as a hero of liberty. Cromwell created a Republic he ruled until his death before passing power to his son. How is that different from the monarchy he sought to overthrow?"

"Luca, I love you amico, but here is the problem: You attempt to cut holes in the story with details that are random. Nothing about this portrayal of Cromwell changes my conclusion. He was but one of many tools used to conquer the kingdoms. The Khazars vowed to destroy Russia so let us again look to the past. Outright invasion by Napolean and Hitler did not bring success. But Babylonian black magic has always pressed, the way to victory was to disguise their intent. Divide and conquer has succeeded at many levels for centuries. The final step is global. The Luciferian Khazar Masonic Jesuit—pick a name—globalists control Russia and China just as much as they control American and European political actors."

John asked for a Marlboro before continuing. "Like other political leaders, Vladimir Putin will sometimes talk like he is anti-globalist, but his relationships tell another story. In Putin's first autobiography, titled *First Person*, he discusses with fondness his encounter with New World Order globalist Henry Kissinger. As Putin rose through the political ranks, he maintained a steady friendship with Kissinger who has been an adviser to multiple branches of the Kremlin. Putin and the Kremlin have also kept a steady dialogue with The World Economic Forum. Last year Russia announced it was joining the WEF's Fifth Industrial Revolution Network focusing on economic socialization, AI, the internet of things, and a host of other globalist interests which all lead to worldwide technocracy and tyranny."

John calmly puffed his smoke and took a sip of beer waiting for a counter. When none came, he reiterated: "Again, the Russian government is not anti-globalist. This claim is nonsense. I would attribute the fantasy of Russian opposition to a steady stream of propaganda. What can be called the false East/West paradigm– the fraudulent notion the globalist agenda is a purely a Western or American agenda—which China and Russia are opposed to. If you look at the close interactions between the East and the globalists, this idea completely falls apart. You must understand most conflicts are engineered where the leaders are not really at odds. The wars are real, but the reason given to the public is not. They achieve covert ends while mesmerizing the masses with terror and calamity. Western military technology has consistently been transferred to China for decades."

"I think I understand the fundamental divide," Laszlo pulled his cigarette harder than ever before. "You both agree World War Three is underway in Ukraine and will become global... And I did see the video of the current King Charles bragging about being a bloodline descendant of Vlad the Impaler... Where you disagree, is John believes all sides are controlled by ancient bloodlines and this will be the final saga in the divide and conquer, problem-reaction-solution, order out of chaos, final war for world domination. Whereas Luca thinks the East—specifically the traditional and historical nation states of modern China, Russia and Iran are fighting a true war of survival, and their leadership has not been infiltrated.

"According to you, John, the battle itself is merely a manufactured narrative from which the solution of a one world government and religion will be presented to the survivors as the only way to make sure the tragedy never happens again. Luca is naïve to think there are good guys, especially ones wearing communist Chinese paper mâché dragon costumes... I'm torn on this gentleman. I really am. I wish I had a joint and a few hours to ponder such a massive substantive question."

"I have marijuana back at the condo," John offered.

"Awesome! I'm going to take you up on that... I agree we are likely already in a not super-hot just yet world war. I've had that feeling since the start of COVID. My thinking was reinforced again at dinner tonight by someone who I don't know well but is well connected. I also have it on good authority of someone I know well who is not connected that Astana—the new capital of Kazakhstan—will be the Eurasian capital of the New World Order after Jerusalem is destroyed."

Laszlo finished his beer prior to finishing his thought. "It's impossible to disprove either of you definitively. In light of the terrible possibility of either scenario being true, it's a kind of mathematical proof of the apathetic anger bubbling beneath the surface across the West. Nihilism is a better term or perhaps not. But this condition of being one of eight billion, soulless, godless, consumers living paycheck to paycheck can be treated to an extent. We see this with hundreds of millions on anti-depressants and the rest self-treating with booze and street drugs. Humans are resilient after all. Yet the WEF and other globalists are on record saying we need to depopulate. We will replace you with AI and robots. So, the unconscious collective majority lacking the knowledge and vocabulary to verbalize the reasons for the coming apocalypse can still feel it approaching in their bones. Modern Western society, driven by fear like a whipped racehorse is exhausted. Most do not have the strength to seek, to struggle, to dare. To stand alone against such odds... To face the inevitable storm."

THE DEVIL'S BIBLE

"Women often don't recall what a man says, but they always remember how you made them feel," John explained to Laszlo after saying goodbye to Luca. He was guiding him to the condo to smoke weed, "In stories, the proportion of exceptional characters—for better or worse—is very high. In the real world, the number of exceptional people is by definition very low. My wife is one of these exceptions and I angered her earlier today, last night to be precise."

Laszlo had not considered whether John was married or anything about his personal life since he disavowed knowing Mike. With this disclosure, his adrenaline shot up and mind wandered. Who was this man walking next to him.

"The fact you appreciate her as you say makes me think she has already forgiven you. Is your wife Italian?"

"Oh no, she is Danish. I fell in love the moment we met. Tall and blonde with mesmerizing blue-green eyes that sparkle like the Ionian Sea in August."

"A model?"

"Could've been but no. Her family is also in the fashion industry. Have been dressing the Nordic royal families for centuries."

"Wait a god-damn minute... You told us earlier all the royal courts of Europe have been infiltrated by ancient Khazarians hell bent on depopulation and introduction of the new world order! Now you tell me your wife plays the role of stylist for the wicked?"

"Relax Laszlo, I did not denounce you for your Hollywood ties. Good people come from all walks of life."

"I apologize John. You're right of course. It's been a super weird trip for me and I'm still coming down from the New Year's Eve festivities."

"It's all good brother. You have the cash Luca gave you?"

"Right here," he tapped his backpack.

"That's my spot there," John pointed to one of two skyscrapers with their façades completely covered by trees and shrubs.

"Oh wow; beautiful."

"I am not quite atop on the 23rd floor of Bosco Verticale, the name of the complex meaning vertical forest. There are more than seven hundred trees and thousands of shrubs and perennials across more than ninety different species. It is quite fantastic. During the spring the buildings assume a delicate pastel aesthetic. A lush green dominates the summer. Darker warm hues become prominent at the end of growing season."

"I assumed you lived in Paris full time. This is yours, not a rental?"

"That's right. When the building opened about a decade ago it housed an art exhibition during Milan Fashion Week. I came with some colleagues and, ironically, that weekend is when I met Luca also. But anyway... I went to the exhibit and there were units for sale. It was new so the trees, the greenery had not matured but I could see the vision. When I met the architects they told me The Hanging Gardens of Babylon was their inspiration. When I heard that I simply knew it would turn out to be a good investment."

"Wait here," John instructed as they reached the entrance. "I'm going to grab the weed and see what kind of mood Clara's in."

"Sure, no rush," Laszlo replied looking at his phone showing 2:24 AM as he settled on a bench. Scarlet's warning against smoking dope popped in his brain for a moment but he was able to dismiss it. Another crazy night. The morning would soon come. He would call his parents before leaving the phone on the train that goes to the airport. Then he would board his real escape vehicle, the train to Budapest. He would not use his credit card until he crossed the border. No. He would not use his card at all. He would go to the dental office of a family friend downtown. She would be able to call his parents and get him funds without using his own accounts. To anyone tracking his phone or card it will appear as though he never left Milan.

John returned and took a seat. "It's got a little tobacco in it too. Figure you wouldn't mind," he handed him the joint and a lighter.

"Perfect. Merci beaucoup."

"Clara will be down shortly."

"Cool. So, she is no longer angry with you?"

"Didn't even bring it up."

"How long have you two been married?"

"Long enough that it's starting to get boring," he looked Laszlo in the eye letting him know it wasn't a joke.

"At least you've achieved that milestone," Laszlo replied in jest. "When I was young, my friends and I would smoke and drive to the beach or through Beverly Hills. We'd spot a beautiful woman and everyone would get excited. 'Check out the trunk on that one'. Stuff young men say. Anyway, one friend would wait until the rest of us calmed down and always make the same comment: 'There's a dude somewhere who is bored of hitting that'. Protests of 'No, no way, never,' would explode from me and the others. And you know what? That dude is the only one out of the whole group who got and remains married."

Clara stepped outside and greeted him. She was as advertised. She reminded him of Daniela Pestova, the Sports Illustrated swimsuit cover model from his teenage years. Clara was wearing a short jean skirt and barefoot, showing off her long legs. Her top was a white eyelet notched blouse housing massive cleavage he couldn't help ogling. A blue-green scarf matching her eyes draped off the shoulders, partially covering her long blond hair. She finished the last puffs of the joint as John excused himself to go around the corner and 'organically fertilize' his favorite tree.

"I'm so happy John convinced you to come back with him," Clara stepped closer and affectionately ran her hand down his left arm.

"It didn't take much convincing. The weed was only a bonus. I had a weird night. It was nice to hang out with him and Luca and distract myself."

"Come upstairs with us Laszlo," she grabbed his hand but didn't pull. "All he is going to do is watch. I'm all yours."

He could feel his temptation growing and pulled his hand away. "I can't, I'm sorry." It wasn't Scarlet. The risk was too high. If he was naked and distracted John could steal his passport or worse.

Wrapping her scarf around his neck she whispered in his ear. "I'll let you put it anywhere."

"I'm truly sorry. You're gorgeous but no… I can't."

"No! Oh, c'mon 'L, you can. You will."

"Why did u call me 'L?"

"You fuck whores in Vegas. You worship that other hooker witch like she is Mother Theresa, but you don't want *me*?"

"How do you know about Scarlet? How do you know about Vegas? Who the fuck *are* you?"

"Quit being so damn naïve Laszlo. For someone your age and caliber it's the biggest negative we have discovered."

"Discovered?"

"Yes, it should've been obvious the whole damn time but certainly by now. My husband is well connected. He wanted to speak with you further. He wants for us... I want you..." Hushing her tone she seductively whispered in his ear again, "To stimulate my mind *and* my body."

"Fuck you and fuck him! Fuck your mind. Fuck your body. And if you have one, fuck your soul!" He backed away facing her like a wild animal one should not turn their back on. "I don't know why Willow wants to do me like this. I am not falling for it. I know who I am!"

"We know who you are too," John Milton said assuredly; returning and taking command of the conversation back from his wife, if that's who she really was. "We like you. We were not sent by Willow. On the contrary, we can show you who she really is. We will reveal who Scarlet is. And, most importantly, we can offer you safety from Willow and a new life. You won't have to question or run any longer. Come up to the room. Join us and I promise by tomorrow morning Willow will be exposed as the minor player she is. You will no longer fear her. You will have mastery over your destiny Laszlo."

"There is no greater gift than manifesting your destiny," Clara purred. "Your time to choose is now. Choose us. Take me and everything you ever wanted will be in the palm of your hand."

He turned and fled. Running a mile, perhaps more; constantly looking over his shoulder before finally slowing to a walk in the middle of an outdoor mall. His heart continued to race like he ran not a mile but a marathon. All the shops were closed. There were no people and multiple routes to exit should he need one. He jumped and pulled himself up, perching atop a six-foot concrete barrier. Breathing hard, he looked at his phone: 2:49 AM. Opening the backpack and pulling out the report there was nothing to read. He remembered what transpired that fateful night. He took one glance at the security camera photos and closed the folder. It was Scarlet. Scarlet was the harlot who drugged him and robbed the group in Vegas. There was no doubt.

For three months he'd been dancing with the devil. His blood boiled. He should have fucked her in Seattle when she passed out. Not payback for Vegas but for breaking his spirit; rape. Not something he could ever imagine prior was where his mind now focused. In school one learns rape is not about sex but power. For the first time Laszlo understood this truth. His heart was empty and cold, deprived of emotion. Love and attraction wholly replaced with the lust for revenge. He jumped down and headed for the nearest main street to find a bottle of whiskey. He had to kill the beast.

He purchased a liter and guzzled half straight away. With his anger still growing he needed to stay safe. There could be no revenge if he did not make the train. No! I will be better than safe, he promised himself. I will regain my old form. Stop boozing and drugging. Start swimming again and get in shape. And once he healed his body, mind, and spirit the spells of these witches would never again have power over him. Then it would be time for revenge! Coming from the depths of communism he had felt satisfied with the financial success he achieved. No more. To seek revenge he would need an arsenal of cash. Those bastards had turned a happy and loving person into someone dark and vengeful. The spell would wear off, but he could never be the same free spirit. Oh, how they will wish they succeeded in killing him. He would find a way out of this and make a $100 million. No, that wouldn't be enough. Billions! He would need billions to exact his revenge.

It was diabolical how they used Abhi after finding out he was a fraud. Nobody shunned him because none of them had respected him in the first place. Laszlo was the only one not constantly mocking him for one reason or another. Abhi was too ashamed to go home disgraced. He didn't look for new friends because he knew this group was his only ticket to the wealth and power he craved. A desperate attempt to prove to his family he could make it big in America. He wasn't going to achieve anything on his own. Always watching YouTube videos of Warren Buffet. Repeating narratives he read on CNBC. Regurgitating Cramer's stock picks to smart people with generational wealth.

It must have been the Indian caste system programming which allowed him to justify this behavior. Rationalize killing a friend for self-promotion. Abhi never saw himself as equals with Laszlo. He saw himself as inferior in the dynamics of the group and was deferential to a fault. Laszlo treated him with mutual respect, but Abhi would kiss his ass as he did the others. Showed them respect that was not earned. This is what Willow used to put an idea in his head: To become more doing good would not suffice. Only through treachery could he ascend. Abhi internalized it as his chance to replace Laszlo in the group dynamic. To become a member of a higher caste required stepping on Laszlo's neck. Friendship and years of goodwill be dammed.

He didn't know what Willow offered Abhi but it wasn't hard to fathom. A combination of financial rewards and invites to more exclusive events. Naturally future advancement would require him to do more dirty work. Having shown he was willing to kill a friend of four years, he had the stuff they were looking for in that regard and another: he was physically weak. All the men in the group were. Power brokers in the industry with large bank accounts and frail frames. Laszlo always believed this was because they could get sex solely based off their wealth. The casting couch is a powerful aphrodisiac. Perhaps, but thinking about all the hours he put into pool and gym workouts made him wonder if the ability to cast spells wasn't what lessened their desire for physical prowess.

These witches and warlocks would toss Abhi aside or kill him without a second thought. If Laszlo died in the bay and there was a real investigation suddenly video would surface showing Abhi as the culprit. But they didn't succeed. He didn't die in La Jolla Cove, and he would start his revenge tour in Hyderabad. It would be easy to pay some Indian gangster to off family members. Leave Abhi alive to feel the pain... But no! That wouldn't do it he realized as soon as the thought materialized. Abhi and the whole clan were too selfish to care about family ties. Hell, they would fain pain for sympathy while rejoicing in the spoils of inheritance. There it is, he realized. True revenge would require stripping them of their wealth and power. But how?

****

The first step was to make it to Budapest. James, John, and Luca all knew his plan was to take the train in the morning. They were likely already making plans to foil him. He took a big swig of the whiskey and attempted to forget or at least temporarily temper his anger. Watching a raven swoop down to make off with some small prey he could not make out in the darkness it hit him: Giulia. He didn't know her address but if he returned to the park he was certain he could find her apartment from there. He would give her the cash. If the cash wasn't enough, he would buy her something valuable on his credit card. Anything in exchange for a ride to Rome. There was a Hungarian embassy in Rome. Embassies are sovereign territory protected by international law. Not even the combined power of the US State Department and local

Italian authorities could get to him once inside the compound.

Locating the park was not arduous. He entered from the east and circled around until he saw the old priest on the bench with his Ephesians sign reminding him which direction to exit. Making a left out of the park he passed a dozen or more women on the street without seeing Giulia. When he rang the buzzer to her apartment it was 3:44 AM. He waited a full minute before ringing it again. No luck. She was probably entertaining a client. He decided to go wait in the park for an hour and try again.

Patiently strolling the path, he again came upon the priest who was now reciting his spiel in English: "The tail of the snake is in Florence."

"Bonjourno… I'm sorry to bother you but I'm looking for my friend. Tall female with dark hair. Young, she lives around the corner there," he pointed back in the direction of Giulia's apartment.

"I haven't seen Giulia in a couple hours."

"Oh… You know her?"

"I know all the women who sell themselves here. Giulia is the only one who knows me… Come sit," he nodded up at a raven perched atop the branch of a Stone Pine opposite. "She will be here soon."

"What is the verse on your sign?"

"Ephesians 6:12. For we wrestle not against flesh and blood, but against principalities, against powers, against the rulers of the darkness of this world, against spiritual wickedness in high places."

"No offense, father, but aren't you in the wrong place? The women selling sex out here and their clients aren't the rulers of anything."

"I have been kicked out of the places the rulers inhabit

and excommunicated from the church. That is why I'm here. You don't need to call me father."

"Why were you excommunicated?"

"Because the last war is upon us. The war between the light and the dark. Between the reptilian bloodlines ruled by the serpent and the human bloodline of our Savior. The reptilians have infiltrated everything, and the serpent now spreads venom without fear of reprisal. The Vatican is the head. Florence is the tail; and its cold blood runneth through us here in Milan."

"That is good news for the faithful in a way, is it not? I never understood this. If this is the last war, doesn't that mean God wins? Ushering in eternal peace?"

"Don't feel bad for not understanding. Priests and pastors mistakenly use the terms 'beast' and 'Babylon' interchangeably. They do not refer to the same. The beast is not the ruler of Babylon. According to scripture the beast destroys modern Babylon."

"Wait... What?"

"Many professing believers will be deceived in these last days. This is because the beast is going to fool them—his only trick—into believing the beast kingdom is the second coming of our Savior by destroying Babylon. Jesus tells us so in Mathew 24:24. If the beast and Babylon were synonymous, representing the same spirit, how could the beast destroy itself? It doesn't make sense... The church, the faithful, are confronted by a secular, leftist, totalitarian, tyrannical, Babylonian agenda of a globalist government. But this is not the kind of deception that could fool true believers."

"OK; I kinda understand. If there is such a thing as the devil, serpent, or beast as you say; it must appear holy and righteous to convince the faithful to follow him, it... To 'take the mark' as prophesied in Revelations... Where do you see this incredibly convincing deception going coming from?"

"The source will be the good people who are standing up against that which is clearly wrong in our society instead of the ones who are pushing these problems forward in modern Babylon. For the *pride* of standing against glaringly obvious social wrongs really inflates one's ego. The rebellion we are currently witnessing is a mere prelude to global unity against the Babylonian world of the present. The rallying cry of the beast kingdom will be: Let's tap our true power by uniting as one and standing against this evil."

"The wrong evil? I do not understand yet again. The greater evil is the beast destroying the lesser evil?"

"In a way, yes... The trap of the false light. It's a very powerful delusion. I am battling against evil and therefore I am good. People who hyper-fixate on the obvious dark side of life believe they're revealing the impending kingdom of the beast. Christians, who are taught satan often presents himself as an angel of light become overly engrossed in unmasking clear signs of black magic, like inverted pentagrams, and get pulled into a New Age mindset of spiritual warfare. This turns their focus toward combating dark forces and labels the left as the spirit of Jezebel in the beast's end game. Black magic at its core is about demonic possession. The world is driven by energy, not matter. Energy moves in waves through frequencies. Black magic rituals are designed to entrain the energy of the participants with dark entities, thereby forming a vibrational match and uncovering the harlot. The very adversary the beast is destined to destroy as foretold in Revelation 17:16. Unwittingly these people build not the millennial kingdom of Christ but a counterfeit version of it."

"I don't know what to believe but I agree it—hey I think —it is... Guilia!"

She was wearing all black and accompanied by two middle-aged men in expensive looking suits. "Hello Father...

Laszlo."

He stood up. "Hi... Can I speak with you privately please?"

"Make it quick it. I can't keep them waiting," she motioned to the two men to wait.

Laszlo and Giulia walked toward the playground alone, "Thanks for the book. It was super helpful. Now I need something else."

"You can come an hour after you see those two leave."

"No, not that. I need a ride to Rome."

"What? Take the train... Why? You said you were going to Budapest?"

"Long story; so much has happened since I left your place. The people who tried to kill me in San Diego have agents here in Milan. I need to get out of the city fast and be inconspicuous in doing so. I will pay you."

"Ok."

"Awesome! You're the best!"

"Listen... I first need to go take care of those two gentlemen. Then I need to get a couple hours of sleep."

"OK, no problem. I'll wait here."

"*And*, this is important: I have plans tomorrow night so I can't take you into Rome proper and risk getting stuck in traffic. I'll take you as close as we have time for. You must figure it out from there."

"Yeah, cool. Do what you need to do. I'll wait here with the old man," he offered the whiskey. She took a shot. He finished the bottle.

Laszlo returned to the bench, "I didn't ask Guilia for *that*, father."

"I know. When you see her with other men—despite

knowing what she does for a living—the physical reality slays your fantasy."

"That's so true... Was your excommunication related to, umm, sexual indiscretion?"

"Of course not. Sexual indiscretions are always covered up unless the offender is targeted for other reasons."

"Sounds like Hollywood or politics. I have a few hours to kill if you wish to share who targeted you and why?"

"It's a long story that goes to the heart of not only church history but all history."

"I have about three hours."

"What year is it?"

"2024 on the Gregorian calendar but I have no idea. I was involved in a weird conversation about the pope changing the calendar a few nights ago, on New Year's Eve."

"Right you are, my son. It is not 2024 as most people understand it. My questioning and subsequent personal discoveries are the reason I sit here destitute surviving off charity from prostitutes."

"You found the secret timeline in the Vatican Library?"

"Don't be silly, son. This isn't a Dan Brown novel."

"OK, so if it's not 2024, what year is it? What year would it be according to the Julian calendar?"

"I lost access to the libraries to continue my research, but I believe the answers lie not in Vatican City but in Florence."

"Really? Florence? Is the Vatican not the true seat of power?"

"It's the public seat, which is precisely why they must hide the truth somewhere else. Far too many scholars have access to the Vatican's vast libraries. It has its morsels to be sure. Teases secret knowledge but my contention is that

Florence is where the missing portion of the serpent's bible–The Codex Gigas—is housed."

"I'm confused again."

"The Codex Gigas, also known as the devil's bible, is a medieval manuscript. It is highly unusual because it contains a full-page depiction of the serpent juxtaposed with one of Heaven. It contains the entire Vulgate Bible, but the first chapters of Genesis are missing. Now this work was created centuries before the printing press. Works such as these took more than twenty years of non-stop work to complete the calligraphy and illustrations. The monk who created it had broken his vows and was sentenced to immurement."

"Sorry father, I don't speak Catholic."

"Immurement comes from the Latin meaning to wall in. Today we would call it being buried alive. To escape death, the monk promised to create a work to glorify the monastery forever. One night he became so desperate he prayed to lucifer to help him finish the book in exchange for his soul. The serpent completed the manuscript. The monk was obliged to draw the serpent as tribute. Can you imagine if the missing first chapters of Genesis—the story of creation—differs from the Vulgate? My contention is the missing pages are in Florence at the seat of the Superior General of the Jesuits."

"The Black Pope is based in Florence? Now way! I thought it would Paris or Barcelona because of Loyola!"

"The powers that be needed Spain and France as the threat posed by the Reformation was key to unifying factions within the church during this period. The mother church of the Jesuits is in Rome, but like the Roman Empire metastasizing through the church, the church—or more accurately—the wealth and power held by the ancient bloodlines has been hidden from the public. Now, I can't prove it to you my son, but my belief is Florence is his seat. And all the Western intelligence agencies are controlled by the Black

Pope."

"I have heard theories about ties between the Jesuit Order and Western intelligence agencies. And if there really is a Black Pope, is there a Grey Pope as well?"

"Yes, I believe there is. His headquarters are here in Milan."

"Milan! So what, like the Duomo houses the Grey Pope?"

"Duomo is the word for church in Italian and the name of the plaza containing Milan Cathedral. Next to the cathedral is the archbishop's palace on which the biscione is prominently depicted."

"Biscione?"

"Yes, the biscione is a child in the mouth of a serpent. It can be interpreted as swallowing the child or giving birth to it. I believe it is the later."

"Whoa... Are you saying the archbishop that excommunicated you is the Grey Pope?"

"No, not the current archbishop. Understand the biscione is displayed throughout Milan as it is the symbol on the coat of arms of the House of Visconti. The Visconti clan had men serve as Archbishop of Milan in the past, but modern day only select him. Their motto is: I will not violate the customs of the serpent. They have run the church, banking, and industry in the Lombard region for a millennium... Intermarrying with the House of Sforza."

"Holy Shit! Sorry father... But Sforza! They commissioned Bramante to build the apse of the convent where The Last Supper is located. I just went there last night!"

"Correct... And the biscione can be seen there as well. On the ceiling of the refectory above Da Vinci's masterpiece. The Sforza bloodline added the biscione to their coat of arms after aligning with the House of Visconti... Did you say you went there last night my son. How in hell did you get in?"

"Are you allowed to use the word *hell* in that manner, father?"

"If you, my son, can fuck a whore in the morning and go to the convent of our Virgin Mary that same night then holy hell, I can damn well say whatever I please."

"Fair enough. My friend... An acquaintance, James and his wife, were invited to a birthday party there. They asked me to join them after dinner."

"That was no ordinary party. A ritual was being performed."

"What kind of ritual?"

"I couldn't begin to guess. All the years I was a priest in good standing and friendly with the archbishop, doing my research and having unfettered access to the Vatican Library— not even then—did I ever enter or even think of entering *that* convent at night. Your friend James is supremely connected."

"If you say so. I don't really know him. Please tell me more about the Grey Pope. I always thought it was a rabbit hole put out by the Jesuits to muddy the proverbial conspiracy water surrounding the existence of the Black Pope."

"This is where the troubles began, my son. A relatively unimportant work, considering its author is DaVinci, is housed at Sforza Castle. The Codex Trivulzianus. Now the most interesting thing about it is that there are seven missing pages. This caused me to research other works of DaVinci that were lost or went missing after his death. What I discovered is the last known location of several of them is in the private Médici collection in Florence.

"Being a curious creation made in the image of God, I began to investigate the history of missing and incomplete works. After years of research into the serpent's bible and many others, I concluded that irrespective of the century of authorship, these works—or the missing parts thereof—all disappeared in the 16th Century. The High Renaissance, Reformation, and exploration of the New World. I briefly entertained the theory that the documents were stolen and sent to the Americas to be hidden because I became convinced at this time that whatever happened to them, they were not in the Vatican. A friend soon pointed out the flaw in my theory. Transatlantic crossings were extremely dangerous and the original work so important, the risk of putting them on a ship would never have been considered by the old men in possession of such treasures.

"For a time, I gave up on the research if not the idea and then a miracle happened. The release of *The DaVinci Code* caused a massive uproar in Catholicism globally."

"You got a clue from Dan Brown's novel?"

"No, my son, don't be stupid.

"As I was saying the church was in an uproar because the accusation put forth in the book that Jesus fathered a bloodline is heresy. Catholic Priests around the world were commissioned to fight back in their parishes and the media. Already known to be an experienced researcher, I was tasked with examining the old manuscripts in Northern Italian libraries to find proofs refuting the outrageous heresies made in Brown's novel.

"For the first time, I was given real access at the same time my superiors were otherwise occupied. I used the time to my advantage and what I learned is three-fold. First, missing Catholic manuscripts and missing works of the High Renaissance artists are closely tied together. Second, the works were last known to be in possession of the ruling bloodlines of Milan, Genoa, and especially the Médicis of Florence. And third, and most important to my current situation, was the discovery that these pieces were consolidated and disappeared through tunnels leading God-knows-where but originating in the dark heart of Florence. This where the oldest manuscript of Jerome's Vulgate Bible is on public display at the Michelangelo designed library attached to the oldest church in the city. The complex is the principal burial spot of the Médicis."

"So this is when the Médicis' crushed the other families and consolidated power."

"I didn't say that. The northern bloodlines could've been working together and bribing the pope into the creation of the Jesuit Order. Alternatively, the Jesuit Order was created as a counter to the Reformation in good faith and went rogue after the discovery of the missing and lost works. Ultimately, my personal lesson was that there is no such thing as pawn promotion in church politics.

"I found this out when I brought my evidence of these findings to the archbishop. Telling him I planted a mixture of eggshells and broken crayons in the diocese gardens to grow Easter eggs would've garnered a more understanding reply. He attacked me with a nonsensical flurry of verbal jabs and unrelated and unreasoned uppercuts of church doctrine, revealing himself as nothing more than a basic phony. Not a false prophet persuasive enough to gain a large audience, but merely your everyday huckster. A husband telling a white lie to his wife after twenty years of marriage that her ass still looks good in a pair of designer jeans would come across more genuine than this man of God. Needless to say, I lost all research privileges immediately. The child sex abuse allegations against me started soon thereafter."

"Wow."

"You must think I'm crazy. Making this all up as a cover story for child abuse."

"No, a crazy man is one who has lost the ability to reason. You have lost everything except your mind. Please continue."

"It is my belief the Grey Pope always comes from the House of Visconti-Sforza and his chief role is to attack—or as you say, muddy—the duality of good and evil, virtue and vice in the public conscience through the media, music, and especially fashion industries. He is the inspirer of materialism and the empty, abstract thinking that now predominates society.

"Grey is the playground of the serpent. We all have free will, but it is the grey where the serpent plants his seeds of deception in the mind of man. For the serpent does not have the power to kill, only to deceive good people of all faiths that another group is responsible for all the ills of their society. Despite their professed belief in forgiveness and redemption and God being the only one who can judge the wicked; the serpent convinces man to take it upon himself to dispense justice. The inventor of divide and conquer is the great deceiver. And this is how you get crusades and intifadas and genocides."

"Ok, I understand the point, but how does this relate to the bloodlines and missing manuscripts?"

"Power. The existing power structure was being challenged on all fronts. It is the early days of the printing press and the Reformation. The authority of the church is being challenged and their ability to control information has taken a severe blow. The pushback is multi-frontal: the pope changes the Julian calendar which had been in use for 1,600 years. The Council of Trent declares Jerome's 1,100-year-old translation is now the authoritative and only true word of God. A list of banned books is created: the Index Librorum Prohibitorum. There are the missing manuscripts from my research we can assume someone didn't want printed even more than the books they banned but named. And lastly, there are new manuscripts coming from the America's telling the history of the natives through the lens of church scholars."

"That last part is very interesting. In the US we always focus on the conquests. Killing the natives and taking the land. Manifest Destiny they called it. But I can see how the history of the native people of the Americas being presented to a wide audience across the Old World would have been seen as extremely dangerous by the power structure. Who controlled this information, the Jesuits?"

"There is much I don't know but I will tell you what I discovered. The Franciscan Order was formed by St. Francis of Assisi with the approval of Pope Innocent III in the 13th century. The Franciscan's founded the Colegio de Santa Cruz in Tlatelolco, Mexico City. It was the first European school of higher learning in the Americas and the first school of interpreters and translators in the New World. Established on January 6, 1536, on the Gregorian calendar, the intention was to prepare Native Aztec men for eventual ordination to the Catholic Priesthood. Students trained at the college were important contributors to the work of Franciscan Bernardino de Sahagún in the creation of the Florentine Codex. It was completed in 1569 and became part of the Médici private collection. Scholars were unaware of its existence for two hundred years."

"Holy hell. Did you have access to the codex?"

"I did but without being able to confirm whether it was the true and complete version. My access was limited to twelve books totaling nearly three thousand pages. There are hundreds of illustrations drawn by native artists. It contains religious beliefs but also covers a variety of topics including cosmology, moral philosophy, politics, anatomy, and natural history."

"And! What did you learn?"

"Remember this manuscript was created by natives but with the Franciscans controlling the final work sent back to Florence. Additionally, the first persons reading it never went to Mexico or the America's and their power in Europe was intertwined with that of the church."

"What does it say?"

"At the same time as Jesus of Nazareth, a child is born in Mexico from a virgin and a feathered being. The name of the child is Vitzliputzli. There is no account of his childhood. When he grows up he assembles a group of twelve followers and teaches them a dark magic which has been outlawed by the local priests. About the time Jesus would've turned thirty years old, and for three years, a violent conflict flares up in Mexico between the Aztec Teōtl Priests and Vitzliputzli and his followers. It said the battle was fought not with physical weapons but with spiritual powers.

"The conflict ended with the defeat and crucifixion of the leader of the dark mysteries. They were hanged on the cross at the same time: Christ in Palestine and Vitzliputzli in Mexico. In the mind's eye of the collective church and the individuals who rule Europe an enormous picture arises: In the East, Christ the innocent hangs on the cross; in the West, Vitzliputzli the black magician hangs guilty on the cross. Image and counter image."

HORSEPOWER

Awaking to a bright sun in his eyes and the cold hard cement steps of the central train station wedged in his lower back, Laszlo remembered everything and nothing. Whiskey does that. Neatly dressed passengers hurrying to trains and homeless drunks conversing in Italian populated his immediate surroundings. The vision of a beastly dream was fading from his mind even as the emotional impression remained powerful. A large but run down and foul-smelling villa was the setting. The doors between rooms and to leave were all locked from the outside. He was trapped. A man he couldn't identify who was more powerful than him held all the keys. Scarlet and Willow were there along with others he recognized, but everyone was lifeless. There was a large spread of food but everything on the table smelling like kimchi spoiled his appetite. He drank the red wine but couldn't catch a buzz. Another weird dream to forget.

"Fuck." His head hurt. The event at the convent and then John and Carla popped in his head. Scarlet... The report. "Fuck." It was Scarlet who drugged him. He looked in his backpack and the report was gone. It didn't matter. There was no amount of alcohol or any other substance that could erase the Vegas images from his brain. His passport and wallet were there but when he went to check the time, his phone was not there or his pocket. He threw the report away out of anger and the phone so they couldn't track him, he surmised.

He recalled leaving the old priest in the park. "Father forgive me but I need to go get more whiskey."

"I think you've had plenty my son."

"You don't understand. Tonight, I discovered the one I love betrayed me."

"You discovered it only tonight, but you laid with Giulia yesterday?"

"It's a long story but you're right; that was wrong."

"We all sin my son."

"I have one final question. Forgive me if I'm out of line. What does it feel like; how do you cope here old and alone knowing you were so close to finding the answers to these mysteries you researched. To have it taken away and know it's all behind you now?"

"I am the same. My spirit has not changed in my entire life. My body of course has aged faster since my excommunication but the voice inside my head does not fear. I have always been my mother's son. The same blood flows through the same veins. This is now my role here on earth. To bear witness to sex without love. The most tragic break in the bond between man and his creator. There is no big mystery. I am the same."

He returned to the present and felt his head and back aching once more. This is what Willow and the gang—what Scarlet too—wanted for him. Planned for him. Dying in the bay could have raised suspicions. If he dies here in Milan, alone, drunk, with the homeless, it would be a tragic end of his own making.

From the position of the sun he could tell he missed the early train. He lit a cigarette. There would be another one later. He didn't know what to do but he damn well wasn't going to die here. He thought of his sick father and his mother. Did he message them before discarding the phone. He couldn't recall and not knowing what else to do, began to recite the Lord's Prayer.

"Laszlo!" It was Giulia in a black sedan.

He ran up to the window. "What are you doing here?"

"You said you needed a ride."

"Uh yeah. I sure do! How did you know I was here?"

"The old priest told me you went to get more whiskey and to dump your phone here. You were really drunk so I assumed you passed out. Get in, let's go. I don't have all day."

He jumped into the passenger seat of the Alfa Romeo. Before his door was shut, she sped away. "This is nice, black on black. I wouldn't have expected any different."

"It's the brand-new 2024 Alfa Romeo Giulia Quadrifoglio."

"Giulia is the model? Like your name? Holy shit… Is that why you got it?"

"What am I stupid. Buying a car based on its name. I bought it for the 500 horse, V6, twin turbo and fine Italian leather seats."

"I love it. Especially that it's manual. Can I drive?"

"Do you have a four-leaf clover in your pants?"

"Excuse me what?"

"I said it's the Quadrifoglio. It means four leaf clover and indicates it's the high-performance version like AMG for a Benz."

"Ha! Sorry, no clover in my pockets."

"Then you can't drive," she laughed.

"I'm an excellent driver."

"No."

"Got it… Thanks for coming to get me. Alfa must mean first. Does Romeo have any significance?"

"Romeo is an Italian masculine name meaning a pilgrim

to Rome."

"Like me now!"

"The popularity of the name is primarily due to Luigi da Porto naming his tragic hero Romeo Montecchi in his novel *Giulietta e Romeo*. Seventy years later adapted by Shakespeare into the famous English play *Romeo and Juliet*."

"I did know that" he lied. "Nobody in the English-speaking world gives him his due... Were you named for Giulietta?"

"No. I was named after Giulia Ammannati."

"Who?"

"The mother of Galileo."

"Cool... Hey I get it. Alfa Romeo. The first Romeo!"

"Yeah; check out the logo on the steering wheel."

"Holy shit. It's the biscione!"

"Yes, the company was founded in Milan. The left half of the logo is a red cross, same as the flag of the city. The right half is the biscione... Is that what you were talking to the old priest about? His theories about Milanese bloodlines and the mysterious Florentine X-files?"

"Uh yeah, actually, it is. He turned out to be an interesting playable character."

"We also have a banging sound system," she exclaimed, raising the volume to Avicii's massive hit *Wake Me Up*.

He turned it back down. "Sorry, I really like that track but I've got a banger of a headache... Are we going south through Genoa and down the coast?"

"No, that is a beautiful drive, but it would add like two extra hours. We will take the main highway, the A1. It is the longest in Italy running from Milan to Naples. It takes us southeast to Bologna where it turns directly south. After we pass Florence—depending on what time it is—I will drop you off somewhere north of Rome. Sound good?"

"Great. Let me know if you get tired. I can drive."

"No."

Leaving Milan's crowded narrow streets she merged on to the A1 with little traffic ahead. As people with new cars tend to do, Giulia gunned it and was doing well over the posted speed limit. "You said the book I loaned you was helpful. What did you learn?"

"Most significantly it confirmed my suspicions as to the evil intentions of the people after me. The sorcery they're into and all that. The weird part is she was right about the triskele. Scarlet told me to look for that."

"The woman you were thinking about when you orgasmed inside me yesterday."

"Yes, her... Anyway, its fucked, please listen. I didn't think she was in on it. I wanted to believe she wasn't. Scarlet told me who pushed me into the bay and to find a book with the triskele. Like you, she told me not to smoke weed. But she also turned out to be one of them."

"She is a weird for sure. You will need to come to terms with that."

"I think you mean *it's* weird."

"No, I mean a weird. She is a witch. Weird used to be a noun—as in, weirds like to transform dudes into frogs—not the popular adjective that can apply to anything these days. Recorded since the 16th century as one pretending or having the power to foresee and control future events, a witch or wizard, a soothsayer. So, a bunch of sorcerers and sorceresses could be called a group of weirds. This use fits like a sibling with the wayward weird sisters of *Macbeth*."

"Interesting. I only skimmed parts of it on the train to

the airport. You are obviously more knowledgeable... What is the significance of doves and ravens? Is there a mythology surrounding them as there is in the general public?"

"Did the old priest give you his version?"

"No... I don't think so. Not that I can recall."

"All three Abrahamic faiths believe in the Ark of the Covenant. The story of Noah and the biblical flood. But only Christianity tells the story as translated by Saint Jerome who identified the raven, which was sent forth and did not return, as the 'foul bird of wickedness' expelled by baptism. More enduringly, the dove and its return with the olive branch came to symbolize the Holy Spirit, the hope of salvation and eventually, peace."

Speeding along the A1 and without a word, Giulia used the controls on the driver's side to lock all the doors and windows, spooking him momentarily. He turned rapidly to check the backseat but there was nobody there. Wondering what nefarious purpose caused such a maneuver, he was perplexed as she began to giggle.

Then it him. "Holy shit!" An astonishingly noxious release of methane filled the car nearly causing him to swallow his tongue. "Am I in the Italian countryside or West Texas," Laszlo wondered aloud gasping for a breath of fresh air.

Giulia laughed hysterically while lowering all the windows. Taking her eyes off the road momentarily she turned to him and flashed a quick bright smile, "We are all made in the *image* of God, male and female; but we *smell* like the devil's asshole."

"I was going to ask where we're stopping for brunch, but I've lost my appetite. Tell me more about the birds."

"Fire is believed to purify in witchcraft and by the illuminati. How this belief came to be synced I do not know. A burning dove symbolizes an active ritual. This is one secret you rarely see revealed by mass media, but it is well known in demonology and practiced by every satanic sect. For them, a burning dove represents the torment and agony of the meek."

"I just remembered something. Talking to the priest before you came, he nodded at a raven as some sort of acknowledgement to, or sign of you. It took off and he said you will be coming soon. Then you appeared."

"I'm not surprised... But I don't know if he told you that because I sell my body or another reason. He has a lot of knowledge. I won't deny him that."

"So he really was a priest and researcher?"

"He was. All the girls working the park thought he was just a crazy person obsessed with *Inferno*, but my mother remembers him from the old days when he was highly respected."

"Interesting. I don't recall him bringing up Dante at all."

"Not *Dante's Inferno*... The Dan Brown novel. Don't you work in Hollywood? It was the last one in the series with Tom Hanks playing the role of Professor Langdon in the film adaptation."

"Must've bombed at the box office because I don't remember it. It does explain why he called me stupid when I brought up *The Da Vinci Code*. Why did the other girls—my bad, women—think he was obsessed with the movie and not a real priest... Besides the obvious old man preaching to working girls motif."

"Because the story starts with Langdon being pursued by the Arma dei Carabinieri—Italian military police—into secret tunnels underneath the old city in Florence, where he discovers the first big clue."

"Not ringing a bell. Does Tom Hanks, I mean Professor Langdon, save the world in the nick of time?"

"In the movie, yes. The novel has a dystopian ending. The antagonist billionaire obsessed with overpopulation of the planet is successful in deploying his gain-of-function virus resulting in the sterilization of a third of humanity."

"No way! Sounds like Fauci gave him the outline and Brown filled out the dialogue. Just imagine: the old priest in that park is telling his story of secret tunnels under Florence. Hang with me here. You're Dan Brown and contractually obligated to write one more book... Only you've run out of ideas. Your fifteen minutes of fame are coming to an end. You take a trip to Italy, to Milan, for inspiration. Perhaps feeling lonely and looking for company you make your way to the park-"

"Hold that thought and remind me to tell you about Eco... I want to finish with Columbus before I forget."

"Finish with Columbus? Did we even start on Columbus?"

"Yeah, doves are classified scientifically as belonging to the Columbidae family," she began. "Now I am not an ornithologist, but I can tell you with certainty this name is much older than the scientific classification of birds. The classification was created by an Englishman who died in Genoa a couple hundred years ago. The Greek root of the word is Kólumbos. The masculine Latin first declension is Columbus."

"Of course you would know about this. Christopher Columbus was Italian. As we were taught to repeat in US elementary schools: In fourteen ninety-two Columbus sailed the ocean blue."

"Yes; but let's not fixate on the specific date because if we believe the official account this was a hundred years before the switch to the Gregorian calendar."

"Right."

Giulia made a couple maneuvers as they exited local Parma city traffic. Picking up speed they were again cruising at 150 kilometers per hour. Glimpses of sunshine poked through the high clouds illuminating the grey-black of the highway surface ahead. "Columbus started out as a business agent for the wealthy oligarchical families of the maritime Republic of Genoa, then a Mediterranean and Black Sea colonial power. After Columbus they expanded to the new world and beginning around 1520 the Genoese controlled the port of Panama, the first European port on the Pacific. But Christopher Columbus was not his real name."

"What?"

"It was given after the fact. He was from Genoa but his mother was born into a prominent force-convert Jewish family. The Church and powerful political players wanted this lineage hidden and gave him a proper Christian name. The discoverer of the Americas was surely one of their own. The name 'Christ-opher' means *follower of Christ*. Now recall the dove that Noah sent out to find land, not knowing whether it would come back, and you have the Columbus part. Combine the two and it's a mythical pseudo-savior named Christopher Columbus—a follower of Christ in the form of a dove—the one sent out to discover America across the endless waters."

"Whoa. School literally leaves out all the interesting parts of history… If Columbus is masculine, then Columbia I'm guessing is the feminine. It was a poetic name for the US that was popular in the 19th century. A goddess-like figure called Columbia exuded the spirit of the country and the capital: the District of Columbia."

"Don't forget Columbia University, Columbia Pictures, and Columbia Broadcasting System, CBS, the network with the all-seeing eye for its logo."

"Like on the dollar bill. How do you know about this illuminati stuff?"

"I've always been fascinated with hidden knowledge. Growing up here in Italy you see the historical connections. Symbolism, veiled power, the idea everything happens for reasons not revealed to the public. It's all around if you know what to look for."

"Like the biscione."

"Speaking of things happening for a reason, you told me you were going to Budapest. Why the change in itinerary?"

"I missed my flight," he tried to keep it vague with the one person in Milan who had turned out to be real with him.

"That I get. You were wasted; drugged on New Year's Eve. Why are you now going to Rome instead?"

Hesitating, he watched as the clock on the Giulia's consol changed from 11:59 AM to noon. "Long story short is last night I confirmed they followed me to Milan. They either have agents in place or sent people after me. I'm not sure. I need to get to Budapest undetected. I dumped my phone at the train station so they can't track me."

"OK. We know they're witches but how are you connected to them. Why are they after you?"

"I don't know. It's the hardest part. Old friends and colleagues."

"And Scarlet."

"Yes, she is in on it too. I will need to come to terms with that. Please don't say her name again. I would go tell the old priest if I had something to confess. I'd do anything to go back and make things right. All I see, all I feel is betrayal. And it all started when the clock struck midnight and the calendar turned from 2023 to 2024."

They sat in silence for some time until traffic picked up again. "We are nearing Bologna. It is nicknamed the Fat City for its rich cuisine. It is also known for the oldest university in the world and most renowned in Italy. Famous alumni include Copernicus, Dante, Saint Charles and more recently, Enzo Ferrari. Umberto Eco was a professor."

"I know Charles is the former archbishop of Milan who presided over the Council of Trent. Eco is a modern philosopher. What is it you wanted to tell me about him."

"Hold on," she veered right and hit the brakes hard. "See that white Maserati three cars back?"

He first glanced in the rearview mirror and then turned around, "Yeah."

"Do you recognize it?"

"No. Why would I?"

"Because you're the one with people following you. That car has been behind us for at least ten minutes. When I slowed and moved to the right it did the same."

"Speed into an upcoming exit and we'll see if they get off too."

"There's an auto-grill ahead. The plaza above the highway up there. I'm going to get off. If they follow us, it's easy to get back on. If not, we can get petrol and there is a bistro."

"Cool." The Giulia sped up the entrance ramp and they watched the Maserati continue on A1.

"That was *weird*," he teased, both bursting out in laughter.

After filling up the car with gas they went inside. Laszlo ordered a cheeseburger and two Peronis. Giulia grabbed a chocolate brioche and an espresso.

"I'm happy to drive. I have a lot of experience driving while eating," he declared as they crossed the parking lot. She ignored him and headed to the driver's side.

"Umberto Eco was a highly acclaimed author who never

found the kind of commercial success Dan Brown achieved. Eco suggested Brown stole the idea for *The DaVinci Code* from a work called *The Holy Blood and the Holy Grail*."

"He almost certainly did but this Eco character sounds jealous. Too many great authors write for the snobby critics they went to school with and run in their circles. Even before the mass depopulation event, there is not a large enough audience for high-brow musings to become commercial hits," Laszlo chuckled.

"Eco fancied his own name was an acronym for *ex caelis oblatus*, Latin for 'a gift from heaven' based on a Jesuit publication in the Vatican Library."

"Sounds about right. What's he known for?"

"Several works including a speculative fiction novel, *Foucault's Pendulum*, in which three under-employed editors working for a publishing house in Milan decide to invent a conspiracy theory. It's about an immense and intricate plot to take over the world by a secret order descended from the Knights Templar. Their goal is to reshape the world using telluric currents called ley lines focused at Foucault's pendulum. The pendulum was first displayed in Paris in the 19th century when the prime meridian ran through it, not Greenwich, London. Sound familiar?"

"Yeah, *The DaVinci Code* ends with Langdon finding the final piece of the puzzle at the Rose Line, the prime meridian, beneath the pyramid at the Louvre in Paris. There he kneels before the sarcophagus of the Virgin Mary as the Knights Templar supposedly did."

The sun, now fully emerged, brightened a green and increasingly hilly landscape. The burger and Peronis miraculously delivered a cure for his hangover. "How much longer to Florence?"

"We are about to cross into Tuscany so like forty

minutes without traffic. I will need to drop you in Florence so I can get back to Milan in time."

"That's cool. Thanks again. Any train station works for me," he assured her more than himself. "I paid you for the ride with the gift card I purchased at the jewelry store in Milan. You owe me a train ticket to Rome."

"That was the arrangement."

"Great. That leaves me two hundred euros for food and drinks."

"You better be smart with that two hundred just in case."

"I know. I need to reach Budapest so my parents can send me cash anonymously."

"You do realize you are getting farther and farther away from Hungary every second going south. Why don't you take the train from Florence to Budapest?"

She was right geographically. He was tempted to tell her his embassy plan. "It's too risky."

"You're hiding something. I hope it works out for you. Whatever it is you're intending."

"Thanks," he decided to change the subject before he accidentally revealed any details of his plan. "After you told me about the Médici's palace in Florence, I looked it up. Turns out Florentine Renaissance architecture—specifically the Palazzo Pitti—was the inspiration for the Bank of Italy Building in San Jose California, the capital of Silicon Valley."

"Wait… Isn't San Francisco the center of Silicon Valley?"

"It's known as the bay area. San Fran proper is on the pacific in the north bay. The east bay is Oakland. Both of those cities have been in decline for decades. The south bay is San Jose and all the places you associate with big tech like Mountain View and Cupertino."

"Oh… I've not been."

"But back to the bank. There have been many mergers over the years. It started with San Jose based Bank of Italy buying Los Angeles based Bank of America in the 1920's. Keeping the later name for obvious reason despite corporate control being exercised in the former."

"You're suggesting the modern Médici bloodline plays a major role in American banking akin to the Genoese bloodlines still controlling Columbia named entities."

"I am. And there is another layer. San Jose is the headquarters of the English Grand Lodge of the largest Rosicrucian organization in the world: the Ancient and Mystical Order of the Rose Cross. The Rosicrucian Park compound in downtown San Jose sits on some of the most expensive real estate on the planet. The complex includes the Rosicrucian Egyptian Museum, the first planetarium with a US-built star projector, the Rosicrucian Peace Garden, Rosicrucian Research Library, the Grand Temple, an Administration Building, Fountain Plaza and Gardens, the Alchemy Garden, and the walking Labyrinth.

"According to its own history, the order traces its Catholic roots to Dante, practices Hermeticism and originated from the Mystery Schools established in Egypt during the joint reign of Pharaoh Thutmose III and Hatshepsut, around 1500 BCE, when they united the priesthoods of Egypt into a single order under the leadership of Hatshepsut's High Priest."

"You're starting me down a rabbit hole, Laszlo, I can feel it. No offense but how can you remember all this after drinking so much whiskey you pass out like a homeless drunk."

"I don't know. I can't remember what I had for supper last night most of the time. It's recent, but unimportant history. Likely I've already passed it, if you know what I mean. But as you said earlier, I too am interested in learning what makes the world turn. As such, I rarely forget the juicy tidbits I encounter... And having made that proclamation I recall I did forget one thing: In August of 2001 the order put out a public manifesto calling for a one world government with a universal religion."

"Sorry to interrupt. I'm now seeing red in the rearview. That old Ferrari has been following us the whole time you were talking and mirroring every maneuver I make."

"Holy Fuck! That's a Ferrari 288 GTO. There were less than three hundred made. No way anyone is putting miles on *that* to follow me around. That's a three-million-dollar piece of art."

"So what do you want me to do?"

"Uh…" he was still mesmerized by the image. "Looks like we are nearing Florence. Drop me as you intended but slow down for a second so I can get a better look. There are a handful of them in North America. I've never seen one in person." Giulia slowed as instructed and the red masterpiece pulled alongside. "Holy mother of God!"

"It's just a Ferrari."

"No! That's Ava driving and James is in the passenger seat."

"Who?" Giulia inquired but he did not respond. Making eye contact with Ava burned his eyes. She did not acknowledge him. Simply turned her head back to face the road. The message had been sent.

"It changed lanes and they're now right behind us again. Who the fuck are Ava and James? Tell me now or I'm heading to the nearest police station."

"Calm down. The police can't help us."

"Who the fuck are they!"

"I don't know but if they wanted to merely kill us, kill me… They would have driven an inconspicuous car with tinted windows. It's a message. I need time to decipher it. We must switch. I'm going to drive."

"You're fucking nuts. No way! Do you have any idea the things I had to do to purchase this car. What are you not telling me. I knew something shady was going to happen as soon as you brought up the banks."

"Never mind that now. Let me drive!"

"You don't know how to drive in Italy!"

"I live in Los Angeles. I can drive anywhere!"

Surprisingly this line worked. Or she realized her life was in danger because she countered, "I'll let you drive on one condition: you tell me everything. The whole truth."

"I promise," he gulped.

"How do we switch?"

"Undue your belt" he stated simultaneously undoing his own. "Relax... After this big curve in the road put it in neutral. Keep ahold of the steering wheel. Good. When I say go, lift yourself up and step over the gear box with your right leg. I will slide behind you at the same time and take hold of the wheel with my left hand. When you feel I've taken control, let go of the wheel and pull your left leg over to the other side. Got it?"

"Yes."

"Three... Two... One. Now!" They did it. Laszlo hit the clutch and threw the Giulia into fourth gear. Punching it he felt more at ease than he had in a week. Driving always came naturally to him, like swimming in the ocean. His need to be in control was the reason he despised being a passenger. How to lose these guys, he wondered and checked the rearview, "Does Florence have a ring road?"

"I'm not answering any questions until you tell me the whole truth as you promised."

"OK. That's fair. The two in the Ferrari are sending a message. I met him on the flight from L.A. I had no idea then who they were. Still don't, but last night they took me to the Santa Maria delle Grazie for a party that turned into a ritual. As soon as I realized what was happening, I ran."

"Why are they following us and how are they connected to the witches of Hollywood?"

"All I know is the two most powerful witches, well, one is a man so one witch and a warlock. Does it separate by sex or can a woman be a warlock?"

"Just tell me how they're connected!"

"Right. So one of them, Willow, I've known for twenty years. She has longstanding ties to Milan but I've never met the people in that car before the flight. Last night I also became friendly with another man from Paris and his wife. They told me they work in the fashion industry. I don't know if the two couples know each other."

"They do. Bet on it."

"OK... My other friend, the warlock now from L.A. is Mike and he worked in Paris too."

"What do they do in Hollywood?"

"Willow's family runs a movie studio and Mike is a big shot in fashion. I don't know who he works for, honest, no idea. He may be a fed or intelligence."

"Which studio?"

"You already know. The one with the Genoan connection, Columbia. What do we do?"

"You're right Laszlo. We can't go to the police. They've connected you to me somehow and tracked us via my phone or the car. I don't want any more to do with this. You need to lose them and then we must go our separate ways. This will be better for you also as they can't track you without me."

"That makes sense. I'm truly sorry for getting you involved in all this."

"You're a bad judge of character and reveal entirely too much about yourself."

"I know. My mother tells me all the time. Should I get off in Florence or stay on the highway?"

"Don't get off in the middle of the city. There are big crowds and many streets where cars aren't allowed. If you run someone over, we are fucked."

"OK I won't but then where?"

"I will tell you. I can't recall the name but south of Florence there is a winding road that runs parallel to the highway through little old villages. I'll recognize the exit when I see it."

He drove the speed limit through the city and made no attempt to lose them. They continued to pursue but Ava was not aggressive in doing so. "OK. This is it. Get off here and go left."

"Nothing behind you. Everything ahead, as is ever so on the road."

"What does that mean, Laszlo?"

"In this instance it means you need to focus only on what's ahead. Traffic patterns, forks in the road, any potential places to hide. I'll worry about the car following us."

"OK. Make the first right after the underpass."

"Fuck."

"What! This is the way. The road I had in mind."

"Not that. I just realized something. In the book you gave me I read about the Kelpie. A mythical shape shifting black horse."

"I know about the Kelpie. So?"

"Many years ago in Cairo, Willow and I were in opposing cars racing to the Great Pyramid. I was winning, but at the last moment she commandeered a black horse out of nowhere and beat me."

"Forget about her and lose them!"

"Listen… On New Year's Eve it was Mike who rented the yacht I was pushed off. It was named *Sea Horse*. Written in black on the white boat. Now what's following us?"

"A red Ferrari."

"And remind me what the Ferrari logo is?"

"A prancing *black* horse."

Passing untold numbers of little churches and ancient cemeteries through tiny towns and smaller villages he was able to pull away on occasion, but he could not lose the 288. "I'm not going to be able to outrun her. I need traffic but not too heavy such that I can maneuver. Create a distraction of some kind."

"Make at left at the next road."

"Now what?"

"It's gonna get more winding for a bit. Then we will cross under the highway into Arezzo. It is a little town set atop a steep hill. The upper part of the town there is a cathedral, the town hall and of course, a Médici Fortress from which the main streets branch off towards the lower parts on the other side. If you can lose them by the time we reach the top, there are multiple roads through the valley toward the highway to Perugia. The Tiber River runs through Perugia. I will drop you there and head home. You can follow the river down into Rome. If that's really where you're headed."

"Perfect. What happens if I see the police?"

"They're lazy. They won't follow much past the city limits."

"Hold on!"

He pushed the Giulia to its limit going up the hill at 6,000 RPMs in third gear. Reaching the town they got lucky. Perhaps it was a blessing from above. A large truck was live-hauling chickens in a trailer and stopped in the middle of making an illegal turn. There was a blind spot and the possibility of disaster. He went for it. Ava came to a screeching halt. They were blinded by the chickens. He took the third right. Now cutting downhill on centuries old roads heading into the valley he was pleased with himself. "I just toasted a 288."

"You're lucky there was nobody turning south, or we'd be toast."

"I know."

Presently heading east from Arezzo he wondered what more could possibly be in store. "I think we lost 'em back there. Now what?"

"Make a right here on Viale Raffaello. No, the next one. The main road."

"Got it," he made the turn and gunned it. "I don't see them in the rearview. We should be good but I'll keep pushing hard. Until we part ways, I'm sure they will continue to track you, track us because of me."

"Excellent. You are now a certified expert Italian driver Laszlo."

"Is that all it takes."

"If you should ever find yourself here again, go straight where we made the right and its only five minutes to the birthplace of Michelangelo," she informed with a mix of jest and joy. For the second time they erupted in laughter.

On a lonely road a few miles east of Perugia, Giulia instructed him to pull into the parking lot of a small ancient fortification. "This is The Church of Saint Bevignate. A 13th century stronghold of the Knights Templar. Keep heading west and the highway will take you into the old city center. There you will find the road heading south to Rome. It follows the Tiber River so if you get lost, simply ask where the river is."

She had saved his life. He endangered hers. Sitting in silence, the air between them grew heavy, as if they wanted to speak, and yet neither knew what to say. They were strangers after all. On a bizarre journey lasting only a moment in time concluding at this fork in the road. Each having their own path to which they must now return.

MIRROR MIRROR ON THE BAR

He watched the Giulia pull away in the direction from where it came and disappear. Compared to the mystique and awe one feels at the foot of Milan Cathedral, the tiny 13th century church was unimpressive. Small and plain, lacking austere decorations. The façade hosting only a single tiny cross above a small circular window. The building is rectangular with a single nave and groin-vaulted roof. On a plaque outside, he learned Bevignate was the patron saint of the flagellants who beat themselves in public processions to repent of sin and share in the passion of Christ. The movement started in Perugia after the outbreak of an epidemic. They were tolerated for a couple centuries before the pope declared them heretics. The compound was then given to a Catholic military order founded in Jerusalem during the crusades. Today they are known as the Knights of Malta.

Laszlo was keen to go inside until he learned it cost nine euros. Money was at times tight when he was a child growing up in the San Fernando Valley. That was many lifetimes ago. Again, the desperate situation he faced hit home. Spending a measly ten bucks stopped him from going inside. Memories of thousand-dollar bottles at the club poured over him. Had he foreseen his situation he could've easily saved enough to retire. New money. Easy come, easy go was his reality. He trekked along the left side of the road with the old town coming into view. He was alone now. Truly alone in a foreign land without a phone and a measly two hundred bucks in his pocket. Thinking about death in this scenario is as natural as believing in God. You don't have time for self-pity, he told himself. This moment is the first step of your eternity.

He attempted to focus his paranoid brain. Be absolutely certain you are not tracked. Arrive in Rome alone, as he was presently. He would not take the train or a taxi. Walking was doable if necessary but would take the remainder of the day and all of the next. A bike would be ideal. Purchasing new would wipe out his remaining cash. He could put it on his credit card and immediately leave town. He prepared for the possibility that, if an opportunity to steal one presented itself, he needed to take immediate action. Grey clouds were forming over the hilltop with each step. He passed a basement pub called Kandinsky and was tempted but decided to keep heading toward the center.

Reaching the Piazza Grimana there was no doubt this was it. On his right was an old government building in disrepair with multiple flags flying. Across the street on his left was a small park. Directly in front up a steep incline he faced a massive fort complex with thick walls more than thirty feet tall. In the center was an equally impressive gate protected by two trapezoidal towers. A keystone adorned the top with writing too distant to decipher. Lost in the moment, he forgot about the immediate mission and went to learn more before passing through.

It was Augustus Gate. Named for the emperor who restored it after his victory in the civil war against the Umbrians of Perugia. A few years later he would begin his reign as the first Roman emperor: Julius Ceasar Augustus. Passing through did not change the timeline or Laszlo's fate. He was still alone. The clouds were now signaling imminent rain. He needed to find shelter and was getting hungry. A talkative bartender or a local patron could help him acquire an old bike for cheap, killing two birds with one stone. He approached the first English speakers who crossed his path. A young couple in their late twenties with a non-American accent he could not identify. "Hello... Apologize for buggering your day. Do you happen to know of an inexpensive pub nearby?"

"Kandinsky," they replied. "It's underground on your left." The young gentleman pointed back outside the gate. "You can't miss it."

Descending the stairs down to the pub and sitting at the bar he found no customers nor staff. It was a quintessential dive bar. Dark with funky lighting and old red recliners posing as seats in a corner. The walls papered over with small posters used as street advertisements for the bands who played here over some thirty plus years. The stage empty but not yet cleaned from the previous night's festivities. A harsh cigarette smell emanated off everything. One room was occupied by a pool table while darts were set up in another. The daily special, likely yesterday's special, was handwritten on yellow cardboard taped above a mirrored bar. Not in a mood to wait, he grabbed a glass and leaned over the counter to pull himself a draft of BrewDog Punk, an IPA from a Scottish brewery.

He took note of an impressive set of old saloon doors painted dark red leading to what he assumed was a kitchen and back office. Catching himself mid-breath, he did not yell to ask if there was anyone back there. He had his beer. Don't rush people in these old rustic towns. They live life at a different pace he reminded himself. It was 3:02 PM according to the big clock on the wall. It was so silent he could hear every second ticking away. January 4th, 2024, according to the calendar whose origins he never thought about before the last week. People have lived in this village for at least the last 2,300 years according to science and history books. Did they ever have a different way of tracking—of seeing—the time, he wondered.

Laszlo was comfortable being alone in this place. The

pretentiousness of Milan and California felt a million miles away. The drugs Willow and Mike poisoned him with were slowly but surely losing their spell. Nobody followed him into town, of that he was certain. Hang out. Get the special to eat and another beer and head for home, technically Rome. He caught himself continuously checking the bar mirror. It gave an unencumbered view of the stairs behind him leading down into the front room. Internalizing harsh truth is difficult. He wasn't afraid Willow or Mike would come down the stairs. He was checking the mirror repeatedly because his mind was considering something significantly more unlikely: of all the little anonymous dive bars in all the world, what are the odds he sees Scarlet's reflection come down those stairs.

Zero. It was obviously zero. Dumb and dumber money combining their bet on a billion to one shot. He hated himself for even wanting to see her. "Fucking cunt. She robbed me," he said aloud as a bald bearded late middle-aged man appeared from behind the red doors.

"What's that you say?"

"Sorry I was talking to myself."

"I see you also helped yourself to some of my brother's beer?"

"Your brother?"

"Yes, my brother. He founded the brewery in Scotland."

"That's cool. I didn't want to bother you. I have money. I'll take a refill and the menu... When you have a moment."

"I have plenty of beer and plenty of time, but we don't open for two more hours."

"Well, that explains the crowd. Listen, it's a long story but it's raining outside. I have nowhere else to go... Oh. And I'm looking to buy a cheap bicycle. Any chance you can help me out?"

"Can't help you with the bike but you can stay for now. I need to take a massive shit. You're in charge of security until I get back."

Nearly an hour and three beers later the man returned. "Not a soul in or out Laszlo vowed." It wasn't a fib. He was obsessively monitoring the rearview mirror as was his habit from driving in L.A. traffic.

"Have you ever seen a dead donkey?"

"Uh... No; is this a joke? Because I'm usually willing to try anything once but I could really go for pizza or something more traditional right now."

"Kitchen doesn't open for another hour. Perhaps my donkey is lost in translation. Look at it like this: Do you have a father? The man who knocked up your mother to create you?" he asked, not rhetorically. Waiting and eventually getting a nod in the affirmative he continued. "Well, if tonight you dream your father died, you'd have a very, very bad night's sleep. But when you wake up in the morning, everything will be all right. You'd know it was only a dream."

Laszlo nodded once again. "OK... Is there a more direct translation?"

"The point is, if he really died, it would be exactly the same thing. Only you wouldn't know it. You would be the one to not wake up until you died yourself and were again reunited."

"I will have to think about it; that's interesting. Got any more?" he asked, again checking the mirror to see nobody coming down the stairs.

"Being naked is good for your health. Our natural state. I stay naked as much as possible but it's awkward to impose on others. You wouldn't want me serving you a pizza nude."

"Agreed. Who would?"

"A woman. Not all because women are generally terrified of being raped, but somewhere in the back of the womb, there is one rebellious nerve ending that tingles with curiosity if the word is spoken aloud. Me serving them whiskey naked and alone in this bar is only one step removed."

Laszlo froze his face in an attempt to hide his reaction and not make an enemy of this psycho. At the same time his body melted into mush. Could he stand on his own two feet. He always prided himself on being a free speech absolutist. Yet... Despite that, he now despised this man's words. They reminded him of his desire to hate rape Scarlet after seeing the pictures proving her deception. Not for the act itself. Drugging him was whatever. He hated her more than all the hate which could be conjured and let loose upon the world for causing him to fall in love with her under false pretenses. Was there anything worse in the heavens above or hell below than to fool someone into thinking you loved them? It was the ultimate betrayal. Even as these thoughts reared their ugly head, hearing such words spoken aloud angered his conscience.

"I'm not following. Is there a deeper lesson here that's lost on me?" he finally queried.

"Don't reveal too much of yourself to a stranger. They may be in search of something you will regret having given away." The words washed over him like the cold shower he was desperately in need of.

"Giu- A friend from Milan told me the same using different words only a few hours ago."

"I can imagine you fitting in with the scenery in Milan. What are doing you in Perugia?"

"I'm trying to get away from... Trying to forget about a woman," he hid the truth of running for his life in a white lie.

"Oh, don't worry too much about no woman."

"How can you say that? I have yet to tell you a single

detail about her."

"I already know. You told me she was a woman, and women have been the same my whole life. From the time I was but a young child and through all the decades since right up to this day. They only love you so long as they can keep changing you, little by little. Hell, I think they love their reasons for loving us more than loving us for who we are. It's not so good this way."

The old man had some weird yet not wholly untrue ideas. Still, there was no reason to stay any longer if he could not help him procure a bike. He asked for the check and as the bartender turned, the mirror reflected a pair of long sexy legs in a short black mini skirt descending the stairs. For the briefest moment his heart rose with excitement. Scarlet! Nope... It sunk into terror with equal fervor. It was Ava. Followed by James, Bella, Carla, John, Luca, and Emilia. His fight or flight response kicked in and he burst through the red saloon doors into nothing. There was no exit but through the front stairs. Panicked, he picked up an old bronze lamp as a weapon.

"Relax mister Laszlo," came the refrain from Bella. "We know you are shocked. Feel weird. That was our goal. But we are your friends. You are safe. We are here to celebrate you!"

With the lamp in hand, he surveyed the scene at the bar over the saloon doors. The four women were in front and the men behind. Four happy couples. The two he was aware of plus Luca behind Bella and the bartender with Emilia.

"What the fuck is going on! How do you all know each other! I walked here. How are you tracking me?"

"Relax," Bella repeated.

"I dumped my phone back in Milan and Giulia is on her way back there now. I walked here alone."

"We have a myriad of ways," James confessed. "For one,

you're still carrying that backpack around. Amy put a nano tracker in it while you and I were enjoying the red wine on the flight."

"And Carla put one in your pocket in the event you dumped the whole bag and not just the report," John revealed. "You also consumed nano trackers with your food and drinks. They don't last long as they exit through the digestive system. Injected directly into the bloodstream they stay in the body for years. There is no reason to run because there is no hiding from us."

"How much is Willow paying you? I don't have the money on me now but let's work something out." His offer was met with a chorus of laughter.

After they gathered themselves, Luca restarted. "We are not here to settle any scores between you and your former travel buddies; however you define your relationship with them now. We have been following you and their—umm, shall we say *behavior* in San Diego forced our hand to have this meeting now."

"Meeting! Is that what you're calling this because I didn't sign up for it. If you know about San Diego but don't work for Willow, then who the fuck are you. Who do you work for and why did you track me here? I need a coherent answer now or I'm going to smash my way out of here!" he screamed, raising the lamp in his right hand.

"Relax Laszlo," Bella repeated in a hushed tone for the third time.

"Mate, think about it," James paused. "You did not know we are all working together but we have been tracking you the whole time. We could've easily killed you. If we were here on behalf of Willow, you would not have seen our faces and the fate she attempted to bestow upon you would have been fulfilled."

Luca attempted to change the topic. "Tonight, amico, we get drunk and party. Tomorrow night is the formal meal and ceremony. On the 6th, obviously we know it's your birthday, you'll wake up in Florence and start your new life."

"Even if I wanted to do that I can't right now. I'm low on cash and I don't know if my card will work. Willow or Mike used one of their banking lackeys to put a hold on it." They again burst out in laughter. Now hooting and hollering, high fiving each other.

"Laszlo, you don't need to worry about money anymore. Your birthday present—one of your birthday presents will be a new bank card with ten million in the account. It will work everywhere and every morning the balance will reset to ten million," James explained.

"If that's the case and you're all rich, why did you fly coach to Heathrow? Why did Ava complain you are a cheap bastard post marriage."

"Think about it. It was all a test. A part of this little game. We were playing our roles. You made it and now we can reveal ourselves. You certainly made things interesting for us. As the tracking is perfected in the near future, your story will become legendary. This party, for example, was supposed to take place at Le Cappelle Medicee Restorante near the train station in Florence. I begged Ava not to let you see us, but she couldn't keep herself from prancing the Ferrari 288."

"OK. Hold up. Wait a minute… You're not all here to kill me. You want me to join you. Doing what exactly? And if I say yes, you'll make me unlimited rich. The fuck kind of strings attach to an offer like this. I have worked in Hollywood for years now. Don't you think I would've already sold out."

"Laszlo, it's not like that," Carla spoke for the first time.

"Then how is it, Carla? Surely you want more than a one-night stand from me after this big production. What is the ask?

You want me to join you in fooling people? And if they fail your test what then. Kill them?"

"You won't be asked to kill anybody. We can find guys—or gals—willing to kill on the cheap. If they've had the right training, they become addicted to it."

"Then what do you want from me! What the fuck was up with the costumes at the party Ava invited me to. Should I expect Dr. Lecter to come down next?"

"He will join us tomorrow night. All will be revealed in due time. Relax. Have a drink. Fuck Ava. Fuck us both on the pool table. I know you want to. Henceforth, the world is your oyster."

It was an incredibly tempting offer but the head on his shoulders remained in command. "I don't want that. I want to know who you are. Who you work for. And why we are here?"

James, having discreetly left the group, now returned with drinks on a large tray. He set them on one of the high-top tables between Laszlo and the others. "Grab a glass and let us toast Laszlo!" he announced.

"To Laszlo!" Everyone toasted save for the honoree.

"OK… If all of you are in on this and following me not to kill me but… I don't understand what, where is Giulia?"

"Who?" Luca questioned but Clara snorted, "The street walker he picked up in the park. The whore who gave him the ride here."

"Oh, yeah," Luca laughed, "She isn't one of ours. A real tart. Could've been a top model but quit and started hooking. Neither of them knows it but the old man in the park is her real father. Knocked up her mom while he was still in good standing after she confessed cheating on her second husband to him. What a mark. Anyway, that's how strong genetic bonds are. And how unaware most people go through life."

"Wait. I don't believe it. The old priest can't be Giulia's father."

"Why not. Not all of them are gay, Laszlo. Only the popes and upper echelons."

"Popes?"

"Think about it, amico. The Bible says take a wife and procreate. Earthly riches make it exceedingly hard to enter the Kingdom of Christ. The synagogue of satan does the opposite. Fornicating themselves from ancient Rome to modernity. All while ruling over the unwashed masses devouring their time and energy. Stealing their productivity, art and ingenuity to build palaces for themselves. Do as I say not as I do. Now they are coming into the open. Apparitions and transhumanism. Anyone standing in opposition they plan to destroy. Mark my words."

Laszlo slowly joined the group and slammed his whiskey.

"Listen mate. The things you've been questioning and the lies presented to you in this life have come to a head here. Don't blame us for how we did it. When you become privy to the details you will understand. Embrace us. We contemplated Orwell and Huxley and *The Hunger Games* in the bar at Heathrow. We talked about CERN and Hollywood. You already know. You must fit the puzzle pieces together to reach your truth. The war is not meant to be won; it is meant to be continuous. To launder tax receipts and the productive capacity of the many into the hands of the few. A transnational elite. You have been selected because you're special."

"How is that possible? You all know I'm against the globalist agenda. I oppose this nonsense."

"You do, as do all of us here. You are creative and have excelled in many fields and yet you have not come to terms with how organized evil operates in the world. You will not succeed as an army of one."

"I'll bite at your flattery. What do I offer to your organization?"

"Look at what's happening. The whole world is being feminized. Their current aim is to separate masculinity from intelligence in the masses. The sports star must be a parrot and not speak freely. The fan is overweight and out of shape lacking the will to fight. The intellectual is still necessary to reach the singularity, but that work must be performed by spineless soy boys and women. After your generation the combination of smart and physically fit men will be wiped from the earth, and with them, any possibility of a revolution against the new order. This is the main reason you've been selected. Despite not coming from a royal lineage."

"And it's why I want you to make love to me," Ava proclaimed. "A nervous hysterical energy seeking only safety and immediate gratification has coddled sensibilities and unleashed a tyranny of mediocrity Huxley could only dream of... It's a gigantic turnoff."

"He clearly hasn't had enough whiskey drinks to be seduced. Let's have another round!" John Milton insisted. "Look at what social media is doing to Generation X. They have mostly accepted the move online across the various platforms. And that generation grew up in the physical world before the public internet. Now they pretend. Live in an online asylum of appearances and fake personas serving as an anti-depressant masking the truth that their society is being destroyed in real time all around them.

"Consider universities when they were small outfits reserved for the intellectual. The math genius John Nash. The hit movie *A Brilliant Mind* was based on his life being discovered in West Virginia. He was cultivated at Carnegie Mellon and Princeton, before being sent to MIT to do research resulting in a Nobel Prize. Today an eccentric boy like him is probably drugged by some angry teacher with they/them pronouns in elementary school. If he makes it through that horror show, he's trashed for his whiteness for years. Upon graduation, he is rejected at all the top universities. Perhaps graduating from a lower tier institution, his credentials don't afford him any interviews for top tier jobs. Off chance he knows someone and does manage to get the interview, he will not be hired because of diversity quotas. One in a million, he gets through, he'll be subjected to diversity training and likely hobbled in promotion.

"The war between the sexes and races is the divide and conquer games of the demons in charge. The first goal is to dumb down society making it easier to enslave everyone. The John Nash type is exceedingly unlikely to be recognized. This is what Western society is doing to itself. We did not deceive you because of ill will Laszlo. We are doing what is necessary to fight back against this menace. To fully reveal its evil intent to those capable of seeing the light."

"I know when something is too good to be true. You're offering me protection from Willow. Unlimited money. Sex with your wives or girlfriends or whatever the fuck is going on there... No thanks." He looked each woman in the eye. "All of you are gorgeous and in different circumstances I definitely would. I will regret this. I will so, *so* regret this," he repeated now locked in eye contact with Ava. "But there is something weird at play here."

"Mate don't be stupid. There is nothing for you in Rome. It's a risk without the possibility for reward."

"How do you know I'm going to Rome? I haven't told a soul... I mean, why the fuck would I go to Rome?"

"Mate, did you tell us you were coming to Milan or Perugia? Because if we figured that out, is it not possible we also know more. Isn't it possible we have your best interest in mind?"

"A good point well made. But you still refuse to answer my most basic question: why are we here now?"

"He is as dense as I was," the old bartender spoke for the first time since the others arrived. "It's an easy choice, Laszlo. Black and white. Survive or thrive? You can run from Willow and go at life alone if you so choose. Buy a little farm in Hungary and in a year or three become a statistic. Best case you survive. Slave in district twelve and enjoy the games once a year."

"He won't succumb like that. He'll suicide himself with booze first." Emilia correctly explained.

"Get me six more whiskeys!" Laszlo demanded. "I'm suiciding myself right now. I can't deal with this obfuscation."

"Relax... Do you remember what you posted to Facebook on June 4, 2009?" The date struck immediately as John intended.

"I don't remember exactly but June 4th is the anniversary of the Tiananmen Square massacre. An event so heavily censored in China it can lead to one's disappearance for merely bringing it up in personal conversation. Post about it online and there is no telling what hell the system will dispense. As you all know, I hate commies in general and the CCP in particular. So no, I don't recall the exact language I used. I remember calling out the Obama Administration. Unbelievably to me at the time, he chose that day to give his now infamous 'A New Beginning' speech in Cairo, Egypt. The media credited this as the spark which ignited the Arab Spring. Only by making such an important speech on the thirtieth anniversary of the Tiananmen massacre, Obama and his very savvy media team sucked up all the oxygen and dominated the news cycle... Mere months into his first term, this outed him as a pawn of the globalist agenda he would serve for the next eight years. The speech was a massive gift to the Chinese. He knew it and they knew it." Laszlo concluded with the righteous indignation he felt fifteen years prior.

The whole gang paused briefly before continuing so he could rejoin them in the present. "Now please tell us about the other Facebook posts you made in the month of June 2009."

"I don't recall any others."

"How about in July?"

"I posted probably a few times a week on average, but I don't recall any from July."

"No problem, mate. Can you tell me about any posts you made in July 2010?"

"Um, I was working in Washington D.C... The soccer World Cup was in South Africa. I probably posted about it at some point in June, July, perhaps both... There was a big release of classified documents by Wikileaks related to the War in Afghanistan that summer. I doubt I posted about it due to fears of it being used against me later... Oh! The H1N1 pandemic hit in August. Mexico was a hot spot according to TV news. My high school friends from L.A. and I used it as an opportunity to take a super cheap trip to the Yucatan. I vaguely recall posting pics of the trip in late August. It's possible I shared news articles about the virus or the booking in July.

"Why do you care so much about these old posts anyway? I permanently deleted Meta almost a decade ago. What are you implying?" Laszlo demanded. "Did you run a program over my old social media history. It allowed you to read my mind and figure out I'd be in this little town headed for Rome? Tell me what the fuck is up or I'm out of here!"

James took a slow sip of his whiskey as if he was contemplating a follow up question. Then—without a word—he physically turned toward John, giving him the proverbial microphone.

John glanced at James and then Luca before beginning. "It's much bigger and more advanced than that and you know it. You're not going anywhere. If for no other reason than your curiosity will not let you. Listen to Ava and breathe. Relax. Think."

"Fine but hurry up and make it good." He shot back in frustration.

"There are layers of technology. Did we know you would come to Perugia when you were driving up Interstate 5 on New Years Day. No. The tech is not so advanced yet. Nevertheless, we learned you would be here today. This is old news. Call it the AI of futures past. Much of it was developed decades ago."

"Yeah, yeah… The intel agencies and government black ops teams have stuff light years ahead of the public. I'm going to need more to stay," Laszlo demanded from John while also making eye contact with the others.

"We cannot read minds as of now, but that is the obvious goal. We can and do make incredibly accurate predictions as to future behavior. The closer in time, the more accurately we can predict it."

"I see the flaw in your whole matrix. It only works against individuals like me. It will never reach perfect accuracy because there are powerful competing entities doing the same to constantly update their gameplan. Like an experienced chess player who has his next ten moves figured out until his grandmaster opponent throws a wrinkle in said plan. You recalculate everything up to the last second. Then what? All players conclude the best move in an inevitable fight is to throw the first punch. A post WWII mindset leading to thermonuclear war."

"You're smarter than this Laszlo. Your anger is controlling your conscious mind. Here it is. The long version very short. While you don't even remember most of your own social media posts, we have it all. We have your email and your chrome browsing history. We have it from work, home, and phone. Did you not hit send? It doesn't matter. We have every keystroke including the ones you deleted. We know you used to masturbate every morning you wake up alone to pics of real women in your present or past. Occasionally there were more rounds in the afternoon while watching porn. The day you met Scarlet you stopped looking at all other women.

"We have your academic records and swim medal count. The editorial the Los Angeles Times didn't print arguing trans men shouldn't be allowed to compete against women. We have your family history. We have your DNA and theirs. We have all the papers you wrote from high school to thesis in law school... But I'm only getting started. We know Ricky was your best friend from fourth grade to eighth. We have every mention of you Ricky ever made, whether it was public or private messages. And not only him but every friend and foe you ever had. If they mentioned you, it's fed into the system. We have the timeline of every trip you took and all ticketed events you ever attended. To say we know more about you than you know about yourself is as overwhelmingly obvious as Ava being a model and having millions of followers."

"So *fucking* what. As you said, I already know all of this... I see the sun peeking in from upstairs. Let's go outside and see if you guys can answer my only question. Why are we all gathered here today?"

Taking a drag off his cigarette Laszlo embraced the weak and soon to be setting winter sun hitting his face. A more pressing question entered his mind. It was now obvious James and company did not come here to kill him. But what would happen if he rejected their offer to join them... "All the women remained downstairs. Does this mean the big reveal is finally here?" He attempted to watch all of them at once to garner whether they viewed this comment as a joke or something more.

"Mate, the answer will come from inside. You must realize we are merely a mature reflection of you. There is more to it than what we know about you and your past. The old world was all about gathering intelligence by any means necessary. We—and they—now possess all such pertinent information. And that information is used to specialize messages tailored directly to you, or anyone, to influence real world behavior. It's algorithmically driven to the populace at large, but it can be tailored by humans if the individual targeted is sufficiently important. We can spoof whoever we want. I can video call you and create a deepfake of Scarlet so real you won't know it's not her even after many hours. You can ask 'her' any question from the past or your shared past and it's a near certainty the correct response has been fed into the program."

"Did you do that to me?"

"No."

"Did Willow do it?"

"We don't believe so. Her access is limited because like you she has a reputation for talking too much."

"Especially when she's drinking and on coke," he agreed.

"I said same as you. Let's move on... How does the system work, Laszlo. What have you learned over time. From the assassinations of the 1960's to 9/11 and COVID. Does the government and media lie?"

"Yeah, they lie about everything!"

"OK, and do you know about systems theory?"

"The purpose of any system should not be arrived at by its intent, design or operation as described by the designer. Instead, the purpose of any system is what it does."

"Exactly. Therefore, the purpose of our systems of government and media is not to represent the will of the people or to inform. Its purpose is what it does: lie."

James stepped on his cigarette butt and looked at John.

"The intel agencies and their controllers know everything about their subjects. The purported free individuals called citizens know nothing about the government, the agents, or the black budget programs. Another example of the system working as intended...

"You profess to hate communists and fascists with equal vigor. Well, Mussolini defined fascism as a marriage between corporations and the state. Is that not what we have with big tech taking control of the information war from the mainstream news created Overton windows of the recent past... Did you go to the square in Milan where Mussolini was hanged after the war?"

"You tracked me so you must know I didn't. I do know about it. And I know Senator Prescott Bush was charged under the Trading with the Enemy Act during the war. The fact not a single media personality ever questioned his sons about that on the campaign trail—across five campaigns for president or vice president—is definitive proof the job of the press has been to cheerlead the deep state for a long time.

"Same can be said about Operation Paperclip which brought high ranking Nazi scientist to the US. Never mentioned in the press even after it was declassified. Many former NAZI's went on to have esteemed careers. Werner Von Braun most famously became Director of NASA. Many others were high-ranking NATO officers."

"Mate, the magicians behind the curtains know human consciousness co-creates reality based on what the mind believes to be true and real. All it requires is for the media to ignore certain stories and amplify the counter image. The whole program is progressively installed in the collective consciousness of the masses. They are projecting what they want onto the minds of the public so you will build it for them. It is nearly complete.

"You are exceptional at seeing false narratives yet you

bought the story I fed you about Hollywood being named for an Irish blacksmith. Of course it's holly trees. A sacred symbol of Druids, witches and wizards who used its branches to craft their 'magic' wands for casting spells in ancient times. Remember Merlin the wizard from King Arthur's legend. You guessed it. His wand was made of holly wood. As is the wand of Harry Potter.

"Today the movies, shows and concerts are themselves the spells. The conspiracy theorists rightly call it predictive programming but argue these evil forces must tell us their plans to exonerate themselves from karmic consequences. That's not accurate. What they're doing is getting ahead of the ordeal by acclimating the mind to the possibility of such events occurring. Whatever you call it Laszlo, the purpose of the system is to implant the subliminal messages and symbolism of the occultists into the public consciousness."

"I listened to your story. That is not the same as *buying* it... What is the real story with CERN. Did you feed me more bullshit. Is it a huge hoax, a portal, or something else?"

"It's a portal of sorts." James replied and they all laughed.

"It transports huge sums of taxpayer cash into a black hole of secret budgets," Luca shrugged. "How can the public verify any of it. Perhaps what they built there is a huge computer that will be the coming AI world government. Or is CERN really a way to lower the planet's Schumann Resonances. Weaponizing it's magnetic frequency to post-pone the awakening until the AI control grid can be fully implemented. How would you know. The purpose of the system, Laszlo, is to hide the truth until it's too late.

"Zappa hinted at the plan. At the point where the illusion becomes no longer necessary, they will take down the scenery, pull back the curtains, move the chairs and tables out of the way, and the brick wall at the back of the theatre will be revealed. Zappa left out the ending: the majority will be liquidated, and the Fourth Reich will begin."

"And you guys are anti-fascists communists fighting the good fight I should join?"

"Of course not. Joining the dark side is not a sales pitch we would deliver even if that was the case. The time is at hand. The electronic surveillance wall has already been built. Only the final reveal remains. An alliance of freedom must survive the coming apocalypse. Only then will there be a possibility to destroy the beast system from within. You are the youngest of us here. To be honest, its highly doubtful any of us live to see the day of its destruction."

"I'm not saying I don't believe you but what's the point if you're right. Why *not* go live on a farm somewhere and avoid this madness."

"Because in the very near future there will be no place to run and no place to hide.

"Mate, COVID was about many things. Control of course. De-population to an extent. About twenty percent of the vaccine lots did most of the damage. They were targeting certain groups in various countries, mainly the West. It was testing to determine how compliant people would be and keeping a list of those who are not. They want a database to house and categorize everyone's DNA, which is what the PCR tests accomplished. As you know, the inventor of the test, Kari Mullis, made it clear before he died in 2019 it was not suitable for viral testing. Swabbing up one's nose is—however —a highly effective method to collect DNA.

"Your friend from Andover was right. *The Hunger Games* is sensationalized but based on a realistic goal or model. A ruling class with access to organic food, unlimited energy and tech, with control of all the programs run by AI. A secondary peasant class without access to any of the above will do the things robots can't. They will be kept isolated from each other and history." James finished his whiskey and turned to John

Milton.

"The plan is to close most airports by 2030. Flying will cost too many carbon credits for the new neo-feudal peasant class to be able to afford. By 2050 all airports will close to the peasant class. The only place you'll be going on holiday is within the metaverse, from the comfort of your prison cell—I mean eco-pod. And don't think you'll be going on any domestic holidays either. You won't be able to afford to keep a car. And even if you could, it will be programmed to shut down if you try to leave your 'fifteen minute' smart city. Beef and lamb will be phased out first, and fertilizer use greatly reduced. If you enjoy eating insects and lab-grown fake meat, you'll be OK. This is not conjecture. The World Economic Forum and a host of other globalist groups publish such plans openly. They are implementing them as we speak.

"Today we offer you wealth, a safe haven, and so much more: the ultimate golden ticket. Your children and grandchildren will be rulers instead of slaves. Historically slave status could be changed. There were avenues to escape. After the coming final war all exits will be permanently closed."

"Permanently? You told me only moments ago you would defeat the system from the inside after its implemented! And still nobody has explained why we didn't have this little chat back in L.A. before Willow attempted to have me killed! Why didn't you at least warn me not to go. How can I trust you now knowing you allowed that low IQ fart in the wind Abhi to try and kill me."

James gave Luca the look. "There was a dive team. Your life was never in danger."

"What!"

"There was a team in a submersible with the assignment to collect you. Top notch team from Camp Pendleton. Even knowing your swimming prowess we never considered you'd make it out with all the drugs and booze in your system."

"Look," John pulled out his phone. "Video of you coming out of the bay and collapsing on the beach. Everyone watching live was very impressed. It went viral internally within the organization. Now watch this next one. It's easier to make out because the lighting is much better," he scrolled left. "It is only two minutes later. The woman coming upon you is with us. You have passed out. She checks your vitals and puts a bracelet on your wrist. You do remember the bracelet, don't you? How about the weird rideshare driver to LAX."

"He was one of yours too?"

"He badly wanted to be here tonight, but he is on another assignment. He and Amy will both be at the formal dinner tomorrow night."

"This is too over the top. Let's go inside. I need more whiskey."

"I'll bring some out, mate. We need to cover one sensitive topic without the women. You guys tell him." James disappeared down the steps.

SHATTERED GLASS

John and Luca hesitated as if neither was sure who should speak. Laszlo was impatient. The sun had now set behind the old city walls. "Somebody spill it. After the last few days there is nothing you can say that will shock me."

"They are clones," Luca blurted and watched his reaction. Laszlo didn't say anything. He was apparently referring to the women. Was this part of the test. A comment meant to throw him off kilter even more. A reintroduction of the offer to have sex with them. In movies secret society initiations always included orgies.

"Amico, I have not seen you stoic, silent. Did you know they are clones the whole time. Is that why you don't fuck them? Because let me tell you they are made to be absolute pleasure dispensers. Dominant, submissive or girlfriend experience, it's the real deal."

James returned with the drinks. "What do you think mate. You'll get your own in due time. A couple of them if you wish. Are you convinced to go try out Ava and Clara *now*?"

Laszlo slammed his drink without making a toast. "No. I don't know what the hell all this is about, but it's getting late. I need to be going. Good evening, gentlemen."

"Don't be silly mate. Have another whiskey and let's continue our discussion. Listen to the whole offer. If you still wish to leave at the end, I will make Ava drive you to Rome in the Ferrari.

Laszlo took him up on the offer of another drink, "OK, friends. You want to talk about clones. Let's talk about clones. I don't know anything, so I'm going to lean back against this railing, sip my drink and listen real close."

"What did we discuss only this morning before you foolishly ran away from Clara," John Milton asked rhetorically. "The third world war has already begun. Only it does not look like the movies made about the second. It is being fought with a new generation of weapons. This why so much tech widely considered fringe conspiracy theory five years ago is coming into the open. From gain-of-function bioweapons to nanotech, weather manipulation, directed energy, drone swarms and hypersonic missiles. And yes, clones. A simple toad was first cloned in the 1950's. Do you remember Dolly the sheep?"

"Uh... late 1990's?"

"That's nearly thirty years ago. It wasn't a whistleblower. They revealed Dolly to the world and the mainstream media talked about it for weeks. It was first done secretly in the mid-80s. What do you know about sheep DNA?"

"Nothing. None of this makes sense. Ava and Clara are young, but Bella is my age and no offense, Emilia looks old as dirt. Are you saying Emilia is one of the first clones from the 1980's?"

The four men not named Laszlo erupted in laughter. "Mate, there is only a two-year difference between Ava and Bella. Emilia is two years 'older' than Bella so four years older than Ava."

"I don't understand. How can that be? Ava and Clara are in their early to mid-twenties."

"They are clones. It's not natural age as you understand it. I'll let John explain. He is the resident expert in this field."

"Clones are created from existing DNA and grown from an embryo. Various external inputs are used to speed up the timeline. Depending on the need, a clone can be rapidly aged from embryo to a real world twenty-year-old in under six months."

"Whoa."

"This is not ideal. The more rapid the growth process the more likely a puffy or plastic look will be the result. If the subject being cloned is famous, surgery is needed to match scars, tattoos and other details consistently being photographed is sure to reveal. Additionally, the process of rapid aging results in mismatches because our physical appearance is not only a result of our genetics, but years of life experiences. Stress, diet and our thoughts and actions contribute to our overall appearance. Recent models like Ava and Clara took almost two years to go from embryo to ready for the bright lights. Emilia was a four-year project back in her day. One of the most sophisticated releases of her era."

"Without life experience, how do they know stuff? I didn't speak much with Clara, but Ava is more intelligent than virtually every young woman I've encountered?"

"Memories, speech, mannerism and knowledge are implanted directly into the brain."

"Wait... So, the stories they told me about stem cell creams and everyone jerking it behind the curtain aren't true?"

"What is truth? How does one define it in the modern world? Those stories are true but did not necessarily happen to the Bella you interacted with. Perhaps it was a real memory in the DNA of the human she is molded from. More likely it was implanted as part of her programming. One of the first lessons learned was the way to create hypersexual females despite them not proceeding normally through puberty was to fill their minds with endless sexual memories. A fucked-up but not wholly inaccurate way to conceptualize it is they have every porn film ever recorded embedded in their brain...."

"Anyway, the nano chips are hardwired at birth when the skull is soft and later updated through the eye socket. We are looking to update with nano-injectables but that's a few years away. Because the initial processing power and memory is so great, some updates can be made the old-fashioned way. What I mean by that is this: if I want Clara to learn a novel theory about physics, I can simply give her the book to read before going to sleep. She does not have the ability to conjure new ideas based on what she learns, but she will be able to recite every detail by morning."

"I'm happy I stayed, gentlemen. I will give you that. I don't necessarily believe any of this, but I also can't imagine four well-off middle-aged men with nothing better to do than follow me around telling weird tales and tempting me to have sex with their cloned wives... Can they bear offspring? Do they have souls?"

"A rapidly aged human clone is unable to reproduce. Flat feet and a lack of wisdom teeth are tell-tale signs. Clone families are installed with cloned children pre-aged to a point, and then allowed to age. It will be extremely rapid, so they have to be killed and replaced frequently. Experiments with naturally aged clones are underway. If they don't accelerate through puberty, it's possible they could have offspring. It is very risky. Obviously, the results are many years away. One of the reasons for the extensive expansion of the childhood vaccination schedule despite obvious and horrific human consequences is the attempt to solve this very issue. Profit is not the sole motivation for bad behavior. Especially if we are talking about the ultra-wealthy who have everything but more time."

"I need more drinks," Laszlo declared. This time the bartender went downstairs. "OK... No offspring capability for now. Do they have souls as I understand that word."

All eyes were back on John Milton. "Human beings are

souls inhabiting bodies. Our consciousness resides within our soul. Memories are stored in the brain. Humans can't affect another's soul or transfer a soul from one body to another. Clones are brain-powered machines and have no soul-based consciousness. They have no soul plan and aren't subject to karma. They can display feelings like joy or anger and recall the memory of past emotions. They do not have an inner dialogue and are not capable of love or spirituality."

"Interesting... If this is all true, what purpose do they serve if they have no soul and can't reproduce? Just soldiers and athletes. Am I watching clones at the Olympics?"

"Athletic prowess has been highly problematic because of the rapid aging process. They are programmed to know the rules and understand strategy but do not possess the muscle memory that comes with daily repetition. Secondarily, even with supplementation and surgery, we have not achieved the ability to create the combination of thick fibrous muscle connected to dense bone which is formed by repeated injury and recovery during the critical early teenage years. Every clone you've seen in high-level sports is often injured. Greg Oden was the first attempt at a basketball player."

"That's the first thing I've heard that makes sense... So, if they aren't athletes, can't reproduce and lack the creativity of a real human, what is their purpose? Other than the obvious sex doll experience you are all tempting me with."

"Amico! I'll let John continue to explain the science but don't underestimate the sexual experience 'til you tried it." Luca slammed the drink in his hand and disappeared down the stairs.

"Luca is not wrong here my friend. From a bottom-up perspective, the ability to clone female supermodels and program them to be intelligent and completely faithful is a bad 1980's science-fiction script. Unfortunately for all the 'I'm perfect as I am' dumb bitches with thirty aging tattoos covering their cellulite farms, it will be a death knell. More interestingly, from a top-down perspective, we have achieved something which has been attempted since MK-Ultra: to completely replace real memories with made up ones."

Laszlo passed his pack of cigarettes around and everyone lit one before John continued. "The military application of clones is to create completely controlled politicians, generals and celebrities. Reprogrammed with new memories and beliefs, their application is as obvious as it is frightening. This is how nearly all the male clones have been deployed to date."

"Do they know they're clones?"

"I'll get to the specifics, but most do not. This is why they need handlers. Some may understand there are doctors or handlers around them. Handlers usually come from intelligence or military to guide the clone. Their responsibilities vary greatly depending on the purpose of the clone. Sometimes a family member, including the spouse of the human cloned, can take the role of handler. Financial agreements and threats coerce people to go along with an arrangement of this kind."

"Are Willow, Mike or any of those clowns clones?"

"No. Remember what I said about rapid aging. But if you come across them years from now and they look the same, you are dealing with a clone. The surest way to tell is the whites of their eyes. Any smoke… Cigarette, ganja, campfire—doesn't matter—turns it yellow instead of pink or red. If it was brighter inside the bar, you would've noticed it immediately when we came down the stairs. Female clones are significantly less dangerous. For this reason, most of the clones created to date are female."

"OK, so similar to true human form the male is more likely to kill you than the female."

"Want you dead, no. Carry out the act of violence, yes. The number of each sex created to date skews the numbers relative to the human population. Currently, there are approximately three thousand three hundred female clones for every male. By the time you look a male in the eye it might be too late. If the whites of its eyes turn yellow quickly and it's not smokey, run! I'm talking a deep foggy yellow, not bright. Yellow like urine after a long night of drinking."

"Why are the males so prone to violence?"

"We don't know. One theory is a consciousness they're not supposed to possess."

"A demon?"

"That's a different theory with more scientific backing which is applicable to both sexes. The clone creating scientists are incentivized to lie to further their own promotion. It is fucked in that respect. My personal theory as to males is that an unknown phenomenon activates the pineal gland of the clone which they cannot completely eliminate and still give it human characteristics. However, the gland doesn't develop normally because of the rapid aging and the only enlightenment the clone gains is that they are not a real human. This causes a rebellion against humanity. It's only a theory. The female clones undergoing the same process react with traditional female actions of undermining the handler or feigning being wronged in some horrible way. The male always lashes out with physical violence."

"I'm now tempted to go downstairs. Not to fuck them; at least not yet... To observe and interact with the information you told me."

"Let's fucking go mate."

"One more question first. If you are good guys fighting against the globalists as you say, why don't you take real wives?"

"The same reason we use drones, nano, and other tech. You can't fight fifth generation warfare with first generation weapons. The pen is not mightier than the sword in the modern world. You can deny it... Attempt to write a book about clones and what you have learned about Hollywood. Will it garner attention from major publishers. Do you think you can make it go viral without big tech algorithmic promotion?

"And suppose it's so fucking interesting that you hand it out like a Revolutionary War pamphlet and raise a militia willing to distribute it on your behalf for free... Even then it accomplishes nothing to stop what is coming. Remember mate, the goat herders won in Afghanistan because the mission was to steal the funds allocated to the war, set up bio labs that created poison shots to sterilize the overpopulated Indian subcontinent, and last but never least: sex and drug trafficking.

"If all the fat asses with arsenals at home going to football games on the weekend ever became a true threat, they would be nuked that instant. The powers that be know there is no need. Like the proletariat in *1984*, they will never rebel until they wake up. And they can never wake up if they don't rebel. As we told you inside: the control matrix is now so sophisticated it can be geared toward the individual. The last generation to grow up without social media addiction is middle-aged and not many of them are likely to reach old age. The first phase in any game of chess is positioning your pieces... Check... Only a few moves remain before it is checkmate."

The five men descended the stairs and joined the four female model clones at the bar. Another round of shots was preceded by another toast to Laszlo. He was distraught and unsure if it was drugs or the spell that had him believing the beautiful women surrounding him were clones created in a laboratory.

Ava appeared keen to speak. "Scarlet is a weird you know. An old school MK-Ultra Monarch programmed 'butterfly'. Whatever they call it, the details revealed to the public are nothing compared to the private programming developed over the course of millennia. It's trauma-based mind control. Once Scarlet or any victim endures so much at a young age, they shut out real memories as a coping mechanism. And when that is multiplied by a skilled teacher, they will develop dissociative identity disorder. The individual is then only able to hold certain information within each personality and each can be triggered or suppressed as needed. It is a permanent condition."

"I fucking know about MK-Ultra! She is *not* one of them. Scarlet is a very real and beautiful woman, not a god damn agent," Laszlo boomed with anger. "And if you know so much about Scarlet, how do you not know yourself!"

James gave him a look which said don't go *there,* and Ava continued, "Well, for one, you're not behaving like you know. If you did you would understand why Scarlet can say she is your soulmate one night and not remember anything in the morning. We had bets on whether you were going to rape her. Those of us here bet that you would not. Everyone else you meet from the organization took the other side of the wager. It will serve you well to remember that should any trust issues arise in the future."

"I need a cigarette," Laszlo declared and headed back outside. James, John and Luca followed. The bartender stayed with the clones. He lit a cigarette but did not offer one to the others.

"Let me get one too, mate... Shakespeare told us 'All the world's a stage'. Over the last five days and your career in Hollywood, you still have not taken this fact to heart. Who are you going to put your faith in? You act like Scarlet is the god damn Virgin Mary... But you know she's been pimped and turned out by Willow and Mike for years. Sacrificing your soul to Scarlet is a dead end leading to everlasting disappointment."

Luca pointed at the cigarettes to convey he also wanted one. "You must destroy Scarlet. Not the woman but the idea of Scarlet you created in your mind's eye. Are you familiar with the story of Apollo and Daphne?"

"Enlighten me."

"Apollo intends to make Daphne his bride. He boasts, pleads, promises everything under the sun shall be hers if she will be his wife. Do you know how Daphne responds?"

"Remind me."

"She begs her father to destroy the beauty which cursed her with this fate of Apollo chasing her. She is willing to give up all earthly riches to be free of him. This is how Scarlet sees you now… It's OK. You swam out of the bay. You were able to escape. Overcame the spell they cast upon you despite the near breakdown. Even after you were forced to confront the evidence against Scarlet, your will to live powered you to continue without access to money and other resources you are accustomed to having. This leads us to conclude you have the potential to become an exceedingly important character for us."

"Again with the flattery."

"Sure, it's part of the game. Here is a truth you can't deny. Everything is a lie: history, school, government and the time… Yet there is another piece of advice men selectively choose to ignore: Women cheat. A lot. Men cheat too of course. Men cheat if there is a hot opportunity, but this scenario is unlikely unless he is extremely wealthy. Secondarily, men cheat if they are not getting any sex for a long time at home. This is a precursor to divorce. It's the wife's plan causing him to take the fall with the family, friends and in court."

"You guys say Willow and the gang can't be clones

because of the rapid aging process. That I've known them too long for it to be possible. Do you believe they're witches?"

"Of course I do, mate. They believe themselves to be, it must be so. Do I believe Scarlet can shapeshift into a raven or Mike into a horse. Of course not, don't be silly. But if I can get one of our operatives to believe such nonsense, that's great power. For if he believes himself to be a shapeshifting warlock who derives his power from me, then getting him to carry out mission specific tasks is an easy ask.

"You will start with two wives as we all did, mate. Most likely you will ditch one after the novelty wears off, but you are allowed to keep both as long as you so desire."

"I think you mean if he can handle it," Luca laughed. "You can have three or more if you so desire. Two is what the programming recommends as ideal. We can't reveal details now but if you are not pleased, adjustments will be made. So, forget this silly plan of going to Budapest. Only by joining us in Florence can you live in a world of milk and honey while also gaining the revenge you seek against Willow and company."

"Revenge sounds good now but how is this a life? My two beautiful wives will be soulless slaves? MK-Ultra created clones of former swimsuit models whose pictures I masturbated to as a teenager. Clara is beautiful on the outside, but no... I refuse to board this MK-Ultra clone train."

"We have come a long way since MK-Ultra. Yes, they will be clones. Could you tell Ava, Bella or Clara are clones before we told you. You had no idea. No one will know. You can introduce them to your parents and friends. We will give you the triggers so you will be in control. You will be doing the manipulating instead of getting played by Scarlet or another woman."

"And if I don't like them?

"You will like them, but we will also give you the termination triggers should an emergency arise."

"So I'll be their handler?"

"No, it's not like that. They will have no public role to play. The cloned politicians we discussed are different. Your wives will be singularly purposed to help you and care for you. She—they if you keep both—will literally never deny you. Over time you will establish a real bond as I have with Ava.

"Why didn't you get two?"

"I never said I did not."

"I don't want two. Only a simple Scarlet clone. No crazy updates or weird powers and you have a deal."

"No. It doesn't work like that. You can ask for certain aesthetics, but a full-on Scarlet is not possibly for several reasons."

"Which are?"

"Most importantly, we wouldn't be able trust you. She... It will be so realistic you will love her like the real thing. This could be used against you and in turn us."

"This is creepy. If y'all know so much about me, how do you not understand I don't want *The Stepford Wives*. I want true love." He lit a cigarette as laughter again erupted.

"Amico, none of us fortunate ones here have the ability to create a perfect story for our lives where we get everything we want. We are limited in this dimension. The human mind cannot understand love without experiencing a lack thereof. We can predict action, but we may be wrong. We determined you will be an addition to the organization. Next year you could be terminated. We offer no guarantees except revenge. Before you are ever asked to do a single task for us, we will make sure that whatever dire fate you envision for Willow, Mike, Abhi, or Scarlet will come to pass."

"Why the hell did you include Scarlet? I could never hurt her."

"Dante is not the only great poet in history. Can you quote Yeats?" Milton asked.

"Uh, no, not off the top of my head right now."

> *Turning and turning in the widening gyre*
> *The falcon cannot hear the falconer;*
> *Things fall apart; the centre cannot hold;*
> * Mere anarchy is loosed upon the world,*
> * The blood-dimmed tide is loosed, and every where*
> * The ceremony of innocence is drowned;*
> * The best lack all conviction, while the worst*
> * Are full of passionate intensity.*

"This is the real world. Not some weird fantasy where one falls in true love at first sight and the good guys always win in the end. The sun has set. Our offer to join us also has an expiration. We were impressed with you before the swim out of the bay. In addition to that already discussed, we are prepared to offer you-"

"Stop! I'm not selling my soul for a stepford wifey and earthly riches. If the organization is as powerful as you portend, why can't I do your dirty work and be with Scarlet. The *real* Scarlet not some clone. You can't implant a chip making her oblivious. Destroy Willow and the others and bring Scarlet to Florence so I can talk to her face to face. This is my final answer."

"Be patient with him, mates." James looked at Luca.

"Keep your head above water and breathe, listen. In Seattle if Scarlet was attacked you would've done anything to protect her."

"Anything." He agreed.

"Given up your own life if it was the only option. Killed a stranger and it would've been completely justified action done to save her... But what if the person attacking Scarlet was another of her victims. Someone she drugged, robbed and left for dead. You would have never known. Think about it. You would've been her knight in shining armor. In reality, it would be saving a hoe who drugs people and steals their belongings. You are shown the image and still you do not believe it. I can see it in your eyes even now. Crafting a story to justify her actions. To mask the truth that she is a bad person. Well, what is real then? Only that which we choose to believe."

"Maybe it's a story in my head but it's possible... It's certainly plausible that Willow and Mike coerced her into robbing me. It was they who put Abhi up to it. I'm not going to allow a soulless clone like Ava to tell me what Scarlet does or does not remember. Ha! We went through that portal together and all that came before was undone. We are united and will be together again. This is some satanic level shit you're spitting at me now: the only reality is that which I choose to believe. No. I feel this reality deep in my gut. I'd rather be locked up in the basement of this goddamn bar than make believe in a reality without Scarlet."

James handed him a whiskey. "All we are doing is showing you the truth. Isn't that what you have been seeking your whole life Laszlo? You never submitted to the lies taught in school, told by the politicians, or programmed into the unconscious mind by the media. Listening to your inner voice, your gut, brought you to us. We did not seek you out. We are merely confirmation that you were on the right path all along."

James gave the last whiskey to John Milton. "Who are you carrying all this baggage for anyway... Scarlet? Your Goddess; is that it? God damn it! Let me give you a little more inside information about Scarlet. Scarlet has always been a bad girl. She's a phony. Think about it. She preys on men's instincts as she preyed on yours. She teases you with an extraordinary gift, untold pleasure... And then what does she do. I swear, for her own amusement, her own private revenge against love and sex itself in a cosmic gag reel of hypocrisy, she sets the rules in opposition. Delivers the greatest blue wrecking ball of all time.

"Look, but don't touch. Touch, but don't taste. She's just not ready for that. But—don't walk away—she likes you; only it's too soon. So, here's a little taste: rub my feet and perhaps we may be soulmates. But don't swallow…

"She made a laughingstock of you and a very long list of others. And while you're jumping from one foot to the next, what is she doing? She's laughing her sick—fucking perfect, I admit—ass off. She's a bad mamma jamma. And like the clones, she too is an absent vessel, worse. Worship her. Love her unconditionally. Anoint her your wife. That *cunt*. Why! Never!"

"Better to be selfish and gratify myself. Better to lust after clones than expose myself to heartbreak. Better to reign in hell than to serve in heaven. Is that it, *John*?"

"Why go there, Laszlo. Heaven or hell? Duopoly is dangerous, is it not? Divide and conquer games. Supposedly the devil's oldest trick. Forget that nonsense…

"We're here on the ground in Milan, in Florence, inside the fucking Vatican! Our noses in everyone's crotch since the war started! Nurturing every sensation woman, witches, and the enchantresses have been inspired to deceive us with! I care about what they want, and I never judge them. Why? Because I never rejected them. Despite all their imperfections: I'm a fan of Scarlet! I'm a fan of witches. Perhaps we are the last wizards. Who in their right mind, Laszlo, could possibly deny the 21st century is entirely depraved. All of it, Laszlo. The hot war is going to start any day now. Everywhere and all at once. That which has been will be destroyed. A new world installed. You may not want it or be ready for it, but it is coming for you!"

****

"C'mon mate let's go get another round downstairs."

"I'm no wizard. I'm not interested in talking to clones. The money is a bit enticing and helping me destroy Willow very much so. I want to know more about your organization. Are you intelligence or other operations. What country? Convince me not with the promise of sex with cloned models but with knowledge and information. Illuminate my mind."

"It's not like the movies. Countries don't matter at this level. Intel is our cover. A get-out-of-jail-free card for a lack of a better term. We work for an organization that's been waging this war since before Rome existed. Some battles have been won. Many have been lost. The technology changes. The goal remains the same: preserve history and defend freedom of thought and speech. Never surrender the realm to the forces of the lower dimensions."

"Organization? Could you be a little more specific."

"An organization of the like-minded."

"The Sforza family?"

"Let's just say Dr. Lecter has a boss none of us here will ever meet. In the end, it doesn't matter who. Remember, even if you do not believe, you must understand what the enemy believes to have a chance to defeat them. Our enemy believes itself to be direct descendants of the line of Cain, who they believe was the offspring of satan and Eve. Their belief drives their behavior. Their first rule is rule by bloodline families. And they believe they are more than human. Born of the fallen angels. The Watchers from the Book of Enoch. The rest of us are mere humans. We can worship God, but never become a god. They want us dead."

"I thought they wanted us to join them in the battle against God?"

"That is only to fool people. To use them as their minions. The ultimate goal is to kill every last human from the line of Seth, born to Adam and Eve after Abel's murder and

Cain's banishment. This is how they defeat God and inherit the earth and all that's in it. This is how they become gods themselves and fulfill the wish of satan."

"I give zero fucks about this ancient biblical battle right now," he crushed his remaining whiskey. "Who are Willow and company? If you can help me destroy them, they must not be a bloodline member of this cult or whatever. They practice witchcraft at the behest of whom? Scottish Rite Freemasons? This is the information I need mate."

"We don't know which family but more or less."

"But Willow is Jewish."

"The official seal of the Grand Masonic Lodge of Israel in Jerusalem includes a Star of David, a Christian cross, and a Muslim crescent. All three are superimposed over a masonic square and compass and encircled by a chain of union...

"In Vegas they were probably only playing the games they play on everyone because they're bad people. It entertained their dark side and made them a little money. Scarlet gave them their stuff back, you paid them, and Scarlet kept the cash she stole. It was for their amusement at your expense. New Year's Eve was different. The people they answer to figured out we marked you. They didn't know if it was to join us or because you were being used to betray them, but it didn't matter. Either scenario results in a contract on your life."

"Thanks guys, you're the best. When I join you, won't the price of the contract go up and with it, a greater incentive to kill me?"

"No. There are agreements. It's not a movie but think of it like the mafia."

"Made men are protected?"

"A little like that, yes. Once the hot war starts we don't know what will happen. We anticipate continued protection, but we cannot guarantee it."

"So, if we destroy Willow and her gang will I be protected from retribution?"

"Yes, but again this is not a movie. Not all masons are connected and not all Jesuits are intelligence agents. Most secret agents are not like James Bond. Look at Tony Fauci. He held a public role his whole career. He did not go it alone. Fauci has spoken publicly and highly of the black robed priests at his Jesuit high school and Jesuit college, Holy Cross. His wife also went to a prestigious Jesuit college, Georgetown. She was not in front of the cameras, but you know her role, Laszlo."

"I do. Mrs. Fauci was director of Bioethics and Human Experimentation at NIH during COVID."

"We know because you pointed it out often to anyone who would listen."

"How could her husband be on TV all day for three years without anybody questioning her role. Even a stay-at-home mom should've garnered a little attention. Perhaps a fluff piece in Marie Claire. Yet the national director for human experimentation during the largest rollout of a novel and experimental medical procedure was ignored by the media."

"Hidden in plain sight mate. Who but the black pope could conceal such information... The best way to control the opposition is from within. You know where Timothy Leary, the 1960's hippie icon and advocate of 'Turn on, tune in, drop out' went to school?"

"No idea but I'll guess Holy Cross for the shits and giggles."

"For two years before the second world war. He was then enrolled in the psychology subsection of an army specialized training program that included study at Georgetown. And yes, Leary also worked at NIH in a mental health role. He briefly moved his family to Florence after being fired for failing to meet with NIH investigators looking at irregularities in his research funding. Despite this termination, he soon returned to the US after being offered a position at Harvard University's Department of Clinical Psychology."

Laszlo lit another cigarette. His mind was made up. He knew what he was going to do. First, he allowed James to continue.

"Freemasonry is partly based on hermetic teaching. In Scottish Rite philosophical lodges discussion of politics is not allowed. They believe in fraternity over truth. The hermetic principle of correspondence, symbolized by the phrase 'As above, so below,' originates from the Emerald Tablet of Hermes Trismegistus. This maxim suggests a symmetry and interconnection between the universe and man. The symmetrical design of the image, with the human figure and the mountainous landscape reflected above and below, reinforces this idea of unity and mirroring between different levels of reality. Masculine and feminine, electricity and magnetism, light and dark, spirituality and sexuality.

"The requirement to join a true masonic order is to have faith in any religion rather than a specific one because as you progress, the truth is slowly being revealed, and you are taught all religions are connected. They believe mainstream religion —like the media—is for the masses. The meaning of the symbols and related esoteric knowledge is reserved for true initiates. They follow the ancient Babylonian religion taught by the so-called mystery schools. Other religions, however pure or innocent as practiced by the faithful, are responsible for creating our current system run by sociopaths.

"The infiltration of the occult by evil corrupts knowledge ensuring most people cannot access ancient wisdom. Originally the purpose of esoteric knowledge was to keep evil people away, but now it's the opposite; good people are kept away by lies. As the deception grows, darkness will be preferred to light. Death will be thought more profitable than life. No one will raise their eyes to the heavens. The pious will be deemed insane, the impious wise. The madman will be seen as brave, and the wicked will be esteemed for their virtue."

"I have a request and a question," Laszlo reported. "First, I propose a toast to the wicked."

"To the wicked," came the group chant as glasses were raised and emptied.

"Kidding aside, if you guys are working against the wicked, why all the secrecy? Why adopt their methods? Are you guys Illuminati? Why not expose this evil instead of waiting for the techno prison to be completed and the hot war to start?"

"It's not that simple, mate. 'You can't handle the truth' is one of the most famous lines in cinema. Many quote it. Lots of people can explain the plot line, name the actors and even know details of the personal lives of those actors. Yet most people still cannot see the light. They cannot handle the truth."

James nodded at Luca and headed downstairs. "Everyone must see for themselves. You and Willow both touched the Great Pyramid in Egypt at the same time. Is your understanding of its significance the same? Is it merely the tomb of a pharaoh or is it more? You and Abhi can each look at a dollar bill. Does he question whether Weishaupt killed and replaced George Washington? Has he read Thomas Paine or questioned why Paine came to hate George and the masons?"

"I see your point. That dumbfuck Abhi does not question mainstream narratives. He will wait in line to be the first to go cashless and give up freedom for the promise of a false security."

"Exactly, amico. Imagine if the world was locked in their homes and forced to watch TV news like the early days of COVID... But! Instead of a fear inducing psychological operation, the programming revealed the hard truths of this world most cannot handle. It would collapse civilization. Many would take their own lives. Others would beg their God to bring back the old illusions at any cost. A majority would be willing to sell out their family like Cypher in *The Matrix* to wipe the truth from their brains and return to the safety of a nine-to-five job and tickets to the big game."

John pointed to Laszlo's dwindling pack and lit another cigarette before beginning to wax poetically. "Even the old priest in the park, constrained by the dogma of his faith, has figured out more than most. Taught it to his hooker daughter who got caught up in ancient sex magic stories as a way to justify her profession. Yet she too is closer to the truth than 85% of the global population who are so distracted, deceived and malnourished they wouldn't accept the truth if it was baked in a cake and handed to them on a silver platter.

"The popular meme on social media is that people who do evil in this world believe they must reveal what they will do first to absolve themselves of the bad karma of their evil deed. You see it referred to as predictive programming. *The Simpsons* is the most infamous example, but you know there are hundreds of others. What utter rubbish. It's psychological preparation. Quelling the angst of people before the event by prepping the subconscious for the unlikely. Putting forth a probable villain to control where their suspicions focus after the fact. Combine this with the massive collective trauma caused by the event itself, and all but the strongest minds will desire an answer, any answer. A safe place for them becomes infinitely more important than questioning who and why. The idea the very people they elected to protect them are in fact the culprits is so repugnant as to not be considered. You saw it after 9/11 and now after COVID.

"Are these the people we should spend time and resources informing? Humans with so little capacity they bury their heads in YouTube and social media while the predators slowly eat them alive. The time is short. They are cannon fodder. All we can do is align with those who have broken free of the programming and prepare for the battle ahead. The Babylonian barbarians are already inside. Our institutions are under their control. They possess most of the keys for the electronic gates and drawbridges of the global internet control grid."

James returned with another round, this time Peronis'.

"Tell me about their numerology. Specifically, why the numbers three, thirteen and thirty-three are significant?" Laszlo questioned.

"The most important science of Freemasonry is navigation. The compass and square. The most visible symbols of masonry are the fundamental tools of navigation and map making. Calculation of speed and location under the heavens is considered the highest form of sacred knowledge from antiquity. Navigation unites time with space and the heavens with the earth. The number three is essential to this computation. Without the geometry of the three-sided triangle, establishing location and distance on a map, triangulation, is impossible."

James nodded at John Milton. "The obvious mainstream connection to thirty-three is Jesus Christ because he was crucified at that age. Many equate this to thirty-three degrees of masonry but to high level initiates it has another meaning traced back through their history to the Phoenicians as preserved by the Knights Templar. The Phoenicians' most well-known legacy is the creation of the world's first alphabet. It facilitated the creation of Hebrew and Greek script which was transmitted across the Mediterranean and later used to develop Latin, Arabic and Cyrillic alphabets. Their international trade network fostered the economic, political, and cultural foundations of Classical Western civilization. Based in the Eastern Mediterranean they administered trade posts throughout the region.

According to the Book of Enoch, the two hundred angels who descended to take earthly wives from the line of Cain swore an oath and bound themselves on Mount Hermon in Phoenicia. It has three distinct summits each roughly the same height where the modern borders of Israel, Syria and Lebanon converge. The three snowcapped peaks melt waters merge to become the River Jordan. There are thirty-three ancient Babylonian Temples on the mountain including the Temple of Baal which dates to Phoenician times. The temple is thirty-three degrees north of the equator and thirty-three degrees east of the ley line which runs beneath the pyramid at the Louvre in Paris. As you know, this is where the Knights Templar hid the sarcophagus of the Virgin Mary."

"What about thirteen?"

"That one is tricky, mate. Jesus had twelve disciples. Of the thirteen attending the last supper Judas was the final, thirteenth man to arrive. He earlier betrayed Christ leading to his crucifixion the following day, a Friday. For the Knights Templar the date is significant for another reason. It was Friday the 13th of October 1307, when the King of France ordered the arrest of the Templars leading to the torture and death of many. That date, however, is according to the Julian Calendar. Using our current Gregorian one, the corresponding date does not fall on a Friday or the thirteenth... Long standing theories speculate there are thirteen bloodlines who have ruled the world since Babylon-"

"Why are you guys holding back? Isn't Dr. Lecter a member or beholden to one of the thirteen bloodlines while Willow and her gang work for another?"

"Mate, we are not holding back. It's possible but we do not know. None of us have met or will ever knowingly interact with a bloodline member. Ultimately it doesn't matter whether the number is thirteen or thirty-three. The pyramidical structure is the same. The tippy top is older than the Babylonian bloodlines. They are the direct descendants of the two-hundred angels who conspired on Mount Hermon. Beneath is the larger but tiny group who trace their bloodlines back to Babylon. This level likely encompasses a similar number, thirteen to thirty-three, per continent or geographical region. We don't know for sure. They will never be on TV, and you won't meet them either. The next level down, I think, is occupied by the majority of the old, now underground, royal families like Sforza." James paused for effect. "You *have* met a Sforza."

Laszlo lit a cigarette. "Only one left; call it if you want it… The pyramidic structure makes sense. What level do you guys occupy?"

"The farther down you go, the murkier it becomes and starts to vary regionally. This next level is where secret societies reside. In practice we are non-state actor intelligence operatives reporting directly to Dr. Lecter. But there are modern public royals, archbishops and other religious leaders as well as prominent industrial families like the Rothschilds and Rockefellers who play very different roles but have great power. Within each sub-group there are counter-intelligence agents. They wield enormous power to monitor everyone and likely report to the very top," James concluded and eyed Luca to continue.

"All of the above happens outside of mass public reporting and therefore consciousness. The next level down is where the revelations begin. Important players like Jeffrey Epstein and P. Diddy have been used for many years. They are granted vast earthly riches but get thrown to the proverbial wolves should the operation be exposed."

"They are led to believe they are made men to go back to our earlier analogy but are tossed aside should the need arise," James interjected.

"How Willow and Mike view Abhi and I: disposable."

"Yes, like that but no longer if you join us. The next level down is where they reside. Top academics, high ranking public officials and new money. Basically, from the perspective of the public, it is the Forbes list of the rich and powerful. Is it any wonder why this is the most depressed group of people on the planet per capita. Can you imagine? The whole world thinks you're the top of the food chain and in reality, you must beg to get a meeting with the guy who knows the guy who holds your fortune in his palm. We call this the sacrificial lamb level. No offense, but before our algo team ran your history, you were below this level. In Willow's world you would've continued to be used indefinitely, and when you finally sniffed this level, discarded as ceremoniously as the attempt a few nights ago.

"The bottom is comprised of the remaining ninety-five percent subdivided by race, religion, income, nationality and now gender. This keeps them divided and distracted. At each other's throats not looking up."

"Should we head down for a final round before going to dinner mate?"

"Let's do it," he agreed, and the four men rejoined the bartender and clones in the main room of the Kandinsky.

"About time gentleman. Laszlo has proven to be a tough nut to crack," Clara joked. "We have an amazing restaurant waiting for us."

"They are closed to the public tonight," Bella added.

"You are all certain they have cracked me and I will be joining you in Florence?"

Ava raised her glass, "We are certain. No one can turn down all we have to offer. To Laszlo! To the Apocalypse!"

This time he joined them in toasting himself.

"To Laszlo! To the Apocalypse!" they cheered.

"Ava... Or any of you beautiful ladies, how do you see the apocalyptic scenario playing out?" He looked each in the eye and noticed the yellowish color John had disclosed.

"COVID was a test. The next virus will be truly biblical," Emilia finished her whiskey. "I'm the oldest so I say bring it on. The sooner the better but we don't know the exact timing. It will be orchestrated to destroy the useless eaters but preserve resources while leaving key infrastructure intact. This time the chosen will survive not in an Ark above the water, but underground."

"You are right about Denver airport," Ava too slammed her drink. "It is the hub of the North American tunnel system. Most of the major bunkers are located near airports and are connect via underground high-speed railway."

"I fucking knew it."

"Kubrick filmed the moon landings. The contractors got paid but much of NASA's budget has been siphoned for this purpose."

"Where is the European hub?"

"Geneva."

"Holy shit! CERN funding to build it and an excuse to cover a massive digging operation. Is it global?"

"Yes. Different facilities serve various purposes. Hardened facilities designed to protect vital servers against EMP is one example. The seed vault in Norway another. The war funding for Ukraine is being used to build the underground storage for chemical and biological agents which have been created but will not be released. The salt mine bunkers under Soledar in Eastern Ukraine will house the soldiers who will be the first to emerge from underground. Their task will be to kill any survivors on the way to securing Astana. Around the same time Asian slaves will emerge and populate China's ghost cities and re-start industrial production. Similar groups will follow them to complete various regional missions. Assuming they execute the clean-up operations safely and successfully, we too can emerge from the bunkers into a new world."

"Why don't you try to stop all this before it's carried to fruition is what none of you can explain. It seems you don't even consider doing so."

"Mate, people tend to project their humanity onto others. As long as they remain unable to comprehend the existence of a limitless and bottomless evil, then that evil has the freedom to grow and flourish. This is what has always been exploited to ensure humanity remains enslaved. We do not have the power and resources to stop what is imminent. If we go on a suicide mission it guarantees that only evil emerges from the bunkers. If we can survive, not as peasants, but as a secret society within the ruling class of the new world order, we have accomplished the great task of preserving our ideals past the cataclysm meant to destroy them permanently.

"Do you think you're a peaceful person, Laszlo?"

"If attacked, I would fight back to the death. But if you mean attacking the innocent, then yes, I am."

"You are not. A person without power and money to raise an army has no choice but to be peaceful. Sure, they can beat up a street thug or three, but sooner or later they end up on the other end or in jail. You are not peaceful. You do not have the ability to afflict harm without near term consequences. The only truly peaceful person is one with great power who chooses to be righteous."

"I see your point," Laszlo finished his whiskey. "I disagree. You may think I'm in no position to disagree. But you fuckers don't have everything figured out. You have sold out. You have all this information. You dare say you know more about me than I know myself. But this cannot be true. For it was, you would have known not to waste all this time and effort only to have me do THIS!" He threw his glass at the mirror behind the bar as hard as he could.

Running up the stairs he heard it and the bottles shatter as they went crashing to the floor. Exiting, he sprinted toward the road to Rome. James, John and Luca followed him upstairs but pursued no further. "You're going to regret this!" He heard James yell.

A second look back confirmed they weren't now coming after him. John was last to go downstairs, "I'm going to send an army of migrant gangsters to rape your precious Scarlet!"

ROME

Waking in the grass with his backpack as a pillow Laszlo sat up. There was a bicycle he vaguely recalled stealing about ten yards away. He was on a hill overlooking Rome, but which one? There were no people around but there was an ominous feeling in his gut because he had the same dream. Again spending the night in the villa where the doors locked from the outside and James held all the keys. He tried talking Scarlet into escaping but she wasn't interested. She said this was now their home. There were other people he recognized and children also in the same lifeless condition. Occasionally men would come with James and although he never saw anything, it was clear the women and children were being taken and forced to perform horrific acts. His mind repulsed, but in the dream knew it to be true. He had no strength to fight back or even to get up. Day after day sitting helpless at the large rundown rectangular dining table filled with various meats, cheeses, pasta, fruits and luxurious desserts from one end to the other. Only everything was moldy and spoiled and reeked worse than Giulia's fart. Endless drums of red wine lined two walls, but it was a lust-less murky brown color. It tasted like vinegar and excrement. The others would occasionally come to eat and drink without emotion. James would ask him to have a toast but when Laszlo asked for water instead, he was told there was none.

This villa was certainly worse than any level of hell Dante conceived of. It was personalized to him. The sum of all his fears. He tried not to dwell on it. Rome lay in front of him. He was mere miles from the safety of the embassy. It was January 5th and tomorrow would be his birthday. He envisioned himself celebrating it in Budapest.

The sun rising in front of him and behind the city meant he was west of Rome. As branches drooped and puckered in the night turn up to the returning sun and spread themselves wide to its renewed warmth and light, so too his wilted spirit rose again as heat and zeal surged through his veins and he was born anew.

Rome in its fallen glory is still more magnificent than the mind can easily imagine. Looking at the city stretched out before him he could see the construction of the whole world. Hard working people raising buildings stone by stone. Planting seed, nurturing, harvesting and repeating year after year. Action is evidence of a rational soul, which abhors irrationality and must combat it in order to not become corrupt. The action of practicing, teaching, creating and engaging in philosophical debate perpetuates civilization, for those reduced to a material life alone are no more than beasts. For when a soul becomes trapped in the material world, not one in ten thousand finds the time to form literary taste, to examine the validity of scientific or philosophic concepts for himself, or to form what, for lack of a better phrase, might be called the wise and tragic sense of an old spiritual soul.

The Tiber River flowed between himself and the city thus revealing he was not atop one of the historic hills of Rome. All seven hills lay inside the old city walls east of the Tiber. West of the river there was Vatican Hill, which he could see to his left, confirmed by the unmistakable dome of St. Peter's Basilica. This meant only Janiculum Hill remained. He believed it a good omen to find himself on the hill named for the Roman god Janus, for whom this month of January is similarly named. Janus is the god of beginnings, gates, transitions, time, duality, passages, and endings. He represented time because he could see into the past with one face and into the future with the other. This too he found comforting as he left the bike and began walking down toward the river. A verse of Lupe Fiasco's *Dots & Lines* repeated in his brain.

The applause and patience of the laws in nature
Override lies and the laws of nations
Pilgrims bear witness at all the stations
Sun positions overcome traditions
Numbers govern our young religions
Dead levels making plum decisions
Perpendicular to the undivision
That's bad curricular to the unconditioned
Any love less than unconditional is so under Christian it's unrepentant
The physical part of my church emits the invisible arts of my work
To make gold from garbage is not the alchemical part of this map
But truth be told it's the pursuit of gold
That turns the goal of men into trash
The souls sold and they turning gold into cash
And your reflection is your connection to more collections or more directions and paths
If your reflection is masked, then you're reflective of mass
To see yourself just look at me then split your reflection in half

You look just like how I wanna be
Sacred geometry
In a line, in a line, in a line, in a line, in a line
Three angels in kind, on time, go straight, don't sign
You look just like how I wanna be
Sacred geometry

Reaching the river, Laszlo crossed over the Ponte Palatino, the bridge next to the economic heart of ancient Rome. The first ports were built in this location and The Forum Boarium, the largest cattle market, extended north to the two millennia old stone bridge. He took note of the Temple of Hercules before reaching and passing through the Arch of Janus, the only quadrifrons triumphal arch preserved in Rome.

Quadrifrons arches are known for four fronts in a rectangular form of monument with arched passages in two directions, at right angles, generally built at a crossroads or geographical focal point.

Could crossing the gate change his trajectory, he wondered. Would Scarlet be a part of his life in this dimension? He had run away. Left everyone and everything that ever mattered. Had he passed through an invisible gate? Could he ever go home again? Was everything he left behind: the richness of life and the grief, dreams that flourished and illusions which never materialized, all forever lost to time?

The enormity of such grand questions reverberated as he traversed Palatine Hill, first past the ancient ruins and then The Colosseum without stopping. Continuing down to San Giovani Plaza, he found himself at the base of the largest Egyptian obelisk standing anywhere in the world, including Egypt. According to the inscription, its creation pre-dates the founding of Rome by a millennium. Originally erected at the Karnak Temple complex near Luxor, it is now topped with a Christian cross by order of Pope Sixtus V. Laszlo was sure there is a counterexample as with everything else. Yet looking up he couldn't help but think that in the history of humanity nearly every tall structure ever conceived, designed, planned and built by men, whether dedicated to a deity or not, was done to impress a woman. How would he build his new life to impress Scarlet? What would be his proverbial obelisk of Budapest? Something so magnificent and eternal that it would draw her soul from half a world away without an invite.

Numerous cafés lined the square. Having not eaten since the highway stop with Giulia, he was tempted for a moment. Recalling the foulness of the food in his dream quickly crushed his appetite. He grabbed a Peroni from a small shop and turned back in the direction where he came. A few quick stops on the way to the embassy were reasonable, but he needed to reach it in time to be processed today. He could eat, drink, and be merry tomorrow night in Budapest.

Passing the Colosseum again, this time on the east side, he couldn't help but think about the education system. The meme of bread and circuses during Roman times was universally taught and understood in the West. Movies like *Gladiator* further drove the lesson home. Despite this knowledge, people vote in favor of a tax to build a new stadium for a team owned by a billionaire. Later they pay admission to the billionaire's stadium to watch the circus. Pay extra to buy official t-shirts available online at half-price. All to cheer on multi-millionaires playing a game. They overpay for shit beer and disgusting hot dogs because they're so fucking exhausted from working all week that any distraction is more tenable than facing reality. And this is now a middle-upper-class activity. The lower-classes gamble on the outcomes and play fantasy at home, unable to afford to bring their children to the stadiums built by their labor.

Marveling at the grandeur of the festivities, many believe themselves a part of an advancing civilization which will soon explore Mars and the stars. Evolution, they call it. Yet only technology has advanced. The Homo sapiens are on the precipice of collapse before the surviving minority is bound by eternal chains. Why do they never shout about anything that mattered like they shout during the big game. Meek and passive except for a narrow circle of home life, and perhaps at the office. No more in control than at the stadium, in the face of major events, people feel as helpless as against the elements. So instead of endeavoring to influence the future, they lie down and allow terrible people to shape the world for them.

Does it make sense to be cheering for people you don't know playing a game that doesn't matter? When he was comfortable and safe and had money coming in, it did. From Wimbledon to the Kentucky Derby, the NCAA Final Four, World Cup soccer and the Olympics, Laszlo had attended them all. Countless Lakers games and weekend trips to San Diego to watch a mediocre Chargers team. Milan is home to two of the top soccer teams in the world. Yet the thought of going to a game did not cross his mind. Being broke and watching people play games or pretend to be fictional characters is a distraction from the intention to change your life for the better.

How many stadiums could be filled by the dead from wars fought over divisions created by and for the benefit of families numbering perhaps no more than a baker's dozen in the whole world. He could not trust any of the specifics discussed with James and the rest of his gang, but the overall picture was clear. A third world war was underway. There was little relation to the first two, at least in the mind of the average person. Nation states were no longer relevant. This final war for the soul of man was being fought between a few trillion-dollar globalist entities seemingly in control of everything. And billions of ordinary people of all races and religions opposing the de-population, AI-robot controlled permanent tyranny control grid the globalists were determined to implement. The differences between the two groups couldn't be starker. The globalists are few but united. Free human beings are legion but divided, lacking control of resources, information and supply chains. All the institutions from banking to healthcare are firmly in the control of the parasites who refer to themselves as the elites. Well paid technocrats and the fearful who desire to be ruled run the institutions on their behalf.

He stopped at San Pietro in Vincoli. The little church houses Michelangelo's famous sculpture of Moses with horns on his head. Horns based on a description in Chapter 34 of Exodus in Jerome's Vulgate Bible which was not affirmed as the official version for thirty years after the sculpture was created. Sigmund Freud famously spent three weeks here in 1913 trying to figure out the sculpture's emotional effect. Laszlo did not have that kind of time. He was in and out in three minutes.

What was real? He continued north. The statute he

looked at certainly was. But the story of its creator and subject, how real were they? Were the clones real? Did he really attend a birthday party for a member of the Sforza family? He had always rejected the idea that ignorance was bliss but in this moment he understood.

Waiting in a short line to enter the Galleria Borghese, he took note of the sky. Like an old dream or the memory of a long dead relative, the clouds told endless stories as they passed overhead. Inside there was only one piece he was interested in: Apollo and Daphne. The most famous story of unrequited love in history. John had thrown it in his face the previous night. Did he mean the threat he made against Scarlet? Was John really going to send people to attack her? Laszlo could deal with anything the future brought but *that.* The thought his actions could reverberate back to hurt Scarlet was as repulsive as the dream. Worse, an even deeper level of hell he had not contemplated. Warning her would be his first act after reaching the embassy.

Still not hungry and thirty-minutes from MAXXI, The National Museum of 21st Century Art, he purchased a small bottle of whiskey for the journey. The walking map for tourists he picked up showed the location of the museum, but he wasn't sure he would find what he was truly looking for. This would be his final stop before heading to the embassy and it gave him a chance to reflect. What was the true purpose of this trip. To save his life? Or to lose the illusions deceiving his world and realize it was not death he was escaping but fear. To learn he could, we all can, partake in the glory of creation, love, and live with hope even in the face of evil.

Reaching the museum, he tossed the whiskey bottle in the trash and focused on his present surroundings. There it was. In the bustling heart of Rome, amidst the ancient cobblestone streets and the unending whispers of a bygone era, is a peculiar sight unnoticed by most passersby. Tucked away within the maze of alleys, where tourists and locals alike traverse, it really exists. The invisible toilet.

This creative homage to modern art and primordial needs is not your typical public restroom. It doesn't have signs or arrows pointing toward it. Instead, it blends seamlessly into its surroundings. Camouflaged like a chameleon against its backdrop of historic buildings and bustling streets. It's called invisibility magic. A clever design where the exterior of this toilet is covered with a special material that mirrors the surrounding environment. From the outside, it reflects the buildings, trees, and passersby indirectly, making it exceedingly difficult to spot. He did not stumble upon it accidentally. Scarlet had sent him a link to a video of it a few days prior to New Year's. They had joked it was a secret portal to another dimension.

Upon entering the concealed chamber, he was greeted by a scene that defies expectation. The interior was not just functional, but adorned with exquisite marble, intricate mosaics, and delicate frescoes—an unexpected oasis of opulence amid the urban chaos. Why do modern architects love asymmetrical structures, he wondered. Ancient Roman architect Vitruvius said a building out of proportion is like a deformed body. Nature herself composed the human body and the rest of creation with due proportions. The first rule of Vitruvius for an up-and-coming architect was: No symmetry, off to the cemetery. The old school Roman way of saying: dead on arrival.

Life needs balance and symmetry is it by definition. Duality is the basis of everything in this realm. Male and female. Yin and Yang. Centrifugal force to the centripetal. Up and down. Even politics must find a balance between left and right; swing too far either way and it becomes totalitarian.

Laszlo believed in courtesy flushes to mitigate the stench for the next person. Not today, not no more. People needed to feel, see, and breathe the collective rotting foul carcass that is

Western Civilization to have any chance to rescue it at such a late hour.

For thousands of years, people have known how to grow food, sew clothing, treat sickness with herbs, build shelters and survive. In two generations, this knowledge and accompanying skills have been erased. People in the West are completely dependent on and at the mercy of the system. Slaves used to be in chains. Now they are in denial. Hardly anyone is wondering what we are actually doing here. Most accept the work-eat-entertainment-sleep cycle as all there is to life and have no desire for a deeper understanding or purpose of their place in the universe.

Technology teases the promise of a coming singularity. Who but the most ignorant minds like Abhi would think this is a good idea. A collective singular worldview of religion, of laws, of acceptable behavior dictated by an algorithm is inherently about creating the last caste system for mankind. A world government is the final act of an inescapable totalitarian system. When he was a child, the beast system foretold in Revelations was a far-fetched fantasy. Even if a character so charming, so persuasive as to fool the whole world was to emerge, how could the system be implemented. A mark without which one cannot buy or sell anywhere on earth. It was science fiction. A global technocracy controlled by a tiny elite and administered by accountants, AI, and robot soldiers was no longer fantasy. The system is in place and has been beta tested for more than a decade. It's called the blockchain. The technology exists in the present. The desire to implement it has been with us since the days Babylon.

Everything is being revealed in real time. Western and most other governments are run by child molesting satan worshipers. They are controlled through honeypot operations such as Jeffrey Epstein and P. Diddy with video tape of them doing horrific things to women and children. They put fluoride in the water to keep IQs low. Vaccines, birth control and microplastics feminize the men and sterilize women. Staple crops like wheat, barley, rice, and soy are sprayed with chemicals known to cause cancer and auto-immune disease. Sunscreen is pushed to prevent a connection to the lifeforce and keep vitamin levels low. Legal drugs with untold side effects make billions for pharmaceutical conglomerates and millions for the news channels they advertise with. Natural remedies such as herbs, marijuana and mushrooms are controlled, taxed, and dismissed.

Karen—the meme referring to a middle-class white woman perceived as entitled—does not have the same biological aversion to being conquered that a man does. When women are conquered, the conquerors take them as wives and their genes become a part of the new population. When men are conquered, they're killed, and their genetic lineage is eradicated. This is why men have a larger aversion to a group of assylum seekers nearly wholly made up of military age men. Men are welcoming their competitors. Women are welcoming their new boyfriends and husbands. Either Western man— a tiny global minority—takes back his country and his rights from the globalist, or he will cease to exist. And Rome will, after two millennia, be finally and fatally conquered.

The plan is obvious for all with eyes to see. James and the old priest were both right within their own worldviews. The goal of the controlling parasites is to foment a hot third world war. To pit political Zionism against the Muslim world. The Christian West ruled by Zionists against the Arab world also unwittingly controlled by the same entity will be forced to fight to total exhaustion and annihilation. The survivors, disillusioned with both religion and atheism, will have nowhere to turn. Facing the depths of hell on earth, they will be presented with and united under the pure doctrine of Lucifer at last brought out into the open.

Flushing before washing his hands, Laszlo exited into the street. Only one destination remained. It was curious to think the sky was the same for everybody. In America, Russia, China as well as here in Rome. And the people were also very much the same—everywhere, all over the world, billions of people living as if ignorant of one another's existence, held apart by walls of hatred and lies, and yet almost exactly the same—people who had never learned to think, were intentionally misled and divided, holding in their hearts and bellies and muscles the power to overturn the world.

In the other corner are the globalist parasites. Their goal is the eradication of humanity as we know it. Understanding the destination, it becomes clear why the psychological conditioning, the biological experimentation, cultural grooming, and educational brainwashing we are subjected to is a preparation for accepting the post human future.

A weak, ignorant, immoral, disconnected, and unhealthy population makes an easy target for the next stage: the creation of an entire generation of androgynous beings. Masculinity is attacked psychologically, culturally and biologically. Women are being replaced in sports, entertainment, and politics by men pretending to be women, and schools are indoctrinating children to believe that gender is a choice.

The transgender movement is not a grassroots movement. It's being pushed from above. It has nothing to do with freedom of expression, sexuality, or civil rights. It is an evil psychological operation with a clear agenda to take us closer to transhumanism by forcing us to question the most fundamental notion of human identity, our gender. If you don't know who you are, if you already identify as a hybrid, it will be easy to convince you to become a machine. It is the last step before extinction.

There it was. The Hungarian Embassy in Rome. Ringing the bell and jumping the fence were likely to yield the same result. The decision made itself. If this tale would truly one day become the story he tells his children of how he met their mother Scarlet, then jumping this fence for no reason other than dramatic effect was the obvious move.

THE EMBASSY

He made it. Laszlo was over the fence on Hungarian soil in Rome. He relaxed for a moment in the grass basking in safety. In theory Willow could find him in Budapest. James certainly had the ability to pursue if he wished. But for the first time in nearly a week he was not running for his life.

Having climbed over the eight-foot-tall fence with a cement base and green spiked bars he anticipated security would come to take him inside to explain himself. They did not appear. Perhaps ten minutes passed before he stood and knocked on the thick wood double doors. No response. Unable to locate the doorbell he banged the door again, this time with his right fist. A middle-aged woman with short hair dressed casually in jeans and a t-shirt opened the door cautiously, "Bonjourno."

"Bonjourno... I don't speak Italian. Hungarian or English?"

"Yes, I speak both."

"Great," he breathed a sigh of relief and started to explain his situation.

"I'm sorry. We are closed for the holidays. We will have regular hours again beginning on Monday, the eighth."

"I don't think you understand. My life is in grave danger."

"Wait here. I will summon the local police."

"No! Please. They cannot help me. The people after me

are much more powerful than the police. I am Hungarian. I need the protection of the Hungarian state." He raised his arm and pointed back over his shoulder with his thumb toward the street, "Out there I'm the walking dead."

"Uh… This is highly unusual. Do you have your passport?"

He handed it over without a word.

"Laszlo Nagy. Your name is Hungarian, but this passport is from the United States of America. The US embassy is only a short walk from here. Perhaps they can help you."

"Légyszíves," he begged in Hungarian hoping to garner favor. She reciprocated and switched languages.

"I understand you're Hungarian. I can see it. You look like the older brother of my own nephew. But the embassy is closed. Your passport states you were born in the US. There is nothing I can do right now. Come back Monday. I will schedule you for the first appointment of the day."

He got down on both knees and clasped his hands. "Please. I haven't had a proper night of sleep in a week. I took many risks to get here. I threw my phone away so they couldn't track me. I am out of money. Two very powerful gangs are looking for me. I need refuge. Please have mercy."

"Wait." She closed the massive hardwood double-doors. He heard the security system engage. Lighting a cigarette, he contemplated the unthinkable. What would he do if she came back with security and threw him out onto the streets of Rome? Steal a car and attempt to drive overnight. Mask the license plate somehow. Fuck. He had no experience living like this. The experts say most serial killers in the past, before technology, were only caught because they wanted to be. He understood. Living in a perpetual state of fear and being followed for less than a week had nearly broken him. What about five months or five years? Everyone has a breaking point.

The door opened. "Laszlo, please follow me. On account of your dire circumstances and your Hungarian ethnicity the ambassador agreed to let you stay here temporarily. She is presently returning from her holiday, and assuming no delay, should be here in about an hour to discuss your predicament."

Inside, she signaled for the guard accompanying them to open the door to an unmarked room. It contained a small brown square table in the middle with brown folding chairs on either side. Five or six more folding chairs were propped against one wall. The room was ground level, but the window was a tiny slit like in a prison cell and covered with steel bars.

"Do not take it personally. Facility security protocol mandates I must place you in here."

"No worries. After the last week, I love it here. I've never felt so safe in my life."

"If you are hungry, we have leftovers from the New Year's Eve party."

"Thank you. I would take an alcoholic drink if that's an option?"

"It's not."

"Can I smoke in here?"

"Technically no, but we never have anyone in this room. Just don't tell the ambassador I said it's OK." She turned to leave.

"Miss, one more thing. You have already done me a tremendous favor and I thank you from the bottom of my heart. There is a woman. I care about her deeply. She too is a potential victim of the gangs. I have not been able to contact her. A secure line or encrypted message would be ideal. The situation is dire. I need to reach her ASAP."

"It has been widely reported the phone calls of the German Prime Minister and other EU leaders were recorded by

US intelligence agencies in recent years. I am in no position to pass judgement on the necessity of such actions. I am only making you aware that if you are, in fact, wanted by such powerful forces as you suggest, necessitating begging your way in here and ruining my quiet time, how can I possibly promise you secure communications? Why would you believe me if I did? Because I speak Hungarian? Don't be so naïve Mr. Nagy."

"You're right. I didn't think it through. Any phone will do."

"I have to go. Someone will be by with food and a phone. The ambassador will get here when she gets here."

He lit a cigarette. There was risk but he had to call Scarlet. A different gentleman in an outfit signaling he was security returned with a tray of Hungarian goodies. Sausages and salami, various cheeses and pickled veggies, Italian bread and a half loaf of Jewish rye. He also placed a phone and ashtray on the table.

"Booze?" Laszlo asked in Hungarian but was rejected with a horizontal shake of the head.

The only phone number he could recall from memory, in addition to his parents, was Scarlet. When he was child, he knew a hundred friend's phone numbers from memory. It was another major break in the human timeline. For all recorded history, having an above average memory was invaluable. It gave one status and meant most people—even those with high intelligence—respected you as wise. In an instant this disappeared. The poorest amongst us now has a phone capable of storing and recalling phone numbers and everything else in real time. The only memory people concern themselves with today is the storage capacity of their iPhone.

"Hello?"

"Scarlet!"

"'L! Holy shit! I was hoping it was you. Are you OK?"

"Yes. Are you?"

"Yeah. I'm back in Seattle. I tried to call you yesterday but your phone was off. Willow is pretending nothing happened. You jumped on your own and nobody noticed until it was too late. I know that's not true. I told her I didn't know where you went. I told her I spoke with you yesterday. It was right after I saw the email that you sent from Heathrow. I told her you probably went to hide out in Panama because of your friend who is powerful in the government there. I hope that was the right thing to say."

"Perfect. Throw them off. Listen... I'm so sorry. I hope you can forgive me. I must tell you something terrible. I got mixed up with some bad people."

"No shit. I'm never going anywhere with Willow or Mike ever again."

"Not them. I somehow got involved with a more powerful gang. Perhaps more powerful members of a weaker gang. There is no way to know and it's not important now."

"It sounds important. What did you tell them?"

"Nothing"

"I don't believe you."

"I was really fucked up. You told me I would be. That turned out to be amazingly helpful. Thank you. But I didn't tell them. I swear. They already knew *everything*. It's hard to explain. It's like a movie. They were tracking me the whole time even before San Diego. They showed me a video they took of me swimming out of the bay and passing out."

"What! Fuck. Why didn't you disappear like I told you?"

"I tried. You won't believe this shit. I was seated next to one of them on my flight. Another pretended to be a street vendor in Milan."

"What the fuck, 'L!'" Don't give away your location. My phone is not secure even if yours is."

"I left Milan. It doesn't matter. They know everything... Scarlet, listen to me. I rejected them. It's a long story and I don't have much time. I pissed them off, I think. They—one of them —made a threat against you... Do you hear me?"

"Why me? If they are not connected to Willow, how do they know me?"

"It's weird. It's like some other dimensional mirror of how you warned me about the witches being weirdly attracted to me while I'm under the spell."

"I'm not following. I meant what I said on New Year's Eve 'L. Now that the drugs are exiting your system what do you remember?"

"I remember everything perfectly. I don't know if it's the nano trackers I ingested, but despite taking your advice to the extreme and drinking almost every waking moment of the last six days, I remember everything. Well maybe not everything. I'll try to explain later. Right now, you must believe me and take precautions. I am safe. I'm not going to tell you where, but relatively speaking, I'm safer than you. I still must process everything."

"Why? If not Willow, who?"

"I don't know, but you have to leave Seattle ASAP!"

"L! Stop. You can't be serious. School starts on Monday."

"Take off. Call in sick. Tell 'em you tested positive for COVID. Whatever. Leave now. Do not accept food or drinks from friends you make on the way. Don't talk to anyone until you get somewhere remote. Don't bring anything with you including clothes or credit cards. Buy new clothes from a random store on the way with cash. They are using wearable and ingestible nano trackers. Any piece of clothing, anything you consume can be used to track your location."

"Jesus, 'L; you're serious?"

"I am. All the tech we imagined. The conspiracy theories. Weather manipulation, portals, clones it's all real."

"Clones?"

"I think so. If the whites of their eyes turn yellow and you haven't known them more than a few years, it's a clone."

"You're scaring me 'L. If it's this deep, why run? They will find me anyway."

"Do not think like that. You told me to be strong and know who I am and I would get through this... Remember?"

"Yeah."

"It's your turn. I'm sorry. Fight! We must fight and find a way. It does not mean running forever, but we need to be very careful with communications. Set up an email account that is a mirror of the one I created to message you. Do you understand what I mean?"

"Yes."

"Cool. Leave your phone charging at the apartment and buy a burner with cash. I should reach my location tomorrow. I will contact you then with a phone number to call disguised in a message to that email."

"OK"

"Listen... Scarlet. I have to ask you one thing. I don't want to do this right now, but I must. What's the worst thing you ever did to me?"

"If you don't need to then why now 'L?"

"I need to know if it's really you on the other end. Perhaps it's the drugs or the spell but they told me things and I'm extremely paranoid. What's the worst thing you ever did or thought about me? I won't be mad. It's only a test to see if it's really you or some voice-over tech they are trying to fool me with."

"Of course it's me. You are paranoid. I'm glad you're somewhere safe. Don't leave before banishing such thoughts from your mind."

"It'll disappear the moment you give me something, anything."

"Are you still upset about me dancing with Mike and Dean on the yacht?"

"I'm not but that's a good enough answer. I don't think their AI is so advanced as to pick that over Vegas in an effort to fool me."

"Vegas? What are you talking about?"

"It's OK. I'm so happy it's really you. We went through the portal in Seattle, remember?"

"Of course I remember. Are you asking if we are on our own timelines, communicating to help each other, to find the right path to be together?"

"No. I'm stating definitively that you and I are on the same timeline. I don't care about anyone else… I do have to ask one more question. Tell me the truth. I promise I will not be upset."

"I promise. I'm not scared anymore… New Year's Eve should've been us alone, together. Going to San Diego was a mistake but it opened my eyes. I'm done with them no matter what."

"Scarlet… Tell me about Las Vegas."

"Huh? I haven't been to Vegas in ages."

"Just admit what you did there."

"'L what the fuck. I told you. I party but I don't participate in the occult shit. You're tripping. Have you taken more drugs?"

ONE NIGHT IN MILAN | 363

"No drugs and I'm not talking about rituals. You drugged me and robbed me on my birthday six years ago!"

"No way! Who told you that?"

"The police report. I looked at it for the first time since the incident after leaving L.A. There is a picture of you and me in the elevator. It's unmistakably you."

"Oh my God 'L, you're serious?"

"Of course I'm fucking serious Scarlet. How the fuck could you do me like that?"

"You don't understand. They made me do it 'L. After I turned down the movie role with Willow's sister and moved home to Seattle, they came after me. They gang stalked me. I tried to tell you without telling you. It's painful. They wouldn't stop until I started doing these things for them. When I met you in New Orleans I didn't know you were one of the victims. One of my victims. They made me do it to many men. Not only Vegas, but all over the world."

"I believe they made you do it Scarlet. The part I'm doubting is that you don't remember. That you didn't know I was one of your victims when we met, when I came and stayed in your bed. It's crushing me to think you knew."

"I didn't know. I swear. After doing the deed, I would take the same drugs I used to knock out the victims so I could sleep and forget about it. I couldn't live with myself. I also couldn't live with the constant harassment and stalking. I'm so sorry. You must believe me 'L. I didn't know it was you. I swear to God. You must believe me. I would get super fucked up to do it. I'm so sorry. Please forgive me. 'L you must forgive me. I won't be able to live knowing I did that to you if you don't forgive me."

"I forgive you Scarlet."

"Really? Truly? Please say it again."

"I *forgive* you Scarlet... Before this trip I would not have forgiven you. I would have sought revenge. Retaliated and justified it by telling myself you deserved it. But I'm in no position to judge. The old priest in Milan said I should not live in the grey. Black or white, image and counter-image. Yin and the yang, wherever we land, we must go for it wholeheartedly. In this case, with all we are going through, how can I not forgive you? I may seek revenge against the others but never you."

"You went to see a priest?"

"Well not exactly. I didn't go to church. I was drunk. He is excommunicated and sits all night in a park preaching to the downtrodden. It's a long story. I hope to be able to tell you in person one day soon."

"Me too, 'L. Me too. I hope we can be together soon."

"We will be. Do not fear or doubt it for a single second. I know it and believe it with all my heart. With all my soul. My spirit is your spirit. Not only since we went through the portal, that was merely confirmation. We have been one spirit since the creation of the universe. And will be always until the last day of the calendar that is time immemorial."

The security guard banged on the door and opened it before Laszlo could react. "I'm sorry Scarlet. Gotta go. I love you."

"I love you too."

A neatly dressed woman followed him in and stood over the desk while the guard settled in the corner opposite him to her left.

"Mr. Nagy?"

"Yes, that's me."

"My name is Enikő Kertész. I am the Hungarian Ambassador to Italy."

"Thank you so much for helping me. You have no idea of the trouble I'm in."

"I have an idea. That is not why I am here. You jumped over the fence. It is trespassing. If you had rung, we could have made an appointment for you when the embassy is open. You interrupted my colleague's holiday and now mine as well."

"I meant no such trouble. I have no other way to get to Budapest. I have been cut off from my bank accounts, but I can repay the state. All I'm looking for is safe passage to Hungary."

"I cannot help you. You are an American citizen. Based on your background, I do believe you could be granted Hungarian citizenship, but you need to go about it the right way. Go home and apply through the consulate in Los Angeles."

"I can't go home."

"You cannot stay here."

"Please help me get to Budapest."

"We cannot help you. All you have is a story about some private citizens who used to be your friends supposedly now aiming to kill you. You don't want to go to the local police." She placed an envelope on the table. "Here is your flight information. Rome to LAX with a layover at Dulles."

"Dulles? I can't go through Dulles! That's Washington D.C. Tomorrow is January 6th. Forget the normal citizenship claim. If you want to send me through Dulles... I don't know... I need to apply for political asylum. Safety from political persecution."

"Stop it Mr. Nagy. You are an American citizen. The US is a NATO ally of Hungary with the rule of law. It is standard procedure to send someone in your predicament home through the capital."

"You don't understand. The District of Columbia is

its own jurisdiction. They've been holding people on simple trespassing charges for years in solitary confinement with no trial. It's a stealth suspension of habeas corpus. It was a set-up to begin with and a huge fraud on the Constitution. On the American people. I turned down an untoward opportunity last night. I don't know how they will react. They made threats against the woman I love. I presume they have the power to have me locked up as well. I will not go through Dulles. Not today and especially not on January 6th!"

"I know more than you think Mr. Nagy. You were warned not to come to Rome. But here you are fucking up my afternoon. So, know this: as much as I'm upset with you, believe me, I will stick this heel" she pulled the five-inch black pump off her foot and in an uppercut motion with her right hand raised it to Laszlo's eye level, "Up all their ass's starting with that prick from New Zealand."

"James! What the hell! How do you know James?" He watched as the whites of her eyes turned yellow.

"The state police, the Arma dei Carabinieri, will be here shortly. They will take you to the airport and make sure you board your flight to Dulles." She turned to leave.

"Please don't do this! Throw me back out into the street instead!"

The guard followed her out and engaged the security system. This was it. The end. Of course James and whoever they work for wouldn't let him live. The remainder of his time at the embassy was a blur. Gazing out through the little window with bars on it, Bob Dylan's somber modern classic about the assassination of President Kennedy kept worse thoughts out of his head.

> Up in the red light district, like a cop on the beat
> Living in a nightmare on Elm Street
> When you're down in Deep Ellum, put your money in your shoe
> Don't ask what your country can do for you

Cash on the ballot, money to burn
Dealey Plaza, make a left-hand turn
I'm going down to the crossroads, gonna flag a ride
The place where faith, hope, and charity died

Shoot him while he runs, boy, shoot him while you can
See if you can shoot the invisible man

Goodbye, Charlie, goodbye, Uncle Sam
Frankly, Miss Scarlet, I don't give a damn
What is the truth, and where did it go?
Ask Oswald and Ruby, they oughta know
"Shut your mouth," said the wise old owl
Business is business, and it's a murder most foul

Tommy, can you hear me? I'm the Acid Queen
I'm riding in a long, black Lincoln limousine
Riding in the backseat next to my wife
Heading straight on in to the afterlife
I'm leaning to the left, I've got my head in her lap
Hold on, I've been led into some kind of a trap
Where we ask no quarter, and no quarter do we give
We're right down the street from the street where you live

The police came and took him without a word. There were two of them in uniform. The car was unmarked. He was not handcuffed, but there was a divider between the front and back and no way to unlock the doors. He wasn't looking to run anymore. Whatever happened now, it would be the will of others. His will was broken. Nothing remained but to live out his fate.

The drive to Leonardo da Vinci Rome Fiumicino Airport took less than an hour. He was not taken into the terminal. They passed through a security gate leading to an unmarked entrance away from any planes. The two officers escorted him, one on either side. They took an elevator five stories underground. Exiting into a narrow cold corridor, they passed numbered rooms with thick steel doors and no windows marked only with a small sign. The numbers decreased by increments of one hundred. 1101... 1001... 901...801... When they reached the second to last room, 101, the door was opened. Laszlo felt a gentle nudge on his back sending him inside before hearing the door lock behind.

The room contained a cot, a table, and a single metal folding chair sitting open opposite the cot. In the back there was a toilet and small shower combo. He sat down and opened the brown paper bag which was the only thing on the table. It contained a sandwich in plastic wrap and a bottle of red wine in a plastic bottle with a screw cap. Laszlo said the Lord's prayer before opening his supper. He knew the sandwich would be moldy and it was. He ate it anyway. The wine was rancid as expected. He drank it all. Laying down on the bed he understood the nightmare to come.

ROOM 101

Laszlo woke from his dream in a state all too familiar: sweaty and depressed. He had the same dream. Every night, the same god forsaken nightmare. On most nights he would wake before it turned villainous but not this time. Being trapped in the villa with the awful food and no water was terrible. Trapped and battered in the depths of hell. Through the window, there was a magnificent pool and garden area he was never allowed to step in. Scarlet was giving fellatio to James before John, Luca, Mike, Abhi and a long line of other men took their turn with her. The door was locked. His body old and frail. He banged on the window with all his strength to no avail. It accomplished nothing. He sank lower and lost the will to live. Turning from the scene, he woke up and found himself yet again alone in Room 101.

It wasn't completely unexpected. His birthday was the probable trigger. It was January 5th, 2057. Tomorrow he would turn sixty-six years old. He never went to Dulles, LAX, or Budapest. For the last thirty-three years he had been held in solitary confinement. The guards and occasional medical staff his only interactions.

After his first night in the room arriving from the embassy, he was greeted on the morning of January 6th, 2024, by a female guard who delivered breakfast and the catch-22 that would be repeated every morning for years.

"What time is my flight?"

"You're not flying today. We need to process your file

before you can see the judge."

"A judge, why?"

"The AI security matrix determined you're capable of committing a violent hate crime. Your social media history is a major red flag. We cannot allow you to fly today."

"Capable? Every person on the planet is *capable* of such an act. I have zero intent to carry one out... Who will make this decision?"

"The judge will determine if you get to fly."

"OK, when do I go in front of the judge?"

"As soon as the matrix determines you are not capable of committing a hate crime."

"But I'm not guilty of anything!"

"You are not. If we believed you were guilty you would see the judge and he would sentence you, or—depending on the circumstances—send you back to the US."

"This is crazy!"

"Mr. Nagy, this is not crazy. This is the law."

A similar version of this scenario played out until he finally relented to his situation being permanent. For a short while things got easier after that. His three daily meals tasted awful yet were nutritious enough to keep him alive. Disgusting to his palate, the food never caused major intestinal issues. He had no access to TV or the internet, but in addition to three books per week, there was a morning paper delivered each day with his breakfast. In those early years he contemplated suicide often. He made several attempts at fashioning a rope from the toilet paper to hang himself. It always broke without doing its job.

Once every three months, approximately, but not necessarily on the equinox or solstice, he was taken from room 101 to a medical facility. A battery of tests was conducted.

This took up a whole day and was a welcome respite from the endless monotony of his room. Each visit he was injected with one or more shots. Sometimes it was before and other times after the tests but not both. He never protested the injections.

The trip frequently involved taking a long high-speed underground train ride. When he returned to his room it always looked and smelled the same but there was no way to be certain he was still beneath Rome. Not knowing didn't bother him as nothing else ever changed. So what if he was being held under Paris, Beijing, or Astana? Only death could bring change. It was akin to trench warfare. A slow grind of potentially fatal harm hung over his head. It was not peaceful nor was it likely to kill him on this very day.

He stopped reading the daily paper less than a year into his incarceration despite the boredom. It was personalized propaganda intended to mislead. There was no mention of the April eclipse Scarlet told him about. Over the summer, the big story above the fold was the beginning of civil war in the US. According to the reporting the former President, Donald Trump, was assassinated while campaigning in Pennsylvania. This was soon followed by reports of civil unrest in England. The Olympics in France, after the glorification of a perverted last supper scene during the opening ceremony, was next to be engulfed in mob violence. What was real? Likely these stories were all fake. Written by an AI with the intent to traumatize him.

Soon thereafter the reports became more dire as basic services began to fail in many countries. Reports of trash piling up on city streets. Dead bodies decaying in homes and alleys because funeral homes were overwhelmed. Nuclear energy plants melting down due to lack of qualified personnel were juxtaposed with stories detailing and praising the use of sentient robots in restoring peace and order. There was no reason to keep up to date with such madness, even if true. He lived in the past. That he at least knew to be true. It was his reality and he needed nothing else down here. The voice in his head they could never get to. The only item he continued to monitor was the date. They didn't fuck with that. Month after month and year after year the Gregorian calendar ticked away one day at a time.

Today, January 5th, 2057, one day before his 66th birthday, he woke up expecting nothing and hoping to die. It was the year of the OX on the Chinese calendar. Laszlo had been harnessed for half his life with no task, no fields needing to be plowed. The definition of a useless eater. Naked, in front of the mirror, he felt ancient and without the tiniest will to survive. His body looked as if it had been the lone source of nutrition for the moths circling the artificial light of his cell. Then, everything changed in an instant.

"Good news Mr. Nagy. Tomorrow you are going home." It was the guard who dropped off his breakfast every morning.

"What? Home?"

"Yes, It was determined you are no longer a risk."

"Home? What the hell is *home*?" Never had he been so frightened in his whole life. "It has only been a few weeks since my last checkup. It must be a mistake."

"It's not a mistake. You are going to see the judge tomorrow morning. You will likely be set free."

"Free? I don't know what that means now. I don't want to be set free. Must I leave?"

"Of course. You must follow the judge's order."

"I'm an old man. I don't think I can survive on the outside. I hold many old grudges. They have festered over all these years. When you first locked me up here, I would not have acted on them but now... Now I *will* carry out the hate crime the program predicted."

"Don't be silly Mr. Nagy. If it says you are not capable

then you are not capable. It is never wrong."

"What else do I have left to do in this life but to seek revenge?"

"That is a question beyond my capacity to answer. All I know is The Grand Court of Astana has taken up the matter. My duty is to inform you of the hearing tomorrow morning."

"Astana! Holy shit! Am I... Are we in Astana?"

"Not physically of course, but yes, we are subject to its jurisdiction like every place on planet earth. One such as yourself, having been incarcerated before the transition, can only be freed by an order of The Committee of Two Hundred."

The idea of being free, something he pleaded for to both God and guards for years now terrified him. There was nothing to do for the next twenty-four hours but to again go over the details of what happened from New Orleans to Rome during those fateful three months of his life which landed him here. Was Scarlet alive anywhere but in his dreams? What if she was. Would she even remember him? Had she been swept up by the mob? Did she get married and have a family? Was marriage still a common practice or had it been wiped out? Had the committee in Astana accomplished what the communists could not and destroyed the family unit? Replaced it with a global village? Was every birth now a transhuman created in a laboratory with chips implemented to control their thoughts and actions from birth to the grave?

He wasn't ready to have this new world thrust upon him at this late stage in life, yet there was at least one single curious cell remaining in his body. Were there millions of tourists still coming, still going to Rome every year? Or was commercial air traffic a thing of the past? Was he the only one being released? Surely countless others were similarly imprisoned over the years before the transition. Had Jerusalem been destroyed? The third temple built, and humanity forever deceived. According to the guard, Astana was the capital of the current world order. Was the technological science fiction of his youth now deployed globally? Implanting a chip in one's hand to track every transaction on earth was already being tested when he was imprisoned. Had it been deployed as Revelations predicted? Would he have to decide to take the mark in order to live on the outside?

Alternatively, the push by the globalist for a post-COVID great reset could've unleashed unpredictable nihilistic forces that led instead to civilizational collapse. The wicked ruled over their minions in the cities without the ability to implement the control grid they desired globally. He fantasized a revival of a nineteenth century-esq world with small local economies centered around farming and barter of repaired manufactured goods produced before the collapse. A full-on rejection of globalism and a tribal renaissance with the family unit as its core.

Surely the sun still rose over the Mediterranean Sea and the stars continued to illuminate the Arabian night sky. These were the things that mattered, he told himself as the door to room 101 opened. He recalled few details from the last twenty-four hours. It was time to leave. A young and weirdly attractive androgynous person in an all-black uniform he had not previously encountered was to take him to court. Laszlo walked the long hallway in silence before stepping into the elevator. For the first time in thirty-three years it was going up.

ALL'S WELL THAT ENDS WELL

The elevators doors opened. The warm, bright, late morning California sun hit his face. It felt better than any high to hear the Pacific Ocean. He could not open his eyes. A massive pounding headache of epic proportions, like taking a baseball bat to the head with no helmet, hit his brain a millisecond later. Laying on his back, he felt the familiar warm smooth skin that could only be Scarlet nestled against the left side of his torso. This was not the usual nightmare. What a wonderful sixty-sixth birthday surprise.

"'L! You're alive! I was getting worried about you, silly."

It couldn't be. He attempted to open his eyes again, but only the right one complied. He wiped the sand from the left. It was real. He was on the beach. Scarlet was next to him. "Ugh… What happened… What day is it?" He raised himself painfully to a sitting position.

"Are you OK?"

"Ugh… My head really hurts and my body too. I think so… What happened?"

She laughed, "I figured you wouldn't remember much."

"Assume I remember nothing. What the hell happened last night… No, first just tell me what day it is."

Scarlet continued giggling, "It's New Years Day!"

"What year?"

"That's a good one! 2024 on the Gregorian calendar. See, you do remember a little bit." She tussled his hair playfully.

"I had the craziest trip ever. It was so real… And weird… So, so weird… Was I normal?"

"Mostly until we got back."

"What time was that?"

"One."

"One… Why so early?"

"You don't remember the storm?"

"No… What drugs did I take?"

"A storm came out of nowhere. The captain insisted we must head back to the marina. This was soon after midnight. We got back to the beach house around one. I had pre-rolled a fat blunt for late night. We smoked it and everyone chilled inside. You grabbed my hand and insisted we go swimming."

"What drugs did I take?"

"All of 'em… 'L, I am not judging, but you were *on one*. I don't know for sure. We think you ate all the mescaline. When I asked, you told me it was a witches brew."

"I said witches brew. I really said that?"

"Yeah… And you thought that shit was hilarious. Laughed for like twenty minutes straight."

"So how fucked up was I. Don't hold back."

"Don't take this the wrong way 'L, you were otherworldly. A barely playable but heartwarming retard like that 1980's Corky character, but drug fueled and straight out of Hunter S. Thompson's weirdest dream kinda fucked up."

"Whoa. I always dreamt of getting to that level. What happened after we went swimming?"

"Nothing. I went inside to get us towels. You insisted we sleep out here on the beach under the stars. When I came back you had passed out. A lifeless corpse."

"And you stayed with me out here on the beach all night?"

"I didn't really have a choice. You wouldn't budge. At first, I thought we were going to freeze. But you were giving off heat all night like a furnace. So I had no choice but to cuddle you up."

"You cuddled *me*?"

"I had to in order to survive. You weren't moving. I could've frozen to death. Don't go assuming it means anything," she smiled.

"Thanks for staying. I would've really freaked out if I woke up here this morning alone."

"Why?"

"Long story... When did you fall asleep?"

"I have no idea. Late... I only woke up about thirty minutes ago."

"Was I talking in my sleep?"

"You said thirty-three a bunch of times this morning after Willow woke me up."

"Willow! Where is she? Where is everyone?"

"They went to brunch like half an hour ago. I figured we would drive separately and join them when you were alive again. That's when Willow told me your thirty-third birthday was coming up on the sixth. Why didn't you tell me, silly? Anyway... I figured you were having a dream. A nightmare about getting old," she couldn't help but smirk.

"We are not going to brunch with them. Go pack your bags. I want you to come to L.A. with me and meet my parents."

"I would 'L but my flight is from here. Early tomorrow morning."

"Don't worry. I'll kindly change it for you... Or we can drive up the coast to Seattle. Wanna take a road trip up the coast with me?"

"Yeah, but don't you have to work?"

"I quit... Am quitting."

"What?"

"Yeah. I'm done with the Hollywood circus."

"You're serious..."

"Very... Maybe I'll rent out that storefront by your condo and open a burrito shop. I mean a Hungarian restaurant. I'll use my parents' recipes and make it real authentic so no one can claim cultural appropriation. I bet you could make a ton of tips being my bartender. You know, just as a side hustle." He winked.

She hit him playfully in the ribs. For a moment all was right in the world. "Go inside and start packing. I want to call my mom and let her know to expect us." Laszlo watched her walk away and pinched himself before clasping his hands.

"Thank you, Jesus, for saving me. Whatever that trip was about, thank you. Thank you. Thank you..." Still in disbelief he sent his mom a photograph of Scarlet and a few moments later called her.

"You're up early. Happy New Year!" was the beautiful refrain on the other end.

"Happy New Year Mom! I love you!"

"We love you too. How was the party last night? Did the weather cooperate? Did everyone have a good time?"

"Yeah. Mom, listen... Quick question: did you get the photo I sent just now?"

"I think so. My phone beeped and then you called. I didn't look at it yet."

"Ok, mom, listen. Please go up to the attic right now. In the bottom drawer of the filling cabinet in the corner by the window there is a police report in a manilla folder."

"What are you talking about?"

"Please! Start walking up and I will explain. You don't have to read the report. Do NOT read the report... Find the folder. It's stamped in blue with a capitalized 'LVPD'. Las Vegas Police Department."

"Oh my dear God! Did you get in some kind of trouble?"

"No. I promise, no. Its old... Let me know when you find it."

"I found it. I think. This must be it."

"Ok, great. Compare the picture in the folder to the one I sent you and tell me if it's the same woman."

"I'm looking... You sent me a picture of Scarlet. You showed me pictures of her before. What's going on? Tell me if you're in any trouble."

"I'm not... Do the pictures match? Is the photo in the police report a younger Scarlet?" Laszlo held his breath. His soul braced for the bad news.

"Not her... Why?"

"Long story. Are you absolutely beyond the slightest doubt sure it's not her?"

"Similar hairstyle but definitely not her. What is going on. Did you two have a fight?"

"No... no fight. We are coming to have a late brunch with you and father. I want her to meet him, to meet you both."

"That's great. We can't wait to meet her... Is mushroom soup and fried chicken livers OK. Or is she on some weird diet?"

"Perfect. Thanks ma!"

After thanking heaven a million more times from his knees in the sand, Laszlo stood up and joined Scarlet inside. She was already packed and ready to go.

"I rolled us a blunt for the drive up. Normally I would've rolled two, but I want to be semi lucid to meet your parents for the first time."

"Good thinking. I could probably forgive you this one time if you weren't. On account of last night."

They packed up the car and hit the road without telling Willow and the others they would not be joining them for brunch. Scarlet sparked the blunt rolled from a real tobacco leaf as Laszlo accelerated onto Interstate 5 North toward Los Angeles.

"You probably don't remember, 'L; but it's your turn to pick a song."

Laszlo knew exactly who he wanted to hear, Bob Marley:

> *Emancipate yourself from mental slavery*
> *None but our self can free our minds*
> *Have no fear for atomic energy*
> *'Cause none of them can stop the time*
> *How long shall they kill our prophets*
> *While we stand aside and look?*
> *Some say it's just a part of it*
> *We've got to fulfill de book*
>
> *Won't you help to sing*
> *These songs of freedom?*
> *'Cause all I ever have*
> *Redemption songs*
> *Redemption songs*
> *Redemption songs*

"Oh my God, 'L, you're tearing up. You really had a crazy trip, huh?"

He grabbed her hand. "Not the worst ever. I once thought

my 2nd grade teacher was peeing on my leg like a dog."

Scarlet found this hilarious. "Tell me about your trip last night."

"I think it was to show me how my life would've turned out if we never went through the portal together in Seattle."

"Seriously? What happened. How did it turn out?"

"It was hell. Willow and Mike wanted me dead. They used Abhi do their dirty work."

"Oh my God! Is that why you want to quit your job?"

"No... Not only that. It's hard to explain. So many things happened. So much is being revealed. I think the whole world is going to change... Do you remember when the Panama Papers scandal revealed that all the richest people in the world are part of an enormous criminal conspiracy to dodge taxes and hoard stolen wealth in offshore accounts?"

"Vaguely."

"When it first broke literally nothing happened except a reporter working on the story was assassinated. This further confirmed they're all in a giant cult and Epstein clients... But maybe things *are* changing. Only slower or differently than we can easily perceive... I'm not sure. It's a lot to make sense of right now."

"Well, we have a long drive to Seattle for you to tell me everything. I'm an excellent listener."

"You really want to do the road trip up the coast?"

"Yeah, let's do it. School doesn't start 'til the eighth."

"Great! Yeah, lets fucking go! We can stay at my place tonight. Chill and smoke and watch football. We'll head out first thing tomorrow morning. Play it by ear."

"Yay! I'm excited now. This is going to be *so* fun!"

"Me too Scarlet. Me too... You have no idea." Laszlo

pinched his left leg to make sure this was real… "You were right about CERN being a portal by the way. Wanna know where to?"

"Obvi!"

"CERN is named for Cerunnos—the Celtic name for the lord of hell. The belief system goes all the way back to Gilgamesh and Babylon. CERN's rings mirror the rings of Saturn. The dark sun. The prison planet of the fallen angels. CERN's real aim is to open a portal to Saturn and unleash the fallen angels from the abyss. To destroy Babylon, install the beast system on earth, and wage war upon humanity and the creator."

"Holy fuck. This was revealed to you during the trip?"

"Yes, and a thousand other things. Nothing happened on the eclipse date. Or I wasn't told the truth. I don't know anything for certain… But Trump was assassinated three months later. That started the civil war in the US and soon thereafter a massive global conflagration."

"You really did take a witches brew, huh?"

"Yeah, it was hell. I was sure it was real and that I would never escape. It lasted forever. Well not forever. I was sixty-six years old when I woke up on the beach this morning. Can you believe it?"

"That's so *weird*… But we did go through the portal, so how do you feel now, awake at last?"

"I think the darkness of this world can be transformed through a spiritual process in our souls. It is meant to burn off the false parts of ourselves so we can strive to live our true nature as the creator intended. It is easy to have faith when everything is going your way. It's when you have nowhere to turn, family and friends gone or turned against you… Rock bottom is when man begs a higher power for help; the dark night exists to help us deepen a connection between our souls and God."

"Yo! That's fucking beautiful. Next trip you must take me with you," she joked.

"You were with me this time. You told me how to survive it and saved me. You have blessed me with the greatest gift of all."

"What are you talking about?"

"Are you familiar with the last line of *Paradiso*, the third and final book of Dante's *The Divine Comedy*?"

"No."

He looked her in the eye. Pulling her arm up to his face he kissed the back of her hand.

> *But already my desire and my will*
> *are being turned like a wheel, all at one speed,*
> *by the Love which moves the sun and the other stars.*